Those in Pe...

Dieter separated th... ...
laces and held it in his hand. It was a letter
that had been handled by Germany's greatest
enemy and would count heavily in his battle
for translators of this treasure. As his eye
wandered over the bulging crates that filled
his office, he wondered how much of
Churchill's confidence would be left if the
great man knew that not only had the letter
fallen into German hands, but also all the
documents and notes relating to the
development of their most secret
anti-submarine weapon. The Allied
Submarine Detection Investigation Committee
had been formed in the 1920s to come up
with effective U-boat countermeasures.
Because the allies shared the German love of
acronyms it was inevitable that the weapon
they had developed was named after the
initials of their committee: ASDIC.

James Follett trained to be a marine engineer, and
also spent some time hunting for underwater
treasure, filming sharks, designing powerboats, and
writing technical material for the Ministry of
Defence before becoming a full-time writer. He is
the author of numerous radio plays and television
dramas, as well as eighteen novels including
Savant, *Churchill's Gold*, *Dominator*, *Swift* and
Trojan. He lives in Surrey.

Also by James Follett
*available in Mandarin Paperbacks

*The Doomsday Ultimatum
Crown Court
*Ice
*U-700
*Churchill's Gold
*The Tiptoe Boys (*filmed as* Who Dares
Wins)
Earthsearch
Earthsearch – Deathship
*Mirage
*Dominator
*A Cage of Eagles
*Trojan
*Torus
*Savant

James Follett

THOSE IN PERIL

Mandarin

A Mandarin Paperback
THOSE IN PERIL

First published in Great Britain 1994
by William Heinemann Ltd
and Mandarin Paperbacks
imprints of Reed Consumer Books Ltd
Michelin House, 81 Fulham Road, London SW3 6RB
and Auckland, Melbourne, Singapore and Toronto

Reprinted 1994 (twice)

Copyright © James Follett 1994
The author has asserted his moral rights

A CIP catalogue record for this title
is available from the British Library
ISBN 0 7493 1963 1

Typeset by Deltatype Ltd, Ellesmere Port, Cheshire
Printed and bound in Great Britain by BPC Paperbacks Ltd
A member of The British Printing Company Ltd

Eternal Father, strong to save,
Whose arm hath bound the restless wave,
Who bids the mighty ocean deep
Its own appointed limits keep:
O hear us when we cry to thee
For those in peril on the sea.

W. Whiting, 1825-78

It was, and will remain for many years,
the longest and most hazardous rescue
in maritime history.

Admiral Karl Doenitz
Commander-in-Chief, U-boats, 1936-43

Part One

1

Paris fell quietly to the German army on Friday, 14 June 1940.

At 6:30 a.m. the sky was already bright, heralding another fine day, when an advance column of military vehicles reached the Place de la Concorde. Within fifteen minutes key government offices were occupied. Early-morning workers, unable to comprehend what was happening to their capital, watched as a huge swastika was hung from the Arc de Triomphe and army engineers strung loudspeakers from buildings along the Champs-Elysées in readiness for the triumphant parade that would take place later that morning. There was some resistance, however: a postman remonstrating with a *feld-gendarmerie* sergeant before a small, sympathetic crowd. He had mail to deliver to the Air Ministry, and he was determined that an army of occupation was not going to stop him. Eventually, to a chorus of cheers from the onlookers, the steel-helmeted military policeman allowed him through.

An open-top field grey staff car leading a convoy of three commandeered Citroën vans scurried past the trucks and armoured cars, intent on its own mission. It was occupied by three Kriegsmarine NCOs – all chief petty officers – and an officer. The CPOs looked suitably imposing in their Marine Artillery field service dress, their helmets and sub-machine-guns gleaming. They kept their gaze rigidly ahead although they were secretly delighted at being chosen to be among the first naval personnel to enter Paris.

At the wheel was Leutnant zur See Dieter Rohland, feeling self-conscious in his navy blue walking-out uniform. His

3

otherwise good-humoured features were drawn into an unnatural and unconvincing impassive expression of someone who was trying to look unworried about the responsibility that had been thrust upon him. He had a tall, gangling frame which had been the despair of his tailor. It was only the second time that he had worn it, but he had promised his chief that he would put on a good show. Normally Admiral Canaris, the head of the Abwehr, the military intelligence service, would not have given a damn what his subordinates wore – he rarely wore a uniform himself – but the occupation of Paris was considered special. It was an army show, therefore the navy had to look their best, even in the tiny role they were playing.

Dieter used back-doubles to avoid the snarl-up around the Hotel Crillon where the army were setting up their headquarters, and nearly lost one of his following vans in the process. He knew this part of Paris well. He had spent long periods the previous year posing as a tourist, looking his part as the son of a wealthy Berlin factory-owner with a passionate interest in photography, because that was exactly what he was. The truth was always the best cover of all. Armed with a Leica, he had spent many happy hours photographing the imposing government buildings, especially in the early hours when the long shadows created interesting variations in light and shade on the over-elaborate façades. The evenings had been spent, or ill-spent, drinking coffee and brandy in the cafés and bistros of Montmartre, and falling in and out of love.

Dieter and his retinue of vans drew up outside the admiralty annexe office block. It was a drab, nondescript structure in reinforced concrete, thrown up by a speculative builder in the 1920s, and tucked down a side street as if the magnificent city was ashamed of the abortions it was capable of producing. Yet the building had featured in a number of Dieter's photographs. On one occasion he had even managed to photograph senior anti-submarine experts from the navies of the allied powers arriving for one of their committee's

4

monthly progress meetings. They had all obligingly glanced towards the camera as they entered the building because Dieter had been photographing a provocatively-dressed model hired for the occasion.

Despite the early hour, the doors of the building were ajar and a party of workmen were dragging crates of box files from the lift. Directing operations was a frantic, arm-waving civil servant. Two hours before he had been asleep in his flat, unaware until his phone had rung that Wehrmacht columns were marching into Paris. Now the lobby was strewn with orange boxes and tea chests crammed to overflowing with bulky manila files, all was noise and bustle, a tone close to panic in the confusion.

'Where's that damned transport!' the official wailed, grabbing the reception desk telephone and frantically rattling the antique hook. 'It should have been here thirty minutes ago.'

'It's right here, Monsieur Dellan,' said Dieter pleasantly.

The workmen stopped unloading the lift. The civil servant gaped and dropped the telephone, his face suddenly haggard. Confronting him was a tall, serious-looking German officer. The Frenchman's startled gaze took in the single gold sleeve stripe on the uniform tunic, and the gold lightning flash on his white shoulder boards denoting a communications officer. Flanking the resplendent officer were the three chief petty officers. There wasn't much doubt about the credentials of the sub-machine-guns they were holding at the ready. Their expressions suggested that they were eager for trouble. In reality not one of them had ever pulled a trigger in anger.

Dieter saluted the official and clicked his heels while peeling off his gloves, finger by finger. 'Good morning, Monsieur Dellan. Leutnant Dieter Rohland at your service. We have both had an early start to our day.' His French sounded good because he had been rehearsing the greeting. It added to the hapless official's confusion: precisely the effect Dieter had hoped for. He crossed to one of the tea chests, picked up a file at random, and opened it.

'Those documents are Government property!' the official protested.

Dieter bowed. His solemn expression covered his delight. He had expected to have to turn the building inside-out in his search for these files. 'Correct, m'sieur. German Government property, and now in the care of the Kriegsmarine. Please do not look so upset – I will give you an official receipt for them.'

2

Eighteen hours later what must have been a tonne of documents – many of the file covers stamped 'Most Secret' in English – were stacked to the ceiling in Dieter's office in the warren-like headquarters of the Abwehr at Titpitzufer 72–76 in Berlin. As the head of Branch I(C) – Submarine Communications Research (research being the polite word for espionage) – Dieter was entitled to his own room overlooking the Landwehr Canal. Despite the prestigious title, it wasn't much of a department; he was also its filing clerk and typist. Nor was it much of an office, barely room for his desk and chair.

He grabbed the nearest file and switched on his desk lamp. It was late and he had had no sleep for nearly twenty-four hours, but he was eager to make a start, even an uncharacteristic haphazard start, because he couldn't bear to return to his flat without taking a peek at his booty. To his astonishment the first document he looked at bore the signature of Winston Churchill. Dieter's English was shaky but good enough to extract the gist. The typed note was addressed to the chairman of a committee and offered heartfelt congratulations for the committee's 'remarkable achievement'.

Dieter checked the date. It had been written in 1938. Churchill was out of office then, but his friend, Admiral Dudley Pound, had taken him to Portsdown to see a demonstration of 'your wondrous new weapon'. Churchill had concluded:

I'm delighted to see that the work of the committee has borne such fruit. That the free nations of Europe can work together with a common purpose and with such success gives me great confidence in the future. In the dark days of 1916/17, when the U-boats nearly brought us to our knees, I never dreamed that the time would come when I would actually hear one of those devilish, damned un-English weapons asking to be destroyed.

Dieter separated the document from the file's laces and held it in his hand. It was a letter that had been handled by Germany's greatest enemy and would count heavily in his battle for translators of this treasure. As his eye wandered over the bulging crates that filled his office, he wondered how much of Churchill's confidence would be left if the great man knew that not only had the letter fallen into German hands, but also all the documents and notes relating to the development of their most secret anti-submarine weapon. The Allied Submarine Detection Investigation Committee had been formed in the 1920s to come up with effective U-boat countermeasures. Because the allies shared the German love of acronyms it was inevitable that the weapon they had developed was named after the initials of their committee:

ASDIC.

3

November 1941

The hounds didn't bay or howl, but Joe Cleary, exhausted to the point of hallucination by the sixty-mile pursuit across the treacherous terrain of the Rio Grande, knew they were close.

The broken, mountainous territory of southern Brazil was behind him. Now he was struggling across the undulating plains of the pampas that stretched through Uruguay to Argentina. He had been on foot for six hours since the front forks of his stolen motorcycle had finally collapsed. He drew comfort from the fact that as the hunted, the choice of route had been his; he knew this region well, and had forced his pursuers to waste at least an hour before finally abandoning their truck which he had led into a swamp.

He breasted a rise and looked back, his chest heaving. When his vision cleared he saw that they were about a mile back, trying to force a straight line through the long pampas grass because they had discovered that following his weaving trail took them through the worst of the swamps. He adjusted the webbing straps of a heavy rucksack so that the harness had a fresh supply of skin to turn to raw meat, and turned his attention ahead. The line of tall parana pines that marked the beginning of the abandoned plantations and settlements along the river was about half a mile away.

Joe's features twisted into a self-satisfied grin of triumph, but the race to the frontier was far from over. His legs were jelly, his heart was steamhammering, and half a mile was the equivalent of ten miles such was the state he was in.

But somehow he made it. Once in the trees and thick undergrowth, he felt more secure. The chase across the plain had left a trail that a blind man could follow whereas here in the plantations he stood a chance of outwitting the two Charrua Indian trackers that accompanied the overseers. Also the plantations meant that the river was close, and the long chase nearly over.

He slid down a steep bank towards the sluggish, silt-laden stream. A protruding root of an aged mahogany tripped him, sending his short but powerful frame sprawling in the mud. He staggered to his feet, and clung grimly to an overhanging branch. Sweat streamed into his eyes. His desperate gasps sucked a mosquito into his lungs. The bout of hacking coughs needed to dislodge the insect drained his dwindling reserves of strength. He struggled on through the gloom-shrouded forest, splashing across small inlets of static water silver filigreed by light filtering through the trees. He reckoned that he was a mile from the abandoned missionary research station.

The tall, quiet-spoken German had been precise in his instructions: a boat with an outboard motor would be tied-up at the station's jetty. All Joe had to do was cross the river where the German would be waiting for him on the Uruguayan bank. One more mile. One mile was all that was left of the vast, pro-British country of Brazil. Then a trip across the river, and the German would whisk him away to safety. So what if he didn't know the tall German's name? Joe prided himself on being a good judge of character; he instinctively knew that the man could be trusted.

He tripped again, fell badly, winding himself, and discovered that he hadn't the strength to get up. He pressed his cheek against the clammy soil and wept — the first time during the gruelling chase that he had come close to feeling sorry for himself. A mile! A poxy, sodding mile! Sweet Jesus, it might as well be twenty.

Come on, Cleary! Another mile, a river crossing, and you'll be $5000 richer.

He saw the money in his mind's eye as bundles of crisp, new $10 bills. With the $2000 he had already been paid for this mission, he would be able to open his long-cherished mining equipment rental company in Rio. He saw a smart office with his name on the door, and the vision bored into an untapped vein of strength. He staggered to his feet and stumbled blindly on.

He came to a second, swift-flowing stream and felt a surge of elation. The Indian trackers employed by the mine were good, they saw things when the dogs had no scent to follow, but they would never see his tracks through this discoloured water. He drove himself on for another ten minutes, stumbling on unseen rocks. The water rose to his knees and then his waist. It slowed his progress while adding to his misery and the drain on his meagre reserves of strength. He rested, clinging to a mango's gnarled cage of roots, his chest heaving, half-blinded with sweat.

The rucksack harness was giving him hell. As he slackened a buckle, he saw the leech clinging to the lacework of knotted veins on the underside of his right forearm. The loathsome creature was bloated with his blood. How long had it been gorging itself? Maybe as long as two hours from when he had led his pursuers through a deep swamp. The things released an anaesthetic from behind their grinders which made their victims unaware of their ghastly presence. There were times when Joe wished that he knew less about the plains, swamps and forests of Brazil. With a grimace of disgust, he tore the leech away and crushed its body. Red spurted beneath his stubby fingers. He looked closely at the laceration caused by the creature's grinders. Another minute and it would have broken through the wall of the vein. The proper way to deal with the disgusting things was with a lighted cigarette, but the scent of tobacco smoke could hang for hours in the still air of the forest. The previous month the overseers had returned with a wretched, half-dead miner trussed-up in the back of their truck. The grinning Charrua tracker, who had earned a five dollar bonus, had found the fugitive by following his nose. Dogs were primarily interested in ground scent, but the Charrua Indians could flit like ghosts through the trees as they tracked an air scent, while their eyes picked out the thousand and one clues left by the passage of an animal – or a man. But the stream would bugger them – provided he was heading in the right direction.

The Charrua had been his main worry when he made his escape from the mining camp the previous night. There were hardly any of the little bastards left – the early settlers had hunted them to near extinction – but the few descendants had been recruited by the mine. That was something he had written in the report for the tall German.

Realising that he had lost his bearings, Joe looked up, but the direction of the mist-shrouded afternoon sun was impossible to determine through the thick canopy. The trees around him were young but neglected – afromosa and sapele – they

10

didn't grow naturally here, therefore he *had* to be near the research station. He lifted what looked like a cheap wrist-watch to his eye. A gentle squeeze on the winder and the second hand floated free. It swung uncertainly on its tiny jewelled pivot before settling to magnetic north. Pleased with the result, he pulled the left-hand pocket of his sodden trousers inside-out. Although the linen map stitched to the lining had been impregnated with wax to make it waterproof, it was scarcely legible, but it was sufficient for his purpose. He ripped off the outer small-scale map of the entire region which had now served its purpose and revealed a large-scale map of the border area. He traced his route with a labour-calloused forefinger. There was the stream he had just crossed, and this was the stream he was standing in now. He followed the pecked line. He was on course: the river and the abandoned agricultural research station were about half a mile away. He stuffed the lining back and pushed on. Such a simple idea, that map; it had fooled the overseers. They made all the miners turn out their pockets during the thrice-daily searches, but they had never thought to check the linings. The map, the compass-watch, the Minox camera and the film had been provided by the German. Good planning. No wonder they were walking away with the war in Europe. Joe was certain that Germany would emerge triumphant. Not that he cared either way – just so long as he received his $5000. Whoever won in Europe would be a customer for the mineral riches of Brazil. The huge country was an ally of the British, but corruption was a way of life; its politicians, wholesalers, distributors and exporters would trade with anyone with money.

Joe Cleary had spent thirty of his forty-five years in South America, winning a precarious and often dangerous living from the mineral riches of the vast continent. Sometimes feast, more often famine. Although it had never been boring, he had learned belatedly that the way to make real money was not prospecting – those days were over – but in supplying the

11

mining industry. His dreams were his source of strength and kept him going.

The stream had shallowed to knee depth when the sound of something crashing through the undergrowth broke in on his thoughts. He wheeled around. Loud panting of straining dobermans held in check on chokers. Snuffling. A volley of curses in Portuguese as the dogs pulled someone over. That would be Perlez. A machete hacking at the undergrowth. Jesus, they were less than two hundred yards away. Despite his mounting terror, Joe took long, unhurried strides, carefully setting down his feet to avoid splashing. Only when he had put another hundred paces between himself and his pursuers did he haul himself out of the stream and force his exhausted body into a shambling run. There was an excited yipping that was quickly hushed; either the dogs or the Indian trackers had his scent; or both. There was no point in trying to hide his tracks now. Distance between him and his pursuers was all that mattered. Once he reached the river, he would be safe.

He came to the once broad track that the Jesuit fathers had cleared through the plantation. Now, after nearly three years' disuse, it was overgrown and overhung with creepers and vines. In another two or three years the once well-managed plantation would be an impenetrable jungle. All that was left of the road were water-filled ruts where the Jesuits' supply trucks had compressed the impoverished soil to a degree that merely slowed the forest's inexorable repossession, but didn't stop it.

Joe followed the waterlogged tracks down the slight slope. The trees thinned and gave way to the now neglected and overgrown field systems where the priests had experimented with new crop strains financed by grants from the big mining corporations. His heavy boots squelched deep into the mud, making every stride an ankle-wrenching misery. Several times his feet sank deep and refused to pull free, usually sending him flat on his face. At one point he lay still for a sacrificed thirty seconds, his lungs frantically hoovering.

Sweet Jesus! The river! He could smell it!

Something crashing through the dense undergrowth in a field behind brought him to his feet and spurred him on. By the time he was staggering drunkenly through the abandoned collection of rusting, corrugated steel huts he was splattered from head to foot with clinging mud, and could barely see where he was going. The steps of what had once been the trading post next to the clinic looked inviting. Through the haze of his crippling exhaustion, Joe had warm memories of his illegal prospecting days when he had spent pleasant evenings drinking bottled beer on the broad stoep. Provided you had money, the Jesuits were not adverse to selling you booze, or even putting up prospectors for the night. But all that had stopped in 1939 when the British had bought the mining concession outright. The new owners had shifted the research station several miles down river. They had cleared and levelled fields, and had provided the fathers with new huts and a fully-equipped laboratory as an incentive to accept the move. Even the Indian settlements around the station had been relocated. The British had spent more than even gold or diamond mine owners would normally spend in such a short time. In the rucksack was the reason why.

But there was no time to rest. With his heart threatening to hammer its way out of his ribcage, Joe reached the river where children had once played. He slithered down the bank and doubled up against one of the jetty's stout uprights while he got his breath back. He wiped the sweat and mud from his eyes and scanned the forest of tall reeds lining the Uruguay bank opposite. He didn't expect to see the German, but he would be there, watching and waiting.

His boots rang on the jetty's sawn boards as he stumbled towards the water. The jetty was more of wooden quay – a substantial structure designed to berth the small, flat-bottomed Sulzer steam launches that had plied the river. He looked down at the long Indian dugout, tugging at its painter as the swollen, silt-laden yellow river oiled past. The river was

13

narrow at this point, about a hundred yards; fordable before the rains which was why the Jesuits had chosen this spot, but when in flood, as it was now, the narrowing meant that it flowed faster. Its apparent sluggishness near the bank was dangerously deceptive; in the centre swift-moving islands of tangled trees and vegetation betrayed the true strength of the current.

The boat's outboard was an ancient Atco – little more than a two-stroke eggbeater. Always a pig to start. It was the humidity that crucified their carburettors. He half fell into the narrow craft, and crouched low, remembering to keep his weight over the centreline. He closed the engine's choke, opened the valve on the gravity fuel tank, and pulled slowly on the recoil cord to prime the float chamber. Next, open the choke to halfway, and give a sharp yank on the cord.

The cylinder ports on the little engine emitted an explosive report and a cloud of blue smoke, but the engine refused to catch. Another pull. Nothing. Another explosive backfire was followed by the crack of a rifle and a bullet splintering into the jetty. He twisted around just as a second round whined and smacked into the dugout's prow.

Five men had appeared on the bank three hundred yards upstream and were splashing towards him – three Europeans and two Indian trackers. The blond European steadied his rifle against a tree and took careful aim. Joe uttered a swift prayer and mustered all his strength for one last, superhuman yank on the outboard. It fired, ran erratically for a few turns, stopped. The effort had ruptured the leech-weakened vein. A thin stream of blood spurted from Joe's forearm without him noticing it as he dived over the side, just as a third round ripped into the dugout where he had been crouching.

He thrust his head above water, snatched a gasp of air, and forced himself under again. The water was only five feet deep here which made it difficult to submerge. Nor did the bulk of the rucksack help. A hard shove against the jetty led to a floundering underwater stroke that churned up the mud on

14

the bottom. It was hopeless; in his present state of exhaustion he stood no chance of reaching the cover offered by the vegetation drifting down the centre of the river. With lungs bursting, he broke the surface and heaved down another gasp of air. He plunged down again, making it look as if he was heading towards the middle of the river, but he twisted around underwater and kicked out blindly for the jetty. He blundered into one of the uprights and hauled himself beneath the boards. His boots sank into the riverbed mud, releasing sluggish bubbles of foul-smelling gas from the decaying vegetation. The sound of his choking gasp as he clawed down air was cloaked by the clump of boots pounding onto the jetty. Through the gaps in the boards he could see the moulded tread on their soles a few inches above his face. There was no sign of the Indian trackers – maybe they were holding the dogs on the bank.

'Perlez! Over there!'

It was Hanlon's unmistakable Glaswegian accent – the mine's day shift superintendent; rough, tough; as bellicose as a bull with gripe. Yet you could have a fist fight with Angus Hanlon at lunchtime, and get drunk with him that evening. Perlez was one of the mulatto guards employed by the mine.

The rifle cracked twice. Two .303 shell cartridge cases rang on the boards and plopped into the water in front of Joe's face. He inhaled a silent lungful of air and submerged by pushing down on the slippery upright. The rucksack rode up; if they looked down through the boards, or if he tried escaping underwater, its bulk would be certain to betray him. His fingers groped for the buckles. He opened his eyes underwater to see what he was doing and saw strands of red lacing the water. They were right before his eyes otherwise he would never have seen them in the yellow jaundice murk. Holy Mother – he had been hit, although he hadn't felt it.

He lashed the rucksack underwater to a central upright where it would be difficult to find. As he did so, he saw the spurts of blood pumping from his arm in unison with his pounding heart. He raised his head carefully above the surface. Thank God they hadn't brought the dogs onto the jetty. Relieved of the rucksack's bulk, he began to feel more confident.

'I tell you he was no condition to reach the middle!' Hanlon was snarling. 'He's got to be close.'

'But if he got even a few yards out, he could be a hundred yards downstream by now!' The second voice belonged to Ian Craddock. Young, well-educated. A cold-blooded public school import from London who worked in the admin block. Joe wondered why he had come on the chase. It was well known that Hanlon and Craddock despised each other.

'There!' Hanlon bellowed.

The rifle cracked again. More cartridge cases danced through the gaps and fell into the water right under Joe's nose.

'We're shooting at logs, Angus,' Craddock observed.

The water flowing from under the jetty was streaked with red. Shit! It only needed one of them to look down . . .

Joe hooked his arm around the upright and jammed his thumb into his armpit, feeling for the pulse of the artery and squeezing hard. But the pressure made no difference: the broken vein continued pumping tendril-like beacons of crimson. Where the hell were the dogs? Could they pick up the smell of blood off the surface of the water? Cayman could. But the alligators would have abandoned this section of the river; the big reptiles steered clear of human habitation. But the station had been abandoned for two years. Maybe the buggers had returned? His imagination shifted up a gear when something brushed against his injured arm. A deep breath of air, a slow submersion, eyes open underwater in time to see a small, bug-eyed fish with a snub, protruding lower jaw dart into the silt-laden murk. Another one shied away when he blew bubbles. A flash of small, needle-like teeth, and it was gone.

Piranha. Not cayman. Thank Christ for that.

Piranha were curious, but timid. With one exception. The

16

exception was the black piranha. But they were rare, preferring the rain forest rivers to the north. And besides, the stories about shoals of black piranhas stripping a horse carcass to a skeleton in a minute were grossly exaggerated: it usually took about ten minutes. After a lifetime in Brazil, Joe had heard of only two cases of piranha attacking people; both on the Amazon, not this tiddly little tributary that marked the border between Brazil and Uruguay.

He lay back, allowed his face to break the surface, and filled his lungs slowly and quietly. The three pairs of boots stumped and shuffled above him. Hanlon and Craddock were still arguing about how far downstream their quarry was likely to be by now.

Joe was about submerge again when a sudden, agonising pain in his injured forearm forced him to give an involuntary gasp. He half jerked his suddenly heavy arm out of the water. The black piranha refused to let go. It was over a foot long and had buried its vicious incisors deep into his flesh. He snatched at it and felt the spasm of its powerful muscles as it tried to tear his flesh away. Another piranha drove its teeth into his shoulder. The yellow water turned red. And then the shoal was upon him: ripping and tearing, their frenzied bodies beating the water, blending Joe's blood with the silt and creating a ghastly orange foam. The scream that rose in his throat was cut off as he lost his footing and slipped under. Then he was beating and flailing blindly, his arms and legs thrashing in a futile attempt to beat off the ravening hordes of snapping jaws that were ripping dementedly into every exposed square inch of his flesh.

'Jesus Christ!' Hanlon yelled. His powerful fingers hooked one of the boards. The rotten, waterlogged timber broke away easily. He tore up a second board. For some seconds the three men were too numb to move as they stared down at the seething maelstrom. In thirty seconds the turbid water had turned from orange to bright crimson. Joe's face broke the surface, and the men saw that the creatures had devoured one

17

of his eyes. Now they were ripping the flesh from his cheekbones. They were even tearing into his throat, turning his screams to obscene glugs that frothed the blood around his severed windpipe.

Craddock and Hanlon yanked up more boards. Hanlon threw himself flat and reached down. He nearly threw up as his fingers closed around a bloody mass of pulp and white bone that had once been a man's hand. He tried to haul Joe out of the water but the sheer weight of thrashing, writhing fish locked by their jaws to the dying man made the task impossible. One of the little bastards even darted for Hanlon's fingers.

Craddock grabbed Joe's wrist. The arm that they used to lift the man half out of water was no longer an arm but an appendage of bone and vestiges of flesh. Some of the evil-looking snub-nosed fish relinquished their grip and flopped about on the boards. Perlez kicked them back into the river but many held on, thrashing their short but powerful bodies in their desperation to tear away flesh from Joe's legs, not relinquishing their hold until Perlez beat frantically at them with the flat of a machete. Hanlon and Craddock pulled Joe right out of the water and joined in, hammering at the frenzied fish with the broken boards. It was several minutes before the last stunned piranha was kicked back into the river, where the injured ones were shredded and snapped up by the rest of the demented shoal. The three men stopped, chests heaving, and stared down in horrified disbelief at the remains of Joe Cleary lying on what was left of his side. The left arm and both legs had been reduced to a virtual skeleton. Even the boots bore marks of the piranhas' murderous jaws.

'Jesus Christ,' said Craddock weakly. 'Jesus bloody Christ.'

All three men saw the movement beneath the shredded remnants of Joe's shirt.

'Still alive,' Perlez croaked, his eyes round with terror.

'He can't be,' Hanlon muttered hoarsely. Tough as he was, this had shaken him badly. Craddock tried to speak but was unable to form any words.

The Brazilian turned the body over onto its back. Joe's remaining eye stared unseeing at the sky from his hideously mutilated face. The eyelid was gone. Shreds of tissue clung to cheekbone and jawbone like carnival bunting of a festival in Hades. The voracious creatures had chewed into their victim's solar plexus. A gasping piranha flopped out of the gaping wound. Perlez gave a grunt of disgust and stamped on it, nearly breaking through the jetty's boards.

The shredded remains of Joe's lips moved.

'He *is* alive!' Craddock cried, ashen faced.

Perlez crossed himself and moved back in fear. For a man to receive such injuries and still be alive was the work of Satan.

Hanlon knelt beside the dying man. 'Cleary!' It took an effort to make his voice sound harsh. 'Where's the rucksack?'

The eye moved in its pulped socket. It seemed to focus on Hanlon. The overseer repeated his demand. There was a ghastly frothing rasp of breath from Joe's neck where his windpipe had been savaged.

Craddock pointed the rifle at Joe so that muzzle was inches from the staring, lidless eye. When the Englishman spoke his voice was quiet, matter-of-fact. 'Where's the rucksack, Cleary?'

The eye regarded the rifle. Another whistle of breath dragged through torn airways and past flaps of shredded tissue.

'He can't talk,' said Hanlon shortly. 'Look at his throat, man.'

'Where's the rucksack!'

'For Chrissake—'

The rifle roared and the eye dissolved. Birds rose in screeching panic from the trees, and the echo boomed back and forth across the river like a salute to the dead man. The dobermans settled on the bank, their heads lowered. They didn't like gunfire.

Craddock met Hanlon's gaze. 'It was the humane thing to do, Mr Hanlon.'

The Scot looked down at the dead man. His working life in this country had been spent kicking the hell out of native labourers to get them to work. He had used everything: fists, boots, even a crop when he worked for one particularly sadistic mine owner. But he had never killed a man. He shook his head and said: 'And I always thought that scientists were bald men with test tubes who were always forgetting things. All I can say is that there must be a lot at stake, Mr Craddock.'

'More than you could ever guess,' Craddock replied. 'I'm sure he had the rucksack on when he fell out of the boat,' he mused, staring dispassionately down at Joe's remains. He went through what was left of the dead man's pockets before turning his attention to the water. The black piranhas were still at work beneath the jetty, fighting and snapping at bits of flesh.

Hanlon swallowed hard, determined not to give this cold-blooded bastard the pleasure of seeing him throw up. 'We were too far off to see clearly. The chances are he dumped it on the trail. The dogs will find it.'

'It was on his back,' Craddock insisted.

The Scot gave a humourless smile. 'Yeah – well if you think that, Mr Craddock, you're welcome to have a swim around. You'll not mind if I watch?'

The Englishman's answer was to stride from the jetty. He drew his machete and hacked three saplings from the under-growth. He signalled to the Indians to carry Joe's body onto the bank. They were reluctant to handle it but they did as they were told. The three men probed the water around the jetty. A few remaining piranhas lunged impotently at the saplings.

'We're wasting our time,' said Hanlon at the end of fifteen minutes when all they had found was a bicycle frame.

'We *have* to find that rucksack,' said Craddock determinedly.

'It's lost,' Hanlon answered. 'And if it's lost, it doesn't matter, does it?'

'The Minox camera we found hidden in the showers had his

fingerprints on it, Mr Hanlon. If he had a miniature camera, it's a safe deduction that he also had rolls of miniature film. And God only knows what else was in that rucksack. So, if you don't mind, we keep searching.'

'Yes, I do mind. It'll be dark in a couple of hours. We have to start heading back to the truck now. It'll take us half the night to dig it out of that fucking swamp.'

Craddock glanced up at the sullen sky. 'Very well. But we return tomorrow. And the day after. We've got to find that rucksack.'

'If you say so, Mr Craddock,' said Hanlon evenly.

The Englishman gestured to the Indians to dump Joe's body in the river.

'We ought to bury him properly,' said Hanlon uneasily as the two men carried the corpse back onto the jetty.

'Why?'

'It's the decent thing to do.'

'I don't believe in doing decent things if they're illogical. Nature will dispose of our friend's body whether he's buried in the ground or in the river. It's worms or fish, Mr Hanlon. The fish started the job so they might as well finish it.'

The Indians dropped Joe into the river and watched the water turn to foam as the insatiable piranhas caught the scent of raw meat and closed hungrily in.

4

There was a witness to Joe Cleary's bizarre death.

Despite the small army of hungry ants that had found a way through the folds of his bush suit, Dieter Rohland kept perfectly still, lying in the reeds while watching the events on the opposite bank through a pair of Zeiss binoculars. During his year in Uruguay he had learned about the legendary hunting abilities of the Charrua Indians, so the only movements he permitted himself were to occasionally wipe the

21

binoculars' lenses which were persistently misting over. It was the humidity, of course. The damned, soul-sapping, will-destroying subtropical humidity. It had probably condensed in the Atco outboard motor's fuel tank. Dieter felt very bad about Joe's death; the miner had trusted him, yet what more could have been done? Dieter had tested the outboard that morning before leaving the dugout tethered to the jetty. It had started first time, every time.

He waited and watched, steadfastly ignoring the fiery attentions of the ants. The three men were probing the waters around the jetty. Dieter knew what they were looking for: he had seen Joe jump into the water with the rucksack on his back, and be pulled out of the river without it. Another futile attempt to polish the lenses before refocusing on the three men. The misting was a nuisance but he had no difficulty in identifying the big man as Angus Hanlon. The mulatto would be one of the guards – the file on the Brazilian mine that Dieter was building up said that over a hundred had been recruited from the rubber plantation workers at Cuaros. But the fair-haired, younger man was an enigma. About thirty to thirty-five. Dieter knew that he had seen that face before; not in the flesh, most likely in a photograph. But where? And when? Dieter cursed the misted prisms that prevented him getting a good look at the man.

They were arguing now. Soon, after a few final prods around the jetty, the party made their way back past the huts. The dobermans seemed pleased to retrace their tracks.

Dieter waited fifteen minutes to be certain the men were unlikely to return before backing out of his hiding place. He rose from the reeds like a giraffe, and stretched, stamping the circulation back into his cramped legs, and scratching bliss-fully at the insect bites.

In uniform, Dieter looked an unlikely naval officer. Out of uniform, he looked an even more unlikely spy. Successful spies merged with their background. But at nearly six foot five inches tall, he had about as much chance of merging with his background as a black panther on an icecap. Moreover, successful spies had colourless, forgettable personalities; whereas after only a few months in Montevideo, the tall, always-smiling Berliner couldn't move without a huge entourage of shrieking children demanding to carry his photographic equipment, not so much because of his generous tips, but because they liked him. Adoring mothers wanted him to photograph their children, and unmarried young women were just adoring. His easy-going charm was such that he could rebuff the former and deter the latter without giving offence. A smile and a joke were usually enough. It was possible that he would have laughed uproariously were he to discover that his presence in South America, indeed the entire expensive operation of which he was a part, was the result of a translation error made by an Abwehr clerk when working on one of the Allied submarine committee's documents that he had commandeered in Paris.

But there was no sign of his customary good humour as he returned in the failing light to his Chrysler saloon parked back on the unmetalled Melo–Centurian road. His expression was cold as he rummaged among some wildlife photographic equipment and produced a vacuum flask. It had been a long, tiring forty-eight hours which had included a six hundred kilometre train journey from Montevideo to Melo where he had hired the car. One swallow of the near-lethal Uruguayan black coffee was enough to banish any craving for sleep for a week. He took two; there was much to be done before sunset without worrying about what the toxins in the brew were doing to his stomach lining. He found a waterproof torch among his photographic equipment, and returned to the river bank.

The dugout with an Atco outboard was hidden in the reeds. Like the outboard he had left for Joe Cleary's escape, it refused to start. Dieter was drenched with sweat and his arm was aching abominably before the motor stuttered into life. Roundly cursing the village trader who had sold him both boats, he crouched his awkward frame over the outboard's tiller arm and steered the craft some distance upstream, staying in the slack water close to the bank before swinging into midstream, playing the torch beam ahead to avoid logs and islands of vegetation.

He judged the crossing well; the current swept him downstream so that he was able to bring the boat alongside the jetty and tie up in one neat manoeuvre. He cut the engine and sat quite still on the stern thwart, staring down at the black, turbid water for any sign of the marauding piranha while trying to ignore the fear knotting his stomach at the thought of what he had to do.

Firstly, think things carefully through. It seemed unlikely that the piranhas would have eaten through the webbing straps of Joe's rucksack, so what would account for it not being on his back when the British had hauled him out of the river? No; the likelihood was that Joe had decided that he stood a better chance of survival if he got rid of it. If so, had he merely unbuckled it and dumped it, or had he concealed it so that it could be recovered?

Dieter had had several meetings with Joe in Montevideo. The Irishman was stubborn and possessed of an animal cunning, and, above all, greed. Perhaps greed was unfair. The few bits of good fortune that had come Joe Cleary's way during his hard life were probably due to an ability to recognise an opportunity when he saw it and grab it. Joe wasn't getting any younger. The days when he could earn a living selling a few gems here and there were numbered. The Brazilian government was tightening its control at one end of the business, and organised crime was closing in at the other. He was desperate to start in the mining supplies business. No, Dieter reasoned, Joe would not have just dumped the rucksack.

He shone his torch under the jetty. There was a gap of several centimetres between the surface of the now black water and the underside of the boards. The sawn planks were nailed to three timber joists which were in turn supported on three rows of uprights driven deep into the mud. He had seen the three men probing the outer uprights, but not the hard-to-reach centre row, apart from those near the gap where the boards had been torn up.

Dieter toyed with the idea of pulling up the rest of the boards, but that would alert the British should they return to continue their search the following day. There was nothing for it but to get into the water. He stripped off, eased his reluctant way down.

The cold touch of the water and soft glutinous ooze closing around his feet played havoc with his imagination. The bubbles were worse: they slid up his legs, brushed past his genitals, and glurped obscenely around him like living creatures, releasing a stench of marsh gas. He clung to the jetty and ran his foot up and down the first central upright.

Nothing.

He jammed his torch into a gap so that it splayed a beam under the jetty, reached under the boards with his foot, and explored the second upright with his foot. A splinter was certain to lead to infection in this muck, but the timbers were worn smooth by the continuous abrasion of the silt-laden current. To reach the third and subsequent supports meant ducking right under the jetty. His nerves screamed at him in the feeble light. The torch created an entire troupe of macabre dancing shadows that whirled the faceless denizens of his nightmares in a ghastly, maddened masque.

There was nothing attached to the third upright. The fourth was near the gap in the middle of the jetty. His foot encountered something – something that the current was pressing against the timber. He reached down as far as he could, head on one side, the cold touch of the river on his temple stirred his imagination to a frenzy. His fingertips brushed against what felt like a strap. There was ragged material attached to the strap. Something shapeless touched his thigh and played a symphony with his tortured nerves. He got a good grip on the strap and heaved.

It was as well that Dieter had allowed the search party to get well away before beginning his own search. Had they been within a mile it was likely that they would have heard his scream as Joe's near fleshless, grinning face broke the black surface beside him. Dieter lost his footing and swallowed water as he went under. A soundless realisation screamed from the very centre of his being that the water flooding his throat was the same black poison that he was sharing with the dead man and he retched, violently and in near-panic. He hauled himself up in blind panic and crashed his head against the boards. The sudden pain brought him to his senses, enabling him to bring his coughing under control. His wild prayer when he opened his eyes was that the apparition would be gone. But Joe was still there. The exposed, now lipless gums and poorly filled teeth leered in ghastly appreciation of Dieter's terror. The terrible head nodded and dipped below the surface. A fleshless hand wearing a gold ring reached talons of bone to Dieter like a priest bestowing a blessing. He beat the claw away in panic and watched the current bear the thing away from under the jetty and into the darkness. Dieter's instincts screamed at him to get out of the water and leave this terrible place as fast as possible. But his professionalism and dogged determination took over, and he resumed his grisly search.

The rucksack was tied to the next upright. There was no mistaking the feel to his probing foot of the steel frame and the bulging canvas pack. His instep traced a strap knotted around the timber close to the mud. There was no point in hesitating. He took a deep breath and plunged his head under water. Luckily Joe had tied a relatively slack knot, no doubt because he had expected to return and retrieve the rucksack. The strap came free without trouble. He pulled the rucksack to the surface, steered it to the end of the jetty, and heaved its waterlogged bulk into his boat.   Scrambling out of the water and allowing the chill night breeze that had sprung up to dry his body was the nearest thing to true bliss that Dieter had ever experienced. He dressed and stepped into the boat. The Atco was still warm and started without trouble. A final sweep with the torch picked out Joe's remains now beached in shallow water a little way downstream. Dieter played the beam on the dead man and offered a brief prayer for his soul. That the man had died for greed rather than for Germany did not matter; Joe had shown great courage. If Dieter had a spade he would have spared the time and effort to give him a decent burial. He felt strongly about such matters.

The sodden rucksack at his feet oozed cold, evil-smelling water onto his ankle. He angrily kicked it clear, opened the throttle, and let in the clutch. For once the usual laughter lines around his eyes were absent. He would have been even angrier had he known that the cause of Joe Cleary's death and his own miserable experience in the river could be traced back to that unfortunate but understandable translation error.

5

'Tammy,' said Mrs Montgomerie reprovingly, not taking her opera glasses from her eyes as she watched the batsman square up to the bowler. 'Your finger.'

Tammy did her best not to pout, and obediently crooked her little finger as she raised the translucent bone china teacup to her lips. She also did her best not to make a noise as she sipped her tea, and failed.

It was the tiniest of slurps, but Angela Montgomerie's hearing was such that while taking a bath in her mansion she could detect a mouse sneezing three floors below in the wine cellar. And such was her rule over her household, that the mouse would have known that it had been heard and would have done the decent thing and committed suicide by picking a fight with the Burmese cat.

Tammy's flawless olive cheeks, framed by her unEnglish black tresses, flushed, but she was saved from a rebuke by a brisk round of applause from the handful of spectators when the works team's ninth batsman was dismissed in a blizzard of flying bails and stumps. Mrs Montgomerie allowed her opera glasses to drop by their gold chain and clapped sedately.

'Oh, well bowled!' she exclaimed. 'Well bowled!'

Tammy dutifully set down her cup and saucer and joined in the applause, although her white lace gloves rendered her feigned appreciation quite soundless. Her Latin temperament told her that it was typical English stupidity to clap the success of opponents, but the eleven years of her seventeen that she had been 'under Mrs Angela Montgomerie's wing' suggested that it was politic to remain silent. The role of a demure English rose did not sit happily on Tamara Derosa's pretty olive-skinned shoulders, but she accepted her lot with stoic fortitude. After all, Mrs Montgomerie meant well; if it hadn't been for her, Tammy would most likely be working as a prostitute in the mean back streets around the port of Montevideo.

Tammy wondered, not for the first time, what it would be like to have a man make love to her. There was one of the young gardeners whom she often watched covertly from her bedroom window – the one who always stripped to the waist. Such a fine, muscular chest, a smooth back, tight stomach muscles, small buttocks. She could imagine sliding her manicured hands down that bronzed back, under his broad, leather belt, and –

'Tammy!'

Tammy jumped. It was as well she had put her cup down. Tea spilt down her fine new white summer dress would never do; Mrs Montgomerie would be certain to notice that she wasn't wearing a petticoat under the skirt. Or anything else for that matter . . .

'What are you thinking, child?' Mrs Montgomerie's voice was kindly.

'No – nothing, Miss Angela.'

'A few claps are sufficient, Tammy. Just to show appreciation of good play. Nothing more. It's all a matter of poise. And etiquette, of course.'

'Yes, Miss Angela.'

'Something you really must learn, Tammy – poise and etiquette.' The Englishwoman gave her ward an encouraging smile and returned her attention to the game.

It was a fine spring afternoon – warm for November. The blossom on the jacaranda trees around the Montevideo Cricket Club green had survived the icy pampero winds of the winter and was now in full bloom. The broad sweep of the River Plate, over seventy miles wide at this point, sparkled in the distance. Today it was possible to make out the rusting mastheads and radio arrays of the *Admiral Graf Spee*. The German pocket battleship had been scuttled two years before in neutral Uruguayan waters, where she had fled after a mauling by Allied surface units. The rumour that had circulated in smart Montevideo circles at the time was that her captain believed that the British aircraft carrier *Ark Royal* was waiting for him over the horizon when, in fact, it was a thousand miles to the north. It was an incident which, in December 1939, had brought the war briefly to this remote country in the South Atlantic: a seven-day wonder that had had the town abuzz. Now the war had receded to its rightful and proper place in Europe and the North Atlantic, leaving the easy, unhurried life of Montevideo's cosmopolitan high society to continue without further unseemly intrusions.

The one positive aspect of the war, as far as Mrs Montgomerie was concerned, was that it had nearly doubled the price of beef in two years. The good lady's inheritance of her late husband's beef canning and drying business had made her a rich woman in 1936. The day after gaining control, she had promptly doubled the size of the business by raising a bank loan with the Banco Uruguay, and buying the second largest canning factory at Fray Bentos. Since then her continuous expansion had turned the Rio de la Plata and Fray Bentos

29

Meat Company into the second biggest meat processing business in all South America. Now she was an exceedingly rich woman. Angela Montgomerie, the aristocratic daughter of an English judge, who had always scorned what she witheringly described as 'trade', had surprised everyone with her unexpected flair for business; not least her husband's managers who had smugly imagined that the day-to-day running of the business would pass to them. But she had turned out to be a dormant dynamo. Mondays to Fridays, with her shapely legs stuffed into riding breeches, she mingled with the stink of the stockyards at the railhead; prodding cattle; bargaining with bolas-toting gauchos; arguing with stockmen, and inspecting the acres of jerked beef racks where strips of meat, known as charqui, were hung to dry in the sun. At weekends she reverted to her fine clothes, her croquet and cucumber sandwich parties on the lawn served by her butler for Montevideo's coterie of English émigrés and ex-patriots who would do anything for England except live there. Business matters had to be pressingly urgent to be allowed to intrude on Angela Montgomerie's weekends.

She glanced about her to make certain that the member of the British embassy staff whom she planned to buttonhole was still in the offing. She didn't particularly like cricket – a dull game – but she enjoyed the social bonhomie and gossip that relieved the season's otherwise boring Sunday afternoons. Today it wasn't gossip that interested her, but the chance to do a little fixing.

Loud cries of 'Howzat!' broke in on her thoughts. The last batsman in her works team had foolishly allowed himself to be caught in the slips by an embassy fielder. The game was over. The stumps were drawn amid applause, and the players and umpires began converging on the tea marquee. Mrs Montgomerie looked around for a steward. To her annoyance they had disappeared.

'Tammy! Quickly child! A fresh tray for two before the rush.'

'Yes, Miss Angela.' Glad of a chance of an unseen flirt in the marquee with a steward that she had noticed earlier, or with any of the younger stewards if the opportunity arose, Tammy jumped up with undignified haste, grabbed the silver tea tray, and employed an ungainly near-gallop to beat the first of the players into the tent. Mrs Montgomerie watched her rapid departure with marked disapproval. Appalling deportment, and was that the outline of her legs visible through her dress? Oh really, seventeen years old and still she couldn't be trusted to wear a petticoat. It was very definitely high time something was done about Tammy.

'Mr Hammett!'

George Hammett had been heading towards the tent, intent on something stronger than tea, when he felt Angela Montgomerie's gaze target him a second before her imperious command stopped him in his tracks like an Austin 7's progress halted by a 4-inch tank shell through its radiator. He was a personable, unmarried thirty-year-old with a promising career in the Diplomatic Service that would be even more promising when he found a suitable wife. He had already found several, unfortunately none were his. He fixed a warm smile in place, and doffed his straw boater which he wore because he thought it made him look rakish.

'Good afternoon, Mrs Montgomerie. All out for 78 against our 130. Your team will have to do better than that if they want to take the Cup from us.'

'I daresay, Mr Hammett. I daresay.' She indicated the wicker chair just vacated by Tammy. 'I've sent for some fresh tea. Won't you join me?'

The embassy official had no choice but to accept. There was a business matter that he been instructed to follow up with Mrs Montgomerie if the opportunity arose.

'Delighted, Mrs Montgomerie. How kind.' He sat and fanned himself with the boater while regarding his hostess with a mixture of awe and appreciation. With her rich blue eyes and remarkably trim figure, Angela Montgomerie was what Victorian novelists would have described as 'handsome', although there was nothing matronly about her. She was forthright, but rarely harsh; demanding without being too imperious unless determined to get her way. Her upright posture, never allowing herself to relax even for an instant when in company, and the confident thrust of her intriguing bosom, spoke of years of breeding and instilled fear in her enemies. The year before Hammett had seen her renewed passport when it had passed through a colleague's hands. He knew her age. Sixty. Remarkable, because she looked fifty. He said conversationally, 'Incredibly warm for so early, don't you think?' A polite enough opening that bore no hint that he was wondering what his hostess would be like in bed.

Mrs Montgomerie nodded. 'And heavy falls of rain on the pampa – just at the right time. My stockmen tell me the grass is fast this year. There'll be top quality flesh on the hoof when the new droves come in.'

Hammett was surprised at her references to business on a Sunday. He was about to make a suitable comment to lead her on, but broke off when he saw Tammy over her hostess's shoulder. The girl was carrying a laden tea tray towards them. The sun was slightly behind her, revealing the outline of her divine legs. And was that shadow . . . Could it be. . .? No. No. A trick of the light. She flashed him a beguiling smile as she placed the tray on the wicker table. Perfect teeth; full, pouting lips; and such eyes – bottomless pools of black allure in which any man would willingly drown. He half rose and gave her a little bow.

'Ah, Tammy,' said Mrs Montgomerie. 'Thank you so much. Perhaps you'd pour for Mr Hammett? Lemon or milk, Mr Hammett?'

'Milk please, Tammy,' said Hammett faintly, not sure if his voice belonged to him. Tammy had turned her back on her guardian as she bent over the table. Surely the girl realised? And surely it wasn't possible to be treated to such a generous swell of breasts without seeing . . . And there they were – lit by dappled sunlight shining through her lace bodice: two full, mouth-watering nipples, as dark and as plump as ripe black olives. Unsqueezed by human fingers.

'Thank you, Tammy,' said Hammett, smiling as he took the offered cup.

'More milk?' Tammy asked shyly.

'No thanks.'

'Sugar?'

Hammett never took sugar but the bowl was nearer him than the girl, which called for an eager: 'Yes please.'

She leaned even further forward and dropped a sugar lump in his tea with the silver tongs. This time he caught a glimpse of her navel. Not the tight little English asterisk, but a deep, dark glade; a tantalising repository where fantasies got lost.

'And another lump please, Tammy.'

This time Tammy treated Hammett to a sultry smile that in a Catholic country was bordering on the illegal. With Mrs Montgomerie partially unsighted, she picked up the second sugar lump with her fingers, dropped it in the cup, and stirred with the tongs. It was the most blatant act of rebellion that the diplomat had ever seen and he would have smiled had he been less intent on olives and dark glades. Great heavens, the dress was so loose, he could see clear down to her white stockings and buckle shoes, although his gaze was waylaid by other delights before it got that far.

'How many times do I have to tell you, Tammy?' said Mrs Montgomerie wearily. 'You add the milk and sugar, and *then* pass the cup and saucer to your guest. And you do not stir – your guest does. Please apologise to Mr Hammett.'

Tammy pouted those wonderful lips, straightened and smirked conspiratorially at the olive-fancier. 'Sorry, Mr Hammett.'

'Now go and help Mrs Williams with serving. I'm sure she can use some extra help. The stewards are so damnably lazy. And see that you help at the tea table, mind – *not* the bar.'

'Yes, Miss Angela.'

They both watched the girl enter the tent. Hammett had a good view of the serving table from where he was sitting. 'You were saying about high beef yields for the coming year,' he said tentatively, hoping to revive the subject.

'We're looking forward to a buoyant charqui market,' Mrs Montgomerie replied, eyeing Hammett carefully.

He wondered if she could read his thoughts. He said tentatively, 'Naturally the Ministry of Food are anxious to know if you'll be able to meet our importers' orders for canned beef for 1942.'

In the tent hardened beer drinkers suddenly became reformed characters and started queuing at the tea table.

'That would mean producing an extra six hundred thousand tons at Fray Bentos alone,' Mrs Montgomerie observed.

'But you are processing the required amounts of beef already.'

'What your Ministry of Food is after is for *all* my production to switch over to canned beef. That will require new canning plants which I'm not planning until 1943–44. That also means substantial investment, Mr Hammett. The war has driven up the price of tinplate whereas the production costs for charqui are negligible. The sun does most of the work.'

Hammett had been briefed on the problem. Although the production of dried, jerked beef was declining in the world's meat production industries, it was still a high percentage. Charqui had a number of advantages: once dried it could be stored indefinitely and could be eaten raw or cooked. Above all it was cheap, which was why it was still popular. In the northern countries of South America and the Indies it was known as pemmican; in South Africa buffalo and antelope meat prepared in the same manner was called biltong. Such meats were virtually unknown in Britain and would take years to gain acceptance, if in fact they ever did. The trouble was that pound for pound, nothing packed the calories and protein of canned beef. Farm labourers and miners working double shifts needed over 6000 calories a day per person. John Drummond, the government's dietician in wartime, food-rationed Britain was urging a huge increase in the importation of bully beef, or corned beef as it was now known. It had been introduced during the Great War and had become the subject of many jokes, but it was acceptable to British palates, and much more was needed. The beef producers were reluctant to desert their traditional markets. But if a major producer like Mrs Montgomerie could be persuaded to change, then others would do likewise. Hammett talked for a minute, outlining as much as he dared of His Majesty's Government's long-term food planning.

'I promise to give it some careful thought,' Mrs Montgomerie declared. 'But you're asking me to invest over a hundred thousand dollars to meet the needs of a market that might collapse overnight if, heaven forbid, that dreadful Austrian corporal Hitler gets his way.'

Hammett wondered if he ought to appeal to her sense of patriotism, and decided not; Queen Victoria had been on the throne when Mrs Montgomerie had left England, and she had never returned. His judgement was at fault, for Mrs Montgomerie was fiercely patriotic; it was just that she deemed flag-waving to be unseemly and unladylike.

A sudden gale of male laughter spilled out of the marquee's entrance. Tammy's sweet laughter could heard above the noise. Hammett couldn't see her but he guessed that she was the centre of attention of a crowd of admirers.

Mrs Montgomerie twisted in her chair and frowned at the tent. 'That sounds like Tammy. I do hope she's not making a nuisance of herself.'

'I doubt it, Mrs Montgomerie. She's such a likeable girl.'

'And soon she'll be a young woman, Mr Hammett. And that's what I wish to talk to you about.'

The official's thoughts were plunged into a brief, maddened whirl. My God – she was about to ask him to marry the girl!

What on earth could he say? 'Yes please' were two heartfelt but rash words that sprang immediately to mind.

'I'm sure you know this because the embassy is such a hotbed of gossip,' Mrs Montgomerie continued. 'But Tammy was the bastard daughter of one of my servant girls – a sweet but foolish child with a weakness for chauffeurs. When Maria died, Tammy stayed. She became as our daughter.' She paused and added reflectively. 'Andrew and I never had children. Of course, we had to send her to the Holy Cross for her education. I suppose that's what her mother would have wanted, but it did nothing for her polish. Besides, there isn't what I would call a really good Anglican school in Montevideo.' The mannered observation was as near as Mrs Montgomerie was ever likely to get to expressing a disapproval of Catholicism.

She fixed her steely blue eyes on Hammett. 'The time has come to complete her education. I have in mind Madame Yvonne Bouvier's excellent finishing school in Zurich. Two years ought to do the trick.'

Despite his training, Hammett fell into the pit that had opened before him. 'Travel to Switzerland is difficult, Mrs Montgomerie.'

The Englishwoman waved a lace-gloved hand impatiently. 'Rubbish. The trouble is that you're too close to this ludicrous squabble with Germany.'

He reflected that only Mrs Montgomerie could refer to the war as a ludicrous squabble. Tammy appeared near the tent's entrance, enjoying the attentions of a circle of admirers.

'Uruguay is neutral, Mr Hammett,' the redoubtable lady continued. 'As is Spain, the United States, Switzerland, Sweden – and even Ireland. Dozens of countries. The rest of the world is going about its business, and that business includes sending my Tammy to Zurich to have some grace and manners and deportment knocked into her before it's too late. Otherwise no man will ever give her a second glance.'

At that moment Tammy was attracting third, fourth and

fifth glances, and plenty of outright lustful stares. She was sitting on the grass, knees drawn up to her chin, and sharing a joke with her gathering of cricketers who had also decided to sit on the grass – in front of her: young blades hypnotised by a magnificent scabbard. Rawlings, the embassy's slow bowler and top man in the crease, was close to drooling.

Hammett reflected that Mrs Montgomerie's hope of turning Tammy into an English rose was doomed to failure because the material held more promise as a juicy subtropical passion fruit.

'The United States would be easier,' he ventured. 'There must be plenty of suitable finishing schools –'

His hostess snorted. 'There's some quite good ones in Boston, but none come within hailing distance of Madame Bouvier's exacting standards. I have a cable from the principal accepting Tammy's admission. She has pointed out the travel problems. But the Swiss authorities have very sensibly made a number of business-as-usual arrangements for those wishing to visit their country. But such arrangements require the co-operation of the Foreign Office. I will, of course, accompany Tammy as a chaperon.' She fixed her gaze on the uncomfortable official. 'Get the ambassador to sort out the travel problems, and you'll get your bully beef, Mr Hammett. Do we have a deal?'

6

After forty days on patrol Kapitanleutnant Ernst Kessler had shed ten of his surplus kilos but he was still a formidable bulk to fall on anyone. He lost his grip on the ladder as he closed the hatch and fell on his second watch officer, Leutnant zur See Klaus Reche. The two men ended up in an undignified tangle of arms and legs on the control room deck plates as *U-395*, her electric motors whining at maximum revs, tilted down in a fast, dynamic crash-dive.

'It is considerate of you to get out of the way slowly and so provide me with a soft landing, Leutnant,' Kessler growled, retrieving his cap. Reche stammered an apology even though it wasn't his fault. Kessler lumbered to his feet like a waking bear, clapped the junior officer amiably on the back, and calmly reeled off a string of orders to the chief engineer. 'Tell you what, gentlemen,' he muttered to no one in particular. 'I reckon that must be a damned big bastard lurking under a masthead that size.'

The ratings at the trim and flooding panels frantically spun their huge collection of coloured handwheels, allowing water to flood into the ballast tanks. The chief engineer called out the order to group down the electric motors. Now that *U-395* was 'in the cellar' and had shed most of her buoyancy, maximum thrust was no longer needed from the motors to keep her down. At maximum revs the two electric motors could flatten all her banks of batteries in thirty minutes.

'Depth – twenty-five,' Kessler ordered.

The hydroplane operator pressed the trim buttons, his gaze riveted on the depth gauge. The column of liquid in the thermometer-like gauge rose above the drawing of the periscope heads. 'Periscopes under,' he reported, and switched his attention to the main depth gauge – one of the few overhead instruments that wasn't obscured by dozens of black sausages hanging from every pipe like crowded stalactites.

'So what was it, Leutnant?' Kessler demanded.

'She looked like a cruiser, Captain,' Reche answered. The junior officer was a serious, fresh faced young man who had given up trying to grow the customary beard and was the only clean-shaven member of the crew. He had the permanently worried expression of a choirboy in fear of being caught masturbating by his padre.

Kessler grunted. A cruiser was what he had thought when the lookout quartering aft from the periscope standard had spotted the warship. Bow on – a bone in her teeth. A good six miles off. Kessler didn't know if *U-395* had been spotted, but he wasn't taking chances. A cruiser could cover six miles in less than fifteen minutes if she'd a mind.

'Damn nuisance,' he grumbled. 'I was enjoying that fresh air. Cruiser, I reckon. I once saw a Queen Elizabeth class battleship close to. Smack in front of our periscope. Rivets like motorbike helmets. Damned big the British build 'em. Never been so scared in my life. What day of the week is it?'

The crew were used to their 'old man's' grasshopper thought processes. 'Thursday, Captain,' someone replied.

Kessler sighed. 'Roll on Tuesday.'

There were chuckles in the control room. As always, Kessler radiated an air of calm even during an emergency. It was difficult imagining him being scared of anything.

'Hydrophone prop effects and Asdic effects bearing three-three-zero,' Karl Pols, the radio operator, reported from his desk where he was crouched in front of his equipment, hydrophone headphones clamped over his ears.

U-395 slid deeper into the clear waters of the South Atlantic. Kessler cursed his misfortune. Thousands of square miles of ocean and he had to run into a British warship. But it had happened within thirty minutes of having transmitted his position to flotilla HQ at Lorient in Western France. His hazy notion that the British had cracked the Kriegsmarine's Enigma codes was crystallising into a certainty.

'Must be the bastard that sank the *Atlantis*,' Kessler commented, chewing ruminatively on his beard. 'Depth – thirty, chief.' He sat on the chart chest and fixed his gaze on the depth gauge, ruminating on the loss of the supply ship.

Ernst Kessler was thirty-one but his luxuriant black beard, besides giving him a piratical air, made him look older. He had joined the navy as a cadet when he was sixteen and had served on the *Gorch Fock* sail trainer. He transferred to Doenitz's fledgling U-boat arm in 1936, and by 1938 was in command of his own U-boat – one of the so-called canoes that were designed for operations in the sheltered waters of the Baltic. He had distinguished himself in the first months of the war laying mines in the Thames estuary. It always rankled that the tonnage of enemy shipping that his mines had undoubtedly claimed did not go on his record. The Knight's Cross was no consolation, not the way they were being dished out these days.

He had a wife and five daughters in Wilhelmshaven whom he rarely talked about apart from occasional joking references about home leave during long refits invariably leading to another daughter. It was his years under sail that he loved to reminisce about. The bridge lookouts were his favourite targets; a captive audience. His tactics served their purpose. To the youngest members of the crew, Kessler was the original ancient mariner, well into his anecdotage with a stock of tales of such wild outlandishness – of maddened whales charging his ship; of brutal officers who had cabin boys flogged for sneezing; of gales that blew for weeks on end – that it seemed to them that they couldn't possibly come to any harm with Kessler as their old man during something as inconsequential as a war.

'All hydrophone effects stopped,' Pols reported.

Kessler stooped and looked questioningly through the door at Pols. 'Nothing?'

'Total silence, Captain.'

'Damn.' It was bad news. It meant that the British had stopped their engines and were using the directional capabilities of their Asdic in passive mode for listening. In the raids on the North Atlantic convoys, Asdic had not been a problem because the U-boats attacked in packs on the surface at night, using their speed, low profile, and the foul weather to escape detection. Asdic had been proved to be useless against surfaced boats in such conditions. But the South Atlantic was very different. There were no 'wolf packs'; no lines of boats lying in wait in which the first one to sight a convoy would shadow it while signalling its course and speed to HQ who would then order other U-boats to close in for the kill the following night. There was no such infrastructure in the South

Atlantic although it was being built-up, much against Doenitz's will. The commander-in-chief of U-boats believed that his 'damned un-English weapons' had one purpose only: the sinking of Allied merchant ships in the North Atlantic. His protests had been overruled and *U-395* was one of several Type VIIC boats to be sent into this new theatre. Kessler had to find, shadow and attack British merchantmen without help. That meant using the traditional and wasteful technique of a submerged attack in which a fan of four torpedoes was fired across the target's bows. Some supposedly lone merchant ships turned out to be heavily-armed decoys, which meant that they had no compunction about coming straight at you with Asdic and depth charges if you missed. It had happened on this patrol already. After three hours of being harried by the strange scraping noise that the Asdic sub-harmonics produced within a U-boat's hull, and being pounded by patterns of depth charges, the attacks had suddenly stopped. Kessler had taken a gamble that had paid off; correctly guessing that the merchantman had run out of depth charges, he had ordered *U-395* to surface and had sunk the astonished ship with his quick-firing 88mm main gun. 'Popping up and popping off', as he called it, was one of his favourite ploys.

If Oberkommando der Marine wanted to take the U-boat war into the calmer waters of the South Atlantic, Kessler's view was that they'd have to start taking the Asdic threat more seriously. When it was pinging, the enemy found you at short range; when it wasn't pinging, they found you at long range if you were making a noise because an Asdic set was a damn good hydrophone receiver. Right now there were no pinging noises from the approaching warship.

'Stop motors,' he ordered. 'Silent routine. Any man breathing too loudly eats the chef's lasagne for a week.'

The word was passed the length of the boat. Fans were stopped, pumps shut down. Even the heads were out of bounds during silent routine. Anyone needing to use the toilets, used a bucket – quietly.

An eerie silence descended.

Kessler chewed thoughtfully on his beard. He sat on the chart table, plonked his feet on a pipe, and thrust his hands into his pockets. Despite his casual attitude, he did not take his eyes off the depth gauge. '*Wabos* next,' he muttered under his breath to no one in particular. 'Damned wasteful things, depth charges.' He caught Reche's puzzled expression. 'Had an armed trawler take a poke at me last year off Iceland. She must have been loaded to the bulwarks with depth charges. Pounded us for three hours. We popped up at night and found ourselves surrounded by dead cod. Millions of them. For every fish that floats, a hundred sink. That's why I don't like depth charges . . . or cod, now. Ate the damned things for a week. Had a worse cook than Poison Ivy. Well . . . almost as bad.'

The control room petty officer and the planesman exchanged grins and the tension eased.

The pointer edged past the thirty-metres mark. Without forward speed for her hydroplanes to bite on the water, *U-395* was slightly negatively buoyant and therefore sinking, albeit very slowly at about one metre per minute. Kessler reminded himself to commend his chief engineer in the log; not only had Brandt dived the boat in record time, but he had also achieved near perfect trim within a few frantic seconds.

Thirty-five metres.

All eyes in the control room kept going to the big depth gauge, the largest instrument on the boat. The swell generated tiny flickers of the hand, but the trend was downward. The attention directed at the instrument reminded Kessler of when, as a child, he used to watch his father's long-case clock, and had always been thrilled to be able to see the almost imperceptible movement of the minute hand.

'Let her sink, chief,' said Kessler. He yawned and scratched his incredibly hairy chest. 'Are you sure it's Thursday?'

Forty metres.

Reche sneezed loudly and went bright red. Kessler said nothing.

'She'll stop at fifty when we hit the cold layer,' the chief engineer muttered. Otto Brandt was a small, balding wisp of a man but tough as piano wire, at his happiest when up to his elbows in engine grease, preferably diesel engine grease. His father and grandfather had been engineers, and his hero was Rudolf Diesel, whom he considered the greatest engineer that had ever lived. There was a framed photograph of the illustrious inventor wedged between the overhead exhaust handwheels in the engine room. Like Rudolf Diesel, Brandt had graduated at the Technische Hochschule in Munich. After four patrols together, the engineer and Kessler had evolved a deep mutual trust. Kessler was fond of saying that if you opened one of the chief's veins, you'd find engine oil.

U-395 stopped sinking at forty-seven metres.

The chief engineer whistled faintly through his teeth in satisfaction. The U-boat was sitting on a layer of colder, and therefore denser water, and could not sink any lower unless more water was allowed into her ballast tanks.

'HE prop noises resumed – bearing three-three-three,' said Pols. He switched-in different directional microphones from the array around the conning tower to select the one that picked up the strongest sounds, and twirled his car-type steering wheel. 'Now bearing three-three-five.'

There was a further easing of the tension. The British warship was making a noise and thus reduced the likelihood of it hearing the U-boat. Also she was no longer heading directly towards them. Kessler waited patiently. That the ship was moving away didn't mean a thing. The British used a box search system for dropping their patterns to cause maximum effect using the least number of charges; they were probably just moving in to a good position to begin their murderous assault. But the expected crump of distant explosions never came.

'Hydrophine effects bearing three-three-six – much fainter,' said Pols phlegmatically.

Kessler stepped through the door to the tiny radio office and pressed the spare pair of phones to his ear. The chirruping of dolphins and whales was particularly noisy. 'I'm not hearing anything,' he complained.

'It's there, Captain,' Pols replied. 'Right underneath.' He switched in another transducer. Kessler concentrated hard and thought he could hear a faint beat underneath the background noise.

'Getting fainter, Captain.'

That was what Kessler liked to hear: HE prop effects getting steadily fainter. He didn't like warships that stopped their engines and played psychological games. He grunted his thanks, returned the headphones to their hook, and stepped back into the control room.

'We'll sit here another hour and then take a look-see. And to think I reckoned that things would be nice and peaceful in the South Atlantic. Life is cruel.' With that he ducked through the watertight door and entered his tiny commander's cabin – little more than a square metre of space behind a heavy green curtain. He sat on his berth and used the stillness of the boat at this depth to write up the log. He reported on the crash dive and noted:

The problem of contaminated diesel fuel still not resolved.

Doenitz would pounce on that. The commander-in-chief hated vagueness. He combed through all the log books and patrol reports of returning skippers and soundly berated his captains on the slightest pretext. Kessler sighed, crossed the sentence out and wrote:

The appearance of warship interrupted investigation into likely contamination of fuel.

He sat back. It was crazy. He was worrying about Doenitz's ire and the wording in his logbook when the truth was that *U-395*'s fuel in 4 and 5 tanks, that the chief had so carefully husbanded for their long return voyage to Lorient, was contaminated, possibly sabotaged by workers in the French yard. *U-395* was in grave danger of being lost.

In the engine room, diesel mechanic Handel unscrewed the

fuel pump pipe on the port engine and pushed the length of hose into place. He nodded to the chief engineer. The port engine turned noisily over on compressed air. Half the cylinder compression valves were open so there was no danger of the engine starting, but the noise caused some consternation the length of the boat. A diesel running while submerged could suck all the boat's air into its cylinders, thus creating a partial vacuum that had been known to rupture eardrums.

The chief kept the engine cranking until there was a litre of fuel oil in the glass flask. He took the vessel from the mechanic and held it up against the nearest caged light bulb. He gave it a swirl. The viscosity looked okay but the colour was wrong.

'It's got a bluish tinge, chief,' said the mechanic.

The chief engineer grunted in agreement. 'Any ideas what might cause it?'

The mechanic shook his head. 'Potassium permanganate, do you reckon?'

'Any idea what potassium permanganate does to diesel oil?'

'No idea, chief.'

'Nor have I. I'm not a bloody chemist. But whatever it is, it makes the engines run like shit. Okay – get this lot cleaned up.'

Brandt made his way forward with the flask, his face grim. He climbed through the watertight doors, taking care not to spill any of the oil. Oberleutnant Hans Maron, *U-395*'s first watch officer, kept the boat spotless.

Kessler knew every tread outside his curtain and called out before the chief had a chance to rap on the locker panel beside the curtain.

'Come in, chief. Sit down.'

The engineer placed the flask on the table and sat opposite Kessler, their knees almost touching.

'That's from the port engine injector pump, Captain. It's the same as the starboard engine – blue.'

Kessler held the flask up to his reading light. 'Any ideas?'

Brandt shook his head. 'If it was something that had been

45

put in the fuel lines or filters from tanks 4 and 5, then I'd expect them to run clean after a while. But they're not running clean, therefore it has to be something that's in the tanks and the oil separators.'

'But you checked the fuel-oil in 4 and 5 in Lorient, chief?'

Brandt knew his captain was eliminating possibilities rather than implying any criticism of his professionalism. 'I did. And both engines burned a tonne each from both tanks on the first day out from Lorient. There was no trouble then.'

Kessler was silent. The unthinkable was that a member of the crew had sabotaged the last of their fuel. 'Any ideas?' he asked again.

Brandt met Kessler's eye. Four patrols together was enough for each to know what the other was thinking. 'I'd rather not say until I've a proper chance to get a dip sampler into those tanks.'

Kessler nodded. Brandt had been out on the after deck casing, about to take samples through the bunkering valves when they had been interrupted by the British warship. There was a sudden passing to and fro in the central companionway. The watch was changing. Kessler glanced at his chronometer. 'We'll take her up now, chief. I want this settled.'

Fifteen minutes later *U-395* was lying stopped, riding the long Atlantic swell under a hot midday sun. Four of Brandt's mechanics had the aft casings open to expose the rows of fuel oil bunkering valves. Kessler watched from the *wintergarten* deck abaft the conning tower deck that housed the 20mm quadruple-barrelled Oerlikon anti-aircraft guns. Two mechanics swung a wrench nearly a metre long to unscrew one of the valves. Once the heavy valve had been lifted clear, Brandt fed a sampler down the pipe. It consisted of a pipette attached to a coiled ten-metre length of flexible drive cable. Most of the cable disappeared before Brandt was satisfied that he had reached into the depths of the tank. He gave several twists and withdrew the cable. One mechanic wiped it clean as it was pulled out and the other coiled it up. The pipette came clear. Brandt studied it for a moment and offered it up to Kessler. There was a thick, blue-tinted sludge trapped in the sample tube.

The test on the second tank produced the same result. Brandt smeared some of the sludge on his palm and rubbed the ball of his finger into it. 'Lumps,' he said shortly. 'You see?'

Kessler nodded. 'Some sort of slow-dissolving tablets,' he said bitterly. 'So how much fuel is contaminated, chief?'

'All of it,' Brandt answered bitterly, wiping his hands on a wad of cotton waste. 'The whole fucking lot.'

7

When Dieter Rohland's station taxi pulled up outside Señora Candelaria's photographic shop, a small horde of shrieking children descended on the car, eager for the pesos that the smiling German always doled out when he had equipment to carry. The taxi driver, who had been hoping that the amount of baggage would result in a generous tip, looked on sourly as photographic carrying cases were seized from his taxi by small, willing hands, and borne into the dark recesses of the shop.

Upstairs in her gloomy bedroom, Candelaria Ramazon, her siesta interrupted, thrust her head into the grubby poncho and wrapped it around her bulk. It was a huge, hand-woven garment that she always wore regardless of the weather. She waddled out onto her balcony overlooking the narrow street and looked down in disapproval as Dieter tousled bobbing heads and paid off the driver. Pocitos Beach was Montevideo's respectable resort suburb, so why was it that her assistant couldn't go anywhere without drawing such attention to himself? As usual, the angry words she had ready were stilled when Dieter met her on the stairs and kissed the back of her gnarled hand with a courtly flourish.

'Some amazing pictures of the rhea, Candel,' he said excitedly in his terrible Spanish. 'You'll be amazed.'

Candelaria grunted. Wildlife photographs of the small ostrich-like plains bird did not interest her. 'I'll be amazed if the pictures Pepe did of the Freemans' wedding are any good,' she sniffed, easing her weight into a rocking chair behind the shop's long counter. 'You know how I hate having to use him. You said that you would be back by yesterday.'

Dieter looked suitably contrite. He and Candelaria had an arrangement. In return for his bed and board, he helped out in the shop and darkroom, and handled the occasional profitable assignments such as weddings and first communions. Dieter had presented himself on her doorstep several months ago. He told her that he was from South West Africa – the former German colony – and was hoping to be allowed to remain in Uruguay. Candelaria had been happy to take him on until his papers came through. There were many German-descent farmers in Montevideo who had left South West Africa when the British had taken over after the Great War. She didn't like them because they preferred to take their own photographs with their Leicas, but Dieter was different from them. His boyish charm could be quite devastating. But she never let him forget who was boss.

'So?' she said gruffly. 'What happened? Why are you late?'

'I'm sorry, Candel. But a guy in Melo told me where there were hundreds of rhea. I went chasing two hundred kilometres across the pampa only to find out that he was lying.'

The woman grunted. 'Why can't you relax in your spare time? Chase after girls like other young men? There's more of them and they like being caught.'

Dieter's grin widened to its most charming. 'How can I be interested in other girls when they have to measure up to you, Candel?'

She scowled at the compliment but was secretly pleased. She watched as Dieter carried his gear into the small back room that served as his bedroom, and continued to sniff her disapproval. She could not understand why he was so keen on galloping off all over the pampa to photograph wildlife. Uruguay was nearly all grassland; what little wildlife there was had been displaced by the huge herds of beef that had made millionaires of the six hundred or so landowners who controlled the country.

'Could I use the darkroom for an hour or so, please, Candel? I'll pay for the chemicals and paper. You'll be thrilled at the pictures I've taken.'

Candelaria grunted indifferently and heaved herself out of the chair. She had learned that the young German was always scrupulously honest about such things. 'Don't bother me with your silly pictures, but do what you like.' She shuffled towards the stairs in the gloomy passage and fixed him with a stern eye. 'I'm going to finish my siesta that you interrupted.'

As soon as he heard the creak of her ancient bed, Dieter locked himself in the humid little darkroom beside his bedroom and switched on the safe light. The low ceiling obliged him to stoop so he sat down to work. He unpacked the case that contained the contents of Cleary's rucksack and tipped the cans of Minox film onto the grubby bench. Each film was packed in a Colman's Mustard tin which had been sealed with electrician's insulating tape. Dieter had already checked one of the tins to ensure that it hadn't leaked. Fortunately Cleary had followed his instructions to the letter regarding the care of the films. At least no water had got into any of the tins; the worry was whether the appalling temperatures on the long train journey from the north might have affected the emulsion.

Dieter's concern turned out to be groundless: all the rolls developed perfectly. The 16-millimetre films were difficult to handle so he spliced them into one length when they had dried. His movements were methodical and unhurried even though the films were the culmination of several months' careful preparation. He drew the miniature film through the enlarger's gate frame by frame, viewing the negative images that were projected onto the platen. The first film, which Joe

49

Cleary had marked as number 1 on the mustard tin, was disappointing. Those images that didn't suffer from handshake were either out of focus or partially obscured by fingers.

The next roll was an improvement although there was nothing on them that was of any use. It was much the same with the third and fourth rolls. Dieter bit on his lip in disappointment. His credibility was on the line now, but his hand remained steady as he pulled the film carefully through the gate.

Roll Five – a few pictures of a camp enclosure that could be anywhere. Some indistinct faces; a group of men eating in a canteen. Dieter could hear Admiral Canaris's wrath ringing in his ears; Dieter and his crazy ideas had absorbed valuable funds and resources that could have been put to better use in the struggle against the Allies. Damn! If only he had spent longer drilling Joe Cleary with the miniature camera. He had shown him how to hold the Minox steady in his palm and operate the shutter while pretending to mop his brow. The Irishman had been an able pupil; so what had gone wrong?

The edge of Roll Six clicked as it entered the gate. The pin-sharp head and shoulders picture of a black-haired man that jumped off the platen at Dieter took him by surprise. For a moment he forgot to read the negative properly. The black-haired man was a blond of course. He bent as close as he could over the platen without obscuring it with his shadow. It was the unknown man in the search party that had hunted Cleary down, the man Dieter had watched from across the river. Even in negative Dieter was now certain that he knew who the man was.

The next picture was of the same man standing beside an ore-crusher. He was examining a large piece of rock with the aid of a magnifying glass. The conveyor belt carrying the spoil was sharp on the negative, showing that it had been stopped. It was a picture that told a complete story. The existence of the big crusher alone was enough to quicken Dieter's pulse. The next picture was stunning: it was an aerial shot of the entire complex. How had Cleary managed that? He looked closer and realised that it had been taken from the top of a watchtower. There were three other towers clearly visible at the extremities of the complex. There were plenty of trucks in the picture – certainly enough for a skilled picture analyst to calculate the exact area of the site. In the distance was wild scrubland and beyond that granite hills.

Dieter could scarcely credit his luck when he came to the seventh roll. Somehow Cleary had photographed the one thing that spoke volumes about any organisation: the notice board. With careful enlarging Dieter was sure that it would be possible to read some of the notices. He moved on. There was a whole series of pictures taken at the mine's rock face. There were even shots showing the gallery numbers painted on the sides of the tunnels. No doubt Cleary had trained his helmet light on them and taken time exposures. God only knew how he had avoided hand shake, but he had. Best of all was a picture of a map of the complex – slightly blurred, taken in a hurry, but everything was there.

Light had seeped into the tenth roll and ruined every shot, but Dieter wasn't worried. He had nearly all the evidence he needed. The next task was to print the results. There was no point in printing all the frames – just enough to prove his point. He took down a packet of 120 photographic paper that was used for the Uruguayans' holiday efforts with their Kodak Box Brownies, and printed twenty of the best pictures. Once they had been dried and glazed, he trimmed them on the guillotine that gave them a ragged edge thus making them look even more like holiday snaps to a casual observer.

When he had finished, he cleared up carefully, making doubly certain that nothing incriminating went into the waste bin. He left a note pinned to the wall listing the chemicals and paper he had used.

Candelaria's snores were reverberating down the stairs when he emerged from the darkroom and entered his bedroom, turning the key in the lock. For all her faults,

Candelaria had always respected his privacy, but Dieter believed in leaving nothing to chance. Unpacking his photographic gear could wait. The important things now were the small sacks of samples that he had found in Cleary's rucksack. At least five kilos, he estimated. Had Cleary lived, he would have most certainly earned his fee. He spread out an old newspaper on his dresser cum desk and tipped out the linen sample bag that Cleary had labelled in indelible pencil: 'All Grade 2 in first class category except two largest which are Grade 1 mother crystals.'

Of the twenty or so chunks of quartz crystal that rolled out of the bag, there were two that shone like a pair of Hope Diamonds in their virgin purity.

They were nearly the size of a tennis ball and were the largest and finest pieces that Dieter had ever seen. For a mine to produce one such crystal was remarkable. And yet Cleary had smuggled out not one, but two. It suggested that the mine the British were working in Brazil and were so desperate to keep secret was a source of the finest quartz crystal in the world.

He picked up the largest rock and turned it over in his hands, peering closely at the strange, pyramidal crystalline structure as though its bizarre properties would be revealed.

Dieter had been well briefed by experts in Berlin on the importance of the curious rock. Of all the minerals in the earth's crust, quartz is one of the strangest for it has piezoelectric properties. That is, passing an electric current through carefully selected slivers causes the crystal to distort. Conversely, distorting the crystal produces a flow of current. The phenomenon had been exploited for many years in microphones where there was a need to convert sound energy into electrical energy. But it was the rapid distortion properties of quartz that interested the Kriegsmarine because the British exploited it in their Asdic submarine detection equipment. Given the right purity and size, quartz crystals could distort with great speed and violence and so produce the underwater sonic ping whose returning echoes revealed the presence of submerged U-boats. From the papers Dieter had captured in Paris, he was convinced that the British were working on a new high-power Asdic system with many times the range of their existing sets. If so, the consequences for the Battle of the Atlantic would be disastrous for Germany. The new sets would come at a time when U-boat commanders were learning not to fear Asdic. Dieter's arguments had not wholly convinced Canaris, Doenitz and the OKM. Nevertheless a small intelligence network with limited resources had been set-up to discover all it could. The first priority had been to find out where the British were getting their quartz. Brazil had been the obvious target because it was the world's largest producer and had close links with Britain. And now Dieter had pinpointed the exact mine that was the source of the high-grade quartz.

The next problem would be to get the samples safely back to Germany for evaluation by Siemens and OKM technicians. Dieter's feelings were mixed as he stared down at the strange rock. His obsession had been vindicated, but the thought gave him no pleasure. The enemy's historical ties with Brazil had given them a huge technological advantage over Germany.

With a hundred such prime quality crystals one could win a war.

8

'Tammy! Come away from that window at once! Dressed like that – what are you thinking of?' Mrs Montgomerie sailed across Tammy's plush bedroom and jerked the girl off the window seat. 'Sitting combing your hair like that when there are gardeners about! Now go and get dressed. An hour is quite long enough for a bath.'

She bundled the sulky Tammy into her dressing-room adjoining the bedroom and returned to the window. The moment her formidable face appeared, the two gardeners, who were hoping for the return of the vision in her underwear, jumped visibly and made a guilty show of tending the immaculate flowerbeds. She glowered down at them, and was about to throw the window open for some verbal abuse when the hall telephone gave a long, strangled ring.

Frobisher, her mulatto butler, answered it.

'For you, ma'am,' he said, holding the handset to Mrs Montgomerie as she advanced down the broad, sweeping stairs.

'Of course it's for me! And how many times must I tell you to wear a glove to answer the phone. Who is it?'

'He didn't say, ma'am.'

'You should ask!' The telephone was an invention for business, not the home. Mrs Montgomerie was used to a world in which visitors presented a card and were shown into a reception room where they were exposed to the householder's taste (or lack of it) in art until the householder deigned to see them. The domestic telephone permitted strangers to barge into one's house without proper formalities. Mindful of germs, she held the instrument her customary few inches from her ear which meant she never recognised callers' voices.

'Who's that?'

'Mrs Montgomerie?'

'Well of course it's me. Whom did you expect?'

'It's George Hammett at the embassy.'

'Good afternoon, Mr Hammett. Do you have some news for me?'

'May I come and see you, Mrs Montgomerie? I'd rather not discuss the matter on the phone.'

'If you call my office tomorrow, my secretary will arr —'

Hammett was firm. 'It's urgent unless you're prepared to wait another five weeks, Mrs Montgomerie. If I could come and see you in about an hour's time. It'll only take a few minutes.'

Any other caller would have been berated for such a

peremptory approach but she had no wish to upset the embassy. Her answer had just the right degree of frostiness without being rude. 'Very well, Mr Hammett. I'll expect you in an hour.'

9

Professor Fritz Haug was one of the few men for whom Dieter had a genuine respect, even though he didn't trust him. Despite his slightly comic appearance, which was largely contrived, the plump little Berliner, a former physics lecturer at Kiel, was a shrewd, clear thinker, and was about as unlikely a naval intelligence officer as it was possible to imagine. The meeting on the Porticus–Montevideo ferry had been his idea.

Dieter watched anxiously from the empty saloon deck as Haug's portly figure in a white linen suit came in sight on the pier just as the deck hands were hauling the steamer's mooring lines clear of the bollards. Haug pushed purposefully through the crowd of bystanders, sun glittering on his gold-rimmed spectacles. He refused the services of a shoeshine boy, and beamed amiably about him at the noisy party of school-children quarrelling over loan transactions in a queue at an ice-cream stall. He gave no indication that he intended to catch the ferry. He even walked past the gangway. The steamer gave a long blast on its siren. Anglers dotted along the pierside quickly twitched their rods clear. The saloon windows shook as the engines went slow ahead. Haug suddenly did a smart about turn, hopped onto the gangway with remarkable agility just as it was about to be pulled clear, and was aboard the ferry before the startled deck hands could voice a protest. A tall man a few paces behind Haug registered momentary alarm as though he had expected the portly German to fall into the sea.

A few minutes later, when the steamer was well clear of the quay, Haug descended into the stuffy saloon and beamed at

Dieter. Only an observer watching the new arrival closely would have noticed that his small, sharp eyes took in every detail in the saloon before he spoke.

'Dieter, my boy,' he exclaimed as they shook hands. 'What a pleasant surprise. I was just taking a stroll along the promenade when on an impulse, I decided to take the ferry rather than a taxi. The purser was a little cross with me – I jumped on his boat just as it was leaving. But I'm sure you saw everything.' He flopped down in the seat opposite and fanned his pink face with his fedora.

Dieter smiled. 'And I expect whoever that was who was following you is a little cross as well.'

Haug gave an impish grin. 'So tiresome, the British. I can't move in this city without them following me around. I was at the mayor's banquet last week and met my opposite number from the British embassy. I suggested that we exchange engagement diaries each week to save on staff and footwear. He wasn't a bit amused.'

Dieter laughed. It was the sort of bizarre logic that only Haug could come up with. He recalled Admiral Canaris's words: 'You'll like Haug, Dieter. Everyone does, but he's dangerous and utterly ruthless. Don't cross him whatever you do.'

The humour faded from Haug's blue eyes as though he was reading the younger man's thoughts. Suddenly the steel beneath that ebullient façade was showing through. 'So tell me about your trip.'

Dieter brought Haug up to date with an account of his visit north and Cleary's death.

'Unfortunate,' Haug remarked. 'But it's one mouth less to talk, and $5000 saved.' He was about to say something else but Dieter handed him the photographs. He went through them once, quickly, to assimilate the overall story they told, and then a second time, more slowly to absorb detail. Dieter noticed that Haug's nails had been recently manicured.

'These are remarkable, my dear Dieter. Quite extraordinary. As I suspected – a huge mining complex.'

'As *I* suspected, professor,' Dieter corrected cautiously. He knew that Haug disliked being called professor but there was no harm in reminding him that his minions had spirit.

Haug chuckled. 'Quite so. As you suspected.'

'Do you recognise the fair-haired man?'

Haug's innocent blue eyes opened wide in surprise. 'Of course I do.'

There were times when the wily professor could be most irritating. 'Then who is he? I know I've seen the face before.'

'You've spent more time combing through the ASDIC documents than I have, Dieter,' said Haug reproachfully. 'Ian Craddock. Professor Jock Anderson's right hand man, and the man who carried out the tests on the prototype Asdic apparatus installed in HMS *Kingfisher* when Jock Anderson wasn't being seasick. There was a photograph of Anderson and Craddock in the 1938 ASDIC papers. They were standing together on the quay at the British Admiralty's research establishment at Portsdown. HMS *Kingfisher* was tied-up in the background. The skipper of the *Kingfisher* was Donald MacIntyre. There was another photograph that showed the Portsdown bigwigs shaking hands with Winston Churchill when he visited them for a demonstration of Asdic on –'

Dieter held up his hand. 'All right. All right.'

Haug beamed smugly. He enjoyed showing off his photographic memory. 'Ian Craddock. Former head of research with the British Post Office. A specialist in quartz crystal technology. We thought he'd been transferred to the Telecommunications Research Establishment at Malvern. His presence at the mine confirms that my hunch about the place was right.'

'It was my hunch first,' Dieter protested.

Haug thought for a moment. 'So it was, Dieter. So it was. My apologies. So what other goodies did your man make off with?'

They broke off as a family, talking volubly in Spanish, burst noisily into the saloon. Mother complained loudly that it was

57

too hot. The retinue did an about turn and returned to the deck where mother could be heard complaining that it was too windy.

Dieter felt in his pocket and handed one of the prime quality crystals to Haug. The intelligence officer peered closely at it. The light burned on its facets and made patterns on Haug's face. His cherubic expression hardened. '*Mein Gott*,' he breathed.

'Mineralogy is not my forte,' Dieter admitted. 'But something tells me a quartz crystal that size is important.'

'A top quality mother crystal,' Haug muttered after a pause. 'Cleaving such a rock would give the British a hundred high power transducers for their Asdic sets.'

'Or a few super-power transducers?' Dieter ventured.

'Ah – your super Asdic apparatus?'

'The *enemy's* super Asdic apparatus,' Dieter corrected.

Haug stared at the iridescent fire burning within the crystal. 'I worry about translated documents,' he said slowly. 'Such an apparatus has always seemed very unlikely to me . . . but now . . . seeing this . . . Perhaps you're right, Dieter.' He held the crystal up so that the sunlight turned it to a liquid inferno. 'Such a rock could cost us the war.'

'I've got another just like it. About five kilos of selected samples altogether.'

Haug was silent for a moment. 'You have the negatives?'

Dieter handed him the single spool of 16-mm film.

'No trouble sending it home through the usual channels,' said Haug as he slipped the roll into his pocket. 'But five kilos of samples will require a courier . . . all the way home.'

'Surely the diplomatic channels would be best?'

Haug chuckled. 'The film is no problem. The frames can be converted to aniline dye microdots. But the so-called diplomatic bags? You wouldn't believe what the British are paying out in bribes to customs officers here. Nothing's interfered with but I'm convinced our British friends have a good idea of what we send and what we receive. No – a courier is the only answer. But who?' He thought for a minute and brightened. 'You've done well, Dieter. In fact, brilliantly well. Your work's finished here. You must be itching to get home – back into the thick of everything. Admiral Canaris will be receiving a warm report on your excellent work.'

The younger man said nothing. Much as he was enjoying his posting to South America, he was ambitious enough to realise that promotion was likely to pass him by if he stayed too long away from Titpitzufer 72–76 in Berlin.

'We must get you home as quickly as possible, Dieter.' Haug's pink face creased as he recalled something. 'Just trying to picture a timetable. Ah yes – there's a ship leaving for Rio on Friday. From Rio it sails on to Bilbao. A mail boat, but it takes a few passengers. Getting you home from Spain won't be a problem. How much money have you got left?'

'There's the $5000 I was issued with for Cleary. Plus another $250.' Dieter was tempted to point out that Haug checked all expenses with great care and probably knew anyway. It didn't pay to be fooled by the older man's affable demeanour. Also he needed that good word from Haug to boost his standing in Berlin.

'That's more than enough,' said Haug easily. 'Bilbao Steam and General Navigation. They've got an office above the Correos on the Plaza de la Independencia.' He glanced at his watch. 'We dock in ten minutes. If you hurry, you'll catch them before they close. You have my permission to book second-class accommodation.'

'What's the name of this mail boat?'

'The *Anaconda*.'

10

George Hammett's taxi turned into the drive of Mrs Montgomerie's neo-Georgian mansion in the fashionable Paso de Molino suburb. He told the driver to wait. A movement at a window above the imposing front entrance caught his eye. Tammy waved to him. Her provocative poise, one leg cocked up on the windowsill, seemed to convey the hope that he would climb the ivy and bear her away into the sunset. He returned the wave and decided that perhaps Switzerland was a good idea for her after all.

Frobisher ushered him into Angela Montgomerie's presence in her elegant drawing room where the ritual tea trolley was waiting like a mobile altar. The portrait of King George VI was a surprise; there was also a photograph of Princess Elizabeth and Princess Margaret over the Adam fireplace. Mrs Montgomerie was more patriotic than he had suspected. A silver-framed photograph was the centrepiece of the sideboard, and he wondered who the young man wearing RAF uniform was. Tucked in the corner of the frame was a telegram envelope.

'My nephew, Michael,' said Mrs Montgomerie after their opening pleasantries and seeing her guest's eyes return to the photograph. 'My sister's eldest. A fine boy. I loved him dearly. He spent two summers with us. He was killed last year over France. His Spitfire was . . .' She was unable to complete the sentence. The bitterness and sorrow in her voice took Hammett by surprise; Mrs Montgomerie was not one to allow her emotions to show. But the lifting of her mask was momentary. Her steely gaze hardened and she became her normal businesslike self. 'You have news for me, Mr Hammett?' she said briskly.

'There are problems with getting you and Tammy to Switzerland –'

'Of course there are problems, you silly man. It's six thousand miles away. Your job is to eliminate them.'

'Will you be able to leave on Friday?'

'Friday! Four days?'

Hammett sipped his tea. 'That's when the *Anaconda* sails for Rio. At ten thirty a.m. She arrives at Rio on Monday, takes on more mail, then sails to Spain: Bilbao.'

'The *Anaconda*! Mr Hammett – I am *not* sailing on a scruffy little mail packet. Where would we sleep? On top of a lot of knobbly registered parcels?'

George Hammett was very patient. The mail packets maintained the strong cultural links between South America, and Spain and Portugal. Despite their name, they were fast, modern ships. 'The *Anaconda* has excellent passenger accommodation, Mrs Montgomerie. It –'

'What about U-boats?'

'So far as I know, they don't operate any passenger services.' Seeing that Mrs Montgomerie didn't appreciate the joke, he added quickly: 'The *Anaconda* is a well-run ship and can cater for up to ten first- and second-class passengers. We've used it ourselves for postings to Spain and Portugal. The first-class accommodation is a weather deck suite with two cabins and a stateroom that I'm sure will suit you and Tammy. It's the best I can do, Mrs Montgomerie. The only other sailings are from B.A.'

'How safe are they from the Royal Navy or U-boats?'

'Have you ever lost a cargo of meat on a neutral ship?' Hammett countered.

'Perhaps not.'

'The *Anaconda* is Spanish-owned. We know that U-boat skippers have strict orders not to interfere with Spanish shipping. And the Royal Navy only stops and boards neutral ships if they suspect they are carrying war supplies.'

'So we disembark at Bilbao?'

'We can arrange for a consular official to meet you there. There's a bus service to Bordeaux. There you will meet a Swiss business travel courier who will escort you to Zurich and back again, but he will charge you for his services. Have you kept your Uruguayan passport?'

'Indeed I have.'

'And Tammy?'

'Yes – we visited Rio last year.'

Hammett nodded. 'Good. Neutral passports make everything so much easier. Can you be ready for Friday? I'm sorry it's such short notice but it's the best we can do.'

His hostess gave him an unexpected, generous smile. 'You've been most helpful, Mr Hammett. I'm most grateful. Tammy is becoming more of a problem each day.'

Hammett could believe it. 'You'll be away some time. Your business affairs . . .'

Mrs Montgomerie's smile broadened. 'I have excellent managers. I daresay they will be pleased to see the back of me for a few weeks. And as for that other business we discussed, I've already accepted a tender to have a new canning plant built at Fray Bentos.'

Hammett had neither the heart nor the authority to say that he already knew. He thanked her for the tea, excused himself, and left.

Once she was alone, Mrs Montgomerie thought hard. Friday . . . getting everything ready and Tammy fully kitted out in four days would be difficult but not impossible. She crossed to a globe and spun it, locating Montevideo. Her finger traced the vast distance to Bilbao on the Atlantic coast of Northern Spain. A quarter of the way around the world – to another world that would have changed since her Grand Tour of Europe at the turn of the century, the culmination of her two years at finishing school. A world that was being torn apart by hatred and war for the second time around. A conflict that had taken her beloved Michael from her.

As she stared down at the globe, she felt that familiar tingling sensation at the nape of her neck that she always experienced at the outset of setting up a business deal. It was usually a mixture of excitement and fear. Excitement at the prospect of pitting her wits against men in a men's world, and fear should she fail. But this time there was little of the fear.

Excitement. That was what she needed. The realisation turned the tingling into delicious little terror sensations that chased up and down her spine: exactly the same feelings that she remembered when she had first ridden on a ghost train as a little girl . . . And some years later on her wedding night . . .

Angela Montgomerie would have vehemently denied it, but the excitement she craved was a substitute for sex.

11

The quiet throughout *U-395* was disturbing. Neither of the two Blohm and Voss diesels nor the electric motors were running, conditions that prevailed only when the U-boat was moored – not wallowing in the swell in the middle of the South Atlantic. A few wire-caged fans whirred softly, sucking air into the boat through open hatches and bringing some respite from the heat.

On the bridge the lookouts and the watch officer, all stripped to their vests, scoured the horizon with binoculars, studiously avoiding their skipper's eye.

Kessler stamped his feet impatiently and tugged at his sweat-saturated shirt. He flipped up the pressure-tight cover on the engine room voice-pipe but changed his mind, and snapped it shut. There was no point in harrying Brandt, the chief engineer was doing his best. Pols was sitting cross-legged on the forward casing busy sketching a flying fish that had blundered into the main gun. The hours that the telegraphist spent listening to the cacophony of dolphins and whales on his hydrophone set had kindled a keen interest in oceanography. *U-395*'s emblem painted on her conning tower – a stonefish with an exaggerated row of five poisonous spines – had been Pols' idea. He had assured Kessler that the incredibly ugly fish was the most dangerous of all marine creatures and was responsible for more deaths each year than any other. Maron disapproved because identifying marks on U-boats were against regulations.

Behind Pols off-watch ratings were diving naked into the sea, splashing about and yelling. Diesel mechanic Eric Handel was showing off his remarkable swimming skills by diving under the boat and surfacing on the other side. Handel had been in the German swimming team at the Berlin Olympics and claimed that the film star turned director, Leni Riefenstahl, had wanted to film him naked. Chances to go swimming on a patrol were rare, but there was little risk here of being surprised on the surface by the U-boats' mortal enemy – aircraft. For the thousandth time Kessler wondered why it had been his misfortune to be sent into the South Atlantic where the pickings were so lousy. Especially with the British jumping all over him whenever he used his radio. The chances of adding swords to his Knight's Cross were fading fast, not that he particularly cared about what he called pretty little lumps of diecast metal.

'What day of the week is it?' he asked no one in particular.

'Friday, Captain,' said the lookout petty officer.

Kessler stared moodily aft where there should be a wake. The external ballast tank's flooding flaps were open in case they had to crash dive. Hans Maron climbed through the hatch looking smart in a freshly-laundered sweater, binoculars gleaming. Kessler glanced sourly at his first watch officer. Maron was usually early for his watches; this time he was thirty minutes early.

'The Führer expects vigilance,' said Maron smoothly in answer to Kessler's comment.

A minute later Kessler came up with a suitable riposte along the lines that the Führer also expected his officers to get some sleep, but it was too late. Which was just as well: Maron had a sense of humour but he kept it under strict control apart from his occasional snide references to Rudolf Diesel in the chief's hearing. Despite always feeling ill-at-ease in his first watch officer's company, Kessler was prepared to make allowances. As an oberleutnant craving a command he too had behaved like Maron – always properly turned-out, always correct. Once you were a skipper you could revert to being a slob provided you looked reasonably smart for the newsreel cameras when leaving for or returning from patrol. Kessler knew that his first lieutenant had only just scraped through his naval exams. He was one of those people who had to work twice as hard as others to get anywhere. A man who needed order and neatness in order to keep his world manageable. Fighting such an eternal battle soured a man. Secondly, Maron's parents were dentists; Kessler reasoned that he must have had a miserable childhood.

'What's the latest situation with our fuel, Captain?' Maron asked.

'That's what the chief is working on now.'

'There's nothing in the control room log,' Maron observed.

'The watch isn't over yet,' Kessler replied blandly. It would be easy to criticise his first lieutenant for being over-zealous, but Maron was a good executive officer. That U-395 was the best-run boat in the service was entirely due to Maron and his flair for organisation. Every item of stores was listed on his clipboard and properly stowed twenty-four hours before sailing. Most boats went on patrol with their gangway piled high. Not Maron's boat. He was so good at squirrelling stores away that he could convince victualling officials that there had been mistakes with their paperwork. The result was that U-395 invariably sailed with more than her quota of food.

'I'll see that the log's written up now,' Maron offered, and disappeared down the ladder.

'Engine room – bridge.' It was Brandt's voice.

'Go ahead.'

'We're ready to give the port engine another test.'

'Very good, chief.' Kessler gave a short blast on his whistle and gestured to the men in the water. They scrambled hurriedly onto the casing, knowing that if the engines behaved their skipper wouldn't want to waste time before getting under way.

In the engine room Brandt awaited confirmation that the port engine was de-clutched and primed before operating the compressed-air lever. The explosive hiss was shattering in the confined space. The valve rockers bobbed up and down like a

65

long row of pecking chickens. The engine wheezed and fired. It ran erratically for a few seconds and picked up. Brandt opened the throttle to 600 r.p.m. and then 800. Further aft in the motor room, the rating watching the voltmeter panel confirmed that the batteries were taking a charge. Handel quickly opened and closed the exhaust chamber check valve on cylinder one. A baleful yellow flame spat fiercely into the narrow gangway between the two engines; it should have been a rich blue. It was the same with the other five valves – a certain indication that the trouble was with the fuel.

On the bridge Kessler watched the exhaust smoke venting through the aft ballast tank. The wind caught it and blew it in his face. As on the previous occasions that morning when the chief had tried to start the engines, the fumes looked wrong and smelt wrong.

The diesel stopped abruptly.

'One minute, fifty,' a rating read off his stopwatch. 'Ten seconds better than last time.'

The only sound in the engine room was the ticking of hot metal. Brandt swore, then, 'Clean out the filters, separators and injectors as best you can,' he ordered, wiping his hands on a rag. 'I'm going up top.'

He made his way forward to the control room. Maron looked questioningly at the chief engineer but Brandt ignored him. Maron had a belief in the spiritual destiny of the Third Reich that Brandt couldn't stomach. Brandt climbed the ladder into the attack kiosk.

'Come on up, chief,' Kessler called down when Brandt's bald pate appeared.

The engineer climbed onto the bridge. Kessler knew from his chief's grey, tired expression that the news was unchanged. The two men moved aft onto the *wintergarten* deck and leaned on the rails.

'Christ only knows what that crap is,' Brandt growled. 'I've tried everything. Filtering it, preheating it. Everything. I've even tried bypassing the filters and separators. The pumps handle it okay, but it fucks up in the injectors by frothing – as you just heard. Goddamn dockyard Frenchies. Sometimes I reckon we'd been better off keeping the flotilla at Wilhelmshaven.'

Kessler chewed on his beard. 'How about the saddle tanks? Any chance of sucking a few drops out of them?'

The saddle tanks were the external fuel tanks. Because they were outside the pressure hull, they were free-flooding; otherwise their buoyancy would prevent the boat from diving, and they would be crushed at any depth by water pressure. The oil actually floated on the water. It was drawn off from the top and pumped through separators to filter out residual seawater before being fed to the engines. Because it was so vulnerable, ballast tank fuel oil was always consumed first at the outset of a patrol.

The chief nodded at the suggestion. 'I've transferred what was left in them to the internal tanks.'

'Uncontaminated?'

'Yes.'

'How much?'

'Two tonnes.'

It was a bleak figure. Kessler did not have to perform any mental arithmetic to know how bleak. U-395's total fuel capacity was 114 tonnes which gave her an operating range of approximately 8000 miles at a cruising speed of nine to twelve knots. Two tonnes meant that the U-boat had a range of around 125 nautical miles – a quarter of the way to the coast of South America. It might be possible to increase that range to 250 miles by reducing speed to five knots if the weather remained good. But the batteries were low, which meant an increased load on the diesels when they were being charged.

The captain was silent for a moment. Like all good U-boat engineers, Brandt wasn't happy unless he had a supply of oil secreted away somewhere.

'How about your special reserve, chief?'

Brandt looked like the teenage mother of an illegitimate

67

child called on to name the father. 'A tonne,' he grudgingly admitted.

Kessler guessed that that meant a tonne and a half; Brandt would *always* have a reserve. He nodded.

The off-watch crewmen were swimming again, creating a racket. Kessler made sure the lookouts weren't eavesdropping: the forward messes were hotbeds of gossip.

'How's the freshwater situation?'

'Two days. If we run the engines until we're dry, the condensers will give us another half day's supply.'

Like most U-boats, *U-395* produced its freshwater by condensing seawater in the diesels' heat exchangers. The boat's freshwater tanks were intended only to provide a limited reserve for use when submerged. Everything came down to fuel oil. Without it *U-395* was helpless.

Kessler gave no indication of his frustration. Eventually he nodded and glanced at his watch. 'A mess,' he remarked. 'Okay – get some sleep, chief. I suppose I'd better bring Kerneval up to date.' He gave a wry grin. 'Let's see if those armchair sailors can get us out of this one.'

12

Kessler's low opinion of the staff at the headquarters of the 2nd U-boat Flotilla at Lorient was unjustified. The four men who met in the conference room at Chateau Kerneval near Lorient to discuss his plight and the plight of three other U-boats in the South Atlantic were all experienced U-boat men. The chairman was Admiral Karl Doenitz himself who had commanded a U-boat during the Great War. They all understood the problems facing the commander of *U-395* which were at the top of the agenda. This was not the first time that fuel had been sabotaged although it was the first time it had put a boat in such grave danger. Charts of the South Atlantic were pored over and *U-395*'s position marked. It was the distance alone that poised the insuperable problem. The loss of the *Atlantis* had created a desperate situation for other U-boats and not just *U-395*. The Kriegsmarine had nothing that could refuel them. The nearest U-boat with surplus oil was on patrol off South Africa, and she would have to burn that and her return fuel just to reach the area. A long-range Type IX boat would not be ready to sail for another five days and would take at least fifteen days to reach *U-395* at a moderate cruising speed to conserve fuel, and that would only be possible if the weather was favourable, which was unlikely.

At the end of thirty minutes' discussion the flotilla chiefs concluded that any attempt to rescue *U-395* could easily result in two U-boats becoming stranded.

'There's nothing for it,' said one. 'Kessler has just enough fuel to reach the Uruguayan coast. His only option is to put his crew ashore and scuttle his boat.'

Doenitz's bird-like features creased into a frown at the prospect of having to tell Grand Admiral Raeder that yet another German warship had been scuttled in neutral Uruguayan waters and the crew interned. *U-395* was not the same as the *Graf Spee* but the jubilant British had scored a major propaganda victory over her and would be sure to make the same noises over the loss of a U-boat.

'I think,' Doenitz said in his reedy voice, 'before we do anything, we must recommend that the situation be reported to the naval intelligence officer in Montevideo. He's nearest, and the problem may end up in his lap, so it's only fair that he is briefed.' He glanced around the table at his subordinates as though challenging them to contradict him. 'There's another reason. It's a slender hope, but Professor Fritz Haug is as shrewd as a ferret and may come up with a solution.'

13

The early hours of the morning, when darkness brought favourable skywave propagation conditions for short wave radio communications across the Atlantic, was when the row of *Geheimschreiber* radio teleprinter machines were busy.

But tonight they were quiet. The duty radio officer in the communications room at the German embassy in Montevideo had little to do. Only No. 6 was clattering away, paper ribbon spooling onto the take-up reel. The duty officer's assistant had decoded the header against the day's one-time pad and had determined that the incoming signal was unimportant. Probably another demand for figures from the statistics department. Didn't those idiots in Berlin have anything better to do in the middle of a war? The previous night the Reichsbank had wanted to know the value of forged pesos that the Uruguayan authorities had seized in 1940. The duty officer had decoded the message because he was bored and on an impulse answered the query himself with a figure plucked straight out of his imagination. An hour later a teleprinter had chattered a 'thank you for dealing with our inquiry so promptly' acknowledgement.

The assistant, a pretty blonde, leaned across his desk with a cup of fresh coffee. The duty officer sipped it appreciatively. One of the big pluses about this posting was the coffee. Real coffee – not the sawdust and shit that was served up at home these days. He eyed the girl as she checked that the machine that had just stopped printing had an ample supply of paper tape. He had been nerving himself to make a pass at her. If the rumours were true, he was the only male on the comms staff who hadn't had a handful of those divine tits.

The bell on No.8 chimed and its type bars started clattering as tape spooled through its printing head. The girl and the duty officer stared at the teleprinter. It was a machine that they kept in good order – watered and fed – but this was the first time in weeks that it had come alive. It was a priority machine.

The officer pulled on his headphones and flipped the channel switch for No. 8's frequency so that he could listen-in to the chirruping tones as heard by the teleprinter's radio receiver. Eventually the paper tape produced a string of Ks to indicate end of message. There was a pause and the message was repeated.

The girl scanned through the code groups. 'All clean on both sends,' she reported.

The duty officer sent an acknowledgement. The girl tore off the tape and gave it to him. He transcribed the header on his notepad. It read:

FLH IMMEDIATE.

'Immediate' on No. 8 meant just that. He picked up his intercom handset and buzzed the messenger room. A sleepy voice answered.

'Send a car round to collect Herr Haug from his flat,' the duty officer ordered.

'What, now?'

'Well I daresay you could leave it until the Führer's birthday, but you might be stood up against a wall and shot.'

By the time Fritz Haug entered the communications room forty-five minutes later, the entire message was decoded and typed on a pink flimsy. It was hard to believe that Haug's sleep had just been interrupted. His moon-like face was pink, his eyes bright and alert. He signed the signal log and read the message. For once his normally good-natured expression faltered. He read the message again. It was only ten lines.

'Did this come through clearly?'

'Two sends – both crystal clear,' the duty officer confirmed. He watched as the portly figure went to the wall map. That's given the smug little bugger something to chew on, he thought; he didn't trust men who had manicures.

Haug's forefinger traced the longitude and latitude and came to a stop in the South Atlantic north-east of Montevideo.

71

'Well, well,' he said softly to the wall map. 'We've got yet another stranded U-boat right on our patch.'

'That makes three now,' the duty officer observed.

Haug nodded slowly. 'OKM have dumped the problem in our lap.'

Haug walked slowly back to his flat along the palm-lined rambla. It wasn't far. He enjoyed the cool night air, also the walk gave him a chance to think.

The marbled walkways through the magnificent gardens of the vast Plaza de la Independencia glistened with dew in the ornate street lights. Lovers sat close on the benches, their dark intertwined shapes merging. The occasional flash of pale, slender fingers curling into the nape of a neck gave the dark masses erotic humanity.

He came to the central post office whose imposing colonnade entrance would have been more appropriate for a department store. There wasn't much that a post office could put on display therefore its windows had been leased to various companies. One such was the Bilbao Steam and General Navigation Company. They were proud of their modern fleet of mail packets and had put on a fine display of cutaway models. The *Cobra*, the *Python*, the *Anaconda* . . .

Haug bent nearer and read the little card. The information was printed in Spanish, German, Portuguese and English. The *Anaconda* was the latest addition to the fleet. Launched 1936. 5000 GRT. None of this interested him. Cursing the small print and the reflections off the glass, he screwed up his eyes and moved his head to a better position.

Top speed 15 knots. Power, 2 Lister diesels . . .

Diesels!

Haug straightened, his mind racing. He stared down at the model for some seconds, still thinking hard. Eventually he continued his journey and stopped, hands thrust into his jacket pockets. There was no reason why the OKM should not have an answer to their problem that night. He turned and retraced his footsteps. The scale of his audacious idea excited him. The British had an apt phrase for what he had in mind: 'Killing two birds with one stone'. None of the details were worked out, but he was confident that the bare bones of a plan would be clear in his mind by the time he got back to the embassy.

He quickened his pace. His patent leather shoes rang crisply in the stillness of the night.

14

Kessler lay on his back in the stifling heat and tried to sleep. What were Kerneval playing at? It had been twelve hours since his situation report. He hadn't pulled any punches. He had even used the word 'STRANDED'.

Someone brushed by, accidentally dragging his curtain open. The dim red light from the radio office on the opposite side of the central gangway shone on the plywood panelling by his head. The entire boat was on night vision lighting to conserve the batteries. Even the intercom speakers, normally churning out a muted selection of Pols' Louis Armstrong favourites, were silent. Maron would be pleased; he hated Louis Armstrong, or so he claimed.

Kessler turned his bolster over in the hope of finding a cool spot. He was wearing only a vest and cotton trousers. An unfamiliar, clean-shaven face groped past. Beards which had been carefully cultivated during the patrol were now coming off. Brumner, an electrician who usually resembled an Old English sheepdog, had even shaved his head nearly bald. All hatches were thrown open to catch any breeze that might find its way into the boat, but the occasional movements of air bore the usual smells of oil and Poison Ivy's cooking. Oddly enough the usual stink of sweat and urine wasn't as bad as usual. With the boat wallowing about like a harpooned whale, most men had taken to a daily swim. Dreamlike snatches of conversation from the petty officers' mess reached him as he dozed:

'. . . bloody French waiters. Every morning he brought me a plate of fried bread cut up into little cubes. Everyone else was getting a decent breakfast but not me . . . I had to stick a fork in them to dip them in the jam. Most of them jumped off my plate onto the floor.'

'What did you order then?'

'Croutons – same as everyone else. Those crescent-shaped rolls the frogs eat.'

'Idiot – they're croissants!'

A gale of laughter.

'Christ – the word's virtually the same as ours and *still* you get it wrong!'

'What's worse than a plate of Poison Ivy's hot lasagne?'

'A plate of his cold lasagne?'

'Our cook's really a British agent.'

'Naw – Italian.'

More laughter.

Kessler reflected that morale was high. By now the entire crew knew that internment in Uruguay was the only option open to them. Reche claimed to have read in an article in an American magazine that the crew of the *Graf Spee* were having a whale of a time. A camp had been set up for them outside Montevideo and they could come and go as they pleased, and even smuggle in girls. Weekends on upcountry *estancias* where German was still spoken and where steaks were served up as thick as a man's arm. And if anyone got bored with that, all he had to do was feign some sort of illness and the Uruguayan doctors would recommend to the Red Cross that he be repatriated home. Maron said that such talk was seditious. Maron would.

From aft came the hiss of compressed air. One of the diesels turned over, coughed, fired, and settled down to a steady beat. The red emergency lights brightened. The miniature hurricane of air that the engine sucked through the boat produced a

74

cheer from the forward compartment. The chief had insisted on running alternate engines for five minutes during each watch to keep the batteries up for the daily trim dive. The boat's rolling eased as the propeller bit on the water and gave it a few knots of way. The chief had kept the clutch engaged because he also liked to keep his stern shafts and steering gear in good order.

'Steer two-two-zero.'

'Steering two-two-zero,' the helmsman's voice acknowledged from his position in the conning tower.

The 220-degree heading was Kessler's standing order so that every turn of the screws took the boat a little nearer Uruguay. Maron didn't approve of the course but had remained silent on the matter.

Kessler rolled onto his side and was about to yank his curtain closed when he noticed that Pols was scribbling on his signal pad. He dozed and was woken when the diesel stopped. The cloying, humid air claimed immediate control. Pols was fishing the Enigma cipher machine out of its cubbyhole. Another bloody weather report from another U-boat. There was the metallic clunk of the machine's typewriter-like keys being pressed, turning cogs and gearwheels. Funny to think that the signals security of the entire U-boat force depended on a little wooden box full of gears and sprockets. The millions of key combinations that the little machine provided would not daunt the British – they'd thrown everything into breaking the encryption. After all, they'd got their hands on an intact boat when Rahmlow had surrendered *U-570* off Iceland. Wardroom speculation on the subject had always got a frosty reception from Maron. During one occasion on watch the control room hand had said that whenever the skipper of his last boat had radioed his position, RAF Hudsons had always pounced on him an hour later.

'We were a hundred miles south of Iceland. One position report and we had the buggers jumping all over us like flies on a jam sandwich. It happened every bloody day for a week.'

Other men had similar horror tales. The British had something.

Pols stood without taking his headphones off, and waved a signal slip through the open control-room door. Someone took it from him. Kessler turned his back on the gangway and shut his eyes, determined to get at least an hour's sleep before the watch bell. The next thing he knew was his alarm clock sounding off in his ear.

The midships heads were free for once. And clean. Most men had taken to doing what they had to do when they went swimming. Also most of the stores that had been crammed into every spare corner of the boat, including the midships 'thunder-box', had been depleted. The giant 20-kilo tins of corned beef that had messed with the forward torpedo compartment because the chief wouldn't allow Maron to stow them in the battery compartments had been the cause of much resentment.

'Question: What's the difference between a having a Hamburg hooker in your bunk and a 20-kilo can of corned beef? Answer: The can of corned beef is warmer.'

Kessler washed, and gave up trying to trim his beard. Sharp scissors, the boat's abominable rolling, and his bleary eyes did not go well together. He entered the control room twenty minutes early, and sensed the electric atmosphere immediately. Maron's grey eyes were alight with fervour.

'Anything to report, Oberleutnant?'

'We are returning to the war, Captain.'

'Really? I wasn't aware that we had left it.'

Maron handed him a signal. 'This was relayed from another boat.'

BDU TO U-T. REMAIN PRESENT POSITION. REFUELLING
WITHIN 72 HOURS ARRANGED. PRECISE ETA UNKNOWN.
RECOGNITION LIGHTS PATTERN 116.

'So Kerneval *have* got a supply ship up their sleeve,' said Kessler phlegmatically. 'I shall have to review my opinions about armchair sailors.'

15

Angela Montgomerie was suitably outraged. Not so much because of the liberties the customs officer was taking by going through her baggage, but because the scrutiny was carried out on the dockside, in the open, under the eyes of a circle of stevedores who were curious to see what fineries ladies packed into their luggage. Those who weren't interested in Mrs Montgomerie's underwear were very interested in Tammy. She looked like a child bride, sitting on a huge trunk, idly swinging her white-stockinged legs, while impatiently twirling a parasol that kept the hot morning sun off her shoulders. She revelled in the admiring looks and occasionally exchanged shy smiles with some of the more muscular dockers.

'This is absurd!' Mrs Montgomerie proclaimed in loud Spanish, glaring at them. 'Don't these men have something better to do?'

The customs officer's answer was drowned by the raucous squeal of a rusty derrick lowering a mail-laden net into the *Anaconda*'s Number Two hold. A shunting engine clanked by and wreathed the group of passengers and their baggage in steam and smuts. Mrs Montgomerie's anger took on epic proportions but her remonstrations had to be acted out in mime such was the uproar.

Dieter followed the dock hand who was pushing a wooden handcart bearing one small suitcase. He could have carried his baggage himself but there was no point in creating resentment that might be communicated to the customs staff. The exception was a small kitbag that hung heavily from his shoulder. The dock hand unloaded his battered case beside Angela Montgomerie's smart luggage, accepted his modest tip with cursory thanks, and trundled his cart away. The crane screeched another load of mail into the hold. Dieter ran his eye over the *Anaconda*. He had little faith in the Spanish and had expected the ship to have degenerated to a rusty tub, but she was surprisingly smart. Her pennants looked crisp and freshly laundered; superstructure shone vanilla white so that it hurt the eyes to look at it in the harsh light. A couple of deck hands were painting one of the six lifeboats. Brasswork gleamed, and the red grain of mahogany handrails glowed warmly under coats of carefully-applied varnish. Partly visible above the quay on the upper half of her hull was was a giant Spanish national flag painted amidships. Doubtless it extended down to the waterline. In common with the shipping of many other neutral countries, the *Anaconda* wanted the world to know that her country was not involved in the war. And not only the world, but eyes peering through periscopes. Across the harbour an American refrigeration ship loading beef bore a huge Stars and Stripes on its hull.

The customs officer escaped from the Englishwoman's wrath and wanted to look in Dieter's suitcase. He pawed through the contents and gestured to the kitbag. Dieter unfastened the straps. The pieces of quartz were packed in labelled muslin bags.

'Examples geographica,' Dieter explained.

The German's Spanish seemed to amuse the officer. He chalked his mysterious runes on the kitbag without further inspection. The young German thought ruefully about the two hours he had spent writing out and tying phoney labels on every muslin bag.

Another handcart arrived laden with several small cases. Their owners were a party of three fairly typical upcountry *estancia* owners. Their leader was a small, rotund little man wearing gold-rimmed glasses and a beaming smile. Dieter was too experienced to reveal his astonishment; he merely regarded the three ranchers with casual interest.

Their leader was Haug.

All three were looking the part of wealthy ranchers. Haug's companions were in their thirties. They wore lavishly-decorated gaucho riding boots that were not intended for riding, and well-cut but grubby linen tropical suits. They laughed and joked loudly in German, appearing to be the worse for drink, particularly Haug, although Dieter knew that he rarely touched alcohol. Not once did the wily intelligence man acknowledge Dieter's existence.

Mrs Montgomerie eyed the trio distastefully. 'I wasn't warned there would be ranchers on board,' she complained in Spanish to the white-jacketed chief steward who was writing luggage stickers to identify which of Tammy's range of smart trunks were wanted in the cabin and which could go in the hold.

'They are going only as far as Rio,' the chief steward confided.

Mrs Montgomerie sniffed her disapproval. Her stockmen made frequent trips to Rio to splurge their wages on girls and nightclubs. At least the captain was unlikely to tolerate such loud-mouths at his table, but one could never be sure with the Spanish.

Dieter became uncomfortably aware of Tammy's gaze fixed on him. Had she been with other schoolgirls no doubt she would have had an attack of the giggles when he looked at her. He was used to them being shepherded in front of his camera by watchful nuns. His height intrigued them. But this girl just stared. It was a crazy role-reversal but he felt that she was mentally undressing him. The complaining Englishwoman had to be her chaperon – certainly not her mother. Dieter enjoyed summing up his fellow travellers, but he was careful to ignore the three ranchers.

The customs officer homed-in on the inebriated trio. He opened one of their trunks, eyed the bottles of spirits, and shrugged. It wasn't his concern if they drunkenly fell overboard before Rio. Haug slapped him affably on the back and pressed a bottle of Johnnie Walker on him. The officer politely declined and chalked his hieroglyphics on their cases. A senior customs man appeared and conducted a brief argument with him in rapid Spanish. The second officer wasn't satisfied with his subordinate's examination of the ranchers' baggage. His rummage through the contents of their cases was quick but thorough. His skilled fingers even checked for false linings. Haug's beaming smile never faltered and his two colleagues seemed deliberately indifferent to the special attention their baggage was receiving. Eventually the senior customs officer slammed the cases shut and slouched away.

A ramshackle charter bus, so crammed with passengers that arms were hanging out of the windows, rumbled onto the dockside and grated to a standstill, its rust-eaten body shuddering in resonance with its badly-tuned engine. The bus's roof was piled high with baggage. Six white-garbed nuns piled out, followed by an assortment of stockyard workers and their wives looking self-conscious in ill-fitting cheap suits and dresses. They stood blinking in the bright light. The driver and an assistant clambered onto the roof, untied ropes and began tossing cases down where they were quickly piled into a small mountain on the flagstones. There was a mêlée of shouts and arguments as the cheap fibre suitcases were reconciled with their owners. The customs officer and two junior stewards, clipboards at the ready, hurried over to the new arrivals to establish order. The bus laid a smokescreen of black diesel fumes to cover its retreat.

Dieter maintained his expression of amused interest as he regarded the new arrivals but his thoughts were a sick whirl. Why was Haug a passenger? Who were his two companions? And who were all these people? A hurried count – God, there were at least sixty! There was even a small, tousle-haired boy aged about nine with a thin-faced, harassed-looking mother. One of the women was nursing a baby. Even the three ranchers allowed their surprise to override their intoxication for a few moments.

The Englishwoman voiced the questions that Dieter needed answers to.

'Who are all these people?' Mrs Montgomerie demanded

angrily. 'The passenger list had only six names on it!'

The small boy broke away from his mother and became a noisy aeroplane intent of strafing Tammy.

'We only find out about them two hours ago,' said the chief steward smoothly. 'They are going to Porto Alegre, but the railway bridge is washed away last night. So we take them and put into Porto Alegre on Sunday morning.'

Tammy intercepted the aviator by extending a shapely foot, causing him to crash. The pilot stopped being an aircraft and became a small boy nursing a grazed knee, howling until his mother rescued him.

'But this is preposterous!' Mrs Montgomerie protested. 'Are we to have our nights disturbed by screaming children and the incessant clatter of rosaries?'

'For two nights only,' the chief steward explained. 'Also steerage passengers are not allowed on the upper deck.'

The Spanish was fast but Dieter caught the gist of what was being said. Porto Alegre was five hundred miles up the coast, about half-way to Rio. He was trying to work out how this might affect his plans when the chief steward headed off further argument by clapping his hands. It was the signal for the waiting stevedores to seize the luggage and carry it up the gangway.

'We will go aboard now,' the chief steward announced. 'First- and second-class passengers first please.'

The six passengers followed him obediently up the gangway.

A cabin boy was assigned to show Dieter and the ranchers to their accommodation on the upper deck. As the only first-class passengers, Mrs Montgomerie and Tammy warranted the attentions of the chief steward. He led them forward along the portside quarter deck, under the shadow of the lifeboats. He unlocked a mahogany door with a louvred lower panel, and showed them into a spacious carpeted cabin below the bridge whose width was nearly half the *Anaconda*'s beam. The wanted-on-voyage trunks were stood on plinths against the far bulkhead.

Mrs Montgomerie looked around while Tammy bounced on the settee. In addition to the master bedroom, there was a small cabin provided with two single beds – not bunks – that led off from the main stateroom. This smaller bedroom was provided with a shower room and toilet whereas the master bedroom had an adjoining bathroom with a deep-sided hip bath. Everything worked, including the overhead electric fans. It was far better than she had expected but Mrs Montgomerie was honour-bound to find something to complain about.

'Too many windows,' she said, waving a hand imperiously at the windows on three sides of the stateroom. 'People walking past all the time, looking in.'

The chief steward sounded suitably apologetic. 'There are good, thick curtains, Señora. Only first- and second-class passengers are allowed up here. The crew's quarters are aft, the steerage passengers are on the lower decks.'

Mrs Montgomerie sniffed.

The chief steward shrugged. 'If you want a window where no one can walk by, there will be a cabin free next to the engine room. It has portholes just above the waterline. Maybe flying fish will look in but no one else.' He looked regretful. 'If you would like me to change your cabin, I will be happy to do so, but the company does not give refunds.'

'We'll make do in here,' said Mrs Montgomerie with even more frost than usual because she sensed that she had been beaten. When he had left she closed the curtains and knelt down to check that it wasn't possible to be spied on through the louvres in the door.

Dieter's cabin, aft of Mrs Montgomerie's quarters, was a good deal more modest, and much hotter. He latched the door open on its hook. His quarters consisted of four bunks and a dresser with a built-in wash basin. The shower and toilet was a little larger than a broom cupboard. He stowed his luggage on an upper bunk. There was no point in hiding the kitbag containing the crystals. Asking the captain if he could store it in the ship's safe would only draw attention to the samples. It was better to leave the kitbag on the bunk with the label prominently displayed. No one would be interested in stealing lumps of rock. Through the open door he could hear the drunken laughter of the ranchers in the next cabin, and was thankful that he did not have to share with anyone. Again the question arose in his mind: why was Haug on the ship? Didn't they trust him? The thought made Dieter uncomfortable. Hitherto his loyalty had never been questioned.

He showered. The cold water was warm, and the hot water was superheated steam. He stepped out of his cabin, feeling more human in white shorts and a clean shirt, and leaned on the port rail. Out of the corner of his eye he noted with some amusement that his appearance led to a hurried repositioning of curtains in the Englishwoman's suite. A feminine hand poked around the edge of a window, tucking the curtains into cushions. A small lighter that served as a tug hauled on a hawser and eased the *Anaconda*'s bow away from the quay. Once the ship's heading was into the centre of the basin, the hawser was cast off. A long, mournful blast of acknowledgement from the *Anaconda*'s siren was followed by the entire boat shaking as the twin propellers, going hard astern and hard forward, brought the packet about on her axis. The breeze that played on Dieter's face would have been more welcome had it not been laden with the smell from the beef packing stations on the far side of the harbour. The engine note changed and settled down to a steady beat. Stiff-winged seagulls followed the ship for a few minutes before they realised that it wasn't a fishing boat and wheeled away, uttering cries of raucous disgust.

The resort beaches of Porcitos and Ramirez came into view, with their rows of gaily-coloured bathing tents. 11:00 a.m. and already the sands were crowded. It was going to be a sweltering day. Dieter made his way forward. The nuns had gathered on the foredeck for matins. The breeze from the ship's brisk ten knots whipped at their habits. The noisy aviator boy circled them, arms outstretched, his mouth twisted into a machine-gun yammer until the sister-in-charge fetched him a cuff that sent him bawling back to base.

They steamed past a long line of American merchantman riding at anchor, awaiting berths to collect their loads of beef. It was the sight of the patiently waiting ships that brought home to Dieter the scale of the wealth that the vast grassy plains of Uruguay produced.

A small motor cruiser, its engine idling, drifted into the *Anaconda*'s path about half a mile ahead. Dieter glanced up at the blank windows of the bridge as though expecting to see a reaction. He wasn't disappointed. A stocky figure wearing smart tropical whites and a brass-bound cap stepped out of a side door onto the wing deck and trained his binoculars on the boat. Legs planted slightly apart, muscles bracing and relaxing in time with the ship's easy motion, bronzed arms jutting confidently out. A strong, capable man. He called out something through the open door. The *Anaconda*'s siren blared. White water appeared around the motor cruiser's transom, and it veered away to starboard like a startled rabbit.

The figure interested Dieter. It was Carlos Juan Valez, the *Anaconda*'s captain. Forty-one years old. A home in Bilbao. Two children aged ten and eleven. Pay – the equivalent of $1500 per annum. Fritz Haug had collected quite a lot of information on the Spaniard but not enough for them to be certain that Plan 1 would work. Dieter prayed that it would.

16

Dinner aboard the *Anaconda* lacked formalities. This did not appeal to Angela Montgomerie. For one thing there was no proper dining salon; the meal was served in the crew's common room, the card tables folded away for the purpose. Nor was there a proper captain's table, rather a long, narrow table that seated everyone – the off-watch deck officers, and the handful of first and second class passengers. There were no place settings – seating was a free-for-all – some had already started on the first course. And worse, far worse, there were no proper introductions.

'You soon get to know everyone,' said Captain Valez dismissively when Mrs Montgomerie raised this glaring breech of etiquette. 'The passengers are the ones in rich clothes, and the crew are the ones in poor clothes. And the crew all dress the same.' He laughed richly into his soup at his witticism.

'I'm Dieter Rohland,' said Dieter, half standing and wondering if it was the done thing to shake a lady's hand across the table. 'You must forgive my poor Spanish.'

Cursory introductions were made around the table. The second officer and the engineering officer had no scruples about pumping Tammy's hand across the table and making her breasts jiggle. Her lovely eyes disembowelled Dieter emotionally when he took her hand. Haug's courtly Prussian manners made a good impression on Mrs Montgomerie.

'Delighted to make your acquaintance, Mrs Montgomerie,' he said in faultless English, clicking the heels of his riding boots while bowing and kissing her hand.

'A rancher with manners,' Mrs Montgomerie observed as Haug rejoined his two companions at the end of the table. 'One never knows where one stands these days.'

The three resumed swapping jokes with each other in German and making no attempt to speak Spanish. Haug gave the impression of being slightly drunk even before the steward opened the wine. They were the only men present who showed no interest in Tammy, and Haug had not accorded Dieter as much as a flicker of recognition when they had shaken hands.

Dieter broke the ice over the second course by recounting some of his mishaps when photographing society weddings in Montevideo.

'There,' said Mrs Montgomerie, 'I knew I'd seen you before. You were the young man who took the photographs at the Foresters' wedding. All underexposed. Colonel Forester wanted to give you a horse-whipping as I recall.'

Dieter grinned sheepishly and caught Tammy's eye. 'The gentleman was annoyed,' he admitted. 'It was a faulty batch of plates.'

Mrs Montgomerie sniffed and wondered what the world was coming to when one had to sit down and dine with servants. Also there was far too much garlic in the steak, and –that sin of all sins – the napkins had been ironed but not cleaned. Wooden napkin rings, too. A disgrace.

Dieter had chosen a seat so that he could see out of the windows. Shading his eyes against the last vestiges of an ochre sunset it was possible to distinguish the thin line of swamp-land that made up the entire coastline of Uruguay to the north of Montevideo. This close to shore the sea was calm.

'So why are you going to Spain?' the captain asked Dieter.

Dieter realised that the question was directed at him. 'The Spanish government have given me permission to photograph the bears in the Pyrenees,' he replied. 'They are the last bears in Western Europe.' His cover story had strength because it was true.

The *Anaconda* altered course a few degrees to starboard and gave a long blast on her siren.

The captain looked questioningly at Mrs Montgomerie. She checked an impulse to tell him to mind his own business. After all, she would be dining at this table for the next three weeks, and another three weeks for the return voyage.

The scattered lights of the Maldonaldo seal hunting fleet passed between the *Anaconda* and the distant swamps. The ship heeled again to resume her original course. The heading worried Dieter. It was too close to land.

'I am escorting my ward to her school in Switzerland,' Mrs Montgomerie volunteered.

Captain Valez nodded. He had guessed correctly. Switzer-land was where many of Uruguay's meat millionaires sent their daughters. France if they were devout Catholics.

'And you, gentlemen? What is happening in Rio to drag you from your *estancias*?'

Haug broke off his voluble chatting to his comrades and turned his glittering gold spectacles on the captain. Dieter saw that his blue eyes were sharp and clear. Obviously he was pretending to drink. 'An exposition of slaughterhouse equipment.'

Angela Montgomerie frowned. 'In Rio? What exposition? I've not heard of it.'

Haug smiled benignly and waved a pudgy hand. 'My Spanish . . . Exposition is not a good word . . . Demonstration . . . I don't know where. We are meeting an agent in Rio.'

The meal ended with excellent coffee. Dieter declined an invitation to stay for liqueurs and cigars. He exchanged 'buenas noches' with his fellow passengers, and returned to his cabin. The Anaconda was making a good twelve knots, forcing a chill breeze through his cabin ventilator and out through the louvred door. He read for an hour. A change in the ship's motion prodded him onto the deck. The wind had veered to the south, pushing up a following sea that caused the Anaconda to give an uncomfortable twist at the crest of each swell.

He had work to do. He made his way to the forward rail and positioned himself in the centre – the best place for a magnetic compass reading because the even distribution of the ship's mass would minimise deflection error. He lifted his watch so that it caught a bulkhead light, and pressed the winder. The needle lifted and swung to the twelve o'clock position. Due north.

Damn! He was hoping for a north-east heading.

A movement to his right, which he saw out of the corner of his eye. His sleeve fell back in place as he lowered his wrist. He remained quite still, staring ahead, trying to see beyond the glare of the foredeck lights. The shadow moved beside him. He would have sensed the man's presence even if he hadn't seen him.

'This course is not good, Dieter,' said the shadow softly in German.

87

Dieter turned his head. Haug's moon-like face was hidden by the turned-up collar of a riding jacket. The amiable, free-drinking rancher was gone. It never had been there as far as Dieter was concerned. Despite the warmth of the night, Haug's demeanour introduced an icy chill.

'Too close to land,' Haug observed.

'Can I ask what you're doing here, professor?'

The intelligence officer chuckled. 'Of course you may. To be fair, my dear Dieter, I do believe that you are owed an explanation.' Haug's words were friendly but the voice was cold.

Dieter remained silent. He wanted to fire a hundred questions at the older man but knew that Haug would tell him what he wanted to tell him; no more and no less.

'The stakes have changed quite considerably,' Haug continued.

'They always were high. But if you don't trust me –'

Haug laid a hand on Dieter's sleeve. 'Oh but we trust you implicitly, my dear Dieter. Getting your samples home is still of the utmost importance.' There was a sudden return of his customary warmth. He smiled. 'My judgement in getting you to carry them was sound; you saw that little charade on the wharf with that customs officer. The British have been very jumpy of late. They know that your man Cleary made off with some prime samples but they don't know for sure if we've got our hands on them.'

Dieter decided to venture a question. 'So how have the stakes changed?'

'What is our exact course, Dieter?'

'Due north.'

A gold ring on Haug's finger flashed as he lit a cigarette. The flame from the cupped lighter threw his soft features into sharp relief. His blue eyes were watching Dieter carefully. 'Another twelve hours' hugging the coast on this course and we'll have to steer almost due east to reach our objective. Such a course will be obvious to even the most stupid passenger.'

'I'll speak to the captain in the morning,' said Dieter. 'As per your instructions.'

'Perhaps it would be best if you spoke to him now,' said Haug. 'It would be better not to delay things.'

'I have not delayed anything –'

'Of course you haven't, Dieter. How were any of us to know that we'd be taking on an extra sixty or so passengers, and then crawl up the coast to Porto Alegre?' Haug inhaled hard on his cigarette and thrust his hands into his jacket pockets. 'The operation to return you home has been . . . shall we say . . . merged with another, equally important operation. I don't think you need know anymore than that just yet. We must learn to be flexible, Dieter. Speak to the captain now please.'

With that he turned on his heel and left Dieter fuming inwardly at Haug's refusal to take him into his confidence. His hand went to his inside jacket pocket and touched the envelope. Rehearsing what he had to say, he walked around the deck to the seaward side. The notice at the foot of the steps leading to the bridge was in three languages:

NO PASSENGERS BEYOND THIS POINT

Dieter climbed the steps and banged on the bridge door. It was opened by a junior navigation officer, silhouetted by the red glow of the wheelhouse lighting.

'I need to see the captain urgently,' said Dieter, cutting short the man's objections.

'The captain has just retired –'

'It is *very* urgent. I'm Dieter Rohland – a second-class passenger. I met with Captain Valez at dinner.'

The officer picked up a telephone by the binnacle, spoke too quickly for Dieter to follow what was said, and beckoned to him. Dieter followed him through the small chartroom aft of the bridge and along a narrow passageway. Everywhere was illuminated with soft red lights to preserve the watch's night vision. He rapped on a door, ushered Dieter into a brightly-lit cabin and closed the door.

Captain Valez was sitting in vest and shorts at a small fold-down desk writing his log. The cabin's panelling was smothered in photographs of two gawky children and a plump wife. The white jacket he had worn to dinner was hanging on a closet door.

'Ah. Mr Roman.'

'Rohland. I am sorry to disturb you, Captain. But this is urgent.'

Valez indicated his bunk. He stood, fished a bottle of beer out of a small bulkhead refrigerator, and poured two glasses.

'Your health, Mr Rohland. Somehow, I don't think you want to marry Mrs Montgomerie?'

Dieter smiled. 'I have a more serious problem.'

'Such a woman,' said Valez wistfully. 'She would be a challenge for any man. So tell me about your problem, Mr Rohland.'

Dieter's hesitation was carefully contrived. 'I have some business associates who are in trouble.'

'Ah . . .'

'They use a fast motor yacht to conduct most of their business.'

Valez sipped his beer while watching Dieter carefully. 'So?'

'Yesterday a long sea chase at high speed caused them to burn up all their oil. They are stranded. Drifting. They need help.'

'My help?'

'Yes.'

'A valuable yacht?'

'Yes.'

The Spaniard's eyes narrowed. 'Under international law it is the duty of all ships to give assistance.' He paused, watching Dieter carefully. 'If they need a tow, there would be the question of a salvage claim.'

'Not a tow, Captain. They wish to buy fuel oil.'

'How much?'

'Eighty tonnes. A hundred if you can spare it. Naturally,

you will be compensated for rendering assistance, and for the loss of salvage.'

'You have their position?'

'Yes. It will involve you in only slight alteration of course provided it is not left too late.'

Captain Valez drained his glass. With exaggerated care he selected a toothpick from a small pot. 'How much compensation do you have in mind?'

'$3000 for you, and another $2000 to be shared among your crew as you see fit.'

The Spaniard probed his teeth with seeming disinterest. 'You have this money?'

Dieter produced the envelope and fanned through the bills with his thumb while watching Valez. The Spaniard allowed his gaze to drop. Dieter was a trained observer; the little flash of greed was a flicker – gone in an instant – but Dieter saw it. 'That's half, captain,' he dropped the envelope on the desk. 'The other half when the fuel is pumped across.'

'I need the position of this motor yacht.'

'I can give you a course. You shall have the position when you've held the course long enough to have committed yourself.'

Valez swept the envelope onto the floor. 'Take your money, Mr Rohland. I do nothing without the position. I never run my ship blind.'

Dieter was unperturbed. 'My business associates are very rich and very powerful. If you double-cross them . . .'

'I do nothing without a position,' said Valez doggedly. The toothpick went back to work.

Dieter picked up the envelope and stood. He met the Spaniard's gaze. They remained frozen for some seconds, wills locked together like the horns of warring buffalo; neither prepared to give way, but Dieter knew that he would have to. He gave a gesture of resignation, picked up a chart pencil, and scribbled U-395's position on the envelope. He offered it to Valez. The seaman took it without a word, glanced at the figures and cleared papers and books from his desk. Underneath was a grubby vellum chart, its surface worn from frequent erasures of pencilled plotting. He marked the position with a cross so faint that there was barely any graphite on the paper, and walked a pair of dividers from the *Anaconda*'s running fix line to the cross.

He straightened and stared hard at Dieter. 'The forecast is good, Mr Rohland. This weather should hold for the next twenty-four hours. We can rendezvous in ... seventeen hours.' He glanced at a chronometer mounted in a wooden box. 'At 1800.'

'Make it twenty-four hours from now,' said Dieter curtly. 'At night. When the passengers are asleep. Will that be possible?'

Valez regarded his guest for a moment. 'Of course. It requires only a small reduction in speed.'

Dieter left Captain Valez's cabin ten minutes later, after they had agreed on several details. He reached the foot of the steps leading to the bridge and felt the *Anaconda* alter course a few degrees to starboard. It was the first of several heading changes that Valez would be making over the next two hours.

There was a light showing around the blinds in Haug's cabin. He rapped on the door. A flurry of movement inside.

'It's only me.'

The door opened. Haug's cherubic face beamed. 'Mr Rohland. We were just turning in.'

'There's no one around,' said Dieter impatiently, pushing his way into the cabin. The other two men were sitting opposite each other playing poker. They glanced disinterestedly at Dieter. The taller stubbed out a cigarette in an overflowing ashtray.

Haug's eyes twinkled. 'Well, Dieter?'

Dieter eyed the card-players distastefully. 'Who are these two, professor?'

'Hugo is a good engineer, and Walter is a brilliant navigator,' said Haug. 'We will have a need of such talents.'

'*Graf Spee* internees?'

'My dear Dieter, it is not necessary for you to know.' Haug sat and indicated for Dieter to do likewise.

'The captain's agreed,' said Dieter, declining a seat and a cigarette. 'No doubt you've noticed that we've already made one small course alteration to starboard.'

Haug beamed. 'Excellent. And the crew?'

'Captain Valez has gone along with the idea of them receiving bonuses. He's promised that they'll keep their mouths shut.'

'And the passengers?'

'We rendezvous twenty-four hours from now, 0100 ship time. At 2300 the captain will announce that he's received radio reports of U-boats in the area not respecting neutral flags. He will order *all* the passengers to portside cabins below deck in order to enforce a strict blackout. The U-boat will be refuelled and supplied on the starboard side. Once we're away on the U-boat, the captain will allow passengers back to their normal cabins.' Dieter paused and added with studied politeness: 'Or does that clash with any other plans you may have?'

Haug chuckled. 'It ties-in all nice and neat.'

Dieter glanced at the two intent on their poker. 'So if all goes well, they're somewhat redundant.'

'We'll see, Dieter. We'll see. You haven't told the captain *what* it is he'll be refuelling, have you?'

'He'll find out.'

Haug chuckled again. 'Of course he'll find out. *U-395* has something in common with all U-boats – it bears an extraordinary resemblance to a U-boat.' His companions enjoyed the joke.

'I will tell him just before we rendezvous,' said Dieter evenly. 'By then he'll will have taken his ship four hundred miles off course. It will be too late for him to back out.'

Haug's bland smile remained steady. 'And Hugo and Walter are the insurance in case he does try to back out.'

Dieter looked at each man in turn. 'How?'

Haug nodded to Walter, the taller of the two. He dropped his cards and pulled a wine bottle from under the bunk. The base unscrewed and a German army pattern stick grenade dropped canister first into the palm of his hand. Walter grinned broadly at Dieter.

'Just a small part of our equipment,' said Haug softly. 'Insurance, my dear Dieter. I have a lot of confidence in you, but I do like adequate insurance cover.'

17

The calm was uncanny.

U-395 was lying in the centre of a disc of motionless water. The haze rose from the surface like a muslin curtain drawn up around the stopped U-boat.

'Like a ballerina on a circular stage,' Kessler grumbled to the four lookouts. 'You get this in this area around this time of year even though we're a long way south of the Doldrums.' He was propped against the torpedo aimer, wearing only his white cap and duck trousers, his beard and hair now neatly clipped. He glanced at the sky, grey with haze, trapping the heat rising off the ocean and pushing the relative humidity to 100 per cent.

The forward hatch and the galley hatch were open. *U-395*'s buoyancy was low, trimmed down by the bow, her forward deck casing just above the water. The boat's bow-heavy attitude made it easy for the off-watch crew in the water to scramble aboard but the reason was to drain the oil forward in the fuel tanks. Brandt and his second engineer had the aft deck grating open over the bunkering valves. One of the valves had a flexible pipe connected to it. Brandt caught Kessler's attention.

'We're ready to start flushing, Captain.'

'Very good, chief.' Kessler ordered the men out of the water and called down a litany of orders to the helmsman in the attack kiosk. 'Port motor 300. Steer two-seven-zero.'

U-395 crept silently over the surface on one electric motor, her bow producing a spreading, perfectly symmetrical vee, like the fluting of a skilled woodcarver. Brandt opened a compressed-air valve. The hose stiffened. There was a series of belches and rumbles from *U-395* like an old man's digestion at war with an incompatible dinner. The hose trailing in the water stiffened and became buoyant. The end appeared on the surface a second before the useless fuel oil glugged from the nozzle and spread across the wake, creating a swathe of iridescent light that broadened to a belt that would eventually be at least a kilometre wide. Even at two knots, the conning tower drew a pocket of air after it so that there was no escape from the stench of haemorrhaging oil.

After fifteen minutes the hose snorted compressed air and lashed about. The two engineers connected the hose to the second valve and repeated the performance. At the end of an hour *U-395* had shed all her contaminated oil and was three miles nearer the Uruguayan coast. The last stage of the operation was to purge the tanks, using some of the chief engineer's precious reserves. The diesels ran clean and evenly for five minutes each.

'Pols!'

The telegraphist's head popped up through the hatch. 'Captain?'

'Get that useless birdcage thing of yours rigged.'

Pols climbed onto the bridge and set up the 'Biscay Cross'. The crude aerial consisted of copper wire wound on a wooden cross-like frame. It was connected to a Metox receiver in the conning tower that was supposed to detect enemy radar transmissions. A telegraphist turned the aerial while Pols sat beside the helmsman and tried to make sense of the howls and whines that emanated from the set's loudspeaker. The Metox receiver's incessant racket and makeshift aerial that had to be unshipped before diving meant that U-boat crews had little confidence in the apparatus. Kessler gave it the benefit of the doubt because he had nothing else. He went below and entered the engine room just as the diesel was closed down after the test run. Brandt and two mechanics were reassembling the filters and injectors.

'How's everything, chief?'

Brandt straightened and wiped his hands on a wad of cotton waste. He was caked to the elbows in oil and grease. 'Whistle-clean, Captain. Now all we need is some fuel for the buggers. We'd better bring the trim dive forward to this watch. We're floating like a bloody cork.'

Having shed forty tonnes of contaminated oil, U-395 was now riding in high buoyancy. The door of Tube 5, the stern torpedo tube, was nudging the surface. Ten minutes later the boat flooded her main ballast tanks and dived to thirty metres.

While the control room watch petty officers and ratings worked the trim and flooding panels to fine tune the boat's buoyancy, Kessler conferred with Maron, the officer of the watch.

The two men pored over the chart spread out on the chart chest. The North Atlantic area of the map looked like a sheet of graph paper. It was a mass of grid squares, each square identified by a two-letter code. These large squares were further subdivided into smaller squares, each one identified by a four-digit number. The system had been devised by Doenitz's son-in-law. Even if the British code-breakers had cracked the Enigma system, it was unlikely that they had worked out the significance of the six character position codes used by the U-boat arm. The problem that Kessler faced was that, as Doenitz considered the North Atlantic the only battleground for his U-boats, the grid squares had not been extended into the South Atlantic. The oversight meant that the Kessler had been obliged to transmit his position several times using the conventional fixing notation that gave degrees north of the equator and west of the Greenwich meridian. If the British *had* cracked Enigma, then they would be certain to know U-395's position.

'I'd give our last 10,000 tonne pennant to know what's

going on in those warped minds at Kerneval,' Kessler growled into his beard. 'Why haven't they given us a rendezvous time?'

'Radio communication problems with the supply ship?' Maron ventured. 'We're five thousand miles from base.'

'Possibly,' said Kessler, unconvinced. 'But if a little tub like us can make contact using an antenna nearly in the drink, then I can't see that a ship would have problems. And the damnable thing is that the quartermaster is over the moon with his star fixes. Perfect bloody conditions for him and his sextant. It wouldn't surprise me if the position we've transmitted isn't the most accurate that any U-boat has ever given.'

Maron made no comment. He knew that it was better to remain silent when his skipper decided to talk things through. All Kessler wanted was a sounding board for his ruminations.

'Right. You're a British destroyer, Oberleutnant.'

'I am?'

'You been given chapter and verse on us. You know our position and you know that we're waiting for a supply ship. What do you do? Come charging in and blow us to glory, or what?'

Maron considered. 'I'd wait and try to catch you with your trousers down refuelling, and get the supply ship as well.'

Kessler chewed on his beard. 'Exactly. Exactly. The British won't pass up the temptation to sink two boats. There's probably a destroyer sitting over the horizon right now with all her radar going.'

Kessler was both right and wrong. He was right that the British had cracked the Enigma system and were reading U-boat signals traffic. He was also right that they knew *U-395*'s position and were aware of her predicament. But he was wrong about a British warship lurking just over the horizon. The cruiser HMS *Dorsetshire* was five hundred miles to the north following her sinking of the *Atlantis*, but she was cramming on every knot so that she wouldn't be late for the party.

18

Mrs Montgomerie saw no reason why a sea voyage should lead to a reduction of her standards of civilised behaviour. Those standards included a sun that was expected to conform. With a sigh of exasperation, she abandoned Jane Austen and squinted at the late afternoon sun that had had the impertinence to creep under her deckchair's sunshade. It was shining straight into her eyes and flooding the *Anaconda*'s upper afterdeck with a brilliant golden light. Tammy was leaning on the rail with her back to her guardian, legs slightly apart, a constant eddy from the superstructure flattening her thin cotton dress against her thighs. A deck boy below was wire brushing a lower deck ventilator. He was thirteen years old, shy and impressionable. Tammy was making a great impression on him – one that he would remember all his life. Childhood folklore had taught him what little girls were made of; now Tammy was providing a first-hand lesson regarding the make up of big girls. Every sly upward glance added volumes to the sum total of his knowledge. He was an apt pupil who had the good fortune to encounter a good teacher. They didn't come much better equipped for further education than Tammy.

'Tammy!'

'Yes, Miss Angela?'

'Go and find that lazy, good-for-nothing chief steward. He's supposed to looking after us but I daresay he's gambling with the peasants in steerage.'

A mischievous smile played at the corners of Tammy's full mouth. 'And what shall I do with him when I've found him, Miss Angela?'

'You will bring the miserable wretch to me, you silly child!'

Tammy went off eagerly on her mission, and Mrs Montgomerie resumed reading *Pride and Prejudice*, her favourite book. Jane Austen's opinions of men tended to underpin her own. Men were really a different species that had, at a primitive early stage in their development, diverted from the main tree of evolution of the human race, leaving women to continue alone but retaining a regrettable degree of downward biological compatibility with men to ensure the continuation of the race.

She read undisturbed for ten minutes until Tammy returned dragging a reluctant trophy by the hand. Mrs Montgomerie sighed. 'Tammy – when one goes off in search of the chief steward, it is not necessary to return holding his hand. Stop manhandling him.'

Tammy released her catch. 'Sorry, Miss Angela.'

'Now go and wash. You'll be reeking of garlic.'

Tammy managed to insert a defiant little flounce into her departure. Mrs Montgomerie skewered the hapless steward with her icy grey eyes. The lightness in his step that day at the news of the bonus he would be receiving had been deadened by the summons. Mrs Montgomerie pointed at the sun, hovering over the *Anaconda*'s whipped cream wake. 'What is that?'

The chief steward glanced nervously in the direction of the accusing finger. '*El sol?*' he ventured.

'Yes – I know it's *el sol*, you silly man. What is it doing there? It should be over there.' She pointed to port.

Understanding dawned. The English lady had brought the subject up at lunch. 'Ah, *si*! We are still sailing east to avoid the storms. Very bad storms, Señora.'

The Englishwoman snorted. 'First I've heard of it – driving all the way to Africa just to get round some rough weather. I shall bring up the subject with the captain at dinner. Very well – you may go.'

19

'Twenty metres,' the control room petty officer reported.

U-395's trim dive was being used by Pols to listen for the mysterious supply ship. Under the right conditions hydrophone effects could be picked up over fifty miles.

Pols' voice crackled over the loudspeaker. 'Hydrophone Effects now bearing two-six-five.'

Kessler stepped through the forward door. 'What sort of HE? Propeller noises?' he asked. The radio office was lit by a solitary red light. He had to wave at Pols to catch his attention.

'Too faint to tell, Captain. But it's not whales or dolphins.' Pols turned his handwheel very slowly, eyes tightly closed. 'Conditions are very good. It could be a ship – perhaps as far as thirty miles.'

Kessler was tempted to grab the spare set of headphones off the hook, but he knew that if Pols said the noises were very faint then it was unlikely that he would hear them. Pols' ability to separate propeller noises from the background cacophony of clicks, whistles and bangs generated by sea creatures was extraordinary.

'I noticed some strange acoustic ducting effects on the last trim dive, Captain. The water is heavily layered. I'm sure I heard the calls of blue whales. I don't think they come this far north. I think the long spell of fine weather has led to a lot of surface evaporation and more salinity of the surface layer. Another ten metres down and I might hear better.'

'Petty officer! Ambient water temperature?'

'Ambient temperature – one-seven, Captain.'

'Thirty metres please. Use main ballast. Trim her sweet, chief. I want to stop the motors.'

Instead of using the hydroplanes to take *U-395* down, the control room watch opened the ballast tanks' valves and allowed them to flood. A three-second flow was all that was required. The main depth gauge hand crept to the maximum reading of twenty-five metres and stopped. The smaller, coarse-reading depth gauge edged down thirty metres and it too, stopped.

'Planes to neutral. Stop motors.'

In the motor room Brumner manning the big rotary switches hauled on the handles that shut off the current to both electric motors.

'Motors stopped.'

'Water temperature?' Kessler inquired.

'One-one,' the petty officer replied.

'A nice cold dense layer to park our arse on,' Kessler grunted. He yawned and scratched his chest. 'Roll on Tuesday.'

The petty officer grinned.

U-395 came to a stop. Being slightly positively buoyant caused her to rise. A squirt into her main aft ballast tanks and the depth gauge steadied just above the thirty-metre mark.

Kessler pulled down the crew address microphone and ordered cessation of movement. The boat was balanced like a pair of scales; even one man moving from fore to aft could upset its delicate equilibrium and would necessitate using the pumps to transfer ballast water. There was no need to order silent routine because every non-essential piece of machinery had been closed down to conserve the batteries.

Pols now had perfect listening conditions. His gaunt face tightened in concentration while his long, capable fingers made delicate adjustments to the handwheel. Finally he opened his eyes and looked up at his commander.

'Propeller HE, captain. Extremely faint. Bearing two-six-five.'

This time Kessler listened in, his gaze fixed on Pols' books on oceanography that were crammed into every spare nook around the radio equipment. At first he wondered if the long hours with headphones clamped over his ears had finally got to Pols; he couldn't hear anything except the usual twittering of dolphins and whales. And then he heard a dull beat, so faint that he slipped the headphones off his ears and listened in case the sound was coming from within the boat.

'I've got it, Pols. Do you still think thirty miles?'

The radio operator listened again before replying. 'I think more like forty – the longest range I've ever heard prop effects. Bearing still two-six-five.'

Kessler allowed normal shipboard activity to resume. Fifteen minutes later he called for silent routine again.

Pols listened on his headphones, fine-tuning the position of his handwheel back and forth.

'Prop HE. Slightly louder but still faint. Bearing two-six-five.'

The propeller noises were stronger fifteen minutes later, and the bearing remained the same.

'Constant bearing,' Kessler mused. 'I do believe the bugger's coming straight for us. Let's give him another fifteen minutes.' He grinned happily. Whatever the mystery ship was, it meant that the long, frustrating period of inaction was over. First the crew: they hadn't had decent food in them for two days since he had stopped Poison Ivy using the electric galley burners. 'Chef!' He went aft and shook Ivy awake, unmindful that he was off-watch. 'Omelettes all round, Ivy. Omelettes so light and fluffy that they float out of your frying pan. Think you can manage that?'

Ivy blinked and sat up. A hollow-cheeked, emaciated beanpole of a man with a permanently worried expression. His physique was useful in the galley because it permitted easy passing to and fro, but it didn't inspire confidence in his cooking. 'Use the burners, Captain?'

'No – you breathe on them with your hot, sultry breath. Start now and keep 'em coming. Serve everyone on watch first. Bearing?'

His voice carried through to Pols.

'Still two-six-five.'

Kessler beamed around at the control room watch, and

clapped his hands together. 'Chief! Let's have some bloody lights and fans on!' He jerked his microphone off the hook and gave orders for Tubes 1 to 5 to be made ready.

The torpedo tubes were flooded and the outer doors opened. The rating at the trim panel spun his wheels to compensate for the increased weight. Pumps whirred. The flurry of activity was a sorely needed tonic. Off-watch crewmen sat up in their bunks and demanded to know what was happening. Petty Officer Hermann Brink was particularly incensed. Goethe's *Hermann und Dorothea* demanded intense concentration.

'What's happening?'

'We're rejoining the war.'

A steward passed through the petty officers' mess bearing loaded plates of omelettes for the forward torpedo room.

Brink sighed, put Goethe back in his cubbyhole, and took down Virginia Woolf's heavily-footnoted *Orlando*. Distractions called for light reading.

20

Dinner aboard the *Anaconda* that evening ended in acrimony between Mrs Montgomerie and Captain Valez. The Spanish officer drained his coffee, threw down his napkin and stood.

'Mrs Montgomerie. I am the captain of this ship, and if I decide that the safety of my passengers and my ship depends on my sailing east to avoid severe hurricanes, then that is exactly what I will do – all the way to Australia if necessary. In Spain we have a saying: it is better to arrive late in this world than early in the next. I believe there is a similar saying in English. Good night. I trust you sleep well.' With that he left the dining salon. The remaining deck officers looked embarrassed and avoided Mrs Montgomerie's eye. It was easier to look at Tammy. On a signal from the second officer, they too, rose, bid the passengers goodnight, and left.

'Manners!' Mrs Montgomerie exploded, looking at Dieter for support. 'These wretched people simply have no idea how to deal with the reasonable queries of their passengers. As soon as we arrive in Bilbao, I shall write a strong letter to the owners. Doubtless you will want to sign it too, young man?'

Dieter smiled self-effacingly. 'Perhaps a night's sleep would be a good idea, Mrs Montgomerie. These things always look different in the morning.'

'The sun certainly will. It'll be in the wrong place. And what about all those people cooped up in steerage? They're supposed to be disembarking at Porto Alegre. I expect they're now wishing they'd waited for the railway line to be repaired.'

'They must be feeling very frustrated,' Dieter agreed diplomatically.

Mrs Montgomerie eyed the three ranchers and wondered if she could drag them into her scheme. But they had taken little interest in the dispute; she doubted if they had been able to follow what had been said. She sighed and folded her napkin. 'Come, Tammy. A game of rummy in our cabin before retiring will put me in a better frame of mind.'

'Yes, Miss Angela.'

The two women left Dieter, Haug and his two cronies at the long table. There were no stewards present.

Haug looked pointedly at his watch. 'Not long now, Dieter. Four hours. Have you told the captain what it is we'll be rendezvousing with?'

Dieter shook his head. 'Not yet.'

Haug studied his manicured nails. The cuticles were perfect half moons. 'I think you should tell him now. If there are complications . . .' He smiled and left the sentence unfinished.

'There won't be any problems, professor,' Dieter insisted. 'In two hours the captain will order all passengers into aft accommodation on the port side.'

'Including us?'

'It would be better. It will avoid arousing suspicions if we all went below.'

'Normally I would agree with you. But on this occasion I think otherwise. I think our next course of action should be determined by the captain's reaction when he learns that he is to replenish a U-boat.'

Dieter controlled his anger. 'The captain and crew have already proved that they can be bought. There is no reason why the operation shouldn't go smoothly, and no reason why you and these two thugs should be involved.'

The two 'thugs' regarded Dieter with ill-concealed dislike.

'The captain and crew can certainly be bribed to assist a boat in distress,' Haug agreed smoothly. 'That is no more than any ship's master would do with or without a bribe. But, my dear Dieter, I don't believe he will help one U-boat, never mind three.'

Dieter stared. 'Three!'

'The loss of the *Atlantis* . . . a grievous blow. Three U-boats stranded in South Atlantic. That's what I mean by the two operations being merged.'

For a moment Dieter was too shocked to speak. 'You knew about this all along!'

Haug smiled blandly. 'I didn't plan the sinking of the *Atlantis*.'

'Look – the captain's already been bought. If he has scruples, then we can increase the payment.'

Haug picked up a knife and made circles on the tablecloth. 'Two problems, Dieter. This ship can't spare the oil to bunker three U-boats. Valez won't part with two hundred tonnes, therefore it will have to be taken from him.'

Dieter couldn't think of an answer to that. 'And the other problem?'

'Do you know where the captain comes from?'

'Bilbao. He has a wife and two children. I checked.'

'So did I, Dieter. That's where Valez lives. But do you know where he actually comes from? Where he was brought up; where his parents live, or rather – lived?'

The ice in Haug's gaze belied the humour lines around his eyes. Dieter sensed trouble. He shook his head.

'He comes from a little town near Bilbao,' Haug continued smoothly. 'Guernica.' He looked up at the younger man and smiled slyly. 'I'm sure you've heard of it. The Luftwaffe helped Franco by bombing it during the Spanish Civil War. Goering saw it as good practice for his airmen. Not just a few bombs, but a concentrated raid. Many civilians were killed. Among them Carla Antonia Valez – our erstwhile captain's beloved mother.'

The silence lasted several moments. Hugo and Walter smirked as Dieter stared back at Haug.

The older man sat back and lit a cigarette. He inhaled deeply and allowed the smoke to stream from his nostrils. A patronising smile played at the corners of his mouth. 'So, my dear Dieter, I think it would be best if *my* contingency plan went ahead.'

21

There was too much toing and froing to extend both leaves of the fold-down table in the officers' wardroom so Kessler and Maron ate with their plates balanced on the narrow centre leaf. A large scale chart of the South Atlantic was spread out on the settee between them. Kessler's thumb traced the likely course of the mystery ship that Pols was tracking with his hydrophones.

'Sailing virtually due east out of Montevideo, Oberleutnant. Not a shipping route. There's nothing in the way until he reaches the Far East.'

'Which means it's either our supply ship or an Allied warship,' said Maron.

Kessler speared a lump of omelette and forked it into his mouth. He chewed slowly. 'Exactly. One or the other. If the British have broken our codes, then I'm damned if I'm going to sit on the surface and exchange recognition signals with a bloody destroyer, then have the buggers open fire on us.'

'Our orders are to remain in this position.'

Kessler grinned. 'That depends on how liberally you interpret our position. Christ, this tastes good. Amazing what Ivy can do with dried egg when he tries. We ought to have omelette every Saturday. That'll give us two days in the week to look forward to.'

'Under these conditions, Brink has obtained very accurate star fixes.'

'Exactly. Too bloody accurate for my liking. I wonder why Ivy is so fond of making lasagne?' Kessler looked at his watch and stood. 'Let's have another listen.'

'Still bearing two-six-five, Captain,' Pols reported when Kessler's shadow fell across him. 'Much louder now.'

Kessler pressed a headphone to his ear. There was no doubt about it; for a bearing to remain constant over such a long period *and* to get progressively louder meant one thing: that the mystery ship was heading straight towards them. He turned back to the control room and gave a succession of orders.

'Start motors. Steer two-six-five. Periscope depth.'

U-395's bow angled up as she turned about her centre of buoyancy.

'Pity really, chief,' Kessler mused to Brandt. 'It would have been interesting to find out how long we could have sat on that layer of cold water.'

Without waiting for an answer, he joined the helmsman and sat on the attack periscope's saddle. In the control room Maron raised the sky periscope. The U-boat was now rocking gently. A heavy swell was starting to run, much to Kessler's relief. Like all skippers he disliked millpond conditions which made the vee wake of a periscope dangerously conspicuous. Another reason why U-boats didn't belong in the South Atlantic.

The sky periscope's head broke clear first. Maron saw that the mist had cleared completely. A moonless night, almost total blackness. Optical distortion crowded the constellations together – but the periscope's precision-ground fluorite lenses provided excellent contrast between the stars and the blackness of their background. A shooting star, but otherwise, nothing.

'Sky clear!' he reported.

The bridge watch mustered in the control room under the hatch. The control room hand passed them clean binoculars.

As the attack periscope hissed up from its well Kessler reversed his white cap so that the peak wouldn't get in the way. He peered through the eyepiece, the electric motor spun him and periscope around as one in response to the foot controls. Around once for a fast scan of the horizon, and then a 360-degree slow pan for a close look. Only a fine variation from black to intense black marked the boundary between sky and horizon.

Nothing.

'Surface!'

Compressed air flushed water from the ballast tanks. *U-395* rose.

'Lid clear! Pressure equalised.'

There was some residual pressure in the hull when Kessler released the hatch clips. It blew the steel door open with a loud clang. He climbed onto the bridge, propped himself against the torpedo aimer, and scanned the horizon while the bridge lookouts took up their positions. Brandt kept the electrics running in case they were needed for a crash-dive.

'Hard aport. Steer two-zero-zero. Send up some omelette if there's any left over.'

The helmsman heard Kessler's orders through the open hatch and brought *U-395* onto the new course that was nearly due south. Kessler's next orders were to switch over to main engines, full speed ahead both, and where was his omelette. The helmsman relayed them to the engine room and galley respectively.

No bloody fuel oil and he orders full speed, thought Brandt savagely when the engine room telegraph rang.

Exhaust valves were wound open. Compressed air hissed. The diesels turned over and fired. Once they were running steadily the engine room rating rolled his eyes at his petty officer and opened the throttles to maximum. The noise from the two six-cylinder engines became a deafening roar. Valve rockers nodded frantically like starving chickens thrown a handful of grain. The petty officer gestured at the fuel gauges and held up all his fingers and thumbs to indicate how long he reckoned they'd got at maximum revs.

On the bridge Kessler enjoyed the feeling of omnipotence as he watched the bow cleaving through the swell at a steady seventeen knots. Occasionally the engine note changed as the exhaust valves in the aft ballast tank were partially submerged, but the hurricane of air being sucked through the coaming induction vents remained a constant roar. Phosphorescence played around the wake as it plaited into the darkness. Looking aft past the hunched shoulders of the lookouts, their eyes glued to their binoculars, Kessler watched the inner wakes fold in on themselves, collide, and separate again. The water had a strange frozen look, possessed of no motion, as though *U-395* were a dagger slashing through the cover of a black satin quilt to expose a gash of fine, white down beneath. The boat was taking a slightly offset course towards the mysterious sound effects. If it turned out to be an enemy ship, *U-395* would be on its quarter, ideally placed for a torpedo attack.

In the radio office, Pols slipped off his now useless hydrophone headphones and turned up the volume on his E52 receiver. He rubbed his ears with one hand while bringing the signals log up to date in his small, neat handwriting.

Fifteen minutes passed.

Kessler clutched the wind-deflector lip around the conning tower's rim; his iron will locked in confrontation with the physical laws that were draining the fuel tanks. He ordered the forward lookout onto the periscope standard. The man shinned into position and trained his binoculars ahead, one arm hooked around the slender tube. The extra two metres' height added very little to forward visibility – maybe a half a kilometre – but it could be vital.

Another fifteen minutes slipped by.

The pounding diesels were now fuelled by the collective prayers of Brandt and his engine room watch.

Kessler glanced aft. A faint flush of light was tingeing the sky. Mercury and Arcturus had already risen. He glanced at his watch. 4:00 a.m. Damn! Dawn in two hours and he'd be sitting between the light and the mystery ship. On a night like this they'd have to be blind not to see a conning tower. Getting the target abeam was vital.

The lookout on the periscope standard suddenly called out, 'Captain! Light! Starboard quarter.'

Kessler glanced up and followed the line of the lookout's binoculars with his own. He could see nothing.

'There it is again!'

And then Kessler saw it: a faint blob of light hard on the horizon. It faded, disappeared, and reappeared. It wasn't a star – stars were sharp points of light. This was a smudge. And then it hardened slightly.

'Looks like a masthead light, Captain.'

Kessler teased the knurled focusing wheel and managed to sharpen the smudge to a distinct light. 'A masthead light,' he agreed. 'Well done.' He bellowed the order to stop engines. No point in wasting fuel. Let the target come to him.

U-395's wake was absorbed into the oil-black sea as the boat lost way. The swell rolled the bridge through an uncomfortable thirty degrees. Kessler requested a hydrophone bearing. The hull transducers were not as sensitive as those around the conning tower but they would confirm that the light and the HE were coming from the same source.

Pols listened carefully, turning his hand wheel left and right to null out the sound. He glanced at the gyrocompass repeater.

'HE propeller noises louder – true bearing two-eight-five.'

Kessler's grunted acknowledgement to the helmsman disguised his excitement. The direction of the light and sound tallied.

Pols went back to his signal log. Had he carried out a 360-degree sweep as he should have done, even with the less-sensitive hull microphones, he would have picked up very faint but definite high-speed propeller effects emanating from ten degrees. HMS *Dorsetshire* was now forty miles to the north. She would be gatecrashing the party in under two hours.

22

Mrs Montgomerie would not be moved.

'Preposterous!' she declared to the hapless chief steward. 'Utterly preposterous! Move into steerage indeed! I've never heard such a load of . . . There's a word that my late husband would have used and which I've a mind to use if I thought you'd understand it.'

The steward looked appealingly at Tammy who studied her bare feet.

'Tammy! Come and sit beside me, child.'

Tammy sat beside Mrs Montgomerie on the bed. Both women were wearing dressing gowns over their nightdresses; Mrs Montgomerie's buttoned high lest any femininity tried to escape; Tammy's unfastened lest any wanted to.

'Now go and tell Captain Valez that under no circumstances will I or my ward be moved to steerage accommodation.'

The chief steward returned to the bridge and reported that under no circumstances would Mrs Montgomerie or her ward be moved to steerage accommodation.

Captain Valez glanced at Dieter who was standing near the helmsman. 'There's always one,' he muttered in Spanish as he left the bridge, pulling on his cap.

111

'*Dos, Señor*,' the chief steward amended. A succinct comment from Captain Valez suggested that the correction was not appreciated.

'Captain,' said Dieter. 'There is something I have to tell you –'

'Sorry, Mr Rohland – it will have to wait,' Valez replied. He adjusted his cap and followed the steward down to the upper weather deck.

'Mrs Montgomerie,' the captain pleaded when she permitted him to set foot over the threshold of her suite. 'It is for your own safety.'

'Rubbish.'

'We've had radio reports that U-boats are in this area.'

Mrs Montgomerie was singularly unimpressed. 'What of it? This is a neutral ship. Or has Franco joined in the squabble?'

'Please, Mrs Montgomerie. U-boats have been stopping neutral ships. They stop them with gunfire – always two, maybe three shells fired at the forecastle. It would be most dangerous for you to remain here. It is only for three, maybe four hours, until we are out of the danger zone.'

'If you hadn't insisted on sailing due east we wouldn't be in any danger zone!' Mrs Montgomerie retorted.

'You are refusing to move?'

'Yes.'

'Very well. I will have to use force. If it is necessary, I will order four men to carry you.' He looked sideways at Tammy. 'And perhaps, another four men for your ward.'

Tammy brightened.

'You are threatening me with physical violence?'

Captain Valez folded his brawny arms and managed to outstare his recalcitrant passenger. 'I am threatening you with firm action to move you below, to a place of safety until we are out of the danger zone.'

All Mrs Montgomerie's instincts were to resist but she knew when to yield. 'We will be allowed to take some things with us? Toilet items?'

112

Captain Valez sensed victory and bowed. 'But of course.'

'Very well, Captain. But I want you to know that we are being moved under protest, and we shall expect to be allowed back to this cabin at the earliest possible moment.'

'It's a promise, Mrs Montgomerie,' said the captain, much relieved. 'I will personally conduct you to your temporary quarters.'

He waited outside the cabin until the women emerged clutching toilet bags, and led them down the aft companion-way to the lower weather deck, and then through another door that was guarded by a seaman with a clipboard. He ticked the names on his list.

'That leaves only the three ranchers from the deck passengers, Captain.'

'The chief steward is bringing them down.'

'We'll be right in the bowels of the ship,' Mrs Montgomerie complained as they were shown down another flight of stairs. 'I won't be able to breathe!'

They entered a narrow, stifling corridor on the port side that was crowded with passengers, most of them arguing simultaneously with a junior steward who was unlocking cabin doors and trying to persuade his charges to accept his offerings. The child aviator was in business, roaring up and down the corridor despite an inability to fully extend his wings. Only the nuns appeared to have calmly accepted their lot, especially the youngest, probably a novitiate. She was playing what appeared to be a clumsily-executed three-card trick with two bemused stockmen, and yet she was winning.

Mrs Montgomerie turned to register her protests, but Captain Valez had done the sensible thing and vanished.

On the passenger deck the chief steward knocked confidently on the door of the cabin occupied by the three ranchers. Although they had not been ready the first time he had called, they had not voiced any protests when the plan to move them below had been proposed.

Haug opened the door and beamed at the chief steward.

The other two rose to their feet and matched Haug's amiable smile.

'How kind of you to come back,' said Haug expansively. 'Yes – we're ready now. So sorry to have kept you waiting. We managed to get everything into one small bag. Much more sensible if it's going to be crowded.'

'It's not too crowded,' said the steward, wishing that all the passengers had been amenable as these three. A stockman had nearly threatened him with a knife when he had been moved.

Haug gave a little bow and stepped aside. 'Perhaps you would assist with my bag?'

'Of course,' said the steward, entering the cabin.

'So embarrassing,' said Haug easily. 'We don't normally make a fuss. I expect all the passengers are below now?'

'Yes, sir.' The steward half turned in surprise as Haug stepped behind him and slammed the door shut. Suddenly a lean, hard arm whipped around his neck and jerked his head back. He felt a sharp pain in the small of his back and would have cried out but Walter clamped his left hand across his mouth and drove the stiletto into his heart with his right. He used a swift upward jab, employing little force, but considerable skill to ensure that the blade passed cleanly and swiftly between his victim's ribs. Hugo followed through with a neck-breaking chop but Walter's blade had penetrated the heart and killed the man outright. Hugo caught the body and allowed it to slip to the floor.

'Excellent work,' Haug breathed, his eyes alight with excitement.

The three men moved quickly. Each had a task to perform. They thrust Lugers and handcuffs in their jacket pockets. Walter and Hugo counted out two handfuls of steel bolts and matching nuts that Haug removed from a suitcase. They spread them out on a bunk. Haug double-checked that they had the right number each plus two spares. Walter left the cabin first on a nod from Haug, Hugo followed. The two men darted off in opposite directions. Their routes had been carefully planned.

Walter did a quick circuit of the upper weather deck, keeping to the shadows under the lifeboats. He paused at a door that was marked for crew only. Like all such doors on the *Anaconda*, it was provided with padlock hasps so that the ship could be made secure when in port. It was a requirement that the Uruguayan Post Office had insisted upon before the ship could be licensed to carry mail. Walter slipped one of the bolts through the steel eyes of the hasps and screwed the nut into place on the bolt. He raced down the steps leading to the lower deck. Six more doors received the same treatment. A deck hand was standing by one of the doors holding a clipboard. He blinked in surprise at the gun in Walter's hand.

'In!' Walter snarled, waving the Luger at the door.

The deck hand did as he was told. Walter secured the door with a nut and bolt. It was all so simple. One could only admire Haug's careful planning. Two greasers smoking and talking loudly by the door leading to the engine room required more careful treatment. Haug's orders were not to alert the engine room crew of the take-over if it could be avoided. Walter decided to deal with them later. Drawing on the clear picture he had of the *Anaconda*'s layout from his frequent tours of the ship, he darted through a door on the port side and raced down the stairs. The door before him opened onto the corridor where all the passengers had been herded together. He was feeling in his pocket for a bolt when the door burst open. A Stuka dive bomber in the guise of a small boy charged into him, its siren howling. Walter grabbed the boy by the neck, stifling the siren with his hand, and hurled him back into the corridor. The startled boy recovered his senses and started yelling in Spanish just as Walter secured the door with a nut and bolt. The boy underwent a rapid change of armament and became a tank, first charging at the door, then shaking it, while bawling in an untanklike rage.

Walter cursed. He should've shot the kid. Now he would have to move fast. He returned to the lower weather deck, taking the steps three at a time. The greasers had returned to the engine room. The door was open, spilling light and the heat and roar of the pounding marine diesels into the night. He slammed the door shut, locked it with a bolt, and raced aft. He was just in time to prevent four passengers bursting out onto the poop deck. They fell back when he waved the Luger at them.

'Back! Back!' he snarled.

One of the passengers, a bull-necked stockman, either didn't see the gun or chose to ignore it. He stared uncomprehendingly at the gesticulating German. Walter shot him in the head. The man crumpled without making a sound. Walter jumped over the body, and secured the door. With only a cursory glance at the murdered stockman, he yanked open a door on the starboard side. The passenger accommodation corridor was deserted on this side of the ship. He ran the length of the corridor, throwing cabin doors open. They were all in darkness. The entire starboard side of the ship was now deserted and the access door at the far end of the corridor was locked. Hugo had done his job well.

Walter ran back along the corridor, fastened the outer door, and dropped down a ladder onto the poop deck. It was the nearest deck to the waterline – a semicircular area across the stern that was piled with heavy coir fenders and tarred mooring lines, carefully coiled and cleated so that they could not be washed overboard in heavy seas to foul the propellers. In the centre was a cluster of bunkering valves and their handwheels protruding above the deck. The only illumination was from a navigation light atop the transom jack staff. It threw a harsh glare on the *Anaconda*'s seething wake. He leaned against a power capstan to get his breath and counted the bolts in his pocket. Three left. One too many! He experienced a momentary flare of panic at the realisation that there was a door he had forgotten. Where was it? From forrard he could hear the muffled yells of the passengers who had discovered that they were locked in. A loud clang made him jump. He spun around and saw a shadowy head and shoulders

116

emerging through the deck.

The access hatch to the steering gear! The engineer cried out and released his grip on the rungs as Walter stamped on his fingers. A hard kick in the face and the man dropped from sight. Walter slammed the hatch shut, thrust a bolt through the steel eyes, and spun the nut home.

He was done. Provided Hugo had done his job, the *Anaconda* was now battened down, and all the crew and passengers locked below with the exception of the bridge watch.

He made his way back to the upper deck. The bulkhead lights continued to burn, the ship's engines held their steady beat. There was nothing to suggest that anything was amiss. He didn't need to rap on the door to their cabin. Haug heard him and whipped the door open. The steel-blue eyes took in the two bolts that Walter was holding.

'Well done, Walter. Excellent work.'

Hugo appeared from the opposite direction, also holding up two bolts, and looking pleased with himself. 'Sweet as a nut,' he declared as he entered the cabin.

Haug shut the door. He had pushed the body of the chief steward under one of the bunks. Blood was pooling across the floor. 'Any problems?'

'No one saw me enter the radio shack,' said Hugo. 'And the radio operator didn't hear me. Too busy with his headphones. I used my knife.' He produced two identical radio valves: 'One from the transmitter, and the other from the set of spares.'

'Did you check the signals log?'

'Clean. Nothing.'

Haug nodded his approval and looked questioningly at Walter.

'I had to shoot one of the hands,' Walter admitted.

Haug's mouth set in a hard line. 'I thought I heard something.' He looked at his watch. 'Rohland is already on the bridge. Well – there's no point in delaying matters.'

The three men left the cabin and split up. Haug and Walter

mounted the port-side steps to the bridge, Hugo took the starboard side. Their timing was perfect. They burst into the wheelhouse from opposite sides, Lugers drawn; Haug panting slightly from the unaccustomed exertion.

Captain Valez was bending over a chart with Dieter at his side. He looked up in surprise. He opened his mouth but Haug's shot hit him in the mouth, blasting away the back of his head. He staggered backwards against the chart chest, his eyes bulging. His flailing hands smashed against the chart table light, sending it spinning round so that grotesque shadows danced before the bulb smashed against the bulkhead and imploded shards of glass on the teak decking. Valez clutched at the edge of the chest, crumpled onto the floor, and lay still.

For a second the scene was a frozen tableau: the helmsman's hands had fallen from the wheel as he half turned; the first officer was resting his hand on the binnacle, his eyes blank and uncomprehending; Dieter staring sightlessly at the blood streaming across the deck, stunned by the killing and the speed at which it was carried out. The only movement was from the tendrils of cordite smoke pooling under the deck head lights.

A junior officer burst in through the aft door from the officers' quarters.

'Over there! Hands against the bulkhead!' Haug shouted in Spanish. 'Move!'

The junior officer did as he was told. His hands shook as he spread his fingers out on the bulkhead near the chart table.

'Hold your course!' Hugo yelled at the helmsman, pointing his gun straight at the man's head.

The man hurriedly spun the spokes to bring the heading indicator back to 80 degrees.

'You!' Haug jerked his gun at the bulkhead for the benefit of the first officer. He refused to move and was about to speak when Haug shot him. 'Three more, I believe,' said Haug softly as the body crumpled to the deck.

The second officer, a junior radio officer, and the second

navigation officer burst into the wheelhouse and stared about them in bewilderment. A shot from Haug's gun ricocheted off the deck plates near their feet and embedded itself in the chart chest. It was enough to persuade them that the portly little German was serious. They obeyed his gestures and lined-up against the bulkhead. Haug moved to a better position where he could keep the four men and the helmsman covered. Hugo and Walter pulled handcuffs from their pockets. They jerked their captives' arms behind their backs and snapped the handcuffs in place. Hugo marched them through the aft door.

'Mission nearly accomplished,' Haug remarked. His beaming smile had returned.

Dieter found his voice. But all he could manage was a strangled whisper. 'Why?'

'The age-old question and such a simple answer,' Haug sighed. 'The conquistadors conquered the Incas with a handful of men by cutting off Montezuma's head. You saw everything and yet you haven't learned. Killing the captain induced a state of shock in the crew that made the capture of the bridge easy.' He looked disinterestedly at the corpse. 'Did you tell the captain that we were meeting a U-boat, or U-*boats?*'

'I never had a chance.'

'A word I hate, Dieter. I never take chances.'

Hugo returned. 'They're all secured in the skipper's cabin.'

'Excellent, Hugo. Walter – check on our position.'

Walter bent over the chart table for some moments. 'Last running fix was thirty minutes ago.' He glanced at the gyro-compass repeater and rudder heading indicator. A rummage in the navigator's drawer for a pair of dividers and a parallel ruler. He laid the ruler on the chart's compass rose and checked that the *Anaconda*'s navigator had applied the correct tidal set against the last position.

'A star sight fix was taken just after dinner,' said Dieter hollowly. 'I insisted.'

Walter looked up and nodded. 'All looks spot on,' he

observed. 'We're fifteen miles west of the rendezvous position. Another hour or hour and a quarter should do it. Nice timing.'

Haug chuckled and spoke in Spanish to the helmsman. He was too fast for Dieter to follow. The man was still in shock. He was staring through the forward windows and holding the *Anaconda*'s heading like an automaton. Eventually he muttered a reply that seemed to satisfy the German.

'Hugo, let's speed things up a little. Full speed ahead.'

Hugo crossed to the engine room telegraph and cranked the lever right over. The note of the diesels picked up. The windows shook. Dieter stepped out onto the port bridge wing and leaned against the rail to collect his reeling senses. The slipstream flattened his hair; spray burst over the *Anaconda*'s bow as it plunged into the light swell and stung his face, but he didn't feel it. The killings had shaken him badly. Were they necessary? Surely Valez would have co-operated? Then he remembered the newsreels of Guernica; the devastated, smoking ruins of what had once been people's homes; the black-shawled women brandishing their fists in impotent anger and grief, and wailing silent curses at the camera; smashed bodies being dragged from the debris – perhaps one of them had been Valez's mother. The appalling scale of misery and suffering that an angry Picasso would later capture on a huge canvas.

Guernica . . .

Other towns and cities were now tasting the horror of high-powered bombers and their enormous payloads of fragmentation bombs. Warsaw, London, Liverpool, Southampton, even Berlin.

But Guernica was first.

'It's all a matter of an equation.'

Dieter turned at the sound of a voice. Haug had joined him at the rail. Dieter said nothing. He had nothing to say to Haug.

'On one side the lives of a few civilians. On the other side the lives of many German sailors and the safety of their U-boats. The U-boats are the only truly effective weapon against the British. Their supply lines are their great weakness.'

'I don't need you to tell me that,' said Dieter shortly.

'Perhaps you don't appreciate the scale,' Haug murmured. He looked at his watch. 'Time for the recognition flares, I fancy. On a night like this they'll be seen for miles.'

23

'Ship's firing flares, Captain!' the lookout called out.

But Kessler had already seen the light arc into the sky. It seemed to hang in the blackness for several seconds. A molten spark of pure crimson. It was joined by two green flares fired in quick succession.

'And now three reds,' Kessler muttered.

It was as if the ship had heard him for three more bursts of crimson raced aloft just as the first flare dipped down and went out. The burning lights drifted down to meet their reflections in the humped masses of the black swell and were extinguished.

The ship came into sight again as Kessler's night vision recovered. He crouched over the torpedo aimer and twirled the setscrew. Range was a little over 4000 metres and coming up to zero bow angle. Tubes 1 to 4 were ready, the outer doors open. He chewed on his beard. He had a natural aversion to revealing his presence, but the sequence of flares fired by the approaching ship had been correct. The other lookouts kept their binoculars trained on their appointed sectors. To succumb to temptation by looking at the ship would arouse the wrath of the watch petty officer. A flare dipped into the sea.

'She's Spanish!' called the forward lookout. 'And I can make out the name! A–N–A–C . . . *Anaconda*.'

The information was relayed below to the control room petty officer who quickly rifled through the Lloyds Register of Shipping.

'*Anaconda* confirmed as Spanish mail packet,' Maron reported from below. 'GRT, 5000. Registered Bilbao.'

'And lit up like a bloody Christmas tree,' said Kessler to the quartermaster. He ordered the gun crews to their stations. Men piled through the hatches and readied the guns. The main gun's ready-use lockers were thrown open and an 88-millimetre incendiary shell slid into the breech.

'Gun ready!'

Kessler crouched over the torpedo aimer. He made fine adjustments to the bow angle and depth settings. The revised data was fed automatically to all four torpedoes in the bow tubes. In the torpedo compartment, a petty officer stood within reach of the red levers that would send them on their way. Two warheads had contact pistols and two had magnetic pistols. Kessler was determined that if the mystery ship was a British Q-boat decoy, then U-395 would bite right back the instant it bared its teeth.

'Make with a red, a green, two reds, and two greens,' Kessler ordered.

'A red, a green, two reds, and two greens,' Brink acknowledged, and used the light from the open hatch to check the cartridges that were passed to him. He slipped the first one into the oversize, snub barrel of the signal pistol and aimed at the sky.

'Eyes closed!' he ordered, and pulled the trigger.

A loud bang and the flare was launched. It blazed a path of light into the sky and burst at the top of its climb like a ruptured blood vessel.

'Eyes open!'

The purpose of the ritual was to preserve the night vision of the gun crews and lookouts. It was repeated until all six flares were hanging in the sky like Chinese lanterns.

The ship reduced speed. A signal light winked from the bridge. Brink took the message down but Kessler read it 'off the lamp'. It banished his remaining doubts.

SEACOW TO UBOAT COME AND SUCK ON MY TITS.

The message was sent in colloquial German. Seacow was the slang expression used for ships or large U-boats that provided refuelling at sea. Good spacing of the dots and dashes; no fumbling or strings of rapid dots to mark re-sends. A trained Kriegsmarine signaller on the lamp.

Kessler unclipped the portable signal lamp from the base of the attack periscope and sent:

COMING ALONGSIDE.

On the *Anaconda*'s bridge Walter cranked the engine room telegraph to finished with engines. Hugo returned from having locked the helmsman in the captain's quarters with his fellow officers and Haug instructed him to remain on watch on the bridge while the rest made their way down to the poop deck.

All was strangely quiet – the passengers had given up hammering on the bolted doors. Through portholes they watched the dark shape of the U-boat going about on its electrics as it approached the drifting ship's stern. The only discernible feature on the conning tower was the occasional pale flash of the captain's white cap.

'No wind – long easy swell,' said Walter. 'Couldn't be better. Don't often have this sort of luck.'

'Didn't you signal them to tie up on the starboard side?' Dieter asked in alarm when he realised that the U-boat's skipper was heading cautiously towards the *Anaconda*'s port side.

'Does it matter?' Haug asked.

'Of course it matters! The passengers will see the boat!' He gestured frantically at the conning tower that was now less than two hundred metres away.

Haug grabbed his arm. 'It doesn't matter,' he said quietly. 'If they talk, they talk. So what? There will be protest notes from the Spanish foreign ministry, an apology from us, and then the incident will be forgotten. The important thing is to refuel that boat and the others if they make the rendezvous. The skipper prefers the leeward side, I fancy. Wise man. Those saddle tanks are vulnerable. We'd better lend a hand.'

Like a marauding cat stealing home in the night, *U-395*'s sleek bow entered the circle of light that the *Anaconda* cast on the swell. Dieter could see ratings in shabby overalls lining the forward deck casing. The anti-aircraft guns and the main gun were manned, the gleaming barrels had the *Anaconda* square in their sights. Another exchange of signals and the white-capped figure on the bridge ordered the gun crews to stand down. Hatches were yanked open with loud clangs, and huge coir fenders to protect the vulnerable saddle tanks were draped over the U-boat's sides. More men climbed out of the galley hatch abaft the conning tower and made ready with boathooks. There was a faint whine as the U-boat's electrics went hard astern. Walter caught the heaving line that was thrown to him, and very soon the two vessels were secured, allowing plenty of slack. The U-boat swung slowly towards the *Anaconda* until the two vessels were rolling together in unison as they shared the same swell with less than three metres between them. The manoeuvre was less hazardous than it looked; provided there were no tight mooring lines between them to upset the dynamics, two drifting ships could lie alongside each other in even a heavy swell with little danger of collision.

Dieter helped Walter swing out the Jacob's ladder on its boom. The foot of the poop deck's folding steps clattered harshly on the U-boat's grating. Kessler and Brandt clumped up the ladder in their cork-soled seaboots and jumped nimbly through the opening in the *Anaconda*'s bulwarks.

'So what have you done?' Kessler demanded, looking curiously about him after the introductions had been made. 'Captured a Spaniard?'

'That's about it.' Haug agreed.

Kessler eyed the plump little man. 'Where's the crew?'

'All below under guard. As are the passengers.'

'Where's your black flag?'

'I beg your pardon?'

'A pirates' flag – you should be flying one.' Kessler turned to

Brandt who was on his knees examining the bunkering valves. 'What do you reckon, chief?'

For once Brandt managed an optimistic report. 'Look like standard threads, Captain. Compressed-air dumping which we can use to push the oil out. Don't think there'll be any problems.'

Two engine room ratings struggled onto the poop deck carrying a rope-handled wooden crate crammed with bunkering wrenches and adaptors. Like all U-boats, *U-395* carried a generous selection of tools and fittings which enabled them to refuel from just about anything that held oil. Brandt screwed an adaptor onto the bunkering valve.

'Bloody perfect,' he said. 'Two hoses joined together, a high-pressure air line to blow the fuel out of the ship's tanks, and we'll have our tanks filled in a blink.'

Kessler knew all about Brandt's blinks. 'How long, chief?'

'An hour.' With that the chief engineer jumped to his feet and rattled off a stream of orders. Poison Ivy and the coxswain came aboard with a team of torpedo ratings, intent on tracking down provisions. Dieter helped haul the bunkering hose across from the U-boat to the poop deck and held it level while the chief guided the threaded coupling onto one of the valves that protruded through the *Anaconda*'s deck plates.

'If it's a decent venting and bunkering system, this valve feeds into the bottom of the tank. We blow compressed air into the tank and it dumps the fuel out through the valve and into our tanks,' said the chief. He jumped to his feet and wiped his dripping forehead with his arm. Any activity in this humidity was uncomfortable.

'Hose attached, chief!' a rating on *U-395*'s aft casing yelled.

'High-pressure line! Come on, lads!' the chief bellowed. 'Look sharp!'

The admonishment was hardly necessary; all the crewmen knew just how vulnerable *U-395* was in her present state, with open hatches obstructed by hoses.

'HP ready!'

There was a deep rumbling sound from below. The bunkering hose stiffened where it ran across the deck. A yelled message relayed from the U-boat: 'She's filling, chief!'

'Still an hour, chief?' asked Kessler.

Brandt grinned, pleased with the results of his exertions. His precious diesels were receiving their life-blood. 'Say forty-five minutes, Captain.'

'Perhaps we could have a word in private, Captain?' Haug suggested smoothly. 'There's a comfortable cabin forward.'

Dieter watched the two men leave the poop deck. He sensed that Haug was hiding something. Some passengers started banging on a door and yelling.

Haug grabbed some bottles of beer from the galley on the way and showed Kessler into Mrs Montgomerie's suite. 'I thought you'd appreciate a bath before your drink.'

Kessler didn't hesitate. He peeled off his clothes, filled the tub with near-boiling water, and dived in. He lathered himself with Mrs Montgomerie's scented soap, and lay back, allowing the hot water to soak away the fatigue and filth of the long patrol.

Haug sat on the toilet, lit two Havana cigars and offered one to Kessler who clenched it gratefully between his teeth. The bath water slopped back and forth in time with the ship's easy motion. He had resisted the temptation to overfill it.

'By heaven, this is bliss . . . and it's not even Tuesday. What was your name again?'

'Haug.'

Kessler watched his cigar smoke mingling with the steam. 'Do you have a rank?'

Haug smiled thinly. 'Oh, yes, Captain. But what is more important is that I have orders from OKM for you.'

'From Befehlshaber der Unterseeboote, surely?'

'Not from Flotilla,' said Haug carefully. 'From OKM.'

Kessler set his cigar down carefully and worked soap vigorously into his hair and beard. 'What orders?'

Haug drew a white envelope from his inside pocket.

'What do they say, Mr Haug?'

'They're your orders, Captain.'

Kessler gingerly picked up his cigar with wet hands. 'And I daresay you know what they say word for word. So tell. I'm wet.'

'You're to take myself, my two assistants and Dieter Rohland back to France. Rohland has a batch of geological samples. It is imperative that they get home.'

Kessler found Mrs Montgomerie's hand mirror and examined his beard. 'Passengers? That's against regulations.'

'We're not civilians. There shouldn't be any problem with space in your boat. I understand that you put to sea with a short crew.'

'Still not enough berths to go around. Never are in a VIIC.'

'Also you are to return to Lorient. BdU will confirm that.'

'That,' said Kessler, 'is the best news yet. Now – you go and pour those beers and allow me to wallow in luxury for another five minutes. See if you can find me some clean underclothes that might fit. Men's if possible, but I'm not fussy.'

Haug's nostrils flared slightly – the only indication that he was angry. 'There's more. I think you should see this.'

Kessler sighed and dried his hands on a towel. He took the envelope from Haug and ripped it open. Inside were three typed sheets.

'The last one,' said Haug.

Kessler read the last sheet. He raised his eyes and stared at Haug in disbelief. He read through the signal again. This time his incredulous expression faded, to be replaced a look that was quite different. For a moment neither spoke.

'No survivors?' said Kessler hoarsely.

'No survivors,' Haug affirmed.

'This is an illegal order, Haug.'

'That's your opinion, Captain,' said Haug blandly, unconcerned by the loathing in Kessler's eyes. 'If you care to read the document carefully from the beginning, you will see that you might not be required to carry out the last order. Only if you're the last boat.'

'Last boat? What the hell does that mean?'

Suddenly there were pounding feet outside and someone shouting.

'*Herr Kapitan! Herr Kapitan!*' It was Poison Ivy's voice.

'In here, chef!' Kessler bellowed, leaping from the bath. He raced naked across the stateroom and threw the door open.

Ivy's skeletal frame half fell into the cabin. He clutched the door frame. 'Another U-boat coming in, Captain! She's just fired a recognition signal!' With that the hard-pressed cook promptly vanished.

'*U-68*, I fancy,' said Haug calmly as Kessler hopped around on one leg and then the other to pull on his leather trousers.

'*What?* You've been expecting it?'

'Of course. You don't imagine that you were the only boat sent south to attack the Cape shipping routes, do you? The loss of the *Atlantis* has caused a major supply problem for several boats.'

Kessler struggled into his vest and pullover, thrust his feet into his boots, and snatched his white cap. '*Several boats!* For Chrissake, how much signals traffic have you goons been splatting all over the South Atlantic?' He stormed out of the cabin before Haug had a chance to reply.

The sighting of the U-boat broke the delicate rhythm of the human chain tossing supplies from the pantries to *U-395*'s galley hatch. A box of tomatoes hit the deck and split open. The watch PO yelled for order and the bobbing flow of cases of fruit and vegetables resumed.

Dieter saw things in a different perspective as he watched the approaching dark outline of *U-68*. Maybe Haug was right to turn the simple idea of bribing the captain and crew of a neutral ship to replenish a lone U-boat into a major logistics support operation for several boats. He realised that the *Anaconda* had become the linchpin of the Kriegsmarine's entire offensive in the South Atlantic. Small wonder that Haug had no interest in bribing the *Anaconda*'s skipper and crew. That he had been used as a pawn angered Dieter but did not surprise him; Haug had a reputation for low cunning.

The chief engineer returned to *U-395* to check that the boat was being trimmed properly now she had taken on nearly twenty tonnes of fuel and supplies. CPO Herbert Kohler, who was manning the bunkering valves, summed up Dieter's worries with one succinct sentence:

'Anyone who thinks the British don't know about all this is a dummkopf.'

At that moment the party's fourth guest announced her arrival with a salvo of shells fired at a range of 8000 yards. HMS *Dorsetshire*'s party poppers were radar-controlled 8-inch guns. She had sighted and identified the lit-up *Anaconda* lying stopped. The radar echo of another shape approaching the ship had all the characteristics of a U-boat, but her captain had held his fire until he was certain. The confirmation from his masthead lookouts of a second U-boat already alongside *Anaconda* and taking on supplies was all he needed to give the order to open fire. Neutral or not, the provisioning of U-boats at sea made the *Anaconda* a legitimate target. Also, she was outside the neutrality zone. Just.

One shell screamed overhead and struck the water beyond the *Anaconda*, exploding on impact. Merging with the first explosion as everyone on the poop deck threw themselves flat was a tremendous thunderclap that lifted Dieter off the power winch that he had blindly fallen over, and hurled him to the deck.

'Jesus!' Kohler yelled. 'They've hit that boat!'

His next sentence was snuffed out by a colossal *WHUUMMPP!* and a sheet of flame, so close that it seemed that either *U-395* or the *Anaconda* had been hit. Dieter struggled to his knees and saw that it was neither: the boat approaching them had taken a direct hit on the stern. A huge geyser of flame and debris expanded upwards and outwards from the boat so that it was not possible to see anything of the target in the core of the inferno, but dancing into the night sky on the demonic fringes of the incandescence could be seen unidentifiable shards of ironmongery that might have been deck casings, hatch covers, and what looked like the cigar-shape of half a torpedo, spinning in the air like a drum-major's baton against a vivid backdrop of searing yellow.

Kessler was half-way along the weather deck when the approaching U-boat erupted. He was thrown against the superstructure and badly winded. Splinters of shattered steel screamed into the ship's side. As he struggled to his feet, he saw that the U-boat was diving, and then realised that the foreshortening of the conning tower was due to the boat being laid over virtually on her beam ends. And then it was diving – going down, fast bow first. How the hell could it do that without righting itself and getting under way? Lights from the *Anaconda* caught the U-boat's stern as it lifted clear of the water to reveal the awful truth: the propellers were stationery, one rudder torn clean away; the boat wasn't diving, it was sinking. It rolled upright as it went down so that it was possible to see that the entire upper after end from the *wintergarten* AA gun deck to the stern torpedo loading hatch had been ripped clean away and the side casing and pressure hull peeled back like a spent firework. The speed at which the boat went under and slipped beneath the swell was sickening. Unlike a surface ship, a submarine has little reserves of buoyancy even with her ballast tanks fully blown – 150 tonnes at the most. There had been no time to take in details; from the cataclysmic explosion to disappearance of the boat had been less than thirty seconds. The scale of the horror was such that for vital moments everyone on the *Anaconda*'s poop deck forgot their own immediate danger. They were all seized by a momentary paralysis as they stared at the huge, spreading oil slick and erupting wreckage on the undulating swell that marked where the mangled stern had vanished.

'Must've hit the spare fish under the deck grating!' someone croaked.

That had to be the explanation: 500 kilos of explosive doing to a U-boat what it was supposed to do to its victims. Nothing else could account for the terrible devastation.

U-395's alarm was blaring. There was frantic activity as ratings fought to unscrew the oiling hose and the compressed-air line. Cases of provisions that had been stacked on the deck casing were now scattered on the surface by the force of the explosion like the looting spree aftermath of a street market riot. Two ratings struggled to free a huge crate of oranges that had been jammed in the galley hatch. Another severed the air line with an axe. White water was foaming from *U-395*'s stern. The Jacob's ladder stays were ripped away just as Poison Ivy fell off the steps and landed on the deck casing.

'Swim for it, lads!' someone yelled.

Some men threw themselves into the sea and swam frantically towards their boat, but the stern was swinging clear as she gathered way, the force of her passage driving the air from her main ballast tanks as water roared in. Jets of water were spurting from the free-flow casing vents; already her bow was submerging, water surging across the foredeck and swirling around the main gun. Dieter saw a flash of white above. It was Kessler. The U-boat skipper half fell down the stairs, picked himself up, and raced towards the bulwark just as a shell from the *Dorsetshire*'s second salvo hit the *Anaconda*'s forecastle.

The deck canted steeply to port. Dieter was rolled helplessly against the bulwark and became entangled in a living mass of ropes and hoses that ensnared him like a giant octopus. A smashed crate of tangerines fell across his chest and an avalanche of fruit rolled over him like scurrying lemmings. Heat and light seared against his face as he struggled out of the clutches of a heaving line. A man was screaming, hanging over the side, clinging in terror to the bulwark, not knowing that it was only a short drop to the black, surging sea. Dieter tried to grab him but his feet slipped on the slick of oil, and the man fell from sight. Men were shouting, then the muffled screams of women.

Someone was bellowing: 'Goddamnit! Goddamnit to hell!' It was Kessler, clinging to the transom flagstaff and staring at *U-395* that was disappearing into the darkness beyond the *Anaconda*'s lights.

Dieter caught a glimpse of the U-boat's shrapnel-riddled wind deflector around the rim of the conning tower as it slid under. Shell splinters had ripped away the fore and aft jumping wires and the HF radio antennae. And then all that was left were the two periscopes, sticking up like masts that had had their sails blown away. They sank lower into the water, and then were gone. A stream of bubbles, venting through the casing, continued to the surface in the wake of the vanished boat.

Kessler stopped swearing and stared in silence. Swearing was futile. What was needed now was what he was good at: fast decisions. He took in the *Anaconda*'s list and realised that she wasn't righting. That meant she had been holed and was taking water. He wheeled on Dieter.

'What's the cargo of this tub other than mail?'

The question surprised Dieter. The U-boat skipper had just lost his command and he was worrying about the cargo. 'Only mail,' he answered promptly.

'Well, that might keep us afloat if that bastard lands another brick on us.'

Dieter suddenly realised he and Kessler were the only ones left on the poop deck. A wind was getting up, but it did nothing to disperse the stench of fuel-oil. A wave slapped hard against the stern, drenching the two men in spray. Men were crying out in the water; the screams of a baby could be heard above the suck and hiss of the strengthening swell.

'Lifeboats!' Kessler snapped. 'Come on!'

'Passengers and crew,' Dieter panted, following Kessler up the companionway. 'They're all locked below decks on the port side.'

'What?' Kessler's eyes were livid as he turned to face Dieter at the top of the stairs. '*Locked* below?'

'Haug's idea. I just wanted the passengers guarded.'

'And the crew? Are they locked below, too?'

'I think so.'

'My God! That little bastard will pay for this!' Kessler broke off and yelled orders to two of his crew to throw lifebelts to those in the sea before turning to Dieter and telling to follow him. The U-boat skipper seemed to know his way around the ship. Miraculously, all the bulkhead and companionway lights were still burning. The first watertight door leading to the engine room was easy to find: men on the far side were hurling their weight against it and yelling curses in Spanish. The door was jumping outwards and jamming against the nut and bolt. Kessler motioned to Dieter to deal with it and raced off to the next door.

Dieter struggled to unscrew the nut from the bolt but the repeated impacts from the far side caused the hasps to jam against the nut, making it impossible to turn. He bellowed in Spanish: 'Stand back! Stand back!'

The clamour ceased. The nut spun free and Dieter was nearly trampled underfoot by the four burly greasers who burst out.

'Port side!' Dieter yelled, holding up the nut and bolt. 'Passengers locked below! Help me free them!'

Another shell smashed into the *Anaconda*, hitting the bridge, causing the list to port to increase. One of the greasers panicked. Before anyone could stop him, he uttered a cry of terror, and leapt over the rail into the sea. Dieter detailed one man to free the other engine-room hatches, and led the remaining two down the companionway to the bedlam of hysterical screams and sobs coming from the lower passenger deck. Kessler was struggling to free the corridor door but, like Dieter, was hampered by the sheer weight of panic-stricken men on the far side who were ignoring his shouts in German.

'Stand clear! Stand clear!' Dieter yelled in Spanish. It had no effect. He thought he heard Mrs Montgomerie's scolding voice, telling everyone to be quiet.

'Mrs Montgomerie!' Dieter bellowed in English. 'Get them away from the door! Get them away!'

It was impossible to tell if the Englishwoman had heard him above the uproar on the other side of the door. The baby was screaming.

Kessler ran back to Dieter. 'Is there another door at the other end of the corridor?' he demanded.

'I think so.'

Dieter translated the query into Spanish.

'Si!' the greaser yelled above the commotion. 'Another door!'

'Get to it,' Kessler ordered, sucking at his fingers that had been nipped by the hasp. 'But tell all the ship's crew to muster on the upper port deck to swing out those lifeboats. They'll know how to work them if they've had proper drills on this tub. And find out why the hell there aren't any officers about. And find the purser – we'll need a list of passengers and crew.'

Dieter passed on Kessler's orders in Spanish and raced forward. A sudden swirl of acrid black smoke stung his lungs. Praying that it wasn't from below, he tumbled down the forrard companionway. The air was clear but the smell of burning was strong. The door to the below-deck passenger cabins wasn't hard to find: men on the other side were attacking it with what sounded like an axe but there was less commotion than aft. They belayed their efforts when Dieter yelled at them; he didn't fancy having his skull split open when he freed the door. He unscrewed the nut and jerked the bolt free. The door sprang open. Four men fell out and looked at Dieter in surprise. One of them was José, the *Anaconda*'s huge, bull-necked bosun. He was wielding an axe. Beyond them the corridor was a seething mass of humanity close to panic. Two of the nuns and the young novitiate were doing their best to comfort a distraught mother clutching her baby. Kessler had got his door open at the opposite end of the corridor at the same time with the result that there was a

134

sudden rush in both directions. A woman was knocked to one side.

'We've got to stop this panic!' Dieter yelled at the bosun.

'*Halt!*' José roared, and stood across the corridor like a colossus. The crowd fell back.

'We're going to get you all to the lifeboats,' said Dieter in Spanish. 'There's no need to rush. There's plenty of time. Are there any other members of the crew here who know how to operate the lifeboat davits?'

A cabin boy aged about fifteen pushed his way through the crowd. A similar scene was taking place at Kessler's end of the corridor.

'You're to show all the passengers who leave by this door to the lower weather deck lifeboat muster station on the port side,' Dieter instructed the lad, doing his best to keep his voice calm. 'Have you got that?'

The boy nodded and repeated the order.

'And see if anyone's got a list of all the passengers and crew.' Dieter spun around without waiting for a reply. 'You!' he said to José. 'Where's the officers' quarters?'

'This way's quickest,' said the bosun. He jammed the axe in his belt and went up the steps three at a time without looking to see if Dieter was following. They raced up a ladder to the uppermost deck that was closed to passengers and emerged into the smoke that was billowing along the side deck. Dieter grabbed blindly at the hand rail because the deck was now listing at twenty degrees. His feet skated on the sloping plates and the smoke clawed at his lungs.

'Shit!' the bosun exclaimed, stopping suddenly so that Dieter cannoned into him. It was like colliding with a wall. The wind caught at the smoke. Through a gap in swirling black fog Dieter saw that the entire upper part of the forecastle that included the bridge was ablaze. Paint was bubbling and blistering on the upper superstructure, windows were shattering with explosive reports. Even at this distance he felt the heat sear his cheeks and prick his eyebrows.

'Officers' quarters abaft the bridge!' the bosun yelled, and disappeared into the poisonous black fumes. Dieter remembered his precious samples of quartz crystal – the reason why he was here and doubtless the cause of this mess. He leaned over the rail and saw that he was almost immediately above his cabin. To his right the first of the three lifeboats was being cranked out on its davits. He climbed over the safety rail and dropped the three metres to the weather deck. He darted into his cabin, slung the kitbag over his shoulder, and ran aft to the lifeboats. The canvas cover on the first lifeboat had been untied and the lifeboat swung out, but not lowered. On the deck below, where the passengers were mustered, anxious faces were leaning out and looking up. He shinned up a ladder and ran aft to help Kessler and the greasers who were struggling to crank the hand winches on the second pair of davits. Slowly the inclined arms that had been tilted inboard swung outwards so that the second boat was hanging over the sea. Dieter realised that the black sluggishness of the surface was due to a thick slick of oil, either from the mystery U-boat or *U-395*. The cabin boy leapt nimbly onto the lifeboat's foredeck and started untying the cover, tugging the rope quickly through its eyelets.

The scene was lit by the snarling, raging flames as Kessler supervised the preparation and lowering of the boats, his calm authority managing to calm everyone's nerves.

'Tell them – women and children in the first lifeboat – the rest in the second boat,' he ordered. 'We'll hold back the third one for us and any stragglers. Someone with a passenger and crew list is to wait for us.'

Dieter relayed the orders.

Two hands on the deck below jumped into the first lifeboat and took the children that were passed to them. All were wearing kapok lifejackets. After the initial panic, everything was progressing in a more orderly manner.

The wind was freshening from the south-east, fanning the fire that was blazing forrard, but fortunately carrying the smoke and heat away from the port deck.

'We'll lower the second lifeboat down to the muster station. By the time we've done that, the first lifeboat will be ready to launch,' said Kessler.

'It's not like the movies,' Dieter remarked.

'Be thankful that it isn't. Ships rarely sink quickly unless they're carrying a cargo of pig iron. That's why I wanted to know what this tub was carrying.'

It took a further fifteen minutes to launch the first and second lifeboats and lower the third boat level with the muster station. Two crewmen in each boat unshipped the oars and started pulling away from the stricken *Anaconda*. Dieter saw Mrs Montgomerie sitting upright on a thwart in the first boat. She had a protective arm around Tammy. Oil clung to the oar blades and streaked the sides of the lifeboats with black. Kessler watched them carefully as they moved into the hellish red light of the fire. The clinker-built boats were a good size – about ten metres long and two metres beam. His experienced eye noted that with about thirty survivors in each, they were not unduly overcrowded, but a third boat would make conditions more tolerable. The second boat stopped to pick up an oil-covered ham.

'Belay that, you idiots!' Kessler bellowed, waving his arms. 'Get clear of the damned oil! We can always come back for flotsam!'

They seemed to understand him without benefit of Dieter's translation and resumed rowing, the two boats staying together. There was a sudden explosion forrard. A ball of fire added to the smoke, sparks and smuts vomiting into the sky before being whipped sideways by the wind. The rowers put on a spurt.

'Paint locker going up,' said Kessler cryptically. 'Time we joined them, but why no deck officers? Where's the hell's the captain?'

'He's dead,' said Dieter. 'Their accommodation's right in the centre of the fire. The bridge must've taken a direct hit.' The truth of Captain Valez's death could wait.

137

The ship lurched a few more degrees to port. The two men went down to the lower deck where a small knot of engine room hands were gathered at the muster station. The third lifeboat was hanging level with the deck but there was a two-metre gap between it and the hand rail owing to the increasing list. The assistant chief steward was among the group, clutching a clipboard. Towering over them was José.

'All officers must be dead,' the bosun announced phlegmatically. 'Couldn't get near the bridge and forecastle. Burning like hell.'

'How many missing?' Dieter asked the steward when he had translated for Kessler.

'Twenty-one.'

'All crew?'

'Eighteen crew and three passengers missing,' the steward replied. 'The three ranchers who were sharing a cabin. I've been forrard but there's no sign of them.'

'Lifeboat two!' Kessler bellowed. 'How many of my men have you?'

Five men put their hands up.

'Where's that oily creep I went off with?'

'Do you mean Haug?' Dieter asked.

'That's him.'

'I haven't seen him since he went off with you,' Dieter replied. 'Why aren't they firing anymore?' he asked, peering into the darkness as though expecting to see the instrument of their nightmarish predicament.

'They'll have other businesses to attend to with their depth charges,' said Kessler grimly. 'Merchantmen don't matter when there's U-boat meat around.'

The U-boat skipper shrugged and eyed the fire. Huge tongues of flame were now racing into the sky, fuelled by the wind that the inferno was sucking into its heart. The superstructure behind them was starting to radiate heat. He had watched enough ships burn to know that the conflagration had reached the point when it would spread rapidly.

'We'd better quit now before the damned oil catches,' he said.

José and two hands held the suspended lifeboat against the rail with boathooks while everyone jumped in before leaping themselves as it swung away from the *Anaconda*'s hull. It dropped steadily under its own weight, the winch crank whirred, its reduction gearing controlling the rate of fall.

'We'll row around the ship once to see if there's anyone in the water,' Kessler ordered.

Dieter translated. The hands released the cables and set to with the oars. He stared at the compulsive sight of the double image of the blazing funeral pyre – the fiery reflection in the rolling black swell was as intense as the fire engulfing the ship. Such was the heat that they were forced to stand off at least two hundred metres from the ship as they rounded the bow. The other two boats tried to follow but Kessler waved them to stay where they were. The hands pulled hard in unison, sweat streamed down their faces from their exertions and the heat of the fireball that was now engulfing the entire ship. The strengthening miniature hurricane of air being sucked into the inferno brought some respite and thrust most of the heat into the sky. Dieter admired Kessler's timing; his own instinct had been to do everything in a tearing hurry.

'Oil will go up soon once it starts evaporating,' Kessler predicted.

Hardly had he finished speaking when the slick burst into flames, creating a curtain of fire and dense black smoke like the finale of a bizarre circus act that drew an impenetrable veil around the *Anaconda*.

They completed their circuit of the blazing ship and had some difficulty locating the other two lifeboats in the swell. José spotted them by standing on a thwart. Dieter was about to comment on the deteriorating weather when a dull boom rolled across the water like the reverberation of distant thunder. Kessler knew the sound and was on his feet, staring into the darkness.

The light from the blazing ship caught his face in profile.

139

Suddenly Dieter saw the young man beneath the matted beard. For a moment the anguish in Kessler's eyes swept away his maturity.

'Bastards,' he muttered.

Dieter stared in the direction of the sound. 'What was it?'

'Depth charges,' Kessler replied. 'They'll be plastering my boat.'

24

'Propeller HE bearing zero-one-zero,' Pols reported from the radio office. 'Getting louder.'

'Sixty metres,' Maron ordered. He was clutching his left shoulder. His jacket was sodden with blood from the burst of shell splinters that had killed PO Gerder.

The hydroplane operators kept their eyes on the plane angle indicators and pressed their control buttons to take U-395 down another twenty metres. The electric motors were running at quarter speed. Ten minutes had passed since the near disastrous crash-dive when Brandt and his petty officers had struggled with a badly-trimmed boat as a result of taking on thirty tonnes of diesel fuel and several tonnes of provisions. With the main ballast tanks fully flooded during the dive, Brandt did not know if the boat had negative or positive buoyancy. Depth was now being held dynamically, using the boat's speed and hydroplanes in the same way that an aircraft maintains height with its elevators. Brandt and an engineer petty officer were frantically working the array of handwheels on the trim panel, pumping water between the fore and aft internal trim tanks to stabilise the boat.

'Propeller HE still getting louder. True bearing zero-one-six.'

'Diving stations stand down,' Maron ordered over the PA. He winced in pain as he returned the microphone to its overhead hook amid the swaying udders of hanging sausages.

The order surprised Brandt. It meant that the crew could now move about although he had not reported the boat as properly trimmed. Kessler would never consider giving such an order until he had his chief engineer's okay. From his perch on the flipdown stool by the trim panel, Brandt could see Reche. The young second watch officer was sitting on the settee in the wardroom, looking even more worried than usual. And with good reason: one man was dead and had been abandoned, the first watch officer was injured, five crewmen were missing, and worst of all the boat was without its 'old man'.

'Boat trimmed,' the control room petty officer reported. He immediately had to cancel the statement and started pumping water again as the forward torpedo room set about stowing the mountain of supplies that had been dumped down their hatch.

Brandt gave rapid orders to the planesmen to bring the boat's bow down. Four torpedo ratings tried to stagger into the control room carrying a huge net stuffed with strips of charqui.

'Take that back!' Maron snapped. 'What hell's the idea? Can't you see we're trying to trim the bloody boat?'

The torpedo ratings froze. Kessler would have simply shooed them out but the first watch officer had demanded an explanation. 'I'm sorry, Oberleutnant,' said the leading rating. 'But we're trying to clear some space around the tubes. Ivy said there was room in the galley netting.'

'Propeller noises very loud,' said Pols, employing the urgent tone that he used only when Maron was the watch officer.

The petty officer at the trim panel spun his handwheels again and worked the pumps to compensate for the shifting weight as the four men moved forward with their load. He gave Brandt a despairing look.

'Propeller noises very loud,' Pols repeated. 'One ship. It's not a destroyer. A heavy cruiser, maybe.'

The high-pitched note of the approaching propellers could be heard plainly throughout the boat.

Maron stepped through the door to the radio office and listened on the spare set of headphones. 'Destroyer,' he commented.

Pols said nothing. Normally he manned the hydrophone set sitting half turned on his swivel chair so that his face could be seen from the control room through the door. This time he stayed hunched pointedly over his hydrophone wheel.

'Down another twenty,' Maron ordered, returning to the control room and wedging himself against the attack periscope.

Brandt whistled gently through his teeth.

'Is there a problem, chief?'

'Not yet,' said Brandt shortly. 'That shoulder's bad. Let Reche take over the watch, and have the quartermaster take a look at your shoulder.'

'The safety of the boat comes before my shoulder.'

The propeller noises stopped abruptly. The sudden silence was eerie but expected. The British warship would now be carrying out a 360-degree sweep, using her inclined Asdic beam like a searchlight. Pols didn't bother to relay the information that the warship's engines had stopped. 'Stating the bloody obvious,' Kessler would have growled.

'Hydrophone report!' Maron snapped.

'Propeller effects stopped,' Pols replied, hunching his shoulders even tighter over his hydrophone set.

Brandt called through the open doors to the engine room to shut down the electrics. The order was relayed to the motor room. He did not use the motor room telegraph buzzer because it was too noisy. It was part of the fast, anticipatory action that Kessler had drilled into his watches. If a lone attacking ship stopped its engines, then U-395's crew went into automatic silent routine an instant before the order was given. It made for a tight-knit, efficient boat.

'I didn't give the order to stop motors, chief.' Maron's tone was icy. He had braced his back against the attack periscope with one foot on the chart chest so that he could stand while clasping his injured shoulder.

Brandt looked resigned. 'Slow ahead both,' he called out. The electric motors whined softly.

'Nor did I give the order to start them again! All right – keep them running. Take her down another twenty.'

Brandt's answer was characteristically blunt. 'We'll be too deep. We're going to get nailed in their Asdic beam.'

The comment seemed to amuse Maron. He tried to match Kessler's relaxed, natural humour when under attack. 'Well I daresay you'd like me to give as much consideration to your ideas on strategy as you'd accord my views on running your Rudolf Diesel grease boxes and electric motors.'

Suddenly there were the harsh, high-pitched impulses of an Asdic beam probing the hull. The propeller noises resumed with a vengeance. The Asdic impulses faded as the beam moved ahead of their target.

'Hard aport!' Maron snapped. 'Group up both. Full speed ahead both.'

The motor room telegraph sounded. The electricians slammed down the rotary levers that switched the motors to parallel loading so that each motor drew a maximum load from the badly-discharged batteries instead of sharing a single, series load between them. The control room lights dimmed. Grouping up at maximum power was a battery killer, used only in dire emergencies. Brandt was appalled by the order: sneaking about in the cellar while the enemy made up its mind where to dump his depth charges was not what the old man would have considered an emergency.

U-395 heeled underwater as she veered ninety degrees to port. Shooting off at a tangent when an attacking ship started its run was a standard evasion ploy that was taught at the Baltic training school. Kessler often eschewed the tactic because the British knew all about it.

'Never do what the buggers expect you to do,' was his maxim. On a previous patrol he had gone to periscope depth when under attack by a warship, and had identified the ship as a 'tiddly little sloop that's lost its mother. Time for them to taste our stonefish's spines.'

143

To the astonishment of the sloop's crew and his own crew, he had surfaced within a hundred metres of the warship, and made off on the diesels at *U-395*'s maximum speed of seventeen knots – a speed that the British warship couldn't hope to match. It tried and had stopped a torpedo fired from the U-boat's stern tube for its trouble. *U-395* had returned to Lorient flying a red pennant indicating a warship sunk above its three white pennants for merchantmen. The sinking had added the oakleaves to Kessler's Knight's Cross.

'Not deserved,' he had muttered. 'Maron should get it – he fired the torpedo. Zero angle, bow-on target from Tube 5 while running flat out. Damned if I was going to sit around and let a jumped-up little boat with a twelve-knot engine and a farting little popgun sprinkle bloody *wabos* all over me. We're entitled to get some sleep.'

Not much hope of do-it-by-the-book Oberleutnant Maron trying anything like that, thought Brandt gloomily. What would the old man have done under these circumstances? He could hear Kessler grumbling into his beard: 'Let's go up and scare the shit out of them with a fan. Make ready Tubes 1 to 4.'

'Depth charge splashes,' Pols announced.

Maron made no response. He had twisted himself around and was half slumped against the sky periscope. Even in the red glow of the control room lights his face was deathly pale. Blood was oozing past fingers clamped around his arm.

The explosion shook the U-boat, but that was all.

'Too shallow,' said the control room hand, grinning with relief.

'It was one,' said Maron. 'Chances are the bastards have set their hydrostatics to go off at different depths.'

A minute passed. The next concussion was louder and closer. Brandt chose that exact moment to signal the motor room to group down the motors. The lights brightened but Maron didn't notice. He was staring at the cluster of depth gauges, his face haggard. He opened his mouth to give an order just as the third charge exploded directly above the boat. The concussion sent a shockwave through the pressure hull, tripping circuit breakers and shattering gauges. The heavy HF radio transmitter sheared its mounting bolts and crashed down onto Pols' desk, hanging by one lug and swinging drunkenly before smashing down on the steel case containing the spare radio valves. His oceanography books were scattered. A solid bar of water jetted downwards from the sky periscope gland. It hissed against the deck plates and was atomised to a fine, drifting mist like a hothouse spray. Brandt, two petty officers and the control hand dealt promptly with the damage. Reports came in from the other compartments. Nothing serious apart from a torpedo rating with a broken wrist.

'Propeller noises fading. True bearing zero-one-zero,' Pols reported. He was standing in the centre passageway, still wearing his headphones, while two telegraphists struggled to heave the radio transmitter back into place.

'Looks like he's running back home,' the control room hand remarked as he hammered caulking around the sky periscope gland to stop the leak.

'Propeller noises still fading,' Pols announced.

'Hydrophone report?' said Maron suddenly.

Pols repeated his report and raised an inquiring eyebrow at Reche. The second watch officer looked away in embarrassment.

Brandt ordered the motors to slow ahead without any reaction from Maron. He broached the subject of the first lieutenant's shoulder again.

'I'm perfectly all right without that butcher Brink adding to my problems!' Maron snapped. 'You do your duty and I'll do mine!'

It was an unpardonable insult. Brandt said nothing but went tight-lipped through to the wardroom where Reche was sitting, now looking utterly miserable.

'Did you hear that?'

The junior officer nodded.

'He's badly injured. You'll have to take over command.'

The navy regulations that had been crammed into Reche at college swam before his eyes. 'But . . . he's still on his feet, chief.'

'Not for much longer, he won't be,' said Brandt grimly. 'He's losing blood fast. I don't think the splinter hit an artery otherwise he would not have lasted this long, but he's in no state to take command.'

Reche looked desperate. 'But, chief, he's different from the old man, but he's done nothing wrong. His evasion orders just now were copybook. A court of inquiry would side with him.'

'Propeller noises very faint now,' Pols reported. 'Bearing zero-one-one.'

'That was probably the last of their depth charges,' said Reche. 'That's why they set the hydrostatics to go off at different depths. We'll be able to go back and pick up the old man. Ivy said that he was right behind him on that ship, so there's a good chance he made it to the lifeboats. Anything we do now will be premature.'

'*If* they managed to get the lifeboats out,' Brandt observed icily.

'I think we should wait, chief.'

The two men stared at other. They heard Maron order to motor room to group down and reduce speed to slow ahead both.

'Silly bugger,' Brandt muttered. 'If he was fit to command, he'd know I've already grouped down. Okay . . . we'll wait.' He returned to the control room.

Maron seemed to have recovered his spirits. He smiled thinly at Brandt. 'Variable depths on that last pattern, chief. What's the betting that they've shot their bolt? Why else would they clear off? 'Phones?'

'Propeller noises very faint, and still fading.'

Forty nerve-wracking minutes of silent routine passed with

the boat trickling along with just enough revs to maintain depth. There was always a chance that the warship would come screaming back at thirty knots to renew the attack. Maron's jacket was now saturated with blood. He had remained slumped against the sky periscope, drawing on unsuspected reserves of strength to stop himself from keeling over. Pols reported that all HE effects had been lost. He had to repeat the report.

A few moments passed before Maron acknowledged. 'Very good. Periscope depth,' he ordered. It was an order Kessler usually gave if he was either in the attack kiosk in the conning tower, or about to climb up. Observations from the attack periscope in the kiosk gave an extra three metres height for scanning the surrounding sea before giving the order to surface. Maron reached for the ladder and gave up, wincing in pain.

'Shall I go upstairs, Leutnant?' the control PO offered.

'I'll do it from here,' Maron said tightly, and gave the order to raise the periscope.

Brandt busied himself with depth-keeping. The main depth gauge swung anti-clockwise as the boat rose. The diagram of the periscopes and conning tower marked on the Papenberg sight glass showed that the attack periscope head was clear of the water.

'Periscopes clear,' the control room PO reported.

Maron did his best to hide the pain as he moved. He operated the attack periscope controls with his right hand which was now red with blood. It left smears of crimson on the knurled grip. He stooped awkwardly to the eyepiece and clicked the twistgrip to maximum magnification. When he stopped panning it was possible to see a red glow on his cheeks and reflected in his eyes.

'She's burning,' he remarked cryptically.

Brandt glanced at the sky periscope but the control room hand had removed the eyepiece head to caulk the leak.

The attack periscope hissed down into its well. Maron sat

heavily on the chart chest. He stifled a groan and his right hand went back to his shoulder. 'Twenty metres,' he ordered. 'Steer one-zero-zero.'

'What about lifeboats?' Brandt demanded.

'What about them?'

'Were there any?'

'What if there were?' Maron inquired. 'They're no concern of ours. We know the ship's identity, therefore . . .' He paused to breathe. 'Therefore there's no point approaching them and asking questions. There's a British warship in the area that has already subjected us to an attack. Our duty is to leave as quickly as possible.'

Brandt took a step towards Maron. 'The old man may be in a lifeboat.'

'What if he is? What matters is that he is *not* in this boat.'

' 'Planes to rise – ten degrees,' Brandt ordered.

Maron's nostrils flared angrily. 'Cancel that!'

' 'Planes to rise!' Brandt repeated. 'Periscope depth.'

Brandt stood over Maron. 'Oberleutnant zur See Maron, as a result of your injuries, you are not fit to give lawful orders. Therefore I am taking over command of *U-395*, in accordance with navy regulations.'

Maron pulled himself to his feet but Brandt reached out a hand with the intention of thrusting him down. Maron gave a scream of pain as the chief engineer's palm connected with his left shoulder and jammed the steel splinter even deeper into his collar bone. Brandt was horrified; he hadn't intended to aggravate his fellow officer's wound but there had been little choice in the confined space. He was about to apologise but had to jump forward to catch Maron as he fainted. He lowered him carefully to the deck plates and called for help. Two ratings carried Maron's senseless form through the wardroom to an empty berth in the petty officers' mess so that Brink could attend to his wound.

'Periscope clear!' the control room PO called out.

Brandt almost threw himself at the periscope as soon as it

148

had hissed from the well. His peaked cap tumbled down his back as he pressed his eyes to the eyepiece. He spun the head and found the distant glow of blazing oil hovering in the humid air. A careful check of the horizon. In the east the dawn sky was a hazy grey streaked with fine ribbons of low cloud. The swell had lost its sluggish evenness. He straightened, snatched down the crew address microphone and called the bridge watch to muster in the control room. The coxswain handed out binoculars. Brandt gave the order to surface and was out through the conning tower hatch as the port diesel's exhaust finished flushing water from the main ballast tanks. Mindful of the torn, jagged plates around the coaming, he called down a course to the helmsman and trained his binoculars on the glow. He could sense the eager anticipation of the watch as they took up their appointed sectors.

He suddenly realised that they had plenty of fuel oil although he hadn't had time to check the exact amount. He gave the order for three-quarters speed on both.

The exhaust ports roared, the propellers bit on the water and powered the boat forward. The elegant, knife-like bow thrust into the swell, shouldering aside clouds of spray that lashed the mangled conning tower.

A rating allowed his binoculars to drift too far towards the bow as the U-boat romped through the spray, but the petty officer of the watch didn't have the heart to bawl the man out.

U-395 was on her way back to collect her 'old man'.

25

None of the *Anaconda*'s survivors in the lifeboats saw the cruiser that had sunk their ship and was now attacking *U-395*. They caught a glimpse of a masthead swinging against the eastern sky, but of the ship itself, not a flicker of light betrayed its awesome presence as it went about its deadly business. Kessler estimated that the crump of depth charges was about three miles off. It gave him hope; *U-395* could not have got that distance in time. Also the cruiser was moving fast which meant that her Asdic would be that much less effective.

'Don't do it by the book!' The others in the lifeboat stared at the U-boat skipper as he beat the gunwale in angry frustration. He had to suppress the streams of orders that sprang to his mind. He calmed down with the realisation that he must concentrate on the immediate problems confronting the survivors. The most serious being that the boat containing most of the women was pulling away from the group. The greasers manning the oars were rowing towards the blazing wreckage.

'We stay together!' Kessler roared at the imperial figure of a woman standing in the bow shouting commands at the two greasers. 'My God! What is the stupid woman playing at?'

'That's Mrs Montgomerie,' said Dieter. 'English. And anything but stupid.'

Mrs Montgomerie had spotted a man clinging to a lifebelt. 'Come on!' she urged. 'Another fifty metres!'

'We're too near the fire!' one of the greasers protested. It was a valid point; even though the lifeboat was still over a hundred metres from the blazing oil, the heat was nearly unbearable.

'Nonsense. Keep rowing, or do I have to do it?'

The mother of the baby started crying in despair when she saw her lifeboat's oarsmen resume rowing towards the fire.

'Ahoy, lifeboat! Stay close to us!' Dieter called out in English.

'Man in the sea!' Mrs Montgomerie yelled in reply. She turned her attention to Tammy who had the foredeck locker open and was ripping open another waterproof bag that held blankets. 'Tammy – break out some more blankets and soak them!' She had worked Tammy hard since they had abandoned ship with the result that the girl had been too busy obeying orders to be either scared or seasick. The children that Tammy had wrapped in dry blankets were clinging to their mothers, the glow of the burning ship reflected in their wide, frightened eyes. One of them was the would-be aviator, now a scared nine-year-old in his mother's arms, his engine silent.

The girl looked confused. 'Soak them, Miss Angela?'

'In seawater, you silly child!' Without waiting for a reply, Mrs Montgomerie snatched the blankets from Tammy and doused them in the sea.

Tammy suddenly realised what Mrs Montgomerie meant. She shielded her face from the approaching wall of heat and helped her haul the sodden blankets from the sea and drape them tent-like over each greaser so that only their eyes were visible.

'Now get down,' Mrs Montgomerie ordered Tammy. 'And keep those children down! Come on, you two! Row!'

Tammy grabbed one of the boys who was trying to stand up to see what was happening. The women did as they were told and huddled in the bottom of the boat while glancing fearfully up at Mrs Montgomerie who had dominated them with her iron will since the lifeboat had been launched.

'Left! Left!' Mrs Montgomerie ordered, waving her hands.

The oarsman altered course. Steam rose in clouds from their blankets as they neared the inferno. The heat was suffocating. Mrs Montgomerie wrapped a sodden blanket around herself and stood on a thwart. The man she had seen raised an oil-covered arm and gave a weak wave.

'Come on!' she urged the reluctant oarsmen. 'Another ten metres!'

Each pitch of the swell brought the burning oil nearer to the exhausted man in the water. He tried to swim towards his rescuers and was gripped by a coughing spasm. Tammy saw that the blanket over the oarsman nearest the flames had dried out and was beginning to scorch. She used the bailer to soak him for as long as she could before dropping flat below the lifeboat's gunwales to escape the terrible heat that seared into her lungs.

Mrs Montgomerie threw herself forward and reached out a

hand. 'Got him!' she yelled in triumph, her fingers closing around what little there was of Haug's hair. 'Go back! Quickly!'

The oarsman willingly reversed their stroke and pulled rapidly away from the fire while the mad Englishwoman hung onto a handful of her trophy's scalp. The man seemed to have lost consciousness.

'I think it's one of those ranchers,' Mrs Montgomerie panted when the greasers shipped their oars near the other lifeboats. They hauled the man out of the water. He flopped lifelessly onto the duckboards. Miraculously, he was still wearing his gold-rimmed glasses. Tammy stared fearfully at him.

'Is he alive, Miss Angela?'

'Only just. I think it's Herr Haug. He's probably swallowed some oil. Oh God – he's stopped breathing. Help me.' The two women yanked Haug's head over the gunwale. Mrs Montgomerie thrust her fingers roughly down his throat and twisted them hard. Nothing happened.

Kessler realised what she was trying to do. He stood up in his lifeboat and bellowed across the gap between the two boats. No one understood his German.

'You!' he snapped at Dieter. 'Can you swim?'

'Yes, Captain.'

'Then get after that damned lifeboat! Tell them to hold him upside-down if he's swallowed oil.'

Dieter settled the kitbag on his shoulders.

'Leave that!'

'It goes with me.' Without waiting for an answer, Dieter dived into the water and struck out towards Mrs Mongomerie's boat, the dead weight of the kitbag dragging at his shoulders. He reached the lifeboat and clung to the gunwale.

'Hold him upside-down!' Dieter gasped in Spanish. 'It's the best way of getting him to disgorge oil.' The nuns helped pull Dieter into the lifeboat. The craft rocked as the two greasers stood and held Haug by his ankles like a carcass in an abattoir. He gave a wracking cough. Not sure if it was the right thing to do, Mrs Montgomerie swung her fist into his back with a force that came close to adding a broken spine to his problems. He retched again, vomited black oil, and filled his lungs with a shuddering gasp. Mrs Montgomerie hit him again.

'That's enough,' said Dieter, allowing Tammy to pull his shirt off and wrap a blanket around him. 'Now sit him upright.'

Mrs Montgomerie noticed Dieter's presence for the first time. 'Get back to your lifeboat, Mr Rohland. We can manage perfectly well without being overcrowded.'

'The captain wants a German-speaker in this boat.'

Haug retched again.

'*Agua, por favor,*' he gasped.

Tammy pulled a water canteen from the locker.

'No water!' Kessler shouted in English from his boat that was now nearly alongside. 'Push your fingers down his throat!'

'Don't you give me orders, whoever you are! You are not the *Anaconda*'s captain,' Mrs Montgomerie declared.

Kessler was in no mood to argue. He stood up, the oil fires blazing behind him, and bellowed across the ten-metre gap between the two boats that he was the captain of *U-395* and that he wasn't taking nonsense from anyone. The English he employed was what he had picked up from the world's sleaziest waterfront dives during his merchant shipping days. It was more fitting for berating lascar seamen than expressing a point of view to an English lady with several nuns present, but it worked.

'Well!' Mrs Montgomerie gasped, too horror-struck to reply. 'Never, in all my life . . .' She was about to tell the greasers to toss Dieter over the side but was silenced by a cry from Tammy. Everyone turned to see what she was pointing at.

Purring softly towards the group of lifeboats was the grey,

shark-like bow of a U-boat. In the half light, ratings in fatigues and woollen hats were gathering on the fore casing by the main gun. A group of men were at work cutting away the remains of the jumping wires. The motors whined and the boat went about, presenting its lean profile to the survivors. Dieter wondered what the spined fish painted on the conning tower was. A searchlight on the conning tower snapped on and swept its beam over each lifeboat in turn. It flitted past Kessler's white cap and snapped back to bathe the commander in a harsh white light. A ragged but spontaneous cheer went up from the men on the casing. Kessler seemed far from pleased. He waved the light aside and stood in the pitching lifeboat, glowering at his command as the motors went forward and astern to swing the bow nearer to his lifeboat. Ratings with boathooks latched onto the lifeboat's gunwale and held it close to the U-boat's rust-streaked saddle tank. Kessler timed the motion of the swell and jumped aboard. Willing hands grabbed him and pulled him onto the casing. He shook them off angrily and scrambled up the *wintergarten* ladder.

Mrs Montgomerie spat with unladylike savagery. 'We were filling a U-boat's petrol tanks!'

Brandt was on the bridge with four lookouts and a petty officer. Kessler returned their salute. The smile the chief engineer had in place faded when he saw his commander's thunderous expression. Kessler ignored Brandt's outstretched hand and wheeled on the watch PO.

'Petty officer!'

'Yes, Captain?'

Kessler banged his fist on the 20-mm Oerlikon. 'Make this gun ready and man it immediately! Train it on those lifeboats and blow anyone out of the water if they look like they're going to throw anything at us!'

'Yes, Captain!' The petty officer jumped to the gun.

'Where the hell's the first watch officer?' Kessler demanded, his expression murderous.

Brandt swallowed. 'Oberleutnant Maron was injured in the attack on the supply ship, Captain. I took over as first watch officer.'

'Serious?'

'No. A splinter in his collar bone. Brink has just pulled it out and is sewing him up. Petty Officer Gerder was killed outright by a splinter in the head. We had to abandon him in the crash-dive.'

'Men missing?'

'Five, Captain. Six including you.'

'They're in the lifeboats,' Kessler rasped. He grasped the *wintergarten* rail with both hands. The touch of the cold steel seem to dispel his anger although he snapped at a lookout who allowed his attention to wander in his direction. The three lifeboats had drifted a little way from the boat. They were rolling uncomfortably in the swell. He could hear Haug coughing.

'It's good to have you back aboard, Captain,' said Brandt.

Kessler flapped his hand in irritation. He kept his voice low. 'You know standing orders, chief. When approaching lifeboats, the AA gun must *always* be manned in case some lunatic has ideas about lobbing a hand grenade onto the bridge. It has happened.'

'A neutral ship —? '

'A neutral ship with British passengers!' Kessler snapped.

Brandt looked crestfallen.

'And why the hell are you here now, lit up like a Christmas tree by that,' Kessler jerked his thumb at the distant blaze. 'When there's a British warship in the offing just waiting to lob more bricks at us?'

'It faded right away on the 'phones, Captain. All its *wabos* were set for different depths. We think it didn't have any more left and decided to clear off before we took a poke at it.'

'And did you? No — don't answer. I think I can guess the answer. Damage?'

'The HF transmitter and the sky periscope have been

knocked out. The sky periscope's repairable but I don't know about the radio. Pols hasn't had a chance to look at it yet.' Brandt gestured to the torn and buckled coaming plates and shredded jumping wires. 'There's this damage to the bridge. The torpedo aimer's finished but the spare is okay. As you can see, the net cutter, jumpers and radio aerials have had it.'

Kessler moved onto the bridge and conned the boat. Apart from the torpedo aimer, the jumper cables and the HF aerials, the damage was superficial. Some splinters had smashed right through the coaming and had shredded some of the wooden slats around the lip that were designed to insulate the lookouts from the cold sides of the conning tower.

'Nothing that can't be fixed,' Kessler grunted. He suddenly held out his hand to Brandt and shook it warmly. The tension snapped. And then he put on his booming voice that was intended to be heard by everyone.

'Thanks for coming back for me, Otto.' He slapped the coaming affectionately. 'Seeing this old tub coming out of the mist was the best tonic I've had since that French waitress shed her underwear at Lorient.'

26

A jolt woke Dieter suddenly, and for a disorientating moment he wondered where he was. His stomach churned and his bladder was bursting. He tried to move and discovered that his head was jammed at an awkward angle between a thwart and a large, snoring nun. Each roll of the lifeboat sent a stab of pain shooting through his shoulder. He sat up. Tammy was sitting opposite him, shrouded in a blanket so that only her lovely eyes were visible, catching the light of the early sun.

'God – I feel terrible,' he muttered in German.

'Seasick?' Tammy asked in Spanish.

He forced himself to think in Spanish. 'I don't know.' He massaged the back of his neck.

'Do you speak English?'

Dieter looked at her in surprise. She had asked the question in perfect English. 'It's better than my Spanish,' he said ruefully. 'I think I am being . . .' He groped for the right word in English.

'Seasick?'

Dieter nodded. 'Seasick,' he agreed.

Tammy looked up at the sky. 'José told me to stare at the Southern Cross and not to look at the horizon. It worked. I feel better now. But it's gone now. All the stars have gone.'

'José?'

'The bosun,' she nodded to a recumbent sleeping form.

Gradually the waves of nausea faded. Dieter glanced around. Mrs Montgomerie was asleep, wedged awkwardly on her side against the bow locker with her head resting on a sack of oilskins. Strange that she had not been loud in her complaints about the indignity of being in a lifeboat wearing only a nightdress and a housecoat. Other shadowy shapes sprawled on the lifeboat's duckboards included the mothers of the two boys and the mother with a baby. Wives of upcountry farmers probably. Dieter felt sorry for them. They had been on a Christmas shopping expedition to Montevideo and had never expected to return home by ship. They had become embroiled in a war they knew little about, had been shelled by a warship, and had ended up drifting in a lifeboat. The six nuns were sound asleep amidships. The two greasers had rolled themselves into blankets at the other end of the lifeboat and were snoring. One of the children whimpered and was hushed by its mother.

'Where's Herr Haug?'

'His shivering was worse. So he was transferred to the submarine.' Tammy's gaze was over his shoulder.

Dieter twisted around and stared at *U-395* lying some four hundred metres away. The other two lifeboats were tethered to his boat by long lines. He could hear the muted throb of the U-boat's diesels.

'Why do they run their engines without moving?' Tammy asked.

'To charge their batteries,' Dieter replied. His bladder was threatening independent action. He kept his back to Tammy and relieved himself over the gunwale. He sat down feeling better. She gave him an embarrassed half smile and looked away.

The *Anaconda* had vanished.

'It was gone when I woke up,' said Tammy in answer to his query. It annoyed her that she had not seen it sink. It had just slipped away and no one had said anything. When the *Graf Spee* had blown itself up, police speedboats had raced up and down keeping sightseers well away from the blazing battleship. Now all that was left of the mail ship was a huge circle of debris. The oil had either dispersed or burned. Something bumped against the lifeboat. She looked down at the charred deckchair and wondered if it was the same one that she had used. She fished it aboard thinking it would make a useful awning.

Dieter felt around for the kitbag containing the quartz samples and realised that he was still clutching the shoulder strap.

'What's in the bag?' Tammy asked.

'Just a few things.'

Her cheeks dimpled prettily when she smiled. 'Something valuable, the way you've been hanging onto it. I don't think anyone here is interested in stealing.'

Dieter tucked the kitbag more securely under his knees.

'Mrs Montgomerie says our ship was filling that U-boat's petrol tanks —'

'Diesel tanks,' Dieter corrected absently.

Tammy nodded. 'She said that we must have been attacked by the British Navy. They would have a right to attack us. She's going to write a letter to the owners of the *Anaconda*.'

Dieter looked sharply at the girl, thinking she was joking. She gave him a lovely, enigmatic half-smile which he couldn't help returning.

The sun climbed higher. The sister-in-charge of the nuns stirred and sat up, grimacing as she stretched. Her wimple was limp and black with oil. Tammy stared at the U-boat. She could see the men on the bridge, gazing in all directions through binoculars. She wondered what they were looking for. Perhaps they did that all the time they were on the surface in case the British came looking for them. There were other men on the deck, cutting and sawing and hammering. Their voices carried across the water. Sometimes they shouted; sometimes a sudden roar of laughter. The normality of their exchanges under these bizarre circumstances was strangely reassuring.

A sudden lash of spray across her face and the taste of salt reminded her that she was thirsty. With a furtive look at her sleeping guardian, she took a sip from her water canteen. Mrs Montgomerie had been very forthright when she had filled the canteens from the freshwater tank that was housed under the little foredeck.

'The rescue boats will be on their way,' she had announced to her charges as she handed out the one-litre canteens. 'Captain Valez told me that the *Anaconda* had the very latest wireless apparatus, so an SOS would have been sent. Nevertheless we will have to be careful with the water. One canteen a day per person. No more and no less.'

Tammy offered the canteen to Dieter. 'Just a sip,' she warned.

Dieter took a mouthful of water and passed the canteen to the nun while Tammy wrapped her blanket tightly around herself and eased her buttocks over the gunwale. Dieter looked away, wondering what was happening aboard the U-boat. Tammy wriggled her pyjama trousers around her thighs under the blanket. The wind and spray stung her buttocks as she relieved herself.

At least I'll be clean, she told herself as she hitched her trousers back up.

The wind freshened from the south-west. It was the

Westerlies—the cold trades that swept up the Atlantic coast of South America from the Roaring Forties and then swung eastward across the wastes of the South Atlantic towards Africa, driving the slow-moving Brazil Current before it.

Tammy was pleased that the motion of the lifeboat no longer affected her although there was the occasional unpleasant jolt when the tether to the other two boats was jerked taut. She momentarily forgot José's advice and looked at the sea. The golden morning light suffused the restless horizon, showing the mountainous swells in hard relief in their relentless march towards the rising sun. Tammy wasn't sure which was the more frightening: being in the troughs and seeing the majestic seas bearing down on her, or breasting the crests and witnessing the awesome panorama of the serried ranks of heaving green mountains merging into the distance. Already the wind was tormenting the crests, forcing them to accelerate so that they curved over and broke in shining streaks of spume that the wind whipped away as trophies. The lifeboat rode the swell with confidence, helped by the drogue—a sock-like canvas sea anchor—that they had streamed in response to José's instructions.

Tammy bit hard on her lip to still her fear of the mighty swells. She saw that José was awake. She returned his smile and immediately felt better because he was looking so unconcerned and was even trying to light a cigar.

'She sleeps well,' said Dieter, nodding to Mrs Montgomerie who was now snoring gently.

Tammy had decided that she liked the tall, dark-haired young man when she had been introduced to him in the *Anaconda*'s dining saloon. 'She didn't get to sleep until an hour ago. She's not a young woman.' She glanced uneasily at the sleeping form, half expecting Mrs Montgomerie to rise from her sleep and upbraid her for talking about her. 'They took a count on the other boat while you were sleeping. I gave them your name. Was that all right?'

'Perfectly all right,' Dieter replied. The blanket drawn

tightly around the girl's face seemed to accentuate her innocent beauty.

The lifeboat rolled alarmingly as it breasted a swell. The sun was now a golden-crimson ball well clear of the horizon. The U-boat's swaying periscopes were like raised swords of pure gold, burning in the morning light. The underside of a dark layer of cloud above the horizon suddenly acquired a shining patina of mottled gold leaf. The men on the deck casing had finished their work and were throwing tools in wooden boxes. Another team went to work with spluttering welding torches. Some were leaning on the main gun, smoking and chattering animatedly. More men emerged from a hatch and stripped off their overalls. A bucket on a rope was used to douse them while they soaped themselves down. Tammy watched, fascinated – they were the first naked men she had ever seen. The smell of frying sausages and coffee drifting across from the U-boat ended her curiosity about the U-boat men and their surprisingly small genitalia. Hunger was also a new experience.

The young mother stirred. One of the nuns took the child from the exhausted woman and cradled it in her arms while her fellow sisters clicked their rosaries, their lips moving in silent prayer. The novitiate's heart didn't appear to be in devotions because she was playing Klondike patience with her grimy pack of cards, demonstrating a remarkable skill at shuffling. The boy watched her with soulful eyes from the security of his sleeping mother's arms.

'What's your name?' Dieter asked the boy.

He turned his gaze to Dieter. 'Marco,' he replied. He accepted the canteen from the nun and drank greedily.

'What will happen to us?' Tammy asked when she had given the boy a packet of biscuits from the lifeboat's survival rations.

Dieter did his best to look reassuring. 'Even if the *Anaconda* didn't get a signal out, the U-boat will radio our latest position so that a rescue ship will be able to find us.'

161

Tammy looked doubtful. 'But that would bring the British. Would the submarine risk that?'

The girl was no fool. Dieter shrugged. 'We'll see.'

The swell seemed to be lifting the lifeboat higher than the U-boat. Tammy caught a glimpse of something in the direction of the sun before the seas rode up. On the next crest she saw them again: a cluster of shapeless black dots bobbing on the golden surface that were too far away to be debris from the *Anaconda*. A lookout on the U-boat had also seen them. He called out and pointed. Kessler appeared, distinguishable by his white cap, and aimed his binoculars in the direction of the dots although the other lookouts kept their glasses trained on their appointed sectors.

Shouted orders. The U-boat's diesels slowed and then picked up. White water creamed from the stern and the boat moved off in the direction of the dots.

27

The stitches in Maron's wound were far from neat, but they were adequate. Kessler regarded the unconscious man and moved aside so that Brink could tape clean dressings into place.

'So how much did you give him?'

'Twenty cc, Captain.'

'My God. He'll sleep for a week.'

'He'll miss Tuesday,' Brink agreed.

Kessler was too old a hand to laugh but it took some effort. 'Well — it'll be a few days before he'll be able to hold a clipboard. If he lost as much blood as you say, keep pumping water into him. Can't afford to lose our Number One. We'll all miss his wardroom recitals of *Mein Kampf*.' Kessler's face was deadpan as he moved to the next bunk where Haug was lying. Brink helped him sit up. 'How are you feeling now, Mr Haug?'

'Much better, thank you.' He gave a wheezing cough. 'Your doctor says I didn't swallow much oil.'

'The Englishwoman in your lifeboat made you throw it up. Don't go calling Brink a doctor otherwise he'll want more pay. He was a vet, not a doctor. We don't have many animals aboard so we let him play with our sextants and get us lost.'

Haug gave a thin smile. Despite his ordeal, his eyes were bright and alert. A tough bird, thought Kessler, feeling no sympathy for the man.

'A word in private please, Captain,' Haug requested.

'Later, Mr Haug. There's a lot of minor damage –'

Haug grabbed Kessler's sleeve. 'It is urgent.'

Brink caught Kessler's eye and moved away.

'Where are my two colleagues?'

'There were only six Germans in the lifeboats,' Kessler replied. 'Dieter Rohland and five of my crew. I've brought the crewmen aboard.'

Haug eased himself up the pillow and gave a self-effacing smile. 'Rohland and his samples are safe, of course?'

'Samples?'

Haug's smile faded. 'His geological samples. The orders I gave you on the *Anaconda* –'

'The last thing on my mind has been any damned samples, whatever they are. There's a passenger named Rohland in one of the lifeboats. You're the only survivor I've permitted aboard – something I'm beginning to regret.'

'You mean you've abandoned him?'

'No one has been abandoned,' Kessler growled.

Haug's moonlike face gazed up at the mass of pipes and cables that passed through the bulkhead above his berth. He was out of his depth. His natural habitat was at the centre of plots and intrigues. 'But the engines are running.'

'We're not under way. We're charging the batteries and carrying out repairs.'

'Captain, it is imperative that—'

'What is imperative, Mr Haug,' said Kessler menacingly,

moving his face close to Haug, 'is that the repairs to this boat are carried out quickly and efficiently. It is also imperative that you understand that I am the captain of this boat.'

'Captain to bridge!'

Glad of the interruption, Kessler scrambled up the ladder and joined Reche's bridge watch.

'Liferafts, Captain.' Reche pointed.

Kessler trained his binoculars and found the craft about a mile distant. He swore softly. 'Where the hell did they come from? One . . . Two . . .'

'Three.'

'Goddamnit – they're packed. They can't be from the *Anaconda*. We didn't launch any rafts.' Spray lashed the lenses. Kessler snatched Reche's binoculars and pressed them to his eyes, nearly dislocating the junior officer's neck with the strap. 'Shit! German merchant navy uniforms! What the hell's going on?' He called down a series of helm orders. The stern shafts were engaged. *U-395* went about and set course for the liferafts at a steady five knots. Kessler continued to stare at the bobbing craft. At five hundred metres the nearest raft spotted the approaching U-boat and fired a flare.

'All right. All right. We've seen you,' Kessler growled.

The loudhailer was passed up from the helm. Kessler gave the order to stop engines and allowed the U-boat's way to take it within a hundred metres of the nearest liferaft.

'What ship?' he called out.

A figure separated from the huddle of anxious faces by standing. '*Atlantis!*'

Kessler lowered the loudhailer in surprise.

'The supply ship!' said Reche excitedly.

Kessler's voice boomed across the gap again. 'Port of registration?'

'Hamburg!'

'This is all we need,' Kessler grumbled. 'Do you ever feel that life can be unbearably complicated, Leutnant?'

'Good job it's not Tuesday,' Reche managed to say without going pink.

Kessler looked admiringly at him. 'I didn't think you made jokes, Leutnant.'

'I won't make a habit of it, Captain.'

Kessler lifted the loudhailer to his lips and aimed it at the nearest raft. 'Row over and come aboard – just one of you.'

28

'They're leaving us!' Tammy cried in Spanish, standing up and staring at the U-boat as it went about.

One of the women started sobbing. José mouthed a stream of curses in Spanish. The sudden commotion woke Mrs Montgomerie. She emerged from under her blankets like an avenging kraken, demanding to know what the fuss was about.

'They're leaving us, Miss Angela!'

'I think they are going to investigate the other lifeboats,' said Dieter, speaking slowly so that his English was correct.

'*Other* lifeboats?' Mrs Montgomerie demanded. 'What other lifeboats?'

'I think I saw two or more lifeboats about a mile off.'

'Only three lifeboats were launched, young man.'

'Maybe they are not from the *Anaconda*?'

It was getting warm. Mrs Montgomerie tossed aside her blankets and stood, oblivious of the fact that she was wearing only an oil-stained nightdress. 'Typical,' she said scornfully, as the U-boat slipped into the haze.

She looked rather how Dieter had always imagined Britannia; jaw set firm; flimsy garment streaming in the breeze. The sun outlined her surprisingly shapely legs in a manner that he found curiously erotic. He wished he had a camera.

'They've got a problem with us,' she continued grimly, 'which they sidestep by running out on us.'

Dieter felt his kitbag pressing reassuringly against his calf. 'They'll be back, Mrs Montgomerie.'

She turned and looked down at him, her expression withering. 'And what makes you so sure? Oh, of course, you're German, aren't you? I expect you understand your fellow countrymen better than anyone.'

'I am from South West Africa,' said Dieter carefully, recalling that he had already explained this to the Englishwoman. 'My grandparents were German. I am not.'

'Ha! A German colony.'

'No longer.'

'You talk German. You think German because you seem to know what that U-boat is up to. You were friendly with those German ranchers. You come from a German colony. As far as I'm concerned, you're a German.'

Dieter attempted to defuse the situation by treating the woman to his warmest, most beguiling smile. Mrs Montgomerie was a remarkable lady; he didn't really expect her to succumb, but, to his surprise, she did. She sat down abruptly and looked away, suddenly ashamed. 'I'm sorry, Mr Rohland. I'm being boorish. Forgetting my manners.'

Dieter shrugged but maintained the smile. He gestured around the lifeboat. 'It is perfectly understandable, Mrs Montgomerie. These are difficult circumstances.'

An apology had been offered and accepted; Mrs Montgomerie wasn't going to dwell on the matter. Everyone seemed to be awake so she clapped her hands for attention and spoke in rapid, forceful Spanish. Tammy saw Dieter's worried expression and explained in slow English that Miss Angela had said that in view of the U-boat abandoning them, the water ration would be reduced to half a canteen per day. Also the blankets were to be used to make a shade and a screen to separate the men from the women. This would also help dry the blankets. And all wet clothes were to be taken off and dried.

'Also we must all turn out *all* our pockets and bags and pool our belongings,' Tammy concluded. 'We must do this now.'

It was surprising just how much in the way of personal

belongings the women had saved from the *Anaconda*. The blanket Mrs Montgomerie and Tammy had spread across the duckboards was soon piled with a large assortment of lifejackets, clothes, balls of wool, kitchen utensils, and even a sewing box. Marco produced a toy aeroplane which he was allowed to keep.

'Pepita,' said the sister reprovingly to the novitiate.

The girl sighed and produced her pack of cards from the folds of her habit.

'Quite right, sister,' said Mrs Montgomerie. 'Everything means everything.' She pointed to a bulge in José's sweatshirt breast pocket.

'But, Señora —'

'*Everything*, José.'

Tammy held out her hand. The big seaman looked embarrassed but there was no arguing with Mrs Montgomerie. His broomstick fingers delved into his pocket. He pressed a packet of Durex Featherlite contraceptives into Tammy's palm. The girl looked curiously at the packet but Mrs Montgomerie snatched it away and dropped it in the sewing box without a word. The novitiate sniggered.

'What are they, Miss Angela?' Tammy inquired innocently, although she knew perfectly well. At school she and some friends had played a game with an inflated condom which had ended up being confiscated by a teacher.

'Never you mind,' said Mrs Montgomerie sternly. She inspected the other contents of the sewing box. 'Excellent. Excellent. All we need to sew some blankets together.' She turned to the young mother. 'The baby's clothes are wet – you must get them dry. We must make the sun our friend, not our enemy. We will use the clothes to make sunshades. If it rains, we have the canvas cover.' Her gaze fastened on Dieter's kitbag. 'What's in that, Mr Rohland?'

'Some geological samples. Pieces of rock – nothing else. It is a hobby of mine.'

'You swam from the other lifeboat carrying lumps of rock?

one wonders why it is the British who have a reputation for being eccentric. We need the bag for the baby's clothes in case it rains.' She held out her hand.

'It is not necessary, Mrs Montgomerie. The U-boat will return.'

The Englishwoman glanced at the other women for support. The greasers and José were accepting her authority. 'We share everything, Mr Rohland,' she stressed. 'We've all agreed.'

'They took me many years to collect,' said Dieter stubbornly, embarrassed by the disapproving stares of his fellow survivors. He cursed inwardly, realising that he was sounding petulant and selfish. He thought fast. 'If the U-boat does not return, then I'll give you the bag. Is this a deal?'

For a moment it looked as though Mrs Montgomerie was going to force the issue, but she accepted the offered compromise. 'Very well, Mr Rohland. But if I know anything about your countrymen, they won't return.'

29

Officer-cadet Karl Valle was eighteen years old; skinny, emaciated, and shell-shocked. His once-white tropical uniform jacket was splattered with blood stains. Every movement aboard *U-395* made him twitch nervously. He brought his hand up to salute Kessler and rasped his knuckles on a net bag bulging with onions. He looked up, bug-eyed at the hanging food.

'I shouldn't be here,' he said lamely. 'There's a more senior officer –'

'You were nearest and I haven't got time for niceties,' said Kessler curtly. He waved at the wardroom settee. 'Just sit down and drink. Don't speak until you've finished.'

Valle stumbled against the central table and sank gratefully onto the cushioned seat. He seized the mug of hot, sweet coffee laced with brandy and gulped it down. An electrician passed through the wardroom. Valle's hunted, hollow eyes followed him. His fingers gripping the mug were trembling. The sugar should help, Kessler decided. Poison Ivy placed a bowl of bread pudding in front of him; an English recipe he had discovered for using up mould-covered bread.

'Now eat,' Kessler ordered.

'I should first see to the men in my life –'

'We have the worst cook in the U-boat service. We have to suffer and I see no reason you shouldn't as well. Now eat.'

Valle ate while Kessler moved to the door and conferred with Pols. The radio officer and a telegraphist had dismantled the transmitter. Circuit diagrams were spread all over the tiny radio office. A junior rating was picking broken glass out of the transmitter with tweezers.

'Plate's damaged, Captain,' said Pols, peering closely at a valve he was holding up to the reading light. 'That makes four of them. It was a hell of a bang. The transmitter fell on the spares box. We should know in a few minutes what we can fix and what we can't.'

Kessler grunted. He returned and refilled Valle's mug. 'Now drink some more.'

The second mug of coffee steadied the young man's fingers.

'Right. Now tell me what happened. Don't rush. Take your time.'

Talking helped further calm the young man's nerves. The *Atlantis* had been replenishing two U-boats at night when shells had suddenly ripped into the supply ship.

'What boats?' Kessler interrupted.

'*U-68* was one. I don't know what the other one was.'

U-68 wasn't 2nd Flotilla; Kessler didn't know its commander.

'The dining saloon took a direct hit,' Valle continued, tightening his grip on the mug to control his renewed trembling. His hollow eyes stared down at the table. 'It was crowded. We were having supper with the off watch U-boat

169

men. One shell . . . People screaming all around me. There was blood everywhere. I thought I'd been hit by a splinter. I couldn't stand. The deck was tilting. Tables, bodies . . . bits of bodies . . . All sliding to one side . . . One shell – that's all it was. One shell . . .'

The trembling would have been renewed but Kessler headed it off. 'Were both boats refuelling at the same time?'

The question diverted the young man's mind from the carnage in the dining saloon. 'No – only *U-68*. The other boat was standing off, waiting. We've never refuelled two boats together. We don't have the bunkering valves. The U-boat could have come alongside for provisioning but the captain preferred to wait until the bunkering valves were free.'

Kessler nodded; it was exactly what he would have done.

'There were more shells but they missed I think,' Valle continued. 'The next thing I remember was being pulled onto a liferaft and . . .' He swallowed and clasped his hands tightly together, knuckles as white as his bloodless face. 'And the *Atlantis* and *U-68* had gone . . . One shell . . .'

There was a movement in the control room. Brink appeared.

'Fifty-seven men on those three liferafts, Captain,' he reported.

'Any U-boat men?'

'None.' The quartermaster's face was impassive.

'The other U-boat surfaced the following morning,' said Valle, his voice steadier now. 'Until then we didn't know it had escaped. It took on all the surviving crewmen from *U-68* and then took us in tow. We were told that we would be rendezvousing with another supply ship.'

'You were towed for a week?' Kessler asked.

'Westward,' Valle confirmed. 'We were all very excited last night when the supply ship was sighted. Then the U-boat's first watch officer told us that his captain was suspicious. After the *Atlantis*'s ambush he thought that the supply ship could be a trap. That's why the tow was slipped and we were left – in case the U-boat had to crash dive.'

170

The picture of the boat approaching the *Anaconda* and taking a direct hit on its after casing burned vividly in Kessler's mind. 'Dear God,' he muttered, shaking his head as though the gesture might banish the memory. 'So there were *two* crews on that boat?'

Valle looked uncertain. 'Were?'

Kessler told him what had happened to the U-boat. 'Two rendezvous ambushed!' he concluded bitterly. 'And two U-boats sent to the bottom. Two!'

'We could hear the sound of explosions just before dawn,' said Valle quietly. 'We didn't know what was happening.'

'What was the count of survivors from the *Anaconda*, quartermaster?'

'Forty-six, Captain,' Brink replied. 'A total of one hundred and three survivors altogether. Their nationalities are –'

'Spare me that,' Kessler growled. 'Pols! What about that damned transmitter?'

But he knew the answer from Pols' expression. 'I'm sorry, Captain, but we're one valve short.'

Kessler bit back an expletive. There was no point in swearing at a competent technician like Pols. 'No chance of using the valves in the receiver?'

'They don't match. It's a power amplifier valve we need.'

Kessler recalled the words of a radio operator on a training U-boat in the Baltic. 'Everything on a boat is repairable with one exception: radio valves. Which is why we'll always send you on patrol with a generous supply of spares.'

'Well,' said Kessler philosophically. 'At least we won't have the British pouncing on our necks everytime we transmit.'

Pols frowned and glanced up at the cubbyhole that housed the Enigma machine. 'You really think the British have cracked our codes, Captain?'

'I'm damned certain of it now.'

'But the combinations run into millions.'

'Tenacious buggers, the British.' Kessler turned to Valle. 'Thank you for your assistance, Mr Valle. The petty officer of the watch will see that you're returned to your liferaft.'

The hunted look returned to the young officer's eyes. He opened his mouth to speak and thought better of it. He obeyed Brink's jerked thumb and returned to the control room.

Kessler brought his log up to date and joined Reche's watch on the bridge. Brandt's working party had cut away the damaged jumping wire and were busy with oxy-acetylene welding gear repairing the damaged coaming, torches hissing and spitting, the intense blue flames nearly invisible in the bright sunlight. The wind had dropped so that the fumes from the diesels hovered around the boat. Kessler moodily surveyed the three liferafts that were lying about fifty metres off. They were tethered to each other on a short line so that they rolled easily together on the same swell. The pinched, exhausted faces of the survivors beneath their jury-rigged sunshades were all turned expectantly towards him. Kessler was grateful that Reche hadn't engaged him in conversation. Fifty-seven men in these liferafts plus forty-six men, women and children in the three lifeboats from the *Anaconda*: one hundred and three souls dependent on him, and no radio to ask for help. Theoretically he didn't need help. Doenitz's rules of engagement were simple and rigid: U-boats were not allowed to take survivors on board. It was a rule born out of practicalities rather than brutality. There was barely enough room in a Type VIIC for a full crew of forty-four. Most skippers bent the rules slightly by passing supplies to lifeboats when they could do so without risk to their boats, but taking survivors aboard was out of the question.

Brandt's stocky figure, stripped to the waist, emerged through the forward hatch. He inspected the work carried out by the damage repair crews and ordered them to clear up. He climbed onto the *wintergarten* deck.

'All repairs completed, Captain.'

'Excellent, chief. It looks as good as new.'

Brandt grunted. 'I daresay Mr Maron will object to all this unprimed steel.'

Kessler never responded to Brandt's digs at the first watch officer. 'A lick of paint can wait. How do your diesels like their oil?'

'Running sweet as nuts. Batteries ninety per cent charged. I'd like a trim dive as soon as possible.'

'How much fresh water have we made since we started charging?'

'I haven't checked, but it'll be about a hundred litres.'

'As much as that?'

Brandt glanced at the three liferafts. 'The condensers are on maximum. It's making the engines run cooler than I'd like, but it's in case you want to give them some water before we leave them.'

Nicely said, chief, thought Kessler. A diplomatic way of reminding me of standing orders. He came to a decision, or rather, a small decision that postponed the big decision. 'Leutnant.'

'Captain?' said Reche without lowering his binoculars.

'We'll take those liferafts in tow and take them to the lifeboats. As fast as you can without swamping them. Should be okay at four knots. Might as well have all six craft together until we decide what the hell to do about them. Wardroom in five minutes please. And you, chief. And tell Brink I want to see him as well.'

30

Kessler walked his dividers across the small-scale chart of the Atlantic. He started at U-395's present position off Uruguay and finished at Lorient on the west coast of France. 'Eighty . . . Ninety . . . There you have it, gentlemen – damn near one hundred degrees home. A quarter of the way around the world – six thousand miles as near as dammit.' He tossed the dividers on the table and sat back, thumbs hooked in his waistbelt, regarding his subordinates owlishly while chewing on his beard. 'Chief says we managed to take on thirty tonnes of the *Anaconda*'s oil before we were so rudely interrupted. But we need sixty to get home even if we take it easy. So . . . any ideas?'

No one spoke. *U-395* was towing the liferafts, making a steady three knots, the diesels a little above a fast idle. The motion was comfortable. Reche broke the silence. 'What are our chances of intercepting a ship?'

Kessler shrugged. 'I fancy you know the answer to that as well as I do, Leutnant. We're off the convoy routes, not that it would be that easy to stop a ship in a convoy and ask them to sell us some oil. And if we do chance on a lone sailing, we might have to burn fuel to get into a favourable position to threaten her with our gun, only to discover that she's an old coal burner.'

'Pols *has* to fix that radio,' Brandt declared. As a mechanical engineer he had a profound faith in his ability to fix anything, especially any machine invented by his hero Rudolf Diesel. He mistrusted the seemingly unrepairable technology of wireless telegraphy.

'He can't mend smashed valves, chief.'

Silence.

Reche, Brandt and Brink stared down at the chart as though the answer to the insoluble problem would suddenly be projected on the expanse of white that was the awesome gulf of the mighty Atlantic. From where he was sitting Kessler could see through the door to the petty officers' mess where Haug was stretched out on a berth reading. Pretending to read more like. Ears flapping. But it was unlikely that Haug could hear anything above the diesels. Not that Kessler much cared. Private conferences aboard a Type VIIC were nigh on impossible. 'Quartermaster?'

'I could plot a rhumb line course home instead of plain sailing,' Brink offered.

'Which would save how much?'

'About two hundred miles over the distance.'

'It's two tonnes of fuel,' said Kessler quickly, seeing Brandt's expression. He made a note. 'So we end up stranded 2800 miles from home instead of 3000 miles.'

'The best thing,' said Brandt slowly, studying the chart, 'is to set course for the Cape Verde Islands.'

'Portuguese,' said Kessler gloomily. 'Not only in bed with the British, but positively fornicating with them.'

Reche did his best to look serious and failed. Kessler regarded him wolfishly, expecting to see the tips of the young officer's ears turn bright pink as they usually did. Instead he stared right back at Kessler without a flicker of embarrassment.

'But they're on our home run course anyway,' Brandt pointed out. 'And it takes us near the west coast of Africa. If we pass between the Cape Verdes and Senegal, we stand a chance of stopping a ship plying between the Verdes and Dakar.'

'The Cape Verdes are well over halfway home,' said Brink abruptly. 'The Brazil Current is against us until we cross the equator. We'll never make the Verdes on thirty tonnes.' He paused and gave Brandt a half-smile. 'Unless our chief has got a special reserve stashed away.'

Kessler looked sharply at Brandt. 'Well, chief?'

The engineering officer shook his head. 'That's the lot, Captain – reserves – everything. Thirty tonnes. We'd need at least forty tonnes to reach Cape Verdes. And even that would need fair weather.'

'And then we'd need fuel to chase after a ship,' Reche added. 'One's not likely to steam right into our sights.'

The four men fell silent. Kessler realised that he missed Maron. Although disliked, the first watch officer was as shrewd as a sackful of ferrets. He would never admit defeat and would be certain to think of something.

There was a flurry of movement in the control room. A stream of orders and movement. The engine-room bell carried through the open watertight doors and the diesels closed down. Kessler raised a questioning eyebrow at the chief.

'My standing orders are not to idle the engines when they're not needed,' said Brandt, reading his captain's mind. 'They're to be shut down at every opportunity.'

Kessler nodded in agreement.

'There is an option that ought to be noted,' said Reche boldly.

You are coming out of your shell, thought Kessler. 'Which is?' he prompted.

'We stay in this area and expend all our fish and shells creating as much havoc as possible. Then we head for Montevideo, set the scuttling charges, and take to the inflatable rafts.'

'And end up in an internment camp?' Brandt sneered.

'It is only an option,' Reche replied hotly.

'A good one, too,' Kessler intervened quickly, not wanting the junior officer's new-found self-confidence undermined. 'If *U-395* is going to be lost, then it ought to be lost after doing what it's designed to do – sinking enemy shipping. And Montevideo has got a full-blown embassy to look after our interests while we're interned.'

The control room petty officer of the watch rapped politely on the open watertight door. 'All lifeboats and rafts tethered together, Captain,' he reported.

Kessler thanked him and turned to Brandt. 'Think we could make one hundred and fifty miles a day, chief?'

Brandt considered. 'Six to seven knots? That would be our most economic speed. Yes, Captain.'

'Forty days to crawl home,' Kessler mused. 'Say fifty. Add another ten days to hunt for a prize ship. A hundred days at sea by the time we get home. We'll never make it by Christmas, or the end of the year. Which means that 1941 will be a year in which my wife didn't get pregnant, and that we'll all qualify for one of those long patrol certificates that Kerneval have dreamed up. Something for us all to look forward to.'

'And it gives you all those extra Tuesdays at sea, captain,' Brink added.

The long faces around the table broke into smiles.

'Right — we're going home, gentlemen,' said Kessler with finality. 'Make the announcement to the crew, Leutnant. A word with you on the bridge please, quartermaster.'

Reche's words over the crew address speakers were heard by the bridge lookouts. A curt warning by the watch petty officer as Kessler's white cap appeared through the hatch stilled their excited chatter. The rating who had the multiple barrels of the anti-aircraft Oerlikons trained on the *Anaconda*'s lifeboats stopped whistling. The U-boat commander propped himself against the torpedo aimer and swept his binoculars over the sea of faces in the six craft. Every blanket and scrap of cloth had been pressed into service to provide protection from the sun. All the craft were tethered bow to stern. The *Anaconda*'s lifeboats were streaming sea anchors, drogues which caused all the craft to defy the slight windage and string out in a neat line. It was a sharp reminder to Kessler of the strength of the Brazil Current. South of the equator the Atlantic ocean was a giant, slow-turning anti-clockwise whirlpool powered by the sun and the coriolis effect of the Earth's rotation. On the South American seaboard, the warm Brazil Current, flowing from the equator, swept southward into the lonely wastes of the Roaring Forties, surrendering its warmth in a savage battle of the elements that raged all the year round with such unremitting ferocity that to the whalers who ventured into those latitudes, it seemed that the very fabric of the Earth itself was being torn apart. In those grim wastes, the mighty West Wind Drift thrust eastward, splitting in two to spawn the icy Benguela Current that pushed north up the west coast of Africa.

Brink leaned on the coaming wind deflector and recoiled when the heat from the sun-baked steel punched through the sleeves of his sweatshirt.

'Damned hot,' he muttered, following Kessler's gaze at the lifeboats and liferafts.

'I have to make decisions concerning those people, quartermaster. I don't want you to have to share in the making of those decisions. All I want from you are straight answers to straight questions without any moral considerations whatsoever. If you don't know the answers, say so.'

'Understood, Captain.'

'How much fresh water can we afford to give the survivors? The chief's got the condensers going flat out.'

'None,' Brink replied without hesitation.

Kessler turned and regarded him. The quartermaster's face was expressionless. 'How much food?'

'I don't know, Captain. I haven't had a chance to list what we got from the *Anaconda*. Poison Ivy and his detail went after fresh food and vegetables on Mr Maron's orders because the crew need them. Anything we give them would have to be from our tinned and dried stock.' He hesitated. 'And that was desperately low.'

'Clothing?'

'I've twenty sets of unissued overalls.'

'Lifejackets?'

'Ten spares.'

'Medical supplies?'

'We can let them have a dozen survival kits.'

Kessler nodded. 'We'd better check on them first; they might have more medical supplies than us. Torches?'

'None spare.'

Kessler was about to ask about spare compasses, but checked himself. What was the point? The tiny craft had neither sails or engines, and only the lifeboats had oars. After three or four days on meagre rations and little water, they'd be too exhausted to row, especially as they'd be towing the liferafts; the survivors would have to drift wherever the wind and current took them. If the current was stronger than the wind, it would carry them inexorably into the middle of the Atlantic Ocean. And if the wind triumphed over the current, it would still take them into the middle of the Atlantic, only .quicker. Impasse. A horrible mess all round. Roll on Tuesday.

'Thank you, quartermaster. Tell Mr Haug that I'd like to see him.' Kessler returned his attention to the lifeboats. He didn't need his binoculars; the nearest was within fifty metres. A woman was sitting amidships breast-feeding a baby. She seemed aware that she was been scrutinised for she suddenly looked up. For a few moments their gazes locked. The woman was dark-haired, nothing like his wife, and yet that look of reproachfulness as she nursed her child reminded him forcibly of Ingrid during his last leave. They both hated goodbyes. She hadn't even come to the door when the taxi had arrived; she had sat on the settee, feeding Lola, their latest daughter. She had looked up from her baby and he had frozen every detail of that moment in his mind as a mental photograph to recall during the long watches. It angered him that this woman feeding her baby in a lifeboat was superimposing her image over that treasured picture. A strange, uncharacteristic rage welled up. He was unable to tell if it was directed at the woman or the circumstances that had led to her wretchedness. The emotion was a volatile alliance of fear and anger whose sheer power disturbed him. He turned away from the coaming and came face to face with Haug who had risen silently through the hatch like a wraith. He was wearing shapeless U-boat fatigues, a size too large, giving him a slightly comic appearance.

'It's customary to ask permission before coming on the bridge, Mr Haug.'

The florid face and piercing blue eyes were fastened on him like a cat hypnotising a mouse. There was nothing comic about that gaze: it signalled danger. 'I did, Captain. The petty officer gave it.'

'What do you want?'

'You asked to see me.'

Annoyed at being caught off guard, Kessler gestured to Haug to follow him. The two men moved to the *wintergarten* deck out of earshot of the lookouts. Kessler dismissed the gunner and braced himself against the AA gun. 'You're recovered?' His tone matched Haug's for politeness. The man's half-smile, as though he were dealing with an idiot who had to be humoured, was particularly infuriating.

'Yes thank you, Captain.'

'Good. You're to return to your lifeboat.'

Not a muscle moved in Haug's face. The irritating smile was frozen. 'Your orders are to return me and Dieter Rohland –'

'The circumstances have changed, Mr Haug. Those orders no longer apply.'

'Oh? In what way have they changed? You have an intact boat. You have fuel.'

Kessler refused to be moved to anger by the man's patronising attitude. 'We've no radio and not enough fuel to return to base. It is possible that I may have to scuttle the boat. If I'm forced to do that, then I shall do it in a manner that safeguards my crew. Perhaps under the noses of the British. If it means my men becoming prisoners of war, then so be it. But you have no means of identification on you. And I don't suppose Rohland has either. As far as the British are concerned, you're spies. And that could jeopardise the prisoner of war status of my entire crew. Well I'm not going to take that risk.'

'We are both naval officers, Captain.'

'So?'

'Servicemen. Citizens of our fatherland.'

Kessler nodded to the liferafts. 'So are the crew of the *Atlantis* – what's left of them. So what? I didn't plan this débâcle, Mr Haug. The powers that be decided to send unsuitable boats to the South Atlantic without proper supply facilities. As a result we are as damn near stranded as the poor bastards on those rafts. The difference is that I intend to keep this as a fighting boat right up to the end. I can't do that with fifty-seven survivors on board. You've seen the conditions below, and I don't even have a full crew of forty-four men. twenty-five berths. Men coming off watch have to crawl into the berths of those going on watch. Food rotting everywhere

180

because the designers forgot that we have to eat so there's no proper storage. So there's a standing order, one of the more sensible ones: U-boats cannot take survivors on board. Sensible because it drives a wide, safe wedge between a skipper and any moral scruples he may have. If I allowed the *Atlantis*'s crew on board, then I'd have to consider letting those women and children on board too. And if I allow that, then any of the men left who become sick would also have to be allowed on board. So I'll stick to my standing orders. I don't like the situation, but I have no choice.'

Haug eyed the cluster of tiny craft. 'You're forgetting something, Captain. You are required to ensure that there are no survivors from the *Anaconda*.'

'An illegal order,' Kessler replied. 'Anyway, the circumstances have changed. Presumably that order was sicked up so that the British wouldn't find out that we were using a neutral ship as a depot ship. If they didn't know then, they certainly know now. Anyway, where are those orders now? I never had a chance to examine them properly. If there was an inquiry, I'd have to depend on your word that they existed. I'd rather not have to depend on you for anything, Mr Haug.'

If anything, Haug's bland half-smile broadened. 'You are questioning my word?'

Kessler suddenly turned, jerked the lock on the AA gun and spun the barrels with considerable force. Haug grabbed the firing yoke to prevent it hitting him in the chest.

'You want carry out those orders, Mr Haug? You go right ahead. Line up the open sights and pull those levers under the handgrips towards you. You shouldn't have any difficulty hitting the lifeboats at this range. A twenty-second burst should do it. Twenty-millimetre rounds – they'll tear everything apart.'

The theatrical gesture left Haug unmoved. He carefully repositioned the multiple barrels so that they were pointing at the sky. 'Very well, Captain. You refuse to take us. But if you recall, Dieter Rohland has some important geological samples. It is imperative that they reach home.'

Kessler was about to dismiss the suggestion out of hand but realised that it would be churlish. He shrugged. 'How imperative?'

'They are samples of quartz crystals that the British are mining in Brazil. The best quality ever found. We have documentary evidence that they are using such crystals to develop a new type of Asdic set that—'

'Asdic,' Kessler snorted. 'Useless in foul weather which is all you get in the North Atlantic. No one's frightened of Asdic anymore.'

'– a set that can detect a submarine in an area of ten thousand square miles.'

The figure astonished Kessler. 'That's not possible!' he exclaimed. He thought fast, seeing a faint glimmer of hope; a possible way around his dilemma.

'Nor was Asdic until the Allies invented it,' Haug replied evenly.

'I cannot believe for a moment that –'

'We captured nearly all the documents of the Allied Submarine Detection Investigation Committee when Paris fell,' Haug interrupted, keeping his voice mild. 'A year ago the British were developing a new Asdic set that will be able to sweep an area one hundred miles square. That's ten thousand square miles, Captain. Think about that figure. It means that the entire U-boat offensive will be neutralised, and the lives of hundreds of U-boat men put at risk.'

'As if they're not already,' Kessler muttered dismissively.

'Needless risk,' Haug emphasised. 'That's why Rohland's samples *must* reach Berlin for evaluation. We have to know if such an Asdic set is possible and what countermeasures we can develop.'

Kessler was silent for a few moments. 'Ten thousand square miles,' he muttered at length. He shook his head dis-believingly. 'It just doesn't seem possible.'

31

Mrs Montgomerie knew a smattering of German but she gave up trying to follow the accents of the seamen on the nearest liferaft. The shouted discourse between Dieter and the sailors lasted several minutes.

'They're the crew of the *Atlantis*,' Dieter reported.

Mrs Montgomerie thought she had read the name in the *Uruguay Post*. 'And what, pray, is the *Atlantis*?'

'A German merchant ship. It was sunk at night like we were.'

'And supplying a U-boat like we were, I don't doubt.' She stared at *U-395*. 'Just what are they planning on that submarine?' Her attention was drawn to Tammy, standing up to take advantage of the breeze having splashed seawater on her chest. 'Tammy – please keep yourself covered. Surely you've seen the way those oafs are ogling you? Anyone would think they'd never seen a woman before.'

Probably not too many like Tammy, thought Dieter.

'Keep yourself down, child!'

'But there's no breeze unless I stand, Miss Angela,' Tammy protested politely, plonking herself on a thwart. Sweat imparted a fine, erotic sheen to her face and shoulders.

'Don't argue with me, child. Wrap this around you.' She passed a heavy, homespun poncho to Tammy, who tossed it aside in disgust. The girl defiantly scooped up a bailer of seawater and poured it over her head, matting her black hair and plumping her nipples like over-ripe morello cherries beneath her clinging nightdress. It was a spectacle that Dieter found quite fascinating, especially the way in which the gleaming rivulets gathered below her collarbones and trickled out of sight between her breasts. The first time she had done it had earned her a scolding from Mrs Montgomerie. This time her guardian rolled her eyes to heaven and declared that the girl had no shame.

'She's hot,' Dieter reasoned. 'We all are.' He noticed that the U-boat was launching its inflatable dinghy. A rating started rowing towards the huddle of lifeboats and rafts. Its appearance caused a stir in the other boats. All faces were turned hopefully towards it. Sitting in the stern was an NCO.

'José,' said Mrs Montgomerie. 'We're too close to those rafts. Pull away, please.'

'But we are all tied together, Señora.'

'Then make the rope longer, you silly man – we've got plenty.'

The bosun muttered something under his breath, but did as he was told.

Mrs Montgomerie spied the dinghy rowing towards them. 'At last some news. They can't keep us in this sun like this.'

The U-boat NCO raised a megaphone to his lips. 'Dieter Rohland. Please identify yourself.'

It was a move Dieter had been expecting. He waved, stood, and slung the kitbag over his shoulder. The rating resumed rowing and pulled alongside Dieter's lifeboat.

'Herr Rohland?' The NCO wore the black-billed cap of a petty officer.

Dieter acknowledged and lifted one leg over the lifeboat's gunwale. The petty officer held up his hand. 'Just the goods that you have please, Mr Rohland.'

Dieter stared, momentarily at a loss. 'I don't understand.'

'You have some goods? Are they in that kitbag?'

'Well – yes.'

'My orders are to collect the bag from you.'

'But what about me? And all these people?' Dieter glanced around the boat. The survivors were watching intently although few of them could follow the conversation. The mother was breast-feeding her baby; Mrs Montgomerie's expression was icy contempt.

'Just the goods, Mr Rohland. Those are my orders.'

Suddenly Dieter understood. 'You're going to leave us?'

'The commander has ordered me to collect the goods you have which I have been told are government property.'

184

The months that Dieter had spent living by his wits had done much to undermine his automatic obedience of orders. Also he had learned to think fast. Right now he was thinking very fast indeed although it didn't require any great flights of reason to realise that Haug was behind this.

'Tell the captain that I would like to speak to him, please.'

The NCO's tone became threatening. 'That won't be possible.'

'Then the kitbag stays with me. It weighs five kilos.' Dieter grinned. 'It will sink like a rock because that's exactly what it's filled with. Tell that to the captain.'

The two men tried to outstare each other. Dieter allowed the kitbag strap to half-slip off his shoulder. Eventually the petty officer gave a curt order and the dinghy pulled away.

'They're going to leave us, aren't they,' said Mrs Montgomerie. It was a statement rather than a question.

'I don't think so,' said Dieter evenly, watching the dinghy heading back to *U-395*. He could see Kessler on the bridge, and Haug's unmistakable rotund figure. Although they were too far away to see clearly, he knew that the binoculars the men were holding were trained on him.

'So you *are* a German,' said Mrs Montgomerie contemptuously.

'I don't think my nationality matters,' Dieter replied equably. He lapsed into English. 'You have a saying in your language, "we are all in the same boat" – yes?'

Mrs Montgomerie's expression of loathing gradually faded as she stared at Dieter. The hard lines around her mouth softened into a smile. And then, to the surprise of everyone including Dieter, she threw back her head and burst out laughing.

32

'I don't think he was bluffing, Captain,' the petty officer concluded. 'The kitbag looked heavy, the way it hung. If he had dropped it, I wasn't close enough to grab it. He said it was filled with rocks.' The NCO looked speculatively at his commanding officer and Haug in turn, hoping that he would be told what was in the kitbag. Kessler thanked him; the NCO left the bridge looking disappointed.

'That damned Englishwoman put him up to it,' said Haug grimly. 'Rohland is not the type to disobey orders.'

Kessler raised his binoculars and studied Dieter. 'That damned Englishwoman saved your life, Mr Haug. She was the one who spotted you in the water, *and* she took her lifeboat into the middle of the fire when the *Anaconda* was burning in order to fish you out.'

'She put Dieter up to this,' Haug persisted. 'Such behaviour is not like him. He has always obeyed orders.'

Kessler glanced sideways at Haug and admired his acting. The little man was outwardly calm but Kessler could sense the turmoil that was seething within him. He stamped on the bridge deck plate. 'Helmsman! Pass the word for Pols.'

The telegraphist emerged onto the bridge a minute later, clutching his Leica in the hope that some exotic sea creature had been spotted.

'Nothing for you this time, Pols,' said Kessler affably. 'I want to pick your brains. What's the greatest distance whales and dolphins can communicate with that infernal racket they kick up?'

The question didn't surprise Pols. Bridge watches often relieved the monotony by holding quizzes. 'I don't think the exact distance is known, Captain. I've got all the Woods Hole bulletins if you'd like me to go through them.'

'Woods Hole?'

'Woods Hole, Cape Cod, Massachusetts. The Marine Biological Laboratory. I think I know the exact bulletin to look up.'

'Please do so, Pols.'

The telegraphist went below and was back five minutes later with a copy of the *Biological Bulletin*. 'Fifty miles, Captain.'

'Fifty miles!' Kessler echoed in astonishment.

'Sperm whales,' said Pols. 'Unconfirmed, but Norwegian whaling fleets have reported on sperm whales responding to distress calls over that distance.'

'How the hell do they do it?'

Haug broke in. 'They have a huge reservoir of oil in their heads. It acts as the sound lens, and the bony material of their skull acts as a reflector so that they can direct the sound in any direction by turning their body. It also works in reverse – for listening. Just like the British Asdic and our hydrophones.'

'Thank you, Pols,' said Kessler.

When Pols had gone, Haug said: 'A radius of fifty miles is an area of 8000 square miles. If whales can do it, then the British aren't far behind.'

'I had worked that out,' Kessler replied.

Haug nodded to Dieter who was sitting on the aft thwart of his lifeboat, watching *U-395* intently, resting the kitbag on the gunwale. 'So what are you planning to do about him?'

Kessler's reply was to call down a string of orders. Haug blinked as the diesels closed down and the electric motors cut in.

Kessler tipped his cap back at a rakish angle. 'He wants to see me, so we'll go and see him. Might as well do it in comfort. I loathe rubber boats. When I was a cadet I had the job of rowing victuals out to the *Gorch Fock* when we dropped anchor at Lisbon. My first command. A rubber boat. Flipped over she did, like a bloody tiddlywink. Lost my supplies and damned near drowned. Four cases of brandy. Thought the skipper was going to have me keelhauled. So, I have a deep-rooted aversion to rubber boats.'

33

Dieter watched *U-395*'s approach with deep misgivings. A court martial would be awaiting him now whatever the outcome of his bravura. But he had only to look at the women and children sharing the lifeboat to harden his resolve. The motors went hard astern, bringing the conning tower within a few metres of the lifeboat. Two ratings on the casing offered boathooks which Dieter told José to ignore.

'Mr Rohland!'

Dieter waved an acknowledgment at Kessler. 'I hear you, Captain.'

'Come aboard please, Mr Rohland. We need to talk.'

'I'm not doing anything without an undertaking from you that you won't abandon these people.'

'Let's talk about it first.'

'There's nothing to talk about, Captain.'

'I give you my word that no harm will come to you and that you will be free to return when we've talked. You can leave your kitbag behind. No one will try to touch it.'

Dieter's initial reaction was to dismiss the offer out of hand. He had survived by trusting no one, but he realised that he would have to talk to Kessler if a way out of the present mess was to be found. It was obvious that Haug had impressed on Kessler the importance to the Kriegsmarine of the crystals.

He picked up the kitbag and looked down at Tammy. 'Tammy, listen carefully to me.'

'Yes, Mr Rohland.'

'You must call me Dieter. I'm going on that U-boat. I want you to balance this bag on the edge of the boat and drop it over the side if anyone tries to take it from you.'

'You will not involve Tammy in your devious schemes,' Mrs Montgomerie snapped.

Dieter ignored her and slipped Tammy's hand through the strap. 'Do you understand, Tammy?'

The girl looked worried but she nodded and smiled.

'Good.' Dieter straightened and addressed everyone in the boat. 'I give you all my word that I will return.' He signalled to José. The bosun grabbed a boathook and drew the lifeboat against the U-boat's bow. 'Stay a good fifty metres away until I return, José.'

'*Claro*,' the seaman confirmed.

Dieter followed one of the ratings down to the cramped wardroom, where Kessler outlined the problems. Haug sat opposite Dieter, watching him intently.

'So that's the situation,' Kessler concluded. 'If anything, we're as stranded as those lifeboats and rafts.'

'Not quite,' said Dieter. 'You have a boat, two engines, and fuel.' He glanced up at the cans of apple juice hanging in nets that were lashed to the maze of pipework. 'And food. You have some measure of control while those poor creatures have no control whatsoever.'

'Our fuel and engines will take us farther and quicker into the mid-Atlantic than the wind and currents will take the lifeboats,' said Haug icily. 'As Captain Kessler has explained, there is a faint chance of us encountering a ship, therefore you have a clear duty to hand over that bag.'

'And what are your duties, Captain?' Dieter asked. 'What about the liferafts? They're all our men.'

'Out here nationality doesn't matter,' said Kessler flatly. 'All that matters is the safety of this boat and its crew.'

'Those crystals are an overriding factor, of course,' said Haug. 'They don't need food and water.'

'They stay in the lifeboat.'

Haug sat back. His cherubic face broke into a beaming smile. 'One has to admire your moral fortitude, Dieter. Under any other circumstances, it would be most commendable.' The smile faded a little. 'But I don't have to remind you of the importance of those samples to our entire war effort.'

189

'No,' said Dieter, 'you don't. They stay in the lifeboat.'

An electrician passed through the wardroom. Dieter was surprised that he did so without asking permission but realised that the free passing to and fro of crewmen without formality was essential for the efficient running of the boat. He turned his attention to Kessler who appeared to be wrestling with a dilemma. 'That's my position, Captain, and I'm not budging.'

'Very well,' said the U-boat captain with finality. 'We will take your lifeboat in tow. I don't suppose the drag of one lifeboat will make that much difference to our fuel consumption.' He looked steadily at Dieter and decided to force the issue. 'You already have all the women and children in your lifeboat. It's a large boat so you should have room for men in poor condition from the other craft.'

'What are you saying?'

'I'm saying that you win, Mr Rohland. We'll provision the other boats with what we can afford, and we'll take your lifeboat in tow.'

'You'll take *all* of them in tow,' said Dieter flatly.

Kessler's raising of his eyebrows gave no indication of the elation he experienced. 'That won't be possible,' he said, hoping that he sounded convincing. 'The lifeboats are okay, but we wouldn't be able to make much better than three knots towing the rafts as well. A hopelessly inefficient speed. We'd burn too much fuel.'

'All of them,' said Dieter stubbornly. 'No one is to be abandoned.'

'Uruguayans and British don't count,' Haug commented.

'The captain has just pointed out that it is nationality that doesn't count out here,' Dieter countered.

'Your behaviour will count against you when we get home,' said Haug calmly, polishing his glasses.

'Very well,' said Kessler abruptly. 'We have no choice but to take all six craft in tow.'

Dieter met Kessler's gaze and had an uncomfortable feeling

that he was being manipulated. 'You've made the right decision, Captain.' He left the wardroom.

Kessler grunted. 'One that's been forced on me.'

'I'm surprised that you went along with Rohland with such ease,' Haug observed.

'Did I have any choice?'

Haug considered. 'Perhaps not.'

'There's no perhaps about it, Mr Haug.' Kessler heaved himself to his feet. 'If those crystals are as important as you claim, then Rohland is holding all the aces. I want a written outline from you of their importance. Everything you told me. I want it in your handwriting and signed.'

'The matter is of the utmost secrecy.'

'It'll go with my papers in the weighted bag,' Kessler replied, refusing to be outstared by those piercing eyes.

'Guarding your arse, Captain?'

'Exactly,' said Kessler. 'I'm going to get this boat home somehow. When I do, there's going to be a lot of head-rolling over all this. I intend that mine will not be among them. So start writing. Consider that an order.' With that he entered the control room and began working out the details of the tow with Reche.

34

Dieter returned to the lifeboat to discover that Mrs Montgomerie had instigated her segregation scheme; José and the other men were sitting disconsolately in the bow, separated from the women by a makeshift screen of heavy canvas from the lifeboat's storm cover lashed to the oars. The men had been assigned less than a third of the boat's length.

'I tell her that it won't last if the wind gets up but she doesn't listen,' the big Spaniard grumbled. He hawked, spat over the side, and jabbed a huge thumb at the nearest liferaft. 'They look bad.'

Dieter had been too preoccupied to pay much attention to the other survivors. The raft nearest their boat was the least crowded, about fourteen men, but their condition was wretched. They were huddled under a tattered awning that was badly ripped, offering scant protection from the sun. Two of the men were lying on their sides, not moving. The others were staring blankly about, their gaunt faces red with sunburn, giving them a deceptive cheery look. It was the listless expression in their eyes that told the truth.

'Those two haven't moved for a couple of hours,' said José. 'Been watching them.'

'They've been on that raft over a week,' said Dieter.

'So we'll be like that in a week?'

Dieter pushed through the canvas screen into the women's section. The mother who had been breast-feeding her baby watched him with large, solemn eyes. Young Marco eyed him anxiously as though he knew that the German held the key to his survival. The voluptuous young woman with dark, close-cropped hair, shapely legs and wearing nothing but an immodest chemise was a surprise to Dieter. She was teaching Tammy the rudiments of blackjack. At first he thought that she had been transferred from one of the other boats but when she turned her head and looked questioningly at him he realised that she was the novitiate, Pepita, sans wimple and habit but no longer sans her pack of cards. Mrs Montgomerie and two other women were busy cutting up her gown.

'In future you will ask permission before entering this section,' said Mrs Montgomerie sternly. She espied something that she found particularly offensive. 'Tammy! You wanton young hussy! Cover yourself!'

Like a mischievous plump puppy making a bid for freedom, Tammy's left breast had escaped as she lolled on one elbow. The girl hid her face from her lynx-eyed guardian and gave Dieter a smile that was as conspiratorial as it was sultry. She deftly corralled the errant mammary back under her nightdress. Pepita's attempt to pretend that Dieter wasn't there was undermined by her self-consciously drawing her knees protectively to her chin, momentarily forgetting that glimpses of breasts weren't the only prizes that men sought. She realised her mistake and tried with little success to tuck the skimpy chemise more securely between her bare thighs. Dieter had always considered it unlikely that he would ever lust after nuns but he was young enough to be adaptable. He had often wondered what they wore under their habits. In subtropical climes, it seemed, not much.

'They're taking us in tow,' said Dieter, sitting on a thwart and watching Pepita as she shuffled the cards with a consummate skill that seemed unbecoming of a nun, or even a would-be nun.

Mrs Montgomerie regarded Dieter quizzically. She didn't know how to treat him and was loath to admit to herself that she was learning to trust him. 'Just this boat?'

'All of them,' Dieter replied. He took the kitbag from Tammy and thanked her. She flushed with embarrassment and looked pleased with herself even though she had just drawn to thirteen after a four-card run.

'What about food and water?' Mrs Montgomerie asked.

'They'll work that out tonight. Right now the captain wants to get out of the area as quickly as possible.'

'I want all the men transferred to other boats.'

'It'll have to wait.'

At that moment the U-boat's inflatable, crewed by Brink and a rating, pulled alongside the lifeboat. Tammy jumped up and tried to grab the line that the rating tossed to her. Normally he was skilled at throwing lines but Tammy's jiggling wares ruined his aim. Brink managed to direct his gaze to Dieter.

'We're going to tow you line-astern. This boat will be first in the chain.'

'Wouldn't it be safer to have a line for each boat?' Dieter asked.

'We don't want to waste time cutting lines if we have to

crash-dive,' Brink replied stiffly, wishing that the girl would stop watching him. 'Also there's less risk of the propellers being fouled with only one line. We'll alternate the chain: a lifeboat then a liferaft. The rafts aren't so handy under tow so the lifeboats will have to keep a watch on them. Each boat is to show a white pennant if anything goes wrong. A handkerchief will do.' He handed Dieter a flashlight. 'And this is for night-time. Two flashes. If you see flashes from the other boats, you're to repeat them in case our lookouts are unsighted by the swell. You'll have to work out a twenty-four-hour watch. Under no circumstances must any other light be shown at night.'

'What is he saying?' Mrs Montgomerie demanded.

Dieter quickly translated the gist of Brink's instructions.

'And that will have to be taken down,' said Brink, gesturing at the screen.

Mrs Montgomerie didn't need a translation for that. 'No!' she said resolutely.

Nor did Brink need a translation for her reply. He glowered. 'It's too conspicuous and it will be a problem if the wind gets up. It must come down.'

'But we need to be conspicuous, you silly man!'

'It will have to come down, Mrs Montgomerie,' Dieter advised.

'Certainly not.'

'Also it's your storm cover,' said Brink. 'It should be kept properly stowed in case it's needed in a hurry – not treated like that.'

Dieter translated. For a moment it looked as though Mrs Montgomerie was going to launch into a tirade, but she realised that co-operation would have to be the watchword for the time being. 'Very well,' she relented. 'But I shall expect *all* the men to be transferred off this boat at the earliest opportunity. Bosun! You're to take this down, please.'

José grunted indifferently and dismantled the screen while the dinghy pulled around to the lifeboat's stern. Dieter climbed over his fellow passengers to talk to Brink.

194

'The men on that liferaft are in a bad way.'

Brink inspected the lifeboat's tiller pintle and attached a line to it. 'Be even worse if we left them.' He tested the security of the fixing by yanking on it.

'The two lying down haven't moved for some time,' Dieter persisted.

Brink glanced over his shoulder. 'Okay, I'll tell the captain, but I can guess what his answer will be.' He gave an order to the rating and the dinghy pulled away towards the first liferaft. After a brief remonstration with the officer in charge which Dieter couldn't hear clearly, he and the rating busied themselves for ten minutes, rowing to all the bobbing craft in turn, replacing all the tethers with fifteen-metre lengths of substantial rope. The main towline was then taken from Lifeboat 1's bow cleat to *U-395*'s conning tower. Hanks of hemp were tied around the line where there was any danger of chafing. Kessler's white cap appeared on the bridge among the lookouts quartering the horizon. He was holding the loudhailer.

'Any problems, quartermaster?' Kessler asked when Brink returned.

'None, Captain.' Brink hesitated. 'There's two *Atlantis* stokers on the first liferaft suffering from sunburn.'

'How bad?'

'They'll be okay provided they don't dehydrate. I've said we'd allow them extra water.' He correctly guessed that that was the sort of answer Kessler wanted.

'Only absolute emergencies allowed on board.'

'That's what I told them. I've got some lotion which will help.'

'Mr Maron is awake,' said Kessler dolefully

'Oh.'

'Leutnant Reche is explaining the situation to him. Our oberleutnant is not a happy man. He's spent the last hour watching little pink things with many legs crawling all over him. He doesn't seem to like little pink things with many legs

195

crawling all over him. In fact, he said he'd rather put up with the pain than have to watch them. I suggested that he hits them with his clipboard but he wasn't amused. He suspects that he was given too much morphine. A scandalous notion. Two cc wasn't it?'

'Twenty, Captain. Diluted . . . I think.'

'Well I've put two in the log. You'd better put the same in your log. He'll check them. You'd better go below and reassure him. Can't have our first watch officer nursing such suspicions.' Kessler raised the loudhailer to his lips. 'Attention! Attention!'

The faces in the lifeboats and liferafts turned to the U-boat. 'We're going to start towing now,' Kessler announced. 'We'll tow for thirty minutes at two knots and then stop to see if there are any problems. Have you all got pennants? Show them please.'

An assortment of white flags were waved from the six craft.

'Keep them out of sight and wave them hard if you have any problems,' Kessler's voiced boomed. 'The others do the same if you see a flag being waved. Two flashes at night with the torches and no other lights to be shown. Do you all understand?'

Dieter translated quickly for the benefit of his lifeboat.

Kessler inspected the quick-release shackle that Brink had attached to the conning tower's wind deflector. He ran his eye along the towrope that lay coiled on the after casing. Two ratings were tying cork floats to it at intervals to minimise the risk of it fouling the screws. Brink's idea probably. It pleased Kessler that he didn't have to think of everything. Doubtless there were many other things he had overlooked – the sort of things an ever-vigilant executive officer like Maron would not forget.

'All ready, Captain,' one of the ratings reported.

'Very good. Stand clear. Helmsman! Course zero-three-zero. Slow ahead on the port diesel.'

The engine room telegraph buzzer sounded from the depths

196

of the boat. Black exhaust smoke vented from the ballast tanks and quickly cleared as the engine settled down to a steady beat. There was the familiar metallic clunk of clutches latching home. Kessler's hands gripping the coaming felt the familiar tremble as the screws bit on the water. *U-395*'s bow went about, bringing the boat onto a north-easterly heading.

He glanced up at the late afternoon sky. A flawless bowl of azure apart from a fine lacework of cirro-cumulus low down on the western horizon where Venus had already put in an appearance. Without radio and weather reports, he drew on his experience and a rock-steady barometer to surmise that the present spell of fair weather would hold for at least another twenty-four hours. He raised his binoculars and watched the towline uncoiling. The floats plopped into the water one by one like synchronised dancers in a Busby Berkeley musical routine and then snapped into the air when the line went taut. The towline to Lifeboat 1 was a good seventy metres long so that its weight would act as a shock absorber. Brink was a first class seaman, Kessler reflected. Like him, the quartermaster had started his maritime career under sail. Not many of us left now, he thought.

The towline pulled Lifeboat 1's bow gently around. And then, one by one, the other craft fell into an obedient line. A blur of pinched, anxious faces, all staring his way. 103 men, women and children who had already been through hell and whose lives now depended on him. Nearly 150 souls including his crew. They would all have relatives, loved ones, close friends. Maybe as many 1000 lives entwined in the fortunes of this hapless gathering of humanity in the lonely wastes of the South Atlantic.

And so it was that under a hot December sun in 1941, a tiny, fragile armada set course for France, a quarter of the way around the world, on what would become, in terms of distance, the longest rescue operation in maritime history.

Part Two

35

Tammy was on stern watch when the towline that disappeared into the darkness to the first liferaft suddenly started snaking and jerking on the rudder pintle.

'Stop! Stop!' she yelled, and groped for the torch. She found it and flashed it frantically. A beam of light stabbed out from the U-boat, momentarily blinding her. Shapes around her were throwing back their covers. The baby started screaming. Dieter was on his feet beside her. The U-boat's searchlight probed back and forth and settled on the capsized liferaft and the men struggling in the water. He ripped off his jacket, dived into the sea and struck out. Tammy tore at the unfamiliar buttons on the U-boat overalls she was wearing and plunged half-naked into the sea, not noticing the shock of the cold water closing around her. She was a good swimmer and covered the fifty metres just as Dieter reached the first man. All the men were wearing life preservers so the disaster wasn't as serious as it could have been, but righting the overturned raft proved difficult in the steep swell until José and the greasers swam to their aid. They followed the big seaman's yelled instructions and struggled to use the swell to help right the heavy liferaft. Eventually it tumbled over with a loud splash. The other lifeboats and liferafts merely added to the confusion as they lost way and drifted into the pool of light from the searchlight. At one point the second lifeboat came close to capsizing as willing hands reached out to pull survivors aboard. *U-395*'s electrics whined as she went about, the screws churning the water to foam to keep the sterngear away from those in the water. The powerful bridge light played on the strange scene, particularly on Tammy, kneeling on the raft, helping to beach already exhausted men by grabbing their waistbands and half hauling, half rolling them to safety.

'We should be towed diagonally, using corners as bow and stern. That way there will less water resistance,' a voice called out in German from one of the other liferafts.

'We'll retie the towlines,' the lookout petty officer answered from the bridge.

The man Dieter manoeuvred back to the righted liferaft appeared to have fainted until Tammy had grabbed his arm. He uttered a loud scream of agony and spluttered something in German.

'Badly sunburnt,' Dieter gasped, remembering to speak in Spanish. 'Be careful.' He suddenly realised that the swimmer beside him, helping him shove the seaman onto the raft was Pepita.

'Another man out there!' the girl cried. She turned and arrowed towards the darkness, the searchlight playing on her strong arms shouldering the water as she made off in a fast Australian crawl. She returned towing the other sunburn victim by his hair. He was the only man not wearing a life preserver. Dieter was about to berate him when he saw the mass of blisters across his emaciated shoulders and realised that anything coming into contact with his skin would cause him intense agony.

'Please! I'm better in the water,' the man managed to blurt out.

'Not when we're under way,' said Dieter, easing the wretch onto the raft.

The searchlight snapped to Mrs Montgomerie who was waving the torch about.

'Mrs Montgomerie!' Reche's voice boomed from the bridge. 'Please do not waste the batteries in that torch!'

'Where's Tammy?'

'Here, Miss Angela.' Tammy stood up on the raft. Bathed in

the harsh white light from *U-395*, and with her underwear clinging to her like a transparent second skin, her appearance did much to boost the spirits of the men who had been dumped into the water, as did Pepita when she too scrambled onto the raft and stood up. They looked like the sirens of mythology, intent on luring sailors onto the rocks. The sister-in-charge let out an anguished wail and unleashed a tirade of rapid Spanish.

'You children will return this instant! Do you hear me?' Mrs Montgomerie shouted.

Children! thought Dieter. 'You'd better get back,' he advised the girls. 'José and I will finish here.'

One of the greasers scooped up Tammy and swam back to the lifeboat with her sitting astride his shoulders, shrieking with laughter and yanking on his hair to steer him. Not to be outdone, the second greaser did likewise with Pepita, preferring to tow her back to the lifeboat. She laughingly wriggled ineffectually in the grasp of a brawny arm that encircled her waist while trying to unprise the huge fingers that had closed around her breast like a feeding starfish. Both girls were elevated into the lifeboat by the simple expedient of hands placed under buttocks, inquisitive thumbs having rendered them both hysterical. The circle of heaving swells lit from the U-boat gave the scene a curious circus-like surrealism. It was, Dieter reflected, as bizarre a spectacle as he was ever likely to see.

An inspection of the liferaft showed that its instability was due to a flooded floatation compartment.

'Shell splinter right through the outer chamber,' declared the petty officer from *U-395* who examined the damage. It was decided to abandon the raft. Its food and supplies were unloaded and distributed among the remaining craft, together with its passengers. Much to Dieter's surprise, when Mrs Montgomerie saw the state of the two sunburn victims, she insisted that they were added to her complement for treatment. She and the sister in charge of the nuns carefully applied calamine lotion to the men's blisters while the damaged raft was cut free and the towline shortened. Dieter returned to his lifeboat and experienced a moment of panic when he realised that he had forgotten all about his kitbag and its precious samples. But it was still in its home, jammed under a thwart. In the confusion everyone else had forgotten about it as well.

The convoy resumed its snail's pace journey one hour after the mishap.

36

Kessler's hunch about the weather holding was correct. By mid-morning the sun was burning down with such unremitting ferocity from a cloudless sky that the off-watch crew had to wear rope-soled shoes before they could set foot on the burning deck casing, and wet patches from the spray when U-395 buried her bow in a steep swell shrank away to nothing in seconds. Conditions were so bad in the boat due to the low speed that Kessler decreed that all those off-watch could come on deck. The normal procedure was to allow only a few men on deck at a time in case the boat had to crash-dive. Conditions were a little better in the lifeboats and liferafts; at least their occupants had awnings and could douse themselves with sea water.

Kessler focused his binoculars on the odd spectacle of an *Anaconda* seaman in the first lifeboat pouring a bailer of water over a nun who had removed her wimple for the occasion. A thought occurred and he summoned the control-room hand from below to take a humidity reading. The hand whirred the hygrometer above his head like a football fan's rattle and reported:

'Relative humidity ninety-five per cent, Captain.'

Kessler grunted his thanks. 'Nice and high. Excellent. Excellent. I guessed as much from the haze.' He saw the puzzled expression of the lookout petty officer even though the man had not taken his eyes off the sector of horizon he was quartering. 'The higher the humidity, the lower the rate of the body's dehydration,' Kessler informed him. 'We dropped anchor once at Jeddah and took a trip into the desert. Zero humidity would you believe. Zero! The sweat evaporated off your skin so fast that you felt chilly. You had to drink a litre of water an hour to stop yourself wasting away. So long as the horizon's hazy, we're okay. But, with the miserable trickle of freshwater we're making at this speed, clear horizons means low humidity which means trouble.' He flipped the voice pipe open. 'Would someone like to suggest to Mr Maron that a breath of sea air will do him good?'

Maron climbed clumsily onto the bridge a few minutes later. As expected, he made no concessions to the conditions; everyone was in shorts but not Oberleutnant Hans Maron. He was wearing his uniform trousers, and his injured arm was tucked out of sight under his tunic in a wrist sling. Hair neatly brushed, beard trimmed.

'Good morning, Oberleutnant,' said Kessler breezily. 'How's the shoulder?'

'Fine, thank you, Captain.' As always, Maron's manner was correct but his expression was decidedly frosty. Especially when he saw the men lolling about on the casing in various states of undress. A stoker was mincing up and down the forward casing, hand on hip and twirling a multi-hued parasol amid a chorus of cheers and wolf-whistles from his comrades. Even Haug, who was sitting in the shade of the main gun and reading a book loaned by Brink, seemed to enjoy the joke. Handel was giving a demonstration of his swimming talents by employing a fast butterfly breast stroke to keep up with the boat. Maron's disapproving eye rested on the chain of lifeboats and liferafts following in *U-395*'s wake like moorhen chicks trying to keep up with their mother. His expression became even more disapproving but he said nothing.

'Damnably hot,' Kessler muttered.

'You sent for me, Captain?'

'Thought you ought to get some air, Oberleutnant.'

'Thank you for your consideration. But by staying below I was observing regulations.'

'Regulations?'

'Only able-bodied men are allowed on the bridge or on deck. A few at a time. A sensible regulation should we have to drop into the cellar in a hurry.'

I'd take great pleasure in kicking you down the hatch if an aircraft showed up, thought Kessler. 'Ah, yes,' he said easily, determined not to let Maron's attitude ruin his good mood. 'Regulations. They can conflict at times. A skipper has to keep the morale of his crew high. Damned if I could do that keeping them all cooped up below in this heat.'

Maron maintained a brooding silence. Might as well have it out now, thought Kessler. He beckoned Maron onto the *wintergarten* deck, out of earshot of the lookouts. 'I know what's on your mind, Hans. Go ahead and speak freely. Get it off your chest.'

Maron steadied himself by grasping the towline that sloped down level with his shoulder. He glanced at the quick-release shackle that anchored it to the coaming. 'This entire business is a ridiculous charade, Captain. And you know it is. Not only is it seriously jeopardising the safety of the boat, but we have little hope of getting these people to safety, and certainly no duty to do so.'

Kessler chose his words with care; he wanted to lead Maron into revealing what he knew, or suspected. 'I believe Haug has briefed you on the situation regarding the crystal samples?'

'Yes, Captain,' said Maron politely, reverting to his model of correctness. 'I understand that he's given you a written statement to that effect.'

We have been busy, haven't we?

'And that the British may be using such crystals to develop a new Asdic set that can sweep an area one hundred miles square?'

'That's what Haug believes,' said Maron cautiously. 'That's an area of ten thousand square miles. It seems highly unlikely.'

'The British are both clever and desperate,' said Kessler. 'A lethal combination.' His manner became confiding. 'Actually I share your reservations, Hans. But Pols tells me that porpoises and dolphins can communicate over huge distances with their infernal squawks and whistles . . . So maybe . . .' He spread his hands. 'Therefore it is my intention to get those rocks home. As matters stand, Dieter Rohland is threatening to dump them over the side unless we do something about the survivors. Not a situation I'm happy with, but one I have to accept.'

'I was told that you accepted the situation with some alacrity,' Maron replied. There was not a hint of reproach in his tone; merely a statement of fact.

Ah, thought Kessler. Gottcha. Now to involve you. But careful . . . Careful . . . He cleared his throat. 'I had to, Hans. Rohland was on the point of sending the damned bag of rocks on a four-mile trip to the ocean floor.'

Maron turned his head and stared at the first lifeboat. 'Rohland is the tall one?' His right hand maintained its grip on the towline.

'That's him. Slippery as an eel.'

'It will be interesting to see how slippery he is in front of a firing squad.'

'Waste of bullets on scum like that,' Kessler growled, wondering if he sounded too out of character for Maron to swallow.

'So I take it that your first priority is to overpower Rohland and grab the crystals?'

'I suppose that has to be our first priority,' Kessler agreed promptly, although he was not ready for the question.

Maron returned Kessler's bland smile. 'And return this boat to normal duties?'

'Of course. I need your help, Hans. Not just your help in accordance with your duties, I wouldn't insult you by asking for that because no skipper could have a better executive officer. But over and above the call of duty. I need proper supply rotas to be drawn up instead of answering the needs of the lifeboats when they yell for help. Proper water-rationing schedules. Meal rotas. See that those children get milk. New watches drawn up. A hundred and one things. I've been standing double watches and I'm dead on my feet.' He paused, knowing full well that he was throwing the sort of problems at Maron that the younger officer relished and excelled at dealing with. Well, there was no harm in adding a little bribery to the ingredients. 'I shall of course be recommending you for a Knight's Cross – the way you took command of the boat, evaded an attack, and stayed at your post until you fainted from loss of blood. That's got to be worth a *Ritterkreuz*. A good start for your new command.'

There. That's put a torpedo in any plans you were harbouring to complain about Brandt taking over command.

Maron was silent for a moment, which led Kessler to suspect that the bribe had found its target. The oberleutnant was due to receive his own command but needed a commendation from his senior officer. Kessler could hardly recommend a gong and not a new command. Maron turned and met Kessler's eye. 'With respect, Captain. Such matters are academic if we cannot get home. We don't have enough fuel and we're hardly producing enough water for our own needs, let alone for the survivors. I've been looking at the figures. In twelve days our fuel and fresh water situation will be desperate. Would you agree?'

'Yes,' said Kessler, wondering what this was leading up to.

'Very well. I will be pleased to draw up the necessary schedules and rotas. The more regular contact there is between us and the lifeboats, the greater the chances of an opportunity arising to grab the crystals. Is that what you have in mind?'

'Exactly,' said Kessler, scenting a trap.

'What I suggest,' said Maron slowly, running his hand along the towline to the quick-release shackle, 'is that if there's no change in our circumstances in ten days – on December 17th – that we implement our standing orders and release this towline. Do you agree with that, Captain?' There was an amused light in Maron's grey eyes.

'Agreed,' said Kessler promptly, as though it was something he had had in mind all along. Inwardly he was cursing; the last thing he had wanted was to get manoeuvred into making deals with his first watch officer.

'At noon?'

'If it has to be at any time, it might as well be then,' said Kessler in bad grace. God – how he wanted to plant a fist right in the middle of Maron's smug face.

'And in the meantime, thought must be given to a method of grabbing the crystals.'

'We must give it a lot of thought,' Kessler agreed.

'And prompt action when appropriate.'

'Of course.'

Maron saluted and gave that infuriating half-smile that made Kessler want to hit him there and then. 'Ten days. Thank you, Captain. I will start work immediately.'

He turned and clambered awkwardly down the hatch leaving Kessler wondering who had manipulated whom.

36

'That's near enough,' Dieter warned the two men in the inflatable dinghy. Brink stopped rowing and eyed the business end of the boathook that Dieter was pointing at him like a pikeman. He hauled on an oar and swung the dinghy out of reach of the menacing boathook. His passenger was Maron, his left arm in a wrist sling and his clipboard strapped to his thigh. U-395 was lying stopped under the burning sun, the liferafts and lifeboats rolling languidly in the long swell.

'Why have we stopped?' Mrs Montgomerie demanded imperiously. Three days in the lifeboat had done nothing to make her change her ways. Deprivations were not something to be borne with fortitude; they were to be met head-on, wrestled to the ground, and overcome by the sheer brute force of her personality and iron will. She had used the time to revive dubious, long-forgotten, and certainly best-forgotten, skills with a needle and thread to make herself a passable, loose-stitched, high-necked dress from deckchair cotton duck that fitted where it touched. The other women had reduced their apparel to the minimum essential to preserve modesty. Even the nuns had fashioned their voluminous habits into garments that bore a fearsome resemblance to shorts. Had Mrs Montgomerie the skills to make a parasol, she would have done so. She would even have knitted a butler.

'Soup,' said Maron, indicating the dinghy's cargo of several five-litre Kriegsmarine-issue aluminium canteens. Brink held one up by its wire handle. 'Those men that were taken off Liferaft 2 yesterday were cooks from the *Atlantis*. We now have a proper galley rota. In future meals will be served up at regular times.' He smiled. 'Sorry it is only soup. We have to use up our vegetables. But you will find it nourishing. Also Mr Brink would like to look at your sunburn patients.'

'They should be transferred to your submarine,' Mrs Montgomerie declared when Dieter translated.

'That won't be possible,' said Maron smoothly. 'We must maintain *U-395* as a fighting boat. Now, surely you're going to agree to let Mr Brink examine those men?'

Brink stood up, his experienced sea legs flexing rhythmically to maintain his balance in the even swell. Dieter moved to the forrard thwart so that the kitbag was at his feet. He gestured with the boathook. 'Very well.' The sister caught the painter that Maron tossed to her.

Brink timed the swell and jumped aboard the lifeboat. He moved midships where the women had rigged up a cover over the sick men. Their condition was much improved; liberal treatment with calamine had dried the worst of their blisters and new skin was showing through. He used a mixture of sign language and a smattering of Spanish to tell the women that they were doing well.

Dieter eyed Maron suspiciously while this was going on. 'Who are you?' he demanded.

'Oberleutnant Hans Maron. First Watch Officer. You must be Dieter Rohland.'

'Does it need a watch officer to deliver food?'

Maron ignored the question. 'What is that?' he inquired. He indicated a complex, crudely-stitched tent-like screen on the side of the lifeboat that had been made from surplus material cut from the nuns' habits.

'That,' said Dieter solemnly, 'is our toilet. Mrs Montgomerie designed it.'

'Ingenious,' Maron commented. He kept his grey eyes dispassionately on Dieter while Brink finished his examination and stepped back into the dinghy. 'Also I need to know how much drinking water you have.'

'We've just started on our last ten-litre canteen,' said Mrs Montgomerie in answer to Dieter's query. 'We've been giving extra to the patients.'

Maron made a note on his clipboard. 'Even so, that is very good. You have been most careful. There will be another meal at eighteen-hundred. On alternate days there will be apple juice.' He nodded to Brink who moved to lift the canteen into the lifeboat.

'No!' said Dieter firmly, swinging the boathook towards him. 'Not that canteen – one of the others, please.'

'Oh really, Mr Rohland,' Maron protested mildly. 'Surely you don't think we would try to poison you?'

'One of the other canteens,' Dieter insisted.

Brink shrugged and hung a different canteen on the boathook. Dieter swung it inboard for Mrs Montgomerie to take charge of.

'*Bon appétit*,' Maron murmured and signalled Brink to pull away. When they were a safe distance from Lifeboat 1 he asked, 'Well?'

'There's a kitbag under the forrard thwart, portside,' Brink answered. 'Under where he sat when I went aboard.'

Maron nodded impassively. 'Excellent,' he breathed. 'Excellent.' His arm had healed sufficiently to enable him to unstrap his clipboard. He studied it for a moment. 'The second liferaft is next, please, quartermaster.'

All the survivors on Liferaft 2 were German. Maron was confident of their co-operation.

37

Dieter shivered, pulled the waterproof sheet over his head and drew it more tightly around him. The heat of the day had been sucked into the clear night sky and a freshening following wind was whipping bursts of chill spray off the humped crests and sweeping them across the stern thwart where he was sitting. A length of twine around his wrist was attached to the towline that extended out into the darkness to the unseen Liferaft 1. The rhythmic tugs and thrums from the line as it slackened and tightened in harmony with the swell told him that all was well. He glanced towards the bow but it was too dark to see the figure of Pepita on bow watch. He looked at his watch. The luminous figures shone like miniature beacons. 3:30 a.m. In thirty minutes Tammy would be taking over so that he could join the rest of the sleeping forms for a few hours of slumber before the merciless midsummer sun burned its way into the eastern sky. At least his thirst was more tolerable during the cold night hours. During previous nights he had whiled away his aft watches by wiping condensation off the gunwales with his fingers and licking them; tonight the spray made that impossible. A movement behind him. It was Tammy.

'You're early,' he whispered.

'I couldn't sleep.'

He made room for her on the thwart. Their exchanges were

quieter than José's thunderous snores. Dieter was impressed by his ability to sleep. The big bosun and the greasers had come close to perfecting the twenty-four-hour siesta.

Tammy pulled the sheet around herself and snuggled up close to Dieter. His arm went around her waist; a perfectly natural movement that helped their balance on the narrow board and stopped the cover slipping off them. His hand closed on a narrow expanse of bare skin between her U-boat fatigue trousers and the tunic. She gave a little shiver.

'You're cold,' he commented. 'You ought to wear something underneath.'

'Everything's wet.' She pressed closer to him. He shifted his hand and realised that the gentle pressure on his thumb was the underside of her breast. Her hair brushed ticklishly against his cheek. She combed it and brushed it for half an hour every morning; unlike the other women's hair, it had retained its lustre. The subtle, indefinable scent of its natural oils stirred him. 'No moon,' she commented. 'José told me that it sets in the afternoon – before the sun sets – and that we won't see it at night for a week.'

'Plenty of stars though,' said Dieter. 'Clear skies. That's why it's so cold at night. Cloud would trap the warm air rising off the sea.'

Tammy looked over her shoulder at the north-eastern sky that they were following. 'That bright one's Mirach. José's been telling me about them. He's studying to be an officer. And that's Sheratan.'

Dieter was wasn't sure which stars she meant and neither of them were keen to disturb the security of the cover by pointing.

'He said that we'll be seeing Polaris soon if we hold this course but it will be very low down on the horizon.'

'That'll be when we cross the equator,' said Dieter. 'Will it be your first time?'

'My first time for what?' There was a mischievous catch in Tammy's voice.

'Your first time for crossing the equator.' He moved his

thumb a little higher and brushed it back and forth on the underside of her breast. He made the movement seem unconscious although every atom in his being was focused on the divine sensation.

'Oh yes,' said Tammy.

'There's a special ceremony. I'll be King Neptune and you'll have to pay homage to me as one of my nubile concubines.'

Tammy gave a subdued laugh and leaned forward. Dieter shifted his hand. A slight movement but enough for all his fingertips to come into blood-stirring electric contact with the side of her breast.

'Does that mean I'll be your slave?' Her voice sounded strained.

'Oh yes.' He stretched his forefinger as far as possible without moving his hand. The sensitive nerves in his fingertip interpreted the slight coarsening in texture of her skin as the edge of her areola. He added jokingly, 'I shall demand absolute obedience of all my slaves. The most obedient will receive special favours.'

'Like what?'

'Like this . . .' He moved his finger back and forth, feeling her delicate skin goosepimple to his touch. He fully expected her to pull away but she was strangely still and rigid.

'Down a hundred!' Maron ordered. The diesel mechanic carefully backed off the port engine's throttle so that the revolution counter dropped back a hundred. The engine room hand felt each of the six cylinder heads in turn and made careful adjustments to the cooling pump valves. The diesels had been running at little above a fast tickover since the towing had started. Perversely, they demanded more attention at low speed. The drop in engine noise was barely discernible.

'And down another hundred in five minutes, please,' said Maron crisply. 'That will be the last reduction.'

The engine room crew acknowledged. Maron ducked out through the watertight door.

214

'So what's he up to?' the hand queried, pulling the door closed.

The mechanic shrugged and entered the change in the engine room log. 'Ours is not to reason why and all that . . . Something to do with Handel. Maybe he wants Handel to give him swimming lessons?' He looked at his watch. 'The old man's off watch so it can't be anything important.'

Maron found Handel in the galley. The former Olympic swimmer was honing one of Poison Ivy's knives on a whetstone. He held the blade up so that it gleamed dully in the red night vision lighting. 'All done, Mr Maron. Be able to slit a rhino's throat with this.'

Maron looked at his watch. 'Ten minutes, Handel.'

The mechanic's grin broadened in anticipation. 'I'll be ready, Mr Maron. I'm looking forward to it.'

'It's a ceremony that must be as old as navigation,' said Dieter, knowing that Tammy wasn't listening. He wondered why he was talking. Perhaps it was a deliberate attempt to assuage any guilt, and shift the focus away from his forefinger as he edged it across her puckering areola. 'I suppose the Portuguese started it.' Her nipple surprised him; steel-hard and as erect as a thimble. He explored its contour, his guilt forgotten, marvelling that such unyielding electric hardness could actually be a woman's flesh.

Woman? Little more than a girl!

The bond between them was such that Tammy must have sensed that he was about to withdraw his hand. She grasped his wrist and held it firmly in place, giving a little sigh as she buried her face in his shoulder. His fingers no longer belonged to him; they were separate entities, bent on their own purposeful sensual gratification. His thumb and first finger teased the areola up into twin ridges that sandwiched the clamouring nipple. He felt little tremors coursing through her body. And then, quite suddenly, his index finger thrust hard down on the nipple, rolling it inwards and trapping it beneath the folds of flesh. A tiny, involuntary cry escaped from Tammy's throat and her teeth sank into his shoulder. Dieter eased the pressure and allowed the engorged, bullet-hard nipple to pop back into place. Tammy gave a muffled sob. He was sure her teeth were going through to the bone. His fingers continued to tease her nipple, rolling it in and out. Tammy dropped her hand to his thigh, digging her nails painfully into his leg as he gently but remorselessly eased her towards an edge that she had been over many times before but never in company.

Handel limbered up and down the aft casing, shaking his arms loosely at his side to stimulate his circulation. He was wearing black long johns, his face and arms were smeared with black grease, and the galley knife that he had honed to razor sharpness was in a sheaf strapped to his thigh. On his wrist was Maron's waterproof watch. Its owner was on the bridge, staring anxiously down at the shadowy figure that was now running on the spot. There was little wake now that U-395's speed had dropped to one knot. Two stokers were struggling in the darkness with the dinghy, cursing the freshening wind that made the inflatable difficult to handle.

'Handel! Five minutes! What are you waiting for?'

'Going now, Mr Maron.' With that the black apparition took a running dive from the stern casing, using a powerful kick to launch himself well clear of Tube 5 and the stern gear. Maron strained his eyes into the darkness. He caught a glimpse of Handel surfacing and grabbing the towline, and then the swimmer was swallowed into the night.

Handel trod water once he was well clear of U-395 and allowed the towline to slip through his fingers. He didn't have to swim to Lifeboat 1 – the lifeboat came to him. Taking care not to make a sound that might alert the bow lookout, he grabbed hold of the gunwale with one hand, manoeuvered himself around to the portside and hung on, waiting.

Tammy came close to chewing Dieter's arm off as she went over the brink. Her fingernails tore dementedly into his leg.

Suddenly her body went rigid and she uttered an embarrassingly loud cry that caused several sleeping forms to stir. Dieter was about to pull her face away from his shoulder and clamp his hand over her mouth when a explosive bang from the darkness aft woke the entire boat. A flare, blinding in its intensity, arched into the sky. There was a sudden pandemonium. The baby started crying and people were shouting. Pepita in the bow screamed. She was struggling with a black apparition that had slithered over the gunwale. Dieter tried to reach her but in his haste went sprawling over Marco who added his yells to the uproar. By the time he reached the hysterical girl, the strange, black shape had leapt into the sea and was gone, taking with it the kitbag that had been lashed by its strap to the underside of the bow thwart.

38

Handel's surprise at the weight of the kitbag changed to alarm and then near-panic when he realised that it was dragging him deeper than he intended when he dived off the lifeboat. Five kilos, Haug had said. It felt more like twenty kilos. He clenched the severed strap between his teeth and clawed desperately upwards, legs and arms fighting to overcome the deadly burden. His head broke the surface. The searchlight could hardly fail to find him, so wildly was he churning the water in a desperate bid to stay on the surface. He went under once, twice, and suddenly hands were grabbing him, trying to pull him into the dinghy; voices cursing as they lost their grip on grease-smeared arms. He slipped under again and was about to let go of the strap when it was snatched from his mouth with a force that nearly jerked his teeth from their sockets. He yelled in pain and swore volubly as he was dragged unceremoniously over the side by his scalp and handfuls of long johns.

'Hey, Handel! I thought you could swim?'

Handel was in no mood for jokes. He shielded his eyes from the blinding searchlight and told his two messmates manning the dinghy where precisely he proposed inserting the kitbag once it had been emptied. Five minutes later he made a fearsome entry into the control room. Leaving a trail of black grease, he half-slid, half-fell down the ladder, dumped the kitbag on the chart table with a crash, and glowered at Maron.

'Your kitbag, Mr Maron.' The tone was perilously close to the insubordinate.

'Thank you, Handel. An excellent job.' Even the normally inscrutable Maron could not keep the excitement from his voice as he stared at the prized kitbag. 'You had better get cleaned up.'

Handel grunted, turned to leave, and came face to face with Haug. The intelligence officer beamed. 'Well done, Handel. I will see that news of this reaches the right ears.'

'You underestimated that bag's weight,' Handel growled. 'It fucking near drowned me.' He pushed past Haug without another word.

The smile faded from Haug's chubby face. He looked questioningly at Maron who picked up the sodden kitbag and quickly lowered it again. 'It's a wonder anyone could swim with this, Mr Haug. And yet you said that Rohland swam with it?'

'So I was told,' said Haug, not taking his eyes off the bag. 'I expect it's waterlogged. Yes – that must be the reason.'

Maron wiped his fingers distastefully on a handkerchief. 'Well, at least we've got it. That's all that matters.' He mounted the ladder to the bridge, his arm now sufficiently healed for him to grasp the rungs with his left hand. He brushed past the lookouts, felt along the coaming for the towline's quick-release shackle, and jerked it open. The towline fell away into the darkness. He returned to the open hatch and called down an order to the helmsman. *U-395*'s idling port diesel opened up to half-ahead. He didn't spare a glance astern towards the five helpless craft that he was abandoning.

The increased note of the engine caused a stir throughout the boat and woke Kessler and Brink. Kessler motioned the chief engineer back to his berth. 'I'll deal with it, chief. Get your sleep.'

Kessler stepped into wardroom, sat on the settee, and passed word that he wished to see the first watch officer. He had to contain his impatience for five minutes before Maron appeared. He was holding the grease-smeared kitbag by its strap. Kessler motioned him to the opposite settee.

'What's going on, Oberleutnant?'

With dramatic deliberation Maron placed the kitbag carefully on the centre section of the fold-down table and sat opposite Kessler so that the kitbag was between them. 'U-395 is returning to normal patrol, Captain. At least, as normal as is possible under our present circumstances. As you can see, I have carried out your orders and recovered the crystals.'

'My orders?' Kessler's voice was mild.

'If you recall, Captain. You said that the recovery of the crystals was your number one priority. I entered that in the log immediately after our conversation.'

Their eyes met across the table. Kessler knew that it would have suited Maron if he started shouting. Well, he wasn't going to give him that pleasure. The calm approach allowed him to retain control of the situation and gave him time to think.

'So how was this ... carrying out of my orders ... achieved?'

Maron told him about Handel's exploit.

'You put a man in the sea? At night. Do you not think, Oberleutnant, that it would have been a good idea to have informed me?'

'The wind strengthened. We've always reduced speed when that happens, therefore it was possible to do the same tonight without arousing the suspicions of anyone in the lifeboats. As you know, Handel is an excellent swimmer. The entire incident took less than ten minutes. Its purpose was to restore normal routine which I'm responsible for and which you had ordered was your number one priority. I saw no point in waking you merely to tell you that I was obeying orders.'

Kessler made no reply. He leaned forward and studied the kitbag. It was creating a small pool of water on the table. 'You refer to an operation as an incident. I must congratulate you on your remarkable ability to rationalise the consequential into the inconsequential, Oberleutnant. A rare talent.'

Maron wasn't sure how to respond so he remained silent.

'So what's our speed, Oberleutnant?'

'Seven knots, Captain. Our most economical cruising speed. In accordance with your standing orders.'

Kessler looked hard at his first officer. 'So obviously we've released the towline?'

'The lifeboats have been provided with food, water, clothing and medical supplies. We have more than fulfilled obligations to the survivors that were not ours in the first place to fulfil. We now have the crystals, therefore there was no point in continuing the tow.'

'Also in accordance with my orders, of course?' This time Kessler could not keep the sarcasm from his voice.

'Your orders are recorded in the log,' said Maron stiffly.

Yes. They would be.

'Well . . . We'd better take a look at these crystals,' said Kessler suavely. He raised his voice suddenly. 'Come in, Mr Haug.'

Haug entered the wardroom, smiling benignly.

'For an intelligence officer, you're not well versed in the art of lurking outside doors,' Kessler growled. 'Shadows can be a real giveaway.'

Nothing fazed Haug. 'I was returning to my berth, Captain.' His eyes alighted on the kitbag. 'A remarkable achievement, getting our crystals back like that.'

'Remarkable,' said Kessler drily. 'So let's take a look at them. See what all the fuss is about. Perhaps you'd do the honours, Mr Haug. Or will it spoil those manicured nails?'

Haug beamed. 'With pleasure.' His pudgy fingers had trouble with the soaked straps and the flap buckles. Eventually he got them open and pulled out a heavy package wrapped in several layers of cotton duck. A note fell out and stuck to the now wet floor. Kessler unpeeled it while Haug unrolled the cloth. The contents of the pack clinked metallically. The intelligence officer's smile faded when he pulled the last layer of cloth aside. The three men contemplated the length of lightweight mooring chain. It had been tightly coiled and secured with twine. It gleamed wet and black under the red wardroom lights. Normally Haug never allowed his expression to betray his thoughts but this time there was no disguising the look of horror in his eyes. His grease-streaked fingers delved into the empty kitbag. He even held it upside-down and shook it before subsiding onto the settee like a deflating Zeppelin to stare uncomprehendingly at the kitbag. It lay wet and limp on the table like a set of raped bagpipes.

'Bit hard to read this,' said Kessler phlegmatically, peering at the note. 'Seawater's made the indelible run. Ah yes. "So sorry, Mr Haug, but I don't have a hacksaw therefore this may be a little heavier than the original contents".' He looked up at the two stunned men who were still gaping at the chain. 'It's signed D. R.'

There was no reply. Kessler rose without another word and entered the control room.

'Course?' he inquired.

'Zero-four-zero, Captain,' the petty officer responded.

'Very good. Hard aport. Reciprocal course. Steer two-two-zero.'

On the bridge one of the lookouts lowered his binoculars as the U-boat heeled. 'Bugger me, lads. We're going about.'

'Eyes!' snapped the lookout petty officer.

U-395 completed its 180-degree turn and the starboard engine kicked in. Spray burst over the main gun, drenching the lookouts as the boat gathered speed.

'Reckon we're going back for those poor sods?'

'Looks like it. Maybe our wonderful oberleutnant has suddenly decided that he can't live without that gorgeous dark-haired piece.'

'Which bloke was that then?'

'Eyes!' the NCO repeated, but was wondering the same thing. And then confirmation from the 'office': they were returning to find the survivors.

Only when he was back on his bunk behind the dubious privacy of his green curtain did Kessler permit himself a deep, rich chuckle. Roll on Tuesday.

39

Dieter didn't wait for the lifeboat to drift alongside the raft but leapt across the two-metre gap, nearly causing the flat-topped craft to capsize when he landed. The other survivors were too weak to stop him grabbing the raft's senior officer and hauling him to his knees.

'So whose idea was the flare, Gemmel!'

The man's sunken eyes went round with fear. 'I don't know what you mean,' he stuttered. 'I thought we'd lost a man over the side so I fired the –'

'Don't fucking lie!' Dieter shouted, shaking the hapless man. 'We've got a torch signalling system! That bloody creep of a U-boat officer put you up to it, didn't he? *Didn't he*!'

For a moment it looked as if Gemmel was going to brazen it out but his spirit and resolve was weakened by the days spent on the liferaft. Dieter shook him again.

'Well?'

Gemmel nodded. 'He said to fire a flare at 04:00 dead.'

'Did he say why?'

'An exercise. To check the crew's response. That's why we weren't to tell anyone.'

Dieter suddenly felt ashamed of his behaviour. He released the man who fell across one his mates in an untidy sprawl.

None of the others made a move to help him. They stared at Dieter in the light from the torches trained on them from the other craft that were gathered accusingly around the liferaft. He moderated his tone a little but the harshness was still there to show that he meant business. 'And you believed him, of course?'

'I didn't think that they'd run out on us.'

'Yeah. You didn't think. I want your flares. All of them.'

'You can't,' Gemmel spluttered. 'Supposing we're separated –'

'You pull another stunt like that and you bloody well will be!'

One of the other men opened a waterproof compartment and handed over four flares.

'Is that the lot?'

The man nodded. Dieter checked all the compartments and found that the man was telling the truth. He stood and addressed the other four craft. 'You're all to hand over your flares to José in Lifeboat 1. Right now. And no arguments.'

The other raft and the two lifeboats passed over their stocks of flares. As he watched them, Dieter realised that they were conferring a leadership on him that he had not given serious thought to. It was too late to back off now. He timed the swell and jumped nimbly back onto his lifeboat. Tammy pushed Marco out of the way to offer Dieter a steadying hand which he accepted in exchange for a conspiratorial wink. Despite the recent shock, everyone with the exception of Pepita seemed in good spirits. The girl was sitting in the bow with a blanket pulled tightly around herself, looking utterly miserable. To Tammy's annoyance Dieter sat beside her and took her hand. She was trembling uncontrollably.

'I'm sorry, Dieter,' she began. 'But –'

'It's all right, Pepita, there's nothing to be sorry about. It wasn't your fault.'

'The way it came over the side . . . I thought it was a sea monster. I screamed just like a stupid schoolgirl.'

223

'You were not stupid. That was the best warning of all.' Dieter squeezed her hand tightly. Gradually the frightened girl's trembling stopped. They stayed like that for some moments while Mrs Montgomerie strived to restore calm.

'They've abandoned us, haven't they?' said Pepita at length, her voice low and scared.

Dieter chucked her under the chin. 'I don't think so.' He stood and signalled to Tammy. 'Look after Pepita. She's had a bad shock.'

Tammy was a kindly girl with a genuine liking for the young novitiate. She sat beside Pepita and slipped a friendly arm around her waist. Dieter glanced quickly around. It was now strangely quiet in the lifeboat; the turmoil of the recent abandonment had given way to a stunned shock. One of the greasers was cradling the baby in a pair of brawny arms. Another was amusing Marco while the mother sat huddled fearfully against the nuns. Mrs Montgomerie was tending the sick men. She treated their burns every six hours in accordance with Brink's instructions, and never once had she neglected them. Dieter suspected that she had even given them most of her water ration. The group was as unlikely a mix as it was possible to imagine and yet a bond had formed between them.

The five craft were gathered together in an untidy group, pitching uncomfortably in the steepening swell that was being pushed up by the wind. All the survivors were watching him intently as though he held the key to their fate, which, he supposed, he did. He stood on the lifeboat's foredeck and raised his voice to be heard above the wind.

'The U-boat has been gone twenty minutes. That is as long as it will take them to realise that they have made a mistake. They will return within twenty minutes.'

It was a blunt, categoric statement without exclusions or exceptions. The anxious faces lit up. Some broke into smiles of relief.

Dieter continued: 'Somebody is to stand in each lifeboat and keep a torch waving. Better still, tie it to an oar and hold it high.' He sat down feeling both self-conscious and guilty at his raising of their hopes when he wasn't really certain.

Mrs Montgomerie had pulled in the long towline. She flashed the torch on the quick-release shackle, pulled open the spring-loaded pin and allowed it to snap closed. 'It wasn't a mistake or an accident, Dieter,' she said quietly, using his Christian name for the first time. 'It was deliberate. They've got what they wanted. Do you still think they will return?'

Dieter avoided her eye and nodded. The woman hesitated and reached out to touch his hand. 'I pray to God that you're right.'

Fifteen minutes later Tammy gave a loud cry and pointed. The swell lifted the five craft and all the occupants saw the bright light that was approaching them.

40

The war was moving apace as 1941 drew to a close.

Hitler's assault on Moscow was halted by the weather and the dogged resilience of the Red Army. In North Africa the British were pushing Rommel back to El Agheila in Libya where he had begun his offensive in the spring. In the Pacific the Japanese launched their devastating surprise attack against the American fleet in Pearl Harbor on 7 December, hitting eighteen ships, destroying two hundred aircraft and killing over 2400 American servicemen and women. Four days later Germany and Italy declared war on the United States.

But none of these momentous events was known to the tiny armada edging its way north-east across the wilderness of the Atlantic. During the day the survivors lay stunned and senseless, steeped in heat and lethargy as they huddled under their makeshift awnings to escape the merciless sun, rarely stirring unless it was to sponge their tortured, dehydrating bodies with sea water. The survivors from the *Atlantis* were already hollow-eyed, lolling listlessly on their liferafts, hardly aware of the passing days. Two of the worst cases were transferred to *U-395* so that Brink could tend to them, but conditions aboard the U-boat were little better. The sun beat down on the steel hull, heating the air inside to an intolerable level despite having all the fans set to maximum. Brandt tried flooding the ballast tanks so that the boat rode low in the water, but that merely increased the hull's drag and increased fuel consumption. At the end of each watch he checked the diesel tanks, looked up the distance made good on the control room charts, and calculated the rate of consumption.

'A man could go insane in this heat.'

Brandt looked up from the figures he was double-checking at his fold-down desk in the motor room. Haug's moon-like face was glistening under a sheen of sweat. The engineer grunted noncommittally. He did not particularly like Haug.

'I have nothing but admiration for you submariners,' Haug continued, mopping his face with a handkerchief. 'Cooped up like this. I'm sure I'd start raving if we had to spend any time submerged.'

'The training sorts out those who can't take it,' said Brandt, not looking up from his fuel consumption tables.

'Ha . . . You have long duration dives on training?'

'Bloody long,' Brandt replied.

'What's the longest dive you had on patrol?'

Brandt looked up. 'On the last patrol we were in the cellar for thirty hours when under attack.'

'Dear me,' Haug muttered worriedly. 'Now that really would drive me insane.' He gestured to the rows of drum-like rotary switches. 'A man losing his reason in a U-boat could cause a lot of damage. He could endanger everyone's life.'

'He could, but it's never happened.'

'And if it did?'

'The old man would deal with it.'

Haug looked puzzled. 'Surely some of the crew would overpower him?'

226

Brandt sighed. Haug's curiosity wasn't helping with his figures. 'Not if they were having to man their stations. If someone went berserk and endangered the boat, then the old man would have to shoot him. But only as a last resort. I've never known it happen, and I don't know anyone who has.'

Haug left the motor room deep in thought. The conversation had confirmed what he suspected – that the captain had a gun. The question was, where did he keep it? Obviously it had to be in one of his lockers, but it would be impossible to step behind the captain's curtain without someone noticing.

In the motor room, Brandt went back to his fuel consumption figures. They made bleak reading. As a rough rule of thumb, U-395 consumed one tonne of fuel oil per 110 miles. It did not require a mathematical genius to work out from Brink's fixes that she was burning a good deal more than that: they had made a little over 1000 miles in ten days and had burnt sixteen tonnes of oil. The grim results were made worse by the cooling effect of having the condensers running at maximum freshwater production. Brandt hated running his diesels both cool and slow; the rate at which the exhaust vent valves clogged up with carbon was indication of how inefficiently the engines were burning their fuel. The vents were normally decoked every other watch so that the valves could be wound hard shut on their seatings for a crash-dive without sea water leaking into the engines. Now they needed to be cleaned every watch.

41

At 1700 each evening, when the sun's savagery had moderated to mere spite, the sluggish routine quickened. This was when Poison Ivy and his helpers set to work preparing nearly one hundred and fifty meals. Maron had juggled the mealtimes of his watches to spare the cooks the misery of having to use the galley burners during the heat of the day.

227

One of the assistant cooks was Haug who had astonished Kessler by actually volunteering for the work.

'Someone my shape in the galley gives confidence,' Haug had opined, beaming at Kessler's surprised expression. 'Cooks should be as fat as pigs. A cook as skinny as Poison Ivy is most worrying for the crew, don't you agree?'

Kessler did not agree. It was doubtful if there was any issue on the face of the planet in which he would agree with Haug. 'What's the real reason, Mr Haug?'

Haug blinked. 'I'll admit to being bored. I've always enjoyed cooking, and I don't relish re-reading Brink's collection of Marcel Proust. I've even started on what he calls his trashy modern fiction: Virginia Woolf.'

At 1730 Kessler climbed onto the bridge and marvelled at the golden glory of a spectacular sunset. But that was as it should be. It was Tuesday, of course. Only a Tuesday could serve up such a glorious finale as this sunset.

Tuesday. Glorious, wonderful Tuesday.

It was the most sacrosanct day of the week in *U-395*'s routine; a day that had become a tradition. Tuesday was the captain's day; the day when Kessler indulged himself with a protracted wallow in hot seawater in a collapsible bathtub that the chief engineer hated; reassembling a stripped down diesel was a simple task compared with the weekly ritual of putting the skipper's bathtub together. The instructions printed on the underside were only readable when all the sections had been bolted together. Once assembled, it was jammed across the wardroom's centre aisle for the occasion and filled with a hot water hose from the engine room. For an hour non-urgent crew movements through the wardroom were banned. Anyone obliged to climb over their belligerent skipper placed their genitals at risk from a long-handled bath brush that he wielded with painful accuracy. Although a crash-dive had never happened during Kessler's cherished ablutions, it was rumoured that if one was necessary, the chief's standing orders were that the boat should be taken down at a shallow angle.

Kessler inhaled deeply, feeling good.

Tuesday.

The day of the week when he had a complete change of clothes, and when the wardroom steward changed his bunk linen. His clean sheets were kept in an airtight tin to prevent mould growing on them. Tuesday was the one day of the week when he always felt civilised. Tuesday was when he paroled either the poet or the artist in his soul from captivity. This Tuesday it was the artist. As he gazed westward, the magnificent yellow light reminded him of the Turners he had once seen at Petworth House during a visit to Portsmouth in the mid-thirties. No artist had ever captured the strange interplay of light and shade at sea as accurately as Turner. He had read somewhere that the great man had once insisted on being lashed to a mast during a storm so that he could witness the tempest at first hand. Turner would have loved this sunset. As the sun's limb touched the horizon, so the sea took on the patina of burnished copper. Even the normally phlegmatic lookouts were moved.

'Beautiful . . . Beautiful . . .' one of them muttered. 'And look at those clouds.'

'Cirrus,' said Kessler, squinting at the horse tail golden strands that laced the stratosphere. He added drolly: 'In these latitudes they usually precede a warm front.'

The lookouts laughed. Natural, spontaneous laughter. Certainly not forced merely because their skipper had made a joke.

Morale high, thought Kessler, pleased.

But this particular Tuesday wasn't over. Another long-cherished tradition was about to unfold. Normally it took place during the afternoon but Kessler had, somewhat sulkily, gone along with Maron's suggestion that it be moved to the evening watch. The galley hatch clanged open. Haug and two stewards emerged and began lining-up the canteens of hot stew that were passed up to them. Everything went into Poison Ivy's stew: raisins, dates, sultanas, dried apples, a few potatoes that were mould-free and many that weren't, sausages that were on their last legs and learning to walk, and any other ingredients from the numerous caches around the boat that had reached the point whereby they were capable of crossing the Atlantic without the help of a U-boat. The bow torpedo compartment circulated a number of malicious rumours concerning certain other ingredients that Ivy added to his simmering pots when no one was looking, but these were dismissed as largely true.

Maron climbed onto the casing. He checked the canteens against his trusty clipboard and ordered two ratings to break out the inflatable dinghy. It seemed to Kessler that there were more canteens than usual. A remarkable officer, he reflected, watching Maron release the clips on a canteen and taste the contents. Despite his opposition to towing the survivors, his attention to their welfare had been exemplary. The daily consignment even included large medicine bottles filled with reconstituted milk for the children, and thin gruel for the two sick men that Mrs Montgomerie and the nuns were nursing. Kessler congratulated himself on putting Maron in charge of the survivors' welfare. There had been no more talk from him about abandoning them. Ten days, they had agreed. Well, more than ten days had passed. Kessler pulled himself up. Had ten days passed or did it just feel like it? What was the date he had agreed with Maron? He recalled their conversation and Maron's closing words in particular:

'What I suggest is that if there's no change in our circumstances in ten days – on December 17th, that we implement our standing orders and release this towline. Do you agree with that, Captain?'

And Kessler had accepted the proposal. He recalled the date he had written in the log that morning: Tuesday, 16 December – with the Tuesday underlined. He swore under his breath.

'All ready, Captain,' Maron called out.

Kessler met the cold, grey eyes and wondered what was going on behind them. He acknowledged and gave the order to stop engines. The throaty roar of the exhaust died away. The flotilla of boats and rafts lost way and gathered around the wallowing U-boat like a flock of hungry, expectant moorhen chicks.

Maron double-checked the canteens. He placed neat, methodical ticks on his clipboard. Kessler decided that he must have forgotten their agreement; it wasn't human to show such concern for a hundred souls while planning to abandon them. He pushed the problem out of his mind. After all, it was Tuesday and there were more pleasant things to think about.

And then the long-awaited event finally happened: a divine aroma that rallied memories of childhood Tuesdays in his mother's kitchen came wafting through the bridge hatch. It was mixed with other odours: diesel oil, grease, stale sweat and urine, but there was no hiding the clamorous, overpowering, salivary gland-squeezing smell of freshly-baked bread.

'Captain's rolls coming up!' a voice called from below.

It was a strict rule: like a high priest invited to sample the latest consignment of temple virgins, the first loaves out of the oven went to the captain. The lookout petty officer took the basket that was handed up through the hatch and gave it to Kessler. He took it with due reverence and hooked it over a cleat. The napkin covering the offering was crisp and white. He drew it aside with all the anticipation of a bridegroom undressing his bride, and the glory lay before him: four small, hot rolls and a jar of sour Cologne pickle with more bite than a shoal of barracuda. But the loaves looked wrong. Dreadfully wrong. Disbelievingly, he picked one up. Not only did it look wrong, but it felt wrong. He sank his teeth into it and he knew the awful truth with the clarity of a medieval saint being confronted by a vision of Satan. He spat the mouthful of bread out.

'Ivy!' he roared. '*IVY!* I want that chef on the bridge! Now!'

Maron's ratings were loading larger versions of the loaves into the dinghy. They looked anxiously up at the conning tower where their skipper was assisting Poison Ivy through the bridge hatch by his collar.

'What the hell's this!' Kessler raged, crushing one of the loaves to a wad of pulp smaller than a golf ball and holding it under Ivy's nose.

Ivy's sunken eyes squinted as he focused on the lump of grey dough. 'Bread, Captain,' he croaked.

'Bread! *BREAD!* This isn't bread! This is shit!'

'It's exactly the same recipe as usual, Captain,' said the hapless chef, looking at his fellow crewmen for support and finding none.

'Open your mouth!'

Ivy did as he was told. Kessler crammed the ball of dough into his victim's mouth.

'Now eat!'

Ivy ate.

'Well?'

Maron was standing on the aft casing, watching. Behind him the ratings had rowed the dinghy to Lifeboat 1 and were distributing the canteens.

'Captain!'

Kessler wheeled 'Mr Maron?'

'The cook steam-baked the bread on my instructions.' Maron's face was impassive.

'Steam-baked?' Kessler echoed.

'Crusty bread is difficult for many of the survivors to swallow. I ordered Ivy to soft-bake the bread.'

'The loaves are sprayed with water when they're half-baked, Captain,' Ivy explained. 'I'm baking some ordinary loaves now but you've always insisted on sampling the first batch.'

'Proper crispy rolls that break teeth?' Kessler demanded suspiciously.

Pols agreed that the fresh batch of loaves would have ivory-shattering properties. Kessler grunted and released his victim. Only when the hapless cook had vanished did he treat the watch petty officer to a conspiratorial wink.

Nothing should be allowed to spoil a Tuesday.

42

A humid, moonless night.

Dieter sat in the stern, watching intently for a light from the following lifeboats and liferafts that would signal that something was amiss. After several nights on watch he had learned not to be tricked by the sudden flash of flying fish, or the eerie flicker of phosphorescence in the lifeboat's wake across the humped, sluggish swell. There was no wind; the heat lay over the sea like a suffocating blanket. The craving for fresh fruit returned. Normally he never touched oranges; now he was plagued by visions of the tall fruit sundaes that were served up by the pavement cafés along the Montevideo waterfront. He took a careful sip from his water bottle. The distilled water from the U-boat's condensers was flat but its aftertaste of diesel oil took away the aftertaste of the stew. He had asked one of the ratings who had delivered the meals that evening why there was more stew than usual and had been given a vague answer about the cook wanting to use up some ingredients. Tammy and Pepita played a game each evening trying to identify its contents, holding lumps up for inspection and collapsing with laughter at their whispered suggestions. Well, whatever went into the stew, at least it was keeping them alive. The freshly-baked soft loaves that evening had been particularly welcome.

A man moaned; probably Mencke, one of the seaman that Mrs Montgomerie was nursing. There was what sounded like a smothered giggle, probably Pepita or Tammy. He wondered if Tammy would ever keep him company again during the night watch and decided, with some regret, that it was unlikely. Ever since those treasured moments with her at his side it seemed that she had been avoiding him. Instead she had become more attached to Pepita. The two girls whiled away the days playing endless games of cards, never tiring of each other's company. They even slept at night in each other's arms.

Someone was stirring, moving towards him. A little pang of disappointment when the heavy breathing told him that it couldn't be Tammy. He turned around and offered a hand to the shadowy figure negotiating the sleeping forms. It was Mrs Montgomerie. The diet had improved her figure. She had been only a few kilos overweight but enough to give her a full look; now she had the slimness of a young girl. He made room for her on the thwart.

'That's the trouble with sleeping so much during the day,' she whispered. 'Can't sleep at night.' She reached over the side and splashed water on her face.

'You're on midnight watch from tomorrow,' Dieter reminded her.

Mencke moaned. Mrs Montgomerie was about to stand but a nun called out in a low voice to say that she would attend to him.

'He's in a bad way,' said Mrs Montgomerie.

'You've done marvels for him,' said Dieter.

There was a long silence before she answered. 'If only that were true. I don't think he'll live, Dieter. Every time we turn him over, he's lighter. There's nothing to him.' It was strange to hear her talking so quietly.

'We could tell the U-boat that they ought to take him on board again,' Dieter suggested.

'No. The bruises he got from the last time he was lowered through the hatch aren't healing, and some are turning septic. Another move would finish him.'

Dieter remained silent. That evening Mencke had been unable to keep his food down and the nuns had had trouble getting him to drink some milk.

'I could pass a message to the U-boat tomorrow,' Dieter offered. She made no reply. He turned his head but all he could see was her profile. She seemed to staring fixedly at the haze-distorted constellations low down on the southern horizon.

234

'I'm worried about Tammy,' said Mrs Montgomerie at length.

'How?'

'This friendship with Pepita.'

'Being friendly with a novitiate? What harm is there in that?'

Mrs Montgomerie lowered her voice still further. 'You must swear not to breathe a word of what I'm about to say.'

Dieter was sufficiently intrigued to agree.

'The sister told me that Pepita had been virtually a prostitute from the age of ten.'

The news didn't altogether surprise Dieter; the girl's amazing dexterity with a pack of cards hinted at a dubious past. 'How is one *virtually* a prostitute?' he inquired.

Mrs Montgomerie sniffed. 'She used to work the beaches. Playa poodles, the police call them. She'd sit beside men on the beach and . . . well – put her sleight of hand skills to good use.'

'Or bad use?'

'It's not funny!' Mrs Montgomerie snapped, suddenly showing her old spirit. She glanced anxiously around at the shapeless, slumbering forms, and lowered her voice. 'The police department handed her over to the convent when she was twelve. It was that or the *deposito*.'

'So what is your problem, Mrs Montgomerie? The girl is no longer working at her old trade.'

'This friendship she and Tammy have. It worries me. Have you seen how they're together all the time? The way they even sleep together? Arms around each other?'

'They are two frightened children, Mrs Montgomerie. Nothing else.'

'Neither of them are children. I've seen the way you look at them sometimes.' There was no accusation in her voice; merely a bald statement of fact which Dieter could hardly deny.

'So what do you want me to do?'

'I want . . .' She broke off, her inner conflict making it

235

difficult for her to find the right words. 'I want . . . Oh God – I don't know what I want.' And then she suddenly blurted out: 'I want you to talk to her. She'll listen to you.'

Dieter didn't relish the idea of being cast in the role of a father figure. 'She's a very headstrong girl, Mrs Montgomerie. I'm sure anything I say would have the opposite effect . . . And I'm not sure I would know what to say.'

'You could show more interest in her.'

'Interest? I don't understand.'

'Enough to head off the way this friendship with Pepita might be going.'

Dieter suddenly sensed the Englishwoman's loneliness. For the first time in many years she was confronted with a situation that she didn't know how to handle and which she knew her acid tongue would only make worse. On an impulse that surprised even himself with its boldness, he took her hand and held it. She returned his grip with an intensity that he was unprepared for.

'I'll do my best,' he promised.

Mrs Montgomerie relaxed and withdrew her hand. 'You must think me a very foolish woman.' She stood and picked her way forward over the sleeping forms. Mencke once again became the centre of her attention.

43

The port diesel stopped suddenly and woke Brandt. The seatings on the outlet valves that vented the exhaust into the ballast tanks probably needed decoking. He heard the shrill, angry buzz of the engine room telegraph. Herbert Kohler was the engine room petty officer on watch. What was the matter with the man? He knew perfectly well that the second engine should be started before the first one was closed down. Brandt lay bathed in sweat in his bunk opposite the galley and listened for the sound of compressed air turning over the starboard engine. When it started he knew instantly from its labouring note that something was wrong. Wearing only his underpants, he rolled out of his bunk, thrust his feet into plimsolls, and entered the furnace-like atmosphere of the engine room just as the engine stalled. Stoker Fenicke tried the starter again.

'Belay that, you idiot! Isn't it obvious that something's wrong?'

'Port engine seized, chief,' Kohler reported. 'Starboard sounds the same.'

To suggest to Brandt that his beloved diesels were prone to seizing was tantamount to treason. He climbed through the watertight door into the motor room and ordered the electricians to disengage the clutches before squeezing himself under the stern torpedo tube and the air compressor to reach the point where the propeller shafts disappeared into their stern glands whence they passed through the hull and into the sea. He wriggled himself as far aft as it was possible to get in a U-boat. He pulled a metre-long steel tommy bar from its clips and applied it to the port thrust block coupling. Normally the stern shafts turned easily by hand, but it was locked solid in both directions. It was the same with the starboard shaft: immovable. He wiped the sweat from his eyes and swore volubly. He looked up at the electrician just as Reche's anxious face appeared.

'Captain wants to know why we've stopped, chief.'

'I'll give you one guess,' said Brandt savagely.

Reche returned to the control room with the bad news.

44

Diesel Mechanic Eric Handel sat on the aft casing, the sun beating down on his muscular body as he exhaled, driving every last vestige of air from his lungs. When he inhaled, he inflated his lungs to maximum capacity, held his breath for a few seconds and exhaled slowly to repeat the process.

'What's he doing?' the bridge watch rating grumbled.

'Hyperventilating,' said Kessler breezily. 'Saturating his blood with oxygen so that he can stay under for about a day like a bloody whale.' Despite his usual ebullient demeanour, Kessler was particularly edgy, and with good reason: U-395 was unable to move. She was helpless, her propellers fouled with God's knows what. The chances of a British warship finding them in mid-Atlantic just south of the equator were remote, but even if as much as an armed merchantman chanced on them, all it would have to do was stay out of range of U-395's main gun and shell them to glory at its leisure.

The lifeboats and liferafts drifted close. Some of the survivors risked the sun by pushing their covers aside and standing to get a better view. Two seamen from Lifeboat 2, taking welcome advantage of the lack of way, peeled down to their underpants and slipped into the sea but remained hanging onto the gunwales in case the U-boat set off again.

Handel took one final deep breath and slipped gently into the water. He swam to the stern and jack-knifed under, lifting his feet well clear of the surface so that the weight of his legs pushed him under with a minimum of effort. He went down three metres and opened his eyes. The water was so clear that he had no difficulty finding the port rudder skeg beneath the barnacle-encrusted stern torpedo tube door. He hung onto it to keep himself down. Surface evaporation due to the hot weather had concentrated the salinity of the seawater which had in turn had led to a marked increase in buoyancy.

The problem was self-evident: a continuous length of heavy, wire-reinforced rope with cork floats attached was wound tightly around both propeller shafts. He struggled for two minutes to untangle it but the wire was too badly frayed and corroded for him to haul on it with bare hands. Two powerful kicks returned him to the surface. He clambered onto the casing, not seeming to be out of breath, and reported to Kessler.

'Skein net main cable,' Kessler grumbled. 'Some damned

fishing smack's lost its tackle and we had to find it.' He checked an impulse to bawl out the lookouts; the chances were that the stuff had been floating below the surface.

45

Tammy and Pepita shared a private joke about U-395's odd nose-down trim. The forward ballast tanks had been flooded and her aft tanks blown with the result that the boat was floating nose down with her Number 5 stern torpedo tube completely exposed and her sterngear nearly clear of the swell. Tammy added something that caused Pepita to dissolve into hysterics.

They were sitting amidships with their arms around each other in their 'home' – a tiny area that consisted of a sewing box covered with an embroidered handkerchief that served as a dressing table. Their kitchen was a small wooden crate where they kept their water canteens. The other occupants of the lifeboat had tacitly accepted the arrangement and did their best not to trespass.

Mrs Montgomerie looked up from her task of spooning soup past Mencke's cracked lips. She frowned in disapproval at the renewed gales of girlish laughter. 'What's so funny?' she demanded.

'It looks like a diving duck, Miss Angela,' said Pepita, struggling to maintain her self-control by avoiding Tammy's eye.

'Sheer carelessness if you ask me,' Mrs Montgomerie sniffed. 'Getting rope tangled round their propellers indeed. And to think I always thought the Germans were efficient. They should look where they're going.'

Watching the six U-boat men in the water taking it in turns to dive down to the fouled screws provided a welcome diversion. One of the ratings, armed with a hacksaw, was wearing a Drager submarine escape set that enabled him to remain permanently submerged. Reche was sitting on the

239

stern clutching Kessler's Luger in case any sharks became too inquisitive. The angle of the late afternoon sun reflecting off the water made his task difficult.

'You don't have to hit them,' Kessler had explained. 'Just whack a round into the water near them. The impact will make them clear off.'

There was a loud splash as another seaman in Lifeboat 2 flopped into the water. Kessler had already told the survivors that they expected to be hove-to for about an hour. A few of *U-395*'s more aquatic crewmen had organised a race around the U-boat and were being lustily cheered by their non-swimming mates.

Kessler seized the loudhailer. 'Don't go in the water if you've got open wounds,' he warned the survivors. 'Sharks can smell blood for miles.'

Young Marco gave a whoop and leapt into the sea before his mother could raise objections. She shouted at him to stay near the splashing seamen. Pepita got into an argument with the nun. Their Spanish was too fast for Dieter to follow. The row got acrimonious with Pepita gesticulating wildly. José's grin got wider as the dispute dragged on.

'What's the problem?' Dieter asked Tammy, declining her offer to take over repair of his underpants.

The girl looked faintly amused. 'The sister says that Pepita can't go swimming.'

'Why not? She can swim well.'

'Because of what the captain just said.'

Dieter was too preoccupied with the needle and thread to work out what that could mean. The sooner he sewed up the open fly, the sooner he would be in the water.

'Are you going swimming?' Tammy asked.

'I most certainly am,' said Dieter emphatically. He finished the repair and moved past Tammy to return the needle and thread to Mrs Montgomerie.

'I would like to go swimming, Mrs Montgomerie,' he said quietly.

240

'I'm not your guardian, Dieter.'

He smiled. 'I think you know where I've hidden the samples.'

'In a seaman's stocking, under the duckboard behind me. I'm not blind you know.'

'They seem to be busy on the U-boat, but you know what to do if they try anything.'

'Aren't you worried that I might throw them over the side anyway? I'm still English, you know. Supposing I don't want your little bag to fall into German hands?'

Dieter grinned. 'I'll have to take that chance.'

He pulled a cover over himself, wriggled out of his U-boat-issue trousers that all the survivors were now wearing and into his underpants. He jumped into the blissful, erotic embrace of the warm water and swam away from the lifeboat.

Haug had been sitting reading in the shade of the main gun. It was pleasant on deck now that the day had expended the worst of its oppressive heat. He saw Dieter's unmistakable figure stand on the bow foredeck of Lifeboat 1 and jump into the sea. He snapped his book shut and climbed onto the bridge when he was given permission. Kessler listened to what Haug had to say and cut him short.

'No, Mr Haug. Right now we're too busy to worry about anything but clearing our sterngear and getting under way again.'

'But, Cap —'

'I said no. Now if you will excuse me. I'm busy.'

Haug saw the uselessness of trying to reason with Kessler. He returned to the main gun and opened his book, but his mind was too busy to take in Proust. Reche appeared by the bridge, clutching Kessler's Luger and peering worriedly into the depths. Haug decided the only way of recovering the crystals would be for him to seize the initiative. His fertile mind went to work.

Dieter was surprised at how quickly he tired, and stopped swimming when he was about fifty metres from the lifeboats.

241

The frugal diet was taking effect. He contented himself by rubbing himself clean while marvelling at the buoyancy of the sea. Treading water had never been so effortless.

Tammy watched him wistfully. 'May I go swimming *please*, Miss Angela?'

Mrs Montgomerie looked critically at Tammy. 'Not in those trousers – they'll weigh you down. And you've nothing suitable.'

'I could wear my nightie,' said Tammy brightly. 'It's long enough – it nearly reaches my ankles – and it'll dry in no time.'

Mrs Montgomerie had been about to refuse but she saw the way Tammy was staring at Dieter and relented. 'Oh very well then.'

Pepita scowled as Tammy scrambled under a cover and emerged a minute later wearing her nightdress. Tammy didn't even glance her way.

'Dieter!'

There was a splash. Dieter twisted around and saw Tammy swimming strongly towards him. She reached him and trod water, splashing him playfully.

'Stop that!' he commanded sternly. 'You're making me wet.'

The way her lovely face broke into a smile at his joke made him want to pull her towards him and kiss her. If he timed it so that they were in a trough between the swells . . . Her attempt to dart away from him with a powerful butterfly backstroke ended with a gurgling little shriek as he grabbed her ankle and yanked her towards him. Her nightdress ballooned, her legs went around his waist and pinioned the two of them together, pelvis to pelvis. As Tammy's thighs opened to encompass him, Dieter saw that she was naked.

Reche jumped onto the saddle tank and threw himself prone to get as near the water as possible, cupping his hands to his face to shade his eyes against the reflected glare from the low sun. He didn't want to start loosing off with the Luger unless he was sure. He heard Handel's triumphant shout that the port propeller was clear.

The mechanics of Tammy's and Dieter's love-making was surprisingly disciplined as though they had rehearsed. Even the seamen in the water near the lifeboats played their unknown role to perfection by wallowing and bellowing their way through a mock battle and so holding everyone's attention. Everyone that is, except Pepita, whose jealous gaze was fixed on the distant couple. She watched them as they lay back in the water, their heads a modest distance apart, Dieter's arms moving languidly. Underwater, hidden beneath the voluminous sea anemone-like spread of the nightdress, it was a different story. Tammy gave shuddering little cries deep in her throat, arching her back, while her fingers worked a frantic compensation for the awkward angle. She spasmed again and again with such intensity that Dieter had no clear idea whether the sublime, almost painful grasping was due to her pelvic contractions or her fingers, and didn't much care.

'Shark!' Reche cried and fired twice at the shadowy shape rising from the depths. The men in the water around U-395's stern scrambled onto the casing. The ugly dorsal fin of a big Mako broke the surface near the U-boat and veered sharply away when Reche fired a third shot. The seamen brawling in the water near the lifeboats and the liferafts were making too much noise for the survivors to hear the reports.

Pepita saw Tammy and Dieter separate and kiss, and she knew. Her jealousy and anger boiled over. She slipped quickly out of her trousers, jumped into the water, and struck out towards the couple. The nun's cry was too late. She pushed a woman away from the gunwale and screamed at Pepita about the captain's warning. The girl ignored the nun's pleas and kept swimming.

'A big one, captain!' Reche yelled.

Kessler spotted the dorsal fin arrowing towards the survivors and snatched up the loudhailer. 'Shark!' his amplified voice bellowed across the water. 'Everyone out of the water! *Raus! Raus! Raus!*'

Marco's mother nearly dislocated the boy's arms as she

jerked him into boat. The fighting seamen piled into their lifeboats and yelled warnings to Dieter and Tammy. The couple saw the dorsal fin between them and the U-boat, and struck out frantically for the nearest lifeboat, their limbs thrashing the water to foam, the mixture of panic and adrenalin adding new power to their muscles. They reached Pepita when they were twenty metres from the lifeboat. The Mako was closing fast. It had caught the scent of blood.

'You were doing *it*!' Pepita screamed at Tammy, swimming furiously after her.

Tammy shouted over her shoulder that it didn't matter, and kept swimming.

'It *does* matter!' Pepita choked, losing the rhythm of her breast stroke in her anger.

The shark was within ten metres of the swimmers when it swung away. It preferred to first circle the source of the powerful scent.

Tammy reached the lifeboat first. Hands stretched out and grasped her wrist. She turned and saw that Dieter's strength was failing. She grabbed his hair with her free hand and yanked him alongside her.

'Get them out first!' she cried, and tried to pull herself into the boat.

José and two other seamen hauled Dieter out the water and reached for Pepita.

The Mako's small brain had all the information needed. It flicked its powerful tail flukes. The sleek grey-white body changed course and torpedoed through the water, arrowing straight at the nucleus of the rich scent cloud that permeated the sea. Tammy actually felt the rush of the great creature surge beneath her feet as she was lifted bodily out of the water. José dropped her inboard and snatched at Pepita as the girl tried to swing her leg over the gunwale.

The Mako rolled over. Tammy caught a glimpse of triple rows of inward-sloping razor-sharp incisors lining a crescent maw, and a dull, almost disinterested reptilian eye. Someone

244

was screaming but she was too terrified to realise that it was herself.

The force of the strike lifted Pepita right out of the water so that for a moment it seemed that she were about to fall into the boat. Her arms flopped over the gunwale like the limbs of a stringless marionette. Her mouth opened in a round O of surprise but no sound came. Her eyes stared accusingly at Tammy, and then she was gone. For a moment everyone stared at the empty side of the lifeboat where the girl had been. Tammy threw herself forward and saw Pepita wave what looked like a languid farewell as she was dragged down and away. Another shark homed-in on the smoke trail of blood that laced the clear water. And then another, and another. The creatures erupted onto the surface, striking repeatedly, shaking their entire bodies in frenzied feeding paroxysms as they tore into the flesh. A giant hammerhead drove its grotesque, misshapen head into the centre of the maddened feast.

The sea churned to a rich froth of cream that quickly changed to a stark, accusing crimson to match the setting sun.

46

Brink straightened up from crouching over the tiny chart table in the control room and deliberately avoided Kessler's eye. He snapped the chronometer box shut. A quarter of an hour had passed since he had taken the noon sight. The entire watch was staring at him expectantly. He enjoyed being the centre of attention but was careful to maintain his customary dour expression.

'Well?' Kessler demanded impatiently.

'Thirty-five minutes of arc south, Captain,'

There was a sudden relaxing of the tension. Kessler grinned. 'Sure it's not thirty-six or thirty-four minutes, quartermaster?'

'We're thirty-five minutes south of the equator,' Brink affirmed huffily. Brink prided himself on his accurate fixes. On the previous patrol, when approaching Lorient, he had miscalculated their position in relation to the minesweeper-boom vessel by one mile. He had argued that his position was correct and that *U-395* had been in the wrong place.

'Thirty miles south of the equator,' Kessler mused, staring down at the chart.

They had made astonishingly good progress over the last few days – far better than anyone had expected despite Brandt's non-stop complaints about his diesels, and the forced stop to clear the sterngear. The fair weather had helped of course, and there was every chance that it would hold because they were now heading towards the Horse Latitudes, the tranquil eye of the North Atlantic's mighty clockwise gyre also known as the Sargasso Sea – an area steeped in legend and avoided in the days of sail, not because of the great masses of floating sargassum seaweed that collected there, but because ships could be becalmed there for weeks.

Kessler clapped his hands together and beamed around at the watch. 'Not that it means much. We're still three thousand miles from home with empty tanks, but, by God, I'm going to feel much happier at the end of this watch knowing that *U-395* and Lorient are in the same hemisphere at last. A bottle of beer for every man if our stocks will stand it, Mr Maron.'

'I think we've got more beer than diesel oil, Captain.'

Maron's jokes were rare enough to be caught and stuffed, so the roar of laughter it provoked was louder and more genuine than if had it been made by Kessler.

The news was passed to the survivors when the evening meal was taken out to them, but they were all too shocked by the events of the previous day to think of celebrating the crossing of the equator in the time-honoured way.

47

Mencke died that night, and the burial in the morning did nothing for Kessler's temper. He jammed his prayer book into its cubbyhole and pulled off his uniform, leaving it on the deck for the steward. He threw himself on his bunk wearing only his underpants, yanked his curtain closed and switched on his fan. He needed time to calm down. He loathed burials at sea and preferred to keep them short, especially coming within two days of the memorial service for the novitiate girl, but one of Mencke's comrades had insisted on garbling his way through a rambling ten-minute speech which no one could hear. When Kessler had snapped his book shut and given the nod to tip the plank, the weighted body bag had slithered onto the saddle tank and stayed there. A rating had pushed it clear with a boathook but it refused to sink because too much air was trapped in it. Luckily Handel had the presence of mind to dive into the sea and slit the canvas.

Kessler looked at his watch. One hour to noon – Maron's deadline.

'What I suggest is that if there's no change in our circumstances in ten days – on December 17th, that we implement our standing orders and release this towline. Do you agree with that, Captain?'

He thrust Maron and his pedantic ways out of his mind and concentrated on the photograph of Ingrid and their children. Gazing at her clutching armfuls of offspring usually had a calming influence but this time her smiling face stirred his anger. But for the stupidity of OKM in sending U-boats into the South Atlantic he would be with his family now, enjoying a two-month refit leave, clean sheets and regular hot baths because every day of the week was a Tuesday; he would be playing with his children, buying Christmas presents, getting Ingrid pregnant again, writing cards, cutting logs in readiness for the bitter cold of the coming new year. Cold – God, how he longed for the cold – real cold that turned your breath to clouds of sparking ice crystals in the still morning air. Instead he was 2800 miles from home, bathed in a film of oily, eye-smarting sweat while inhaling fetid, foul-smelling dragon's-breath air, and cursing the ludicrous shambles that this patrol had become. How many enemy convoys loaded with arms and munitions from the United States had slipped unnoticed through the thin patrol lines of U-boats strung across the North Atlantic? The restricted visibility of U-boats meant that they had to be within twenty miles of each other to ensure interception. Fat chance of tight patrol lines with boats being sent south, and even into the Mediterranean. The U-boat was the only real tool Germany had to defeat the British and her decadent empire, and Germany didn't know how to use it.

He looked at his watch again. Forty-five minutes to noon. What were the chances that Maron had decided to forget the matter?

He could hear Maron and Haug talking in the wardroom. He couldn't make out what they were saying but the studied politeness of their exchanges suggested an argument. They broke off when he shambled in to join them.

'What's the trouble, gentlemen?'

'Mr Haug doesn't like your order that the towline must be released at noon,' Maron explained.

Kessler met his watch officer's steady gaze. *Stupid of me to think that you'd forget*. He turned to Haug. 'We're down to five tonnes of fuel, Mr Haug. Barely enough to cover another four hundred miles even under these good conditions. I don't see that we have any choice.'

Haug turned and regarded Maron frostily. 'Have you read the report I've written on the importance of those crystals?'

'I've read it,' Maron replied dispassionately.

Haug nodded. 'In that case I see no point in reiterating what I've already said.'

Kessler considered his dwindling options. There was one

course open to him. He wasn't optimistic that it would work but it was worth a try. 'Mr Maron, pass the word to Dieter Rohland that I wish to talk to him. Tell him he has my guarantee of safe conduct and that no move will be made against him or his damned samples while he's aboard.' For a moment he thought that Maron was going to raise objections. A stupid notion: Maron knew that he didn't need to object – he was getting his way. Instead he clicked his heels and ducked into the control room.

48

Dieter gulped down the glass of apple juice that the steward placed on the wardroom table.

'Another?' Kessler asked.

Dieter shook his head. The litre per day of thick stew had prevented him from becoming emaciated, but being thin to start with meant that he had little reserves of body fat; already he was becoming even more hollow-cheeked than usual. 'I feel guilty enough about that one.'

The two men were alone in the wardroom, facing each other across the table. Both watertight doors were closed with petty officers posted outside to ensure that they were not disturbed. Kessler had put on a clean, short-sleeved shirt but already huge sweat stains were spreading from his armpits. His beard and hair were matted despite the whirring fan trained on him.

Kessler was leaning forward, brawny arms resting on the table, but Dieter was not intimidated. 'So what's the deal you're offering, Captain?' he inquired.

'No deal,' said Kessler bluntly. 'Just a bald statement of facts. Our fuel is nearly finished. Therefore I'm taking on as many German nationals as I can without impairing the efficiency of the boat, and I'm slipping the towline.'

'Then why have I been invited on board?'

'Go and fetch your rocks and you can stay on board. Not

that I care much either way what you decide, Mr Rohland. But you'd be a fool not to accept my offer. Our chances of survival are not good, but they're a damn sight better than being stuck in a lifeboat.'

'So you're abandoning us?'

Kessler's scalp went back but otherwise he kept his temper on a tight rein. 'It's not a question of abandoning you. We're going our separate ways.'

'Cling to that belief if it helps your conscience.'

Kessler was damned if he was going to let this upstart make him lose control. 'You might as well come aboard, Mr Rohland. We're leaving, with or without you and your damned lumps of rock. And if you don't want to come, then hand the rocks over so that we can at least salvage something out of this mess.'

Dieter sat back and regarded Kessler thoughtfully. 'Are you under pressure, Captain?'

'Under pressure!' Kessler echoed angrily. 'I'm over 2500 miles from home and sucking air from my fuel tanks. Of course I'm under pressure!'

'I was thinking of pressure from your executive officers. Mr Maron, perhaps?'

The younger man's perceptiveness irritated Kessler. 'If it wasn't for Oberleutnant Maron, you'd all be starving right now,' he growled. 'Listen. If we do get home, you'll probably face a court martial – disobeying orders, retention of government property, a host of charges.'

'I would not have thought that there's any "probably" about it,' Dieter remarked drily.

'I'll be prepared to give evidence in mitigation saying that you acted out of humanitarian considerations. That's something I can salute. But I can't salute stubborn stupidity.'

Dieter rose. 'Thank you for the offer. If you don't mind, I'll return to my lifeboat.'

'What about those stupid rocks?'

Dieter gave a thin smile. 'Well – they might continue to be a useful bargaining chip, so they stay with me.'

Kessler sat back, his broad shoulders sagging in resignation. 'As you wish.' He held out his hand. 'I suppose we might as well wish each other good luck.'

49

The next hour was spent ferrying the sickest members of the *Atlantis*'s crew from their liferafts to *U-395*. There were ten of them: eight could walk but two had to be lashed to stretchers. Manoeuvring them from the dinghy and onto the deck casing proved difficult in the uneven swell. A further thirty minutes was spent transferring all the remaining crew of the *Atlantis* to the liferaft that was in the best condition and stripping the unwanted raft of its meagre supplies before setting it adrift.

'Where are you putting them, Mr Maron?' Kessler called down from the bridge as the last stretcher was eased through the forward hatch.

'Petty officers' mess and bow compartment, Captain.' Maron answered, and followed the stretcher below.

Kessler grunted and turned his attention to Brink who was by the main gun having just finished the noon sight and was carefully putting his sextant back in its wooden case. Brink was such a remarkable perfectionist. The sea-level tables in his almanacs meant just that as far as he was concerned; when an accurate fix was required, he even took his sightings from a kneeling position on the casing. It wasn't hard to guess why Brink was taking pains over this particular fix. It would be entered in the log as the precise position where the survivors had been abandoned. The quartermaster slung the box from his shoulder and squinted up at the bridge. He glanced at the lifeboats and back at Kessler, uncertain how to begin what he wanted to say.

'Man on bridge, Captain?'

'Come on up.'

Brink scrambled up the ladder and ducked under the *wintergarten* rails. Kessler avoided looking at him by keeping his binoculars trained on the horizon. The atmosphere below had been bad when the word had spread that the survivors were to be abandoned. 'Captain – the petty officers and men in the bow compartment say that they could make room for the women and children. They've offered to rig up a central screen.'

Kessler realised that continuing to stare through his binoculars was a coward's way out. He lowered them and met Brink's hard gaze head on. 'Thank you, quartermaster. Convey my thanks to the bow compartment and tell them that matters must stand.'

Brink opened his mouth to say something but thought better of it. He gave a perfunctory salute and disappeared down the hatch without a word.

Damn! Kessler valued Brink's esteem.

Maron climbed onto the bridge. Kessler pretended not to notice him and swept his binoculars over the four craft on tow. The survivors stared blankly back at him. He tried to take in the overall picture but, very much against his will, he found himself concentrating on individuals: the pretty dark-haired girl in Lifeboat 1 who was talking to Dieter. He heard that she cried all day after the death of the Uruguayan girl. Next was a boy who looked no more than eight or nine years old; then the woman with her baby who reminded him of Ingrid. It would be so easy to order Brink to collect the children. But that would mean either separating them from their mothers or allowing them on board as well. Women in the boat . . . Discipline was stretched as it was . . .

He swung his binoculars to the horizon in silent anger. There were no humanitarian options open to him. And forcing an option open led to endless complications; the U-boat was not designed as a lifeboat – it was a killing machine, plain and simple. You had to keep that bleak concept in sharp focus throughout; the alternative was an agony of recrimination. He envied Maron's ability to see matters only in the stark, simple terms of naval regulations and Admiral Doenitz's standing orders.

'Captain . . .' said Maron tentatively.

Kessler lowered his binoculars.

'We're ready to resume normal duties.'

'What you mean, Mr Maron, is that *you're* ready to slip the tow.'

Maron remained silent.

'Your arm seems much better.'

Maron flexed his fingers. 'Much better, thank you.'

'Good. In that case, Mr Maron, you can do the honours.'

There was no hesitation; Maron stepped onto the *wintergarten* deck and reached for the quick-release shackle.

'Wait!'

He turned and looked quizzically at Kessler.

'Loudhailer, please!'

The bridge watch petty officer passed the loudhailer to Kessler. Feedback caused the instrument to emit a shrill whistle as Kessler turned the volume to maximum. His voice boomed across the swells that separated the lifeboats from *U-395*.

'Mr Rohland!'

Dieter stood and stared at him, one foot resting on a thwart, his legs flexing in harmony with the lifeboat's motion, hands on hips; a posture that conveyed arrogance and heightened Kessler's irritation.

'A last chance for you to reconsider, Mr Rohland. We're about to leave.'

Dieter's answer was to sweep an imaginary hat from his head and give a mock, courtly bow followed by an exaggerated farewell wave. Such was Kessler's anger that he barked his next order into the loudhailer.

'Cast off, Mr Maron!'

Maron shrugged and reached for the quick-release shackle.

'Smoke!' yelled a lookout suddenly, pointing frantically. 'A ship! Hull down!'

50

Erlicht was the smallest and most athletic member of *U-395*'s crew but had he climbed any higher up the periscope standard the chances were that even his slight weight would have bent the slender tube. He struggled to clean his binocular eyepieces while keeping his arms and legs crooked grimly around the periscope.

'Three mastheads!' he yelled excitedly.

'Jesus,' Maron muttered. 'A battleship?'

Kessler was beside himself with impatience. Had he been more agile he would have ordered the man down and shinned up himself. 'What sort of mastheads!'

'Lost them, Captain – No – got them! . . . It's a sailing ship – a big one!'

'Mr Maron! Slip that towline!' Kessler snapped. He yelled a string of engine room and helm orders down the hatch. The telegraph buzzed for full speed ahead both. The shackle hit the deck, grated across the casing and fell into the sea as *U-395* went hard about on both diesels. No one paid any attention to the dwindling lifeboats as the U-boat got underway; all eyes were fixed north in the direction of Erlicht's sighting.

'No topsails!' Erlicht called down from his perch a few minutes later. 'Bare masts.'

'Galley smoke do you suppose, Captain?' Maron queried.

'Christ knows.' Kessler looked up at Erlicht and bellowed: 'Give me her course, man!'

'Can't tell, Captain! Still too far off. Her mastheads look close together so we could be on her quarter.'

U-395 drove her bow into a steep sea. Kessler steadied himself against the coaming and pressed his elbows hard on the spray deflector as he held the binoculars to his eyes, willing the sailing ship to appear. And then he saw a streak of black smoke against the sky and caught a brief glimpse of mastheads and halliards showing themselves above a dip in the rolling crests.

'My God! She's a full-rigger!' he exclaimed.

'A training ship?' Maron queried, standing alongside Kessler and also keeping his binoculars trained ahead.

'Could be . . . Could be . . .' Kessler replied impatiently. 'But she won't one of ours – they're four-masters and they're all sewn-up in the Baltic.'

'We're overhauling her and we're astern of her,' Erlicht called down ten minutes later. 'She's only got one little sail hoisted on the after mast.'

'A mizzen!' Kessler growled. 'Didn't they teach you anything on your basic training?'

'Taught me to recognise the Stars and Stripes, Captain,' Erlicht replied impishly.

'He's right!' said Maron suddenly.

Kessler saw the ensign streaming from the ship's mainmast at the same time. And then he got a clear view of all three masts and their rigging.

'A barque!' Kessler shouted jubilantly, thumping the coaming in excitement. 'She's magnificent!'

Five minutes passed and the hull of the fine ship came into view. A graceful clipper bow and the long spike bowsprit favoured by American builders. Kessler's love of sail was such that he felt privileged to be in the same waters as a full-rigger such as this barque. His U-boat was the result of forty years' development; this incomparable sailing ship he was feasting his eyes on through his binoculars was the majestic culmination of four thousand years' development. Magnificent. Everything about the sleek ship looked just right. Little about her was original of course. There had been alterations such as her aluminium yards and the addition of a radio shack abaft the foremast that spoilt her flush deck, and a curious smokestack between the mizzen and main mast that was making the trail of black smoke, but that was how it should be; real ships were like fine buildings: dynamic, alive;

undergoing constant change, whose adaptability to suit changing needs guaranteed their survival.

With the exception of two small jibs and a mizzen to provide stability, she was ploughing regally along at a steady six knots with all her sails furled and neatly gasketed to her yards. Once her course and speed was established, Kessler ordered the port engine stopped so that *U-395* could shadow the ship at a safe distance.

'Boston-built,' Kessler breathed. 'Middle of the last century, I'll be bound. Around three thousand tonnes. Composite construction – iron frames and keel, and a teak hull. Get yourself snarled-up in pack-ice in a ship like that and you just sit back and wait for a thaw. Have you ever seen such lines?'

'With respect, we need diesel fuel. What's the point in chasing after a sailing boat?'

Kessler's impatience showed in his voice. 'She's making six to seven knots, Mr Maron. How do you suppose that a ship that size is clipping along at that speed with only a couple of jibs and mizzen set when there's no damned wind anyway?'

'I wouldn't know. Naval college didn't devote much time to sailing boats.'

'Look at the wake under her stern! Turbulence. And not the sort you get from an auxiliary engine. That lovely lady is packing a pair of diesels. Big ones. A lot of full-riggers had their top masts reduced and topsails removed after the last war. Cuts down on the number of crew and makes them easier to sail. Replace the auxiliary with diesels and you've got a ship that can ply the world using the wind when it's favourable, and her engines when it isn't. My betting is that she'll have midships fuel tanks with a capacity of at least four hundred tonnes.'

Maron was unimpressed by his captain's reasoning. 'Stop me and buy some? The Americans haven't been too friendly towards our U-boats recently.'

Kessler was momentarily lost for an answer. His main

concern had been to get close enough to the ship to shadow it before working out a plan. What Maron said was true: US warships had attacked U-boats on several occasions. President Roosevelt had justified their actions saying that one didn't wait for a rattlesnake to strike before destroying it.

'Our need is greater than theirs,' Kessler muttered. 'They've got sails.'

'Very well, Captain. We overhaul them, fire a round across their bows, and they heave to. But what else are they going to do? They'll transmit their position. A ship that size is going to be carrying proper HF antenna arrays. Full-length resonate aerials. She'll be heard all over the Atlantic, and that'll bring the British down on us in no time. We've hardly any fuel left; our batteries need a twenty-four-hour charge. We're in no state to engage as much as a sloop.'

Kessler made no reply. The damnable thing was that Maron was right.

'*Maid of Avalon* – Boston, Captain!' Erlicht called down.

The news was relayed to the control room petty officer who reported that the ship did not appear in the Lloyds register.

'Looks like she's heading for home,' Kessler commented while thinking fast. 'I reckon her course will take her smack into Boston in about twenty days.' He flipped the voice pipe open, summoned Brink onto the bridge, and grinned wolfishly at Maron. 'I've had a brilliant idea . . . Ah, quartermaster. Do we have a Stars and Stripes in our flag locker?'

'Only a courtesy pennant, Captain,' Brink replied, his head and shoulders half out of the hatch.

'That won't do. You'll have to make one. The same size as our ensign.'

Brink looked nonplussed. 'I'm sorry?'

Kessler sighed. 'It's a simple enough order, Brink. I want you to make a large Stars and Stripes. Use a sheet and some blue and red material. Anything so long as it looks good at a distance. Get the steward to help out. He's a wizard with a needle and thread. I want it on our jack staff in two hours . . .'

257

Brink acknowledged and disappeared down the hatch. Kessler turned to Maron. 'I want ten men clean-shaven, washed and smartened up and in their number ones, and paraded on the casing. And you may ask why. I'll be disappointed if you don't.'

'A ruse of war,' said Maron flatly.

'Exactly. We have to get that ship to heave-to without them using their radio. And the only way we can do that is if they think we're American.'

'But –'

Kessler held up his hand. 'I know what you're going to say: *U-395* looks embarrassingly like a German boat. To most people, even sailors, one submarine looks very much like another. The crew of the *Maid of Avalon* will see the Stars and Stripes, a row of clean-cut all American boys – not the U-boat scruffs they're used to seeing on the newsreels – and they'll also see a friendly greeting on the lamp. Put that lot together and what they'll see will be a US submarine. Simple.'

51

At 15:30, with the sun beating down on a stunned sea, *U-395* was nearly ready.

A passable Stars and Stripes made from a sheet and coloured blanketing fluttered from her jack staff. Kessler had washed and shaved (even though it wasn't Tuesday) and was wearing a short-sleeved shirt. He had even forsaken his stained cap and was wearing an all-white peaked cap he had scrounged off Maron. Mustered on deck was a party of ratings lined-up for Maron's critical inspection. Clean-shaven, transformed, caps well forward in the American fashion.

'Make the guns ready, Mr Reche,' Kessler ordered. 'But I don't want them manned. Leave them centred and covered and stay near them. Understood?'

'Understood, Captain.' Reche's face was alight at the prospect of action. He gave a crisp salute and snapped out orders to his gunners. The tampon was removed from the main 88-millimetre gun and an incendiary round slid into the breech. Ammunition belts were fed into the Oerlikon anti-aircraft gun. Both guns were then shrouded in canvas covers so that they could be ripped away in an instant. Below in the bow compartment the four torpedoes, ready loaded in their tubes, were given a final once-over.

Maron joined Kessler on the bridge. 'All ready, Captain.'

'Impressive, Mr Maron,' said Kessler, waving an appreciative hand at the pristine men mustered on the casing. 'Very smart.'

'I think we should make a habit of it.'

'What? Driving around the ocean looking like a Yank?'

'Having a smartly turned out watch. It's good for morale. Men that look good, feel good.'

Kessler touched his shorn chin. 'I certainly feel much cooler. Maybe you've got a point.'

Maron looked uncertain.

'Say what's on your mind, Oberleutnant,' Kessler invited.

Maron squared his shoulders to stress his formality. 'There could be a diplomatic furore over what we're about to do.'

Kessler grinned. He wasn't going to let Maron's old-womanish attitude to anything out of the ordinary spoil his good humour. 'Siphoning petrol out of an American boat? Bound to be. I don't mind your noting your objections in the log. Mustn't have your association with me ruining your promotion prospects, must we?'

'I've no objections, Captain. I think it's an excellent idea.'

Kessler opened his mouth and promptly shut it again. He stared at Maron. 'You do?'

'It's just that I think it can be improved on to minimise diplomatic repercussions.'

'Pray tell.'

'I think we should pay for the fuel whether the skipper of the

Maid of Avalon likes us taking it or not,' Maron replied.

'Well . . . I've got a few marks. I suppose we could have a whip-round, and we might be able to include some of Poison Ivy's lasagnes in the deal.'

Maron was not amused. 'Mr Haug has over two thousand US dollars that Dieter Rohland was to have used as bribe money. We could also pay for any food and fresh water we take. Thirdly, before leaving we could escort the barque back to the survivors to pick them up. That way we solve all our problems.'

Kessler looked at his first watch officer in admiration and regretted his joke. He should have known better; Maron's ideas were always sound. He nearly clapped him on the shoulder but remembered his man's wound. 'Brilliant, Hans. Absolutely, stunningly brilliant. Now why didn't I think of that?'

He picked up the loudhailer and exhorted his crew to look American and think American. One wag responded with a passable impersonation of Donald Duck which provoked a gale of laughter. 'Right, men,' Kessler concluded. 'If all goes well, we'll be on our way home by nightfall.' The news was greeted with a ragged cheer. He called down an order to increase speed and spent the next ten minutes going over the final details of the plan with Maron and Reche.

52

The *Maid of Avalon*'s watch was not what it should have been. *U-395* was within a quarter of a mile of her starboard quarter before she was spotted. The wheelhouse door burst open. Several figures darted to the bulwarks and trained binoculars on the diminutive submarine that was overhauling them. More men appeared on deck as the word spread. Some even climbed into the rigging for a better view. They all returned the U-boat men's friendly waves.

'Ten men so far,' Reche reported from his post near the anti-aircraft gun. The young officer sounded manfully calm but his omission of the customary 'Captain' betrayed his excitement.

The elderly barque didn't look so good close to. Her paintwork was faded and peeling, her varnish work non-existent judging by the state of her handrails, doors and hatches which were bleached white by sun and salt. Such shabbiness only increased Kessler's regard for her; she was a working boat, not some millionaire's floating gin palace that was decked out once a year for a warm-water cruise. His nose twitched when he caught a whiff of the black smoke she was making.

My God – I know what she is now.

'She's a sealer, Mr Maron. That smoke's from her separator boiler. No wonder she looks so scruffy. They usually work a long way south – Georgia, Patagonia.'

'How do they catch them?'

'Simple. They heave-to off an island, send a boat ashore with a rifle party, and shoot or club the buggers. The skins are what they're really after, but the oil and meat can fetch a good price too. Damn fine seamen.'

The smell got stronger. Maron's aquiline nostrils registered his disgust. 'Please don't ask me to go aboard if we establish good relations with them.'

Kessler laughed. 'Can't be any worse than a U-boat. Sing out if anyone goes near that radio shack.' He unhooked the portable signal lamp. He had rehearsed in his mind what he was going to say: a short, friendly message in his best colloquial English. The lamp's louvres rattled, flashing out the Morse. By now the distance between the towering sailing ship and *U-395* had narrowed to two hundred metres. A big man in grimy, once-white shorts appeared at the wheelhouse door. It was the way his binoculars slowly and steadily traversed the length of *U-395*, taking in every detail, that twisted a snake of unease in Kessler guts. The man seemed to shout something that caused the crewmen to promptly vanish. He aimed a rail-mounted Aldis lamp at *U-395* and requested a resend. Maron was also uneasy at the sudden disappearance of the crew. He turned to say something but Kessler was rattling the lamp again.

HI FELLERS WE HAVE MAIL FOR HOME AND WE COULD USE A BEER.

The delay before the acknowledgement winked out across the narrowing gap between the two craft heightened Maron's disquiet.

'Come *on*,' Kessler muttered impatiently.

The big man worked the Aldis lamp again:

OKAY WILL STOP COME ALONGSIDE.

Kessler banged the coaming in delight and fired a string of orders as the *Maid of Avalon* lost way. *U-395* reduced speed and turned towards the great ship like a chick seeking the sanctuary of its mother's wing. 'Thought that would work,' said Kessler, chuckling smugly. 'I told them we were dying for a drink. They've taken pity on us. US Navy ships are all bone dry. Dropped anchor once near a US destroyer in Singapore. The sound of a Schnapps bottle popping its cork had its officers swarming all over us.'

The big man appeared at the head of the Jacob's ladder. He stared down at the approaching submarine hands on hips. Reche's ratings dropped fenders into place to protect the saddle tank. Stoker Hartmann was holding a coiled heaving line at the ready.

'What happened to those crewmen?' said Maron worriedly as the bow closed to within fifty metres of the *Maid of Avalon*. They could see the sailing ship's green, barnacle-encrusted copper sheaving as she took the swell on her quarter. 'They've all vanished.'

'Too close to see them at this angle,' Kessler grunted. He ordered the electric motors to take over from the diesel so that they could manoeuvre. They were close enough now to see the big man's suspicious expression. Hartmann heaved the line to him. He tried to catch it but the coils fell short. Later Kessler would learn that the stoker had uttered a profanity in German. At that moment, the big man suddenly stiffened, yelled an order, and darted into the wheelhouse. There was the sharp crack of rifle fire. A round ricocheted off the coaming near Kessler's elbow and whined past his ear. Maron moved fast despite his injured shoulder. He yelled at the crew of the main gun and half fell down the outer ladder. Kessler bellowed down the voice pipe for full speed astern on both electrics. Reche tore away the cover from the Oerlikon, yanked the firing yoke around to bear on the *Maid of Avalon*, and opened up. The harsh yammer of the four barrels raking the bulwarks with a wall of 20-mm lead drowned the sound of return fire from the sailing ship's scuppers.

'Aim lower!' Kessler bellowed.

A gunner bringing *U-395*'s main gun to bear gave a scream and fell writhing to the casing, clutching his shattered leg. Maron ordered the gun crew to fire at will. There was no need to aim at such close range. The gun boomed. An 88-mm shell tore through the *Maid of Avalon*'s wooden side and exploded, showering *U-395* with teak splinters as she backed away. Another stutter of rifle fire and a round zinged off the *wintergarten* rails. Kessler's surmise that the unseen riflemen had been told to concentrate on the U-boat's guns was confirmed when Reche uttered a cry and fell back from the AA gun, blood pumping from a hole in his temple and the gaping exit wound at the back of his head. Kessler shoved his lifeless body aside, grabbed the yoke and stitched splinters along the scuppers. He fired a long burst, unmindful of the deafening staccato from the spewing barrels, the crazy dance of the ammunition belt jerking through the breech, or the blizzard of hot, smoking cases raining around him. He stopped firing long enough to swing the quadruple barrels towards the radio shack, and opened up again, bringing down a tangle of antenna wires and halliards that crashed onto the deck. The barrels jerked in and out on their recoil dampers like the jabbing assagais of Zulu warriors. The main gun boomed again. The *Maid of Avalon*'s teak-planked deck heaved and splintered from the force of an explosion below. The big man jumped onto the midships hatch cover and was about to throw something when Kessler's murderous fire cut him down. The grenade rolled from the big man's fingers and exploded, silencing the last of his crewmen who was still putting up a fight. Two more rounds from the main gun ripped into the stately sailing ship and detonated below decks. A hit on the blubber boiler caused a cataclysmic explosion that burst through the after deck and snapped the mizzen mast which crashed partially down and hung, swaying drunkenly like a marionette from a tangle of halliards and shrouds. The smoke that boiled from the gaping hole in the deck preceded a deep rumbling like the preliminaries of a volcano on the point of major eruption. Kessler's continuous burst swept the entire length of the deck from bowsprit to Samson post, chewing handrails, hatch covers and doors to matchwood, ricocheting off capstans and winches. The blurred feed of the convulsing ammunition belt suddenly ceased when it was spent, and the overheating barrels fell silent. Flames tongued through the hole in the deck and danced like hellish imps through the running rigging, fastening greedily onto tarred shrouds and leaping skywards.

'Cease firing!' Kessler yelled, but too late. The main gun roared again and another incendiary round smashed into the stricken ship. Maron acknowledged the order and straightened, coolly surveying the devastation that the U-boat's guns had wrought.

'By God, we'll have her diesel oil, Mr Maron!' Kessler shouted. He wiped sweat and powder grime from his eyes and rattled orders down the hatch. *U-395* stopped going astern and closed on its victim. Hatches clanged open and men swarmed onto the casing unreeling firehoses. Both diesels started and roared up to maximum revs in neutral. Mechanics frantically spun handwheels to divert the streams of cooling water through the fire hoses. Brandt and his men appeared and yanked open the casing hatches over the bunkering valves. Kessler was the first man to board the *Maid of Avalon*, not out of bravado, but because he was the only man with a gun. His swashbuckling arrival on the sailing ship's weather deck, by grabbing a hanging shroud and swinging Tarzan-like aboard, was spoilt by his loss of footing on planking that was slippery with blood. He jerked the Luger from his waistband and shot dead an injured sealer who was reaching for his rifle. He dived down a companionway to reconnoitre, racing along a gloomy passageway and kicking open mahogany-panelled doors. There was no one below. By the time he returned to the weather deck, Brandt had discovered the barque's bunkering valves and was connecting hose adapters. The men on the fire hoses had doused the rigging blaze and were concentrating their jets of water through the smoking hole in the afterdeck.

Maron ordered men to search below to salvage anything in the way of supplies. 'Any foodstuffs that look as if they might float! Just throw them in the water! Come on! Move!'

'What's the problem, Mr Maron?'

'I think she's sinking, Captain,' Maron replied after he had ordered Pols and a telegraphist to salvage anything that might be of use from the mangled remains of the radio shack. 'One of the explosions was too big to be a shell. A boiler or something. It must've blown a hole in her bottom. The aft hold's empty and making water fast.'

A gout of diesel oil erupted from one of the refuelling valves when Brandt opened it. He shut it off hurriedly.

'We won't need to pump, Captain,' he said, grinning broadly. 'Something's forcing the oil out.'

Maron was right. The explosion had even ruptured the fuel tanks. The pressure of flooding seawater caused by the ship's settling weight was forcing the fuel oil up and out through the valves. It simplified transferring the fuel but it also meant that they had to work fast.

The barque, now smoking and blackened but with most of her yards and rigging still intact, was bearing herself like a proud dowager fallen on hard times. She settled lower in the water, borne down by the even burden of her massive keel that had kept her upright and regal for nearly a century. It was obvious that she wasn't going to indulge in an undignified stern-first sinking, but was intent on going gracefully to the depths like a disappearing cinema organ.

The salvaging operation became an orderly but hurried race against time as the water level rose around the hull. Once the bunkering hoses were connected, there was little Brandt and his men could do but will the precious fuel to flow as fast as possible into *U-395*'s tanks. The *Maid of Avalon* continued to settle lower, now ramming the fuel through the hoses with enough force to make them stiffen. Brandt hung on as long as possible as the deck sank beneath him and his men: every extra tonne pumped into *U-395* meant an extra sixty to a hundred miles range.

'Come on, old girl,' he prayed. 'Forty tonnes . . . Forty tonnes will get us home . . .'

But after an hour, with the swell surging across the weather deck, he was forced to disconnect the bunkering hoses and order his men back to the U-boat.

Kessler clattered down the ladder into the control room and pushed past the watch. Poison Ivy was in heaven; he had salvaged a packing case of dried garlic and was dragging it lovingly along the central aisle. Kessler caused the hard-working chef much grief by stepping on the priceless trophy to reach his cabin. He pulled aside the curtain, sat at his tiny table, and dismantled the Luger. He had hoped that cleaning the firearm would give him time to think, but all it did was focus his mind on what he had just used it for. He yanked the wire brush angrily through the barrel.

Christ – you're a hypocrite. What's the difference between killing people with a torpedo or killing with them with a gun? Does the fact that you can't see the poor bastards dying when you use a torpedo make any difference? If it does, should it? They die just the same.

'Captain . . .'

It was Haug, standing by the open curtain, watching him wrapping an oil cloth around the Luger.

'Not now, Mr Haug.'

'I wanted to say –'

'I said *not now*!'

Not interested or not caring that Haug was watching him, Kessler jammed the gun back in an overhead locker and returned to the bridge. He ordered *U-395* to stand off a safe distance from the *Maid of Avalon* and leaned moodily on the coaming. Rather than look at the magnificent ship he had destroyed, he concentrated on the huge slick of seal oil and diesel fuel and the way it created patterns of iridescent colours in the bright sunlight.

'What's in those cans, Mr Maron?' Kessler demanded as the last giant tin disappeared down the aft hatch. The ten-kilo catering tins had been scattered over a large area. They and sides of ham and other floating foodstuffs had been rounded up and piled on the casing by two ratings manning the inflatable dinghy.

'Peaches, Captain. Either the crew liked them or they had picked up a cargo somewhere.'

Kessler grunted and forced his reluctant gaze to dwell on the *Maid of Avalon*. Her hull was now completely submerged; doubtless pockets of air were keeping her afloat, but they couldn't last. Her masts and rigging, still upright apart from the mizzen, were reflected eerily in the oil slick. The sea seemed strangely still and silent. It was the effect of the oil, of course, but Kessler couldn't help the absurd thought that it was as if the Atlantic were expressing a mute farewell to an old and respected adversary and her crew.

A hundred years she's plied the world. A hundred years of braving storms, tempests and just about anything that the world's weather systems felt like chucking at her. She's probably sailed a million miles in her lifetime. Running spice, tea, coffee, probably arms now and then. Home, wife and a business to hundreds of men in her time. And what was her reward for that long service? Being shot to matchwood and her crew murdered by a stupid, bungling cretin from a country she wasn't even at war with.

Kessler's thoughts turned to Reche, whose body hadn't been found, and the recriminations mounted. He roundly cursed himself. How could he have been so crass to have made so many mistakes? Sealers were a suspicious lot. Their business made them so. Half of it was clandestine: operating on lonely coasts; always exceeding quotas; always on the lookout for naval ships of any country. Navies represented authority, and authority invariably meant trouble. The *Maid of Avalon*'s captain would have known the profile of every damned warship afloat. The homemade Stars and Stripes would not have fooled the canny sealer for an instant. Also, sealers carried rifles and their crews were crack shots. So many stupid, unforgivable mistakes. With a guilty start he realised that he didn't even know if Reche had been married. The young officer had never talked about himself. If it came to that, either through shyness or reticence, he had hardly ever talked about anything.

There was a sudden eruption of air from the stricken barque and she began to go. Kessler knew that he should leave the area as quickly as possible, but the irrational side of his nature told him that he could not leave the proud ship to die alone.

There was a movement beside him. He sensed Maron's presence without turning his head.

'Does the chief know how much oil we salvaged?'

'About ten to twelve tonnes,' Maron replied stiffly. 'Plus plenty of tinned food, some hams, two tonnes of canned peaches, and about two tonnes of corned beef. And a load of garlic.'

The *Maid of Avalon* sank. It was sudden. One minute her masts were still visible as though she were about to rise again. Then a swirl of oil-slicked water. An explosion of bubbles bursting sluggishly through the leaden ocean. And then nothing. Not even wrecked rigging. She had gathered up all her belongings like a careful maiden aunt finishing a social call, and left.

Kessler swore bitterly. 'A dozen men killed and a fine ship destroyed. And for what? A thimbleful of oil that won't take us two thousand miles.'

'A fine ship, but an enemy ship,' Maron remarked casually.

Kessler turned and regarded the younger man. He didn't notice the book that Maron was holding. 'What the hell are you talking about, Hans? You mean her Stars and Stripes was as phoney as ours?'

'Pols didn't find anything of use in the radio shack. You did a good job on it. But he did find the signal log.' Maron rested the book on the coaming and opened it. He pointed to an entry. 'Your English is better than mine, Captain, but I don't think I've made a mistake. We declared war on the United States a week ago.'

Kessler grabbed the log. 'My God,' he muttered when he had finished scanning through the last entries. 'And look at this! "Rio news bulletin. Japan attacked US fleet in Pearl Harbor"!' Holy shit – the whole damned world's at war – again!'

'So it would seem.'

The two stared at the spreading oil slick. Kessler expected Maron to make his usual comments about the invincibility of the Fatherland and how it was inevitable that it would triumph over its enemies, but he remained silent.

'And I used to think it would all be over by Christmas,' said Kessler at length, his bitterness mirrored in his expression. 'I used to read about U-boat aces like Kretschmer and Prien and the rest when I was stuffing mines up England's arse, and worry that there'd be no ships left for me.'

Maron levelled his binoculars at the spot where the *Maid of Avalon* had disappeared. 'When I was about ten years old my parents took me to visit some relatives in Ohio. Dentists, like my parents. The train passed factories . . . Hundreds and

269

hundreds of them. They went on for a whole day. I couldn't believe it. I remember asking my father what they all made but I think he was just as puzzled as me . . . It's strange to think that I've seen more of the world than the Führer.'

Kessler turned and looked at Maron in surprise. It was a tiny admission of loss of faith. If the comment was a criticism, it was first time he had heard such a thing from Maron's lips, but the fine, aristocratic features were as impassive as ever, giving nothing away. Kessler glanced through a few more pages of the log. He seemed to age as he read. He snapped the book shut. 'I made a deal with you about the survivors, Hans.'

'We agreed that the boat should return to normal routine today,' Maron corrected, lowering his binoculars.

'It was a deal. But this changes everything.'

'In what way, Captain?'

That supercilious look was back that made Kessler want to plant his fist right in the middle of Maron's face. 'It'll be like when America came in the last time. The seas swept clear because every nation will be convoying their ships. Those poor bastards in those lifeboats didn't stand much chance of a ship finding them before this happened. They stand none at all now. We're going back for them.'

It was as if Maron was expecting it. He merely nodded and said: 'If it is going to turn into something big involving America and Japan, then we're going to need those crystals more than ever.'

Kessler stared at his subordinate.

My God — first a veiled swipe at the Führer and now a climb-down. A small one, but a climb-down nonetheless. Maybe there is a human being lurking under that cold-blooded exterior after all.

'There's still a lot of food floating around,' Maron added. 'With your permission, we ought to round it all up. We're going to need it.'

53

Dieter opened his eyes and saw the outline of Tammy's head and shoulders framed against the dawn light. She was resting on one hand, her face near his, a blanket pulled around her.

Dieter eased himself up and looked quickly around. He could see the vague shape of *U-395* with the dawn light on its quarter as it rose on the ragged crests, and he could feel the familiar tremors as the towline slackened and tightened in harmony with the swell. He turned his head and was reassured by the sight of the other two lifeboats and the liferaft following line astern. Marco was beside him, curled into a tight ball. For some reason, since the business with the sharks, the boy had come to see Dieter as a great hero and now insisted on sleeping near him. The seaman on stern watch seemed to have nodded off.

'It's not my watch yet, is it?' Dieter asked.

'Not for another hour.'

'Did you wake me, young lady?'

Tammy put a warning finger to her lips and nodded towards the seaman sitting in the stern. As she turned her head, Dieter noticed how fresh and flawless her skin looked again. The week that had passed since the U-boat had abandoned them, only to return some hours later, had been marked by a huge improvement in their diet. The daily measure of soup had thickened to a stew that contained meat, and there had been an additional ration of two peach halves in a sweet syrup for everyone. On several occasions Dieter had quizzed the U-boat men who delivered the food but they were under strict orders to say nothing.

Tammy took a tiny parcel from under the folds of her blanket and held it out to Dieter.

'For you,' she said. 'I couldn't wait.'

Dieter looked at the package in surprise. The wrapping consisted of a piece of grubby notepaper held in place with cotton thread. 'Couldn't wait for what?'

'It's Christmas Day,' said Tammy simply.

Dieter had forgotten the date.

'The German ranchers always give cards and presents on Christmas Day,' Tammy explained. She smiled and added, 'They never wait for the Three Kings so I thought you wouldn't want to wait either. Careful with the cotton – I promised Miss Angela that I'd return it.'

Dieter unpicked the thread without breaking it and opened the package. Inside was a lady's handkerchief, neatly folded, so small that it hardly covered his hand when he unfolded it.

'It's really a Christmas card,' said Tammy shyly. 'I embroidered it myself.'

The 'card' was a work of art. Tammy had acquired a remarkable skill with a needle and thread despite her hatred of the many embroidery afternoons on the lawn that she had been obliged to endure under Mrs Montgomerie's watchful eye. It was a simple winter scene crowded with tiny Lowry-like figures skating on a frozen pond. In the foreground was a snowman, complete with scarf and pipe, all worked into the fabric with beautiful, almost microscopic stitching. With the addition of stitches to suggest light and shade, Tammy had cleverly used the handkerchief's white background to represent snow. The message was picked out in English using a different coloured thread for each letter:

FOR DIETER. MERRY CHRISTMAS AND A HAPPY 1942. WITH LOVE FROM TAMARA.

Dieter was so moved that he was unable to speak for some seconds. He had noticed Tammy working long hours alone, sometimes crying silently to herself, and had assumed that she had been repairing clothes.

'This is lovely, Tammy. I don't know what to say.' He smiled at her. He was tempted to cradle that lovely face in his hands and kiss her but Marco had woken up.

272

Tammy looked away, suddenly embarrassed. 'I did it from memory. A picture in a book. I've never seen snow. Does it look all right?'

Dieter slipped an arm around Marco who was craving attention. 'It looks so realistic that . . .' He pressed the handkerchief to his face and gave a blissful moan. 'Ah – snow. It feels wonderful.'

Marco joined in with Tammy's laughter. The first time she had laughed since they had made love in the sea. The sleeping shapes around them began stirring.

'I don't know how to thank you, Tammy,' said Dieter, giving the handkerchief to Marco for him to look at.

'I do,' said Tammy mischievously.

'Oh? How?'

She took his hand. 'I'd love to see snow, Dieter. Will you take me to see snow when we reach port? *Please*.'

'Why – yes – of course. With any luck there'll be snow at Lorient when we arrive.'

'Snow? In December?'

Dieter chuckled. 'Now that we've crossed the equator, the seasons are stood on their head.'

Her lustrous black eyes became alive with excitement. 'But I want to see real snow on mountains where people go . . . sheeing.' She stumbled over the word.

'Skiing,' Dieter corrected.

'Promise!'

'Yes – I promise.' He would have kissed her but Marco had climbed determinedly onto his lap.

54

Haug was the only man on *U-395* who disliked the daily trim dive. Everyone else relished the forty-minute respite from the heat when the lifeboats were cast adrift and the U-boat was taken down to fifty metres. But for Haug every minute separated from Lifeboat 1 and its priceless cargo was a worry.

'Standing orders,' said Kessler when Haug queried the necessity of the daily ritual. 'Damned sensible orders too. Every day we get through over a tonne of supplies and every hundred miles we burn about a tonne of fuel. For a boat to be controllable during a crash dive, it has to be perfectly balanced. Chief likes his centre of gravity and centre of buoyancy to be around the sky periscope. The trouble with a VIIC U-boat is that it's not a true submarine: it's a surface boat. It fights best on the surface and spends ninety-nine per cent of its time on the surface. The difference is that it has the ability to dive if an aircraft pounces. Last year there were boats returning home that hadn't dived once on their patrol. Several were damned near lost in the Bay of Biscay because they were badly trimmed when the RAF jumped on them.' He grinned at the portly intelligence officer. 'The RAF look upon the Bay of Biscay as their private hunting ground. So, Mr Haug, we take a trip into the cellar everyday and to hell with your crystals. Okay?'

Haug did not appreciate the lecture but treated Kessler to a beaming thanks. The other problem preying on his mind was the weather. Rather than risk another lecture, he decided that the first watch officer might be more amenable.

Maron came on watch at noon. Haug carefully closed the book he was reading in the scant shade of the main gun and approached the bridge.

'A word with you please, Mr Maron.'

Maron eyed the portly figure and motioned Haug to climb onto the bridge. The exertion of the short climb up the ladder left Haug breathless and perspiring. He wiped the sweat from his eyes and glanced aft at the lifeboats. Most of the survivors were out of sight, huddled under the protection of their makeshift awnings.

'This weather is remarkable,' Haug began.

'Uncomfortable,' said Maron guardedly.

'To think that such conditions could persist for so long in the Atlantic. I would never have thought it possible.'

'We're nearing the Doldrums,' Maron replied. 'But the rest of the Atlantic's weather will be going about its business of creating hell for those who venture into its midst.'

'And for us soon?' said Haug speculatively.

'I don't doubt it, Mr Haug.'

Haug hesitated for some moments. 'Oberleutnant, what are the chances of us losing the lifeboats when we run into bad weather?'

'That depends on how bad the weather is,' Maron replied equably.

'I was hoping for a straight answer,' said Haug acidly.

'Mr Haug – you are asking me to make predictions about the weather in the North Atlantic in January. The only thing I can predict with any degree of certainty is that it won't be good. It will be bad, but I can't say how bad.'

'But bad enough for there to be a risk of losing the lifeboats?'

Maron wanted the conversation at an end. He knew what was behind Haug's questioning. 'There is a risk of losing the lifeboats *and* the crystals, if that's what's worrying you. A very real risk.'

Haug thanked the first officer and returned to his book. Before opening it he stared back at Lifeboat 1 and picked out Dieter's head. Haug's hatred welled up although he was careful not to give any outward sign of his seething emotions. Dieter Rohland was a traitor, and like all traitors, would pay dearly for his crime.

55

Brandt tapped the fuel gauge and swore when the float indicator jumped to a new position. Diesel Mechanic Eric Handel couldn't hear the chief engineer's curses above the roar of the engine, but Brandt's expression said it all. He adopted a suitably crestfallen expression when Brandt cupped a hand to his ear and bellowed a number of suitably cutting general observations concerning Handel's tree-dwelling ancestors in general and the doubtful marital status of his parents in particular.

'So how many!' Brandt concluded.

Handel held up four fingers.

'Cretin!'

Handel's crest fell even further. He nodded glumly, ignoring the sweat trickling into his eyes.

'You'll dipstick the damned lot and I want the revised figures in thirty minutes! And try not to wake everyone up when you open the hatches!'

The hapless diesel mechanic went to work while Brandt moved to his berth, switched on his electric fan, and sat before his open engine room logbook, indelible pencil at the ready, while he waited for the correct figures concerning *U-395*'s fuel oil supplies. Handel busied himself for twenty minutes, ducking back and forth between Brandt's berth, the engine room and the casing as each fuel tank was sampled. Brandt's expression became progressively more thunderous as the true contents of each tank were relayed to him. When Handel had finished, he totted up the figures and treated the unfortunate mechanic to one more paint-blistering glare.

'I'm going to report this to the old man now, Handel. If it transpires that he develops a sudden hankering to have your kidneys or any other part of you on toast, then I shall help him roast them.'

With that Brandt tucked the logbook under his arm, donned his cap, and passed through the control room. Maron's midnight watch were taking over. As usual Brandt ignored the officer. When the port engine had played up on his last watch Maron had made another snide remark about the fate of Rudolf Diesel.

Kessler had just kicked his boots off after a four-hour stint on the bridge and was dozing, his electric fan going full blast, when he saw Brandt through a gap in the curtains. He swung his feet to the deck and invited the chief engineer to sit.

'Damn me if it doesn't feel a bit cooler tonight, chief. Or am I imagining it?' Brandt's tense expression alarmed Kessler but he was careful not to show it. He was about to say 'Something on your mind, chief?' but that would win prizes for stating the obvious.

Brandt positioned the logbook carefully on the tiny table. 'I'm very sorry, captain, but following our bunkering from the *Maid of Avalon*, you were given incorrect figures concerning the amount of fuel we were able to transfer aboard.'

Kessler's eyes widened a little. He absently scratched the matted hair on his chest. 'You mean we didn't tank-up with twelve tonnes after all?'

Brandt shook his head and avoided his captain's eye. 'When bunkering I always insist that the balance valves are closed,' he said stiffly. 'That way I know exactly what each tank has received without a lot of blow-backs and airlocks. Once the tanks are full, I then order the balance valves to be opened to fill the reserve tanks, and then top-up the main tanks again. I have just learned that the balance valves were open when we bunkered. I accept full responsibility for the mistake, captain and will ensure that –'

'So *how* much oil did we manage to salvage, for God's sake?' Kessler interrupted, showing uncharacteristic impatience when his chief engineer was making a report.

Brandt opened the logbook. A grease-stained hand prevented the electric fan from riffling the pages. 'Twenty-five tonnes, captain.'

One by one, Kessler's fingers stopped scratching. Their owner stared at Brandt in rank disbelief. '*Twenty-five tonnes!*' he echoed. 'You mean we have *double* the oil we thought?'

'Diesel Mechanic Handel disobeyed my standing orders,' said Brandt grimly. 'I am requesting that a severe reprimand be entered in the boat's log.'

Kessler looked lost for a moment. 'What?'

'I'm requesting that the man is subjected to a severe reprimand,' Brandt repeated.

Kessler collected his thoughts. 'Actually chief, I was thinking more along the lines of a commendation for an Iron Cross.'

Five minutes later Kessler entered the control room and beamed around. It was Maron's watch, therefore everyone in the control room was properly dressed instead of wearing the usual vests and shorts that Kessler permitted. Not even the sight of a perspiring Haug bustling around in a tight-fitting steward's jacket and clutching a tray could spoil his otherwise good mood.

'You seem to be making yourself useful, Mr Haug.'

'I like to keep my mind occupied, Captain,' Haug replied primly, and disappeared through the hatch on some mysterious errand.

'Where's Mr Maron?' Kessler asked the control room petty officer.

'On the bridge, Captain,' the NCO replied, adding boldly: 'You look pleased, Captain.'

'Oh I am. I am,' Kessler replied breezily as he mounted the ladder.

'We're all feeling the same, Captain.'

Kessler paused and glowered. 'Oh? Why? Who gave you permission to be cheerful? Right now I'm monopolising any good spirits that happen to be around.'

The petty officer pointed to the gauge that was showing the control room temperature as 29° Celsius. 'It's the first time in God knows how long that the mercury's dropped below thirty.'

Kessler peered at the thermometer and grunted. 'What the hell do you expect? We're in the northern hemisphere now and it's January. It's midwinter, damnit.'

For some reason the comment provoked roars of laughter.

Haug was an opportunist. He decided to act now because it could be several days before Kessler was out of his cabin during the first watch – the quietest time of day when movements in the boat were at a minimum. Unhurriedly, so that his inner excitement was disguised, he set down his tray in the galley and half filled a tumbler with apple juice. It was Kessler's own glass; a fine piece of Irish lead crystal that had to be wrapped in a towel during rough weather. The captain was fond of his little luxuries. Haug returned forward, balancing the tray and glass on one hand like a professional as he passed through the control room. The central passageway was deserted. He stepped through Kessler's green curtain and made sure it was closed behind him before searching the overhead lockers. The gun wasn't in the locker where he had seen Kessler stow it. Obviously the captain had decided on a new hiding place. He was on the point of giving up the search when his prying fingers found the Luger in its leather holster under a pile of clean vests in a cubby hole over the bunk. A sound outside. He picked up the tray and backed unhurriedly out of the cabin. The telegraphist paid him no attention as he pushed past. Haug returned to the galley. He was pleased with his little foray. Although he hadn't been able to purloin the Luger, at least he now knew exactly where it was.

Dieter opened his eyes and stared up at the stars, wondering what had woken him, knowing that it couldn't be the fitful coughing or snores from the shapeless masses around him. Those sounds were now stamped indelibly on his consciousness. As his mind cleared, he realised what it was: the surge of water hissing past the lifeboat had taken on a more urgent quality. He eased himself into a sitting position, taking care not to disturb Marco who was sound asleep with an arm flung around him.

'We're going faster.' Angela Montgomerie's lips were so badly cracked and swollen that he didn't recognise her voice right away. Dieter turned his head. Although not on watch, she was sitting bolt upright on a thwart, staring in the direction of the unseen U-boat.

Dieter moved Marco's arm and leaned over the gunwale. He tried to gauge their speed from the bioluminescent turbulence of their wake. He splashed water onto his face and allowed the rapid evaporation to suck the warmth off his skin. The night air felt a little cooler than usual but he couldn't be sure. Perhaps it was due to their increased speed.

'About a knot faster. Maybe a little more.' He spoke automatically in German but the Englishwoman understood him.

'I thought they couldn't afford the fuel to go faster?'

Dieter shrugged. 'Perhaps they've discovered that the engines are more efficient if we go faster. Or perhaps they have bought more oil from that ship they met than they say?'

Mrs Montgomerie snorted. 'If you believe that story about buying supplies from a ship, then you're a bigger fool than I thought. There were fresh bullet holes in the conning tower when they returned, and one of the officers is missing. The boyish-looking one. I've looked for him every day and he's never appeared.'

The young German remained silent. He had noticed the fresh damage that U-395 had sustained, but he hadn't noticed that an officer was missing. Not that he doubted Mrs Montgomerie's observations for a moment; nothing escaped her. Whatever had happened, it was a Kriegsmarine matter and was best not discussed with an English national. 'There is still some hours before the sun,' he said. 'We should sleep.'

56

Kessler sighed, planted his feet on the wardroom table, and leaned back on the settee, hands hooked together at the back of his neck while he regarded Brandt and Maron.

'Bit of a bugger, eh, gentlemen? Still not enough oil to get home.'

Maron slid the chart of the North Atlantic from under Kessler's soft shoes and made a show of brushing it clean. The noon sight that Brink had marked in pencil showed U-395's position as twelve degrees north of the equator – almost dead mid-Atlantic, pushing north-east through the throat that was formed by Trinidad in the west, and the Cape Verde Islands in the east.

'I have an idea that's certain to help,' Kessler continued. He smirked, adding: 'And, of course, like all my ideas, it's quite brilliant. But I'm anxious to hear your humble offerings. Chief?'

Brandt stared at the chart. The distance to Lorient said one thing, the amount of oil in *U-395*'s tanks said another, and the fuel consumption figures for his beloved diesels that were recorded with painstaking care in the engine room log, said yet another. And the equation didn't balance. He shook his head.

'Mr Maron?'

As always, the oberleutnant weighed his words with great care. 'I have an idea that will require careful working out, Captain.'

'We might as well hear it without the working out,' said Kessler ungraciously.

Maron turned the chart around and pointed. 'Instead of following our existing north-easterly heading towards Africa, it may be advantageous if we swung north-west towards the West Indies. That way we'd be moving with the North Equatorial Current.'

Kessler's smirk faded.

'That will help take us north,' Maron continued, 'and enable us to pick up the Gulf Stream to push us north-east towards Western France.' With his eyes on the chart he didn't see his captain's expression as it became thunderous. Brandt did, and looked forward to the verbal roasting that he felt certain Maron was about to receive. Maron sensed that something was amiss and looked up.

'Go on,' said Kessler grimly.

'It will certainly be a more circuitous route,' Maron stressed, not flinching from his captain's hard gaze. 'But if we

281

continue our present course, we'll be battling against the Canaries Current all the way up the coast of Africa and Spain.' He unfolded an ocean current chart and pointed to the tranquil eye of the huge clockwise gyre that dominated the North Atlantic. 'The Doldrums . . . Also known as the Horse Latitudes.' He caught Kessler's infuriated eye and mustered a supercilious smile. 'I understand that sailing skippers used to avoid them, Captain?'

'No wind for weeks at a time,' Kessler muttered in bad grace. 'So-called because the Spanish conquistadors resorted to eating their horses when they were becalmed there.'

Maron nodded. 'So if they're as calm as legend has it, then it might be worth us taking advantage of the conditions and cutting straight across the Horse Latitudes to intercept the Gulf Stream. As I say, my suggestion will need careful working out before it can be considered.'

'*Your* suggestion!' Kessler echoed indignantly. 'It's my idea! You've been reading my mind without permission!'

'Great minds think alike, Captain.'

'I'm sure they do,' Kessler replied. 'And so do ours it seems.' He stood, stuck his head through the control room door, and ordered a course alteration in his usual flamboyant manner:

'Petty officer!'

'Captain?'

'Set sail for the Sargasso Sea.'

The petty officer of the watch was a knowledgeable type often called upon to help solve crossword clues, and therefore didn't deserve Kessler's blast of invective when he inquired if it was either the title of a poem or a song, or a well-known phrase or saying.

57

The slight drop in night temperatures turned out to be a cruel hoax. For the next seven days *U-395* maintained an average four knots, forging steadily northward across an ocean that lay stunned and senseless under the sun by day, and smothered by a cloying, soul-sapping mist by night that eroded the will to live. Despite the hardship they were suffering, the physical condition of the *Anaconda*'s survivors remained remarkably good, largely due to Maron's careful attention to their diet. The extra milk and fresh water for the children ensured that they thrived. It was a different story for the survivors of the *Atlantis*. Their days at sea on liferafts before *U-395* discovered them had led to a irreversible decline in their mental and physical state. Generally it was the older members who were worst affected, but not always. On the second night, Karl Valle, the 18-year-old cadet-officer from the *Atlantis*, slipped into sea from Lifeboat 3 without telling anyone, and allowed the tiny armada to sail on into the darkness without him. Kessler recorded the incident in the log but didn't stop for a service. If Valle opted for an easy way out, that was his affair; his duty lay with the living, but to maintain morale in the three lifeboats, such as it was, he ordered Brink to keep a closer watch on the survivors and to transfer to the U-boat those likely to succumb. There were two more deaths during the following three days: one was a Spanish seaman who had taken to drinking copious quantities of seawater before being forcibly removed to the U-boat, and the other was the wholly unexpected sudden demise of José, the big, amiable bosun, who died of a heart attack.

'It happens,' said Kessler phlegmatically to Maron, snapping his prayer book shut when the weighted body bags were slid into the sea at night from the deck casing. 'Four days out from Hong Kong in '33 we had a cook keel over in the galley. Big man. Full of fun, full of life. But he went out just like a light being switched off. That's the way I'd like to go.'

Maron followed his captain onto the bridge. The lookouts made room for them. Kessler leaned against the torpedo aimer and stared ahead into the thin mist that was being rolled aside with sluggish reluctance by *U-395*'s unremitting four knots across the eerie, lake-like, black stillness. The strange, ethereal fog, swirling back into place in the boat's silvery wake, had even subdued the diesel to a sullen beat.

'My God, I loathe these conditions,' Kessler grumbled, mopping his forehead with his cap. 'It's all wrong. What the hell's happened to the Atlantic weather systems, eh? All around us but not here. Doesn't seem right.'

'It's certainly weird,' Maron commented. 'But it's enabling us to make excellent progress. One hundred and twenty miles made good yesterday.'

'But made good into what, Hans? The damned Sargasso Sea, that's what.'

The first-name informality within earshot of the lookouts surprised Maron. He looked sharply at Kessler and wondered how rattled the older man was. And then Kessler gave a deep, rich chuckle.

'Damned stupid sail superstitions. Ninety-nine per cent ignorance and one per cent fact. I spent so long under canvas that I've let too much of the ninety-nine per cent rub off. Mention the Sargasso Sea to the old-timers and they'd smother themselves in good luck charms. It makes them think of huge islands of floating seaweed that ensnare ships. All rubbish, of course. There is a good deal of floating seaweed but it's harmless. Ships drive through it and don't even notice.'

'*Sargassum natans*,' Maron murmured. 'And *Sargassum fluitans* – The two main varieties of pelagic weed in the Sargasso Sea.'

Kessler looked admiringly at his first watch officer.

'I've looked it up in Pols' oceanographic library,' Maron confessed. 'It's also the spawning area of all the world's eels, and most flying fish.'

'I didn't know about the flying fish,' Kessler admitted. 'Wonder what it is about the place that attracts eels? Damned if I'd swim ten thousand kilometres for a quickie.' He was about to enlarge on the theme but remembered Ingrid's propensity to get pregnant whenever he returned from a long patrol. He yawned. 'Ah well. Even if the tales about the Sargasso are ninety-nine per cent superstitious sealore, there's no doubt that it's a very strange place.'

Maron gave a rare smile. 'Well if we do come across a derelict ship ensnared in seaweed, let's hope it's a laden tanker.'

'That's two jokes in two months, Oberleutnant,' Kessler observed.

'It's the sea air, Captain.'

58

Haug treated Tammy to a sunny smile when he had finished collecting the empty canteens from the nuns in Lifeboat 1. His now somewhat slimmer but still rotund figure wobbled dangerously as he stood in the inflatable dinghy and held out a magazine to the girl. He addressed her in Spanish.

'*Señora* Derosa? I think this is exactly what you want.'

She reached for the offering, and Haug's weakness for young boys was not sufficiently pronounced to prevent his quick, questing eyes from being seduced from their usual evening task of searching the interior of the lifeboat to dwell on the mouth-watering spectacle of her generous breasts moving with a life of their own beneath a sweat-soaked, clinging nightdress. Then his gaze dropped to the clear outline of a darkly matted pudendum imbued with Latin prominence.

'Whatever it is you're looking for, Haug,' said Dieter in rapid German, 'I promise you they're not there.'

'It belongs to a member of crew who comes from Bavaria,' Haug continued, ignoring Dieter. 'He would like you to keep it.'

'Oh please,' said Tammy. 'You must thank him for me.'

Mrs Montgomerie shaded her eyes against the sun. 'A suitable magazine for a young girl, I trust?' she said sternly.

Haug managed a little bow. He considered Mrs Montgomerie a fine woman. Almost Wagnerian. 'Most suitable, Mrs Montgomerie. Alpine scenes. A travel magazine.' His bow was a little too ambitious. He had to sit suddenly to avoid losing face and balance. He gave a curt order to the rating and the dinghy pulled towards the second lifeboat.

Tammy flipped through the magazine and came upon a double-page colour photograph that showed a family smiling at the camera. Mother, father and two children all in full skiing regalia. But it was the magnificent backdrop of snow-covered mountains that had captured her attention. She held her prize up for everyone to see. 'Look everyone! Snow! Real snow!'

Marco scrambled over his mother and reached out a tentative finger to touch a mountain peak. 'Can't feel it,' he said, grinning.

Tammy laughed and tousled his hair. She moved to the stern, wriggled down beside Dieter, and traced the outline of a mountain with her forefinger. 'Isn't it beautiful? How can you have such bright sun and snow?'

'It melts eventually.' He smiled at her. The touch of hair on his shoulder sent tingles down his arm.

'Have you ever been skiing, Dieter?'

'When I was a kid. I never learned properly. I kept falling over.'

Tammy smiled and fanned herself with the magazine. 'I'd want to roll over and over in the snow. Naked.'

'I don't think Miss Angela would approve.'

'And I'd make you make love to me.'

'I know she wouldn't approve of that. And you wouldn't have to make me. But not in the snow – it's wet and cold.'

She found another Alpine scene. 'It can't be,' she said dreamily. 'It looks so beautiful. Will there really be snow in France when we arrive?'

Dieter squinted into the setting sun that was illuminating the forbidding upper anvils of ragged thunderheads far to the west. The mighty columns of black cumulonimbus had been taunting them all day. 'It doesn't seem possible at the moment but there could be. If there isn't, there will be in the mountains.'

Tammy snuggled her head down on his chest so that her hair spilled across his chest. 'Will you take me to the mountains to see snow if there isn't, Dieter?'

Dieter had hardly given any thought to what would happen to Tammy and Mrs Montgomerie if they did reach France. Tammy would most likely be interned. But what about Angela Montgomerie? Would she be treated as British or Uruguayan? British, most likely.

Tammy interpreted his hesitation as reluctance. '*Please*, Dieter.'

He stroked her chin and kissed her on the temple even though Mrs Montgomerie was watching them surreptitiously. 'Of course.'

'Promise?' she persisted.

'I promise.'

That night the sudden howling of the Klaxon propelled Kessler out of his bunk and into the sudden pandemonium in the control room before he realised that he was awake.

'Aircraft!' he bellowed incredulously through the conning tower attack kiosk to the bridge. 'In the middle of the bloody Atlantic! I don't believe it!'

The watch petty officer appeared at the hatch, the red night lighting giving his contrite expression a curious glow of health. 'I'm sorry, Captain. A mistake. But an understandable one.'

Muttering curses, Kessler climbed the ladder in his bare feet. He was about to bawl-out the lookouts to still their excited chatter but the extraordinary spectacle confronting him temporarily robbed him of his power of speech. Kessler had spent all his adult life at sea; he thought he had seen everything, but nothing had prepared him for this. All round the U-boat and as far as the eye could see the usual black water was awash with light from countless millions of what looked like tiny Christmas lights, each one emitting a vivid blue light. The aft hatch clanged open and men piled onto the casing, and promptly disappeared down the hatch again when the ghostly blue lights danced towards them across the deck.

'*Pols*!' Kessler bellowed. 'Get Pols up here immediately!'

The hapless amateur oceanographer was hauled from his berth and catapulted onto the bridge. He gaped at the seething carpet of vivid blue lights.

'Well?' Kessler demanded as though Pols was personally responsible for the bizarre phenomenon.

The powerful beam of the searchlight swept the sea, neutralising the strange lights where it touched them. There were cries of alarm of the lifeboats.

'I've no idea, Captain,' Pols admitted.

The solution to the mystery came from an unexpected quarter. A familiar beanpole-like figure emerged from the galley hatch and set about gleefully scooping up the lights and dumping them in a basket. Kessler swung the searchlight on him. The lights became greyish white shapes tossing and heaving in the basket like giant shrimps.

'Ivy!' Kessler barked. 'What the hell do you think you're doing?'

Poison Ivy stopped work and held up one of his writhing catches in triumph. 'Squid, Captain! I need men with nets to catch as many as possible!'

Kessler thumped the coaming. 'My God – fresh food and it's not even Tuesday.' He bawled orders down to the control room for the petty officer to muster a working party. The men set to work with a will, using shirts with knotted sleeves attached to boathooks to land the catch. Anything that could house the squid was passed up through the hatches, even the dinghy was inflated. At the end of an hour's feverish activity Ivy was proudly surveying several tonnes of seething cephalopod mollusc lined up on the casing in an assortment of ammunition boxes and packing cases.

'Do you know how to cook them?' Kessler demanded.

'Oh yes, Captain,' said Ivy enthusiastically. 'I've plenty of garlic so I'll be able to make squid soup, squid stew and even squid lasagne.'

Down below Haug was also pleased with his night's work. The commotion above had presented him with the opportunity he had been waiting for. He had slipped into Kessler's cabin and removed the Luger from its holster. He repositioned the holster under the vests exactly as he had found it and returned to his berth. The gun was easily concealed behind the plywood panelled bulkhead that separated his bunk from the petty officers' mess.

59

Even without the evidence of the falling barometer Kessler claimed that he could smell the impending change in the weather. At 13:00 he was called onto the bridge to survey the grey, leaden slab of cloud ahead that lay across the horizon like a fallen granite tombstone.

'Nimbostratus,' he announced for the edification of the lookouts. He allowed his binoculars to swung from their neckstrap and rubbed his hands gleefully. 'Nature's boundary markers for a depression. You'll all be in shirts and sweaters in a couple of hours.'

At 15:00 *U-395* slipped under the welcome shade of the great canopy of cloud like a desert insect crawling under a rock, and the temperature plummeted to just below 20 degrees for the first time in many weeks. Kessler duly recorded the event in the log.

Maron was the only member of the crew who didn't welcome the respite from the heat. 'They'll all start growing beards again,' he complained over dinner in the wardroom. Since their compulsory shearing for the *Maid of Avalon* interception, most of the crew had discovered the advantages of being clean-shaven and keeping their hair close-cropped.

'A return to tradition,' Brandt muttered into his squid soup.

Maron regarded the chief engineer speculatively. 'I didn't know you were a traditionalist, Chief.'

'I see no harm in a service as young as the U-boat service forging its own traditions.'

'You moan about my bathtub tradition on Tuesdays,' Kessler pointed out.

'That's because it's a pig to put together,' Brandt replied.

'It's tradition that hampers innovation,' Maron commented, cutting the mouldy corner off his bread and covering the slice with a generous spread of squid paté. 'If Rudolf Diesel had been a traditionalist, we wouldn't have diesel engines today. We'd be operating steam-driven submarines like those stupid K-boats that the British built.'

Brandt refused to take the bait. Kessler saw Maron about to make another cutting remark about the chief engineer's hero and intervened quickly. 'The K-boats had to be steam-powered,' he pointed out. 'They were intended to keep up with the fleet. In the 1920s and 1930s the British saw submarines differently from us: as fleet escorts rather than hunter-killers operating alone.'

'A stupid concept,' said Maron. 'The sort of thing we come to expect of them.'

'Don't underestimate the British, Oberleutnant,' Kessler warned, glad to have steered the conversation away from the fate of Rudolf Diesel. 'Especially where the sea is concerned. How did your parents relax at weekends?'

Maron looked surprised. 'How do you mean?'

'A simple enough question. What did your parents do during summer weekends?'

'We had a mountain lodge near Ravensberg.'

Kessler looked inquiringly at Brandt. 'Chief?'

'Camping in the Black Forest with ants and earwigs and mosquitoes.'

Kessler nodded. 'Exactly. No Englishman lives more than

one hundred kilometres from the sea. Look at the map if you don't believe me. At weekends we flock to the mountains and the forests – they're a part of our racial psyche – we defeated the Romans in the forests. But the British swarm to the seaside by the coach-load. While our kids are learning to ski and climb mountains and read forest trails, English kids are learning about the sea and what it can do to their sand castles. When they're older they take to sailing dinghies. And as young adults they sink their savings into small yachts. Thousands upon thousands of them. Look at Dunkirk. A whole army evacuated in small boats. We could never do that. Those corvettes and sloops that dump their damned *wabos* all over us when they get a sniff of our periscopes are all crewed by England's vast army of weekend sailors – the bloody Royal Navy Volunteer Reserve. We'll never beat the British at sea.'

'A defeatist attitude, if you'll forgive me saying so, Captain,' said Maron coldly.

'A pragmatic attitude,' Kessler countered, chewing on a piece of squid. 'Our best bet will be to make peace with Britain and America, and concentrate our efforts in the East.' He grinned at Maron. 'Didn't the Führer say that he was a hero on land but a coward at sea?'

For once Maron didn't respond to a dig at his hero.

'Germany needs a merchant navy,' said Brandt suddenly. 'Not a Kriegsmarine. I look forward to a long life in the engine room of a real ship. Not one of these damned iron coffins.'

'I'll drink to that,' said Kessler, raising his glass. 'A long life to all of us.'

'Rudolf Diesel would have had a long life if he hadn't invented the diesel engine,' Maron remarked.

Kessler sighed. He had tried.

Brandt pushed his bowl aside. 'I'd better see how the repairs to that injector are going.' He rose, instructed the steward to serve his main course in the engine room, and left.

'You shouldn't needle him, Hans,' said Kessler reprovingly,

warily contemplating the steaming oven dish of squid lasagne that the steward had just placed on the table.

'I was merely trying to make conversation, Captain.'

'Yes, but your conversation always turns to the demise of Rudolf Diesel.'

Maron shrugged and helped himself to a ladleful of pallid tentacles dressed with garlic and a crust of hard-baked Parmesan cheese. What sat on his plate looked as if it had already been eaten once.

'As a matter of interest,' said Kessler, also digging into the offering but with a marked lack of enthusiasm. 'How *did* Rudolf Diesel die?'

'He disappeared while travelling across the English Channel on a ferry.'

Kessler looked surprised. 'He fell off?'

'So it would seem,' Maron replied, tugging a piece of elasticated squid from between his teeth.

'But surely he would have cried out?'

'Very likely. No doubt he would have been heard if the ferry was steam-powered. But its steam engine had been removed and replaced by one of his diesels. Consequently he wasn't heard above the racket it was making.'

Kessler helped a half-chewed, half-cooked tentacle to slide down his throat with the aid of a swig of apple juice. 'It's a cruel world,' he observed.

The steward served them with peach and pineapple pie. It tasted of squid.

60

It was 21:30 on Wednesday 28 January 1942. Brink was sitting on *U-395*'s aft casing with his eyes shut to enhance his already excellent night vision. The collar of his jacket was turned up, and he was gripping his sextant between his knees. He was cold and uncomfortable, which helped with his working up of a hatred for the horizon-to-horizon blanket of cloud which was refusing to break despite the brisk sou'wester that was pushing up a choppy following sea. The towline above him thrummed softly in the wind whenever it was pulled taut as *U-395* lifted her stern to the steepening swell. Four times since sunset the lookouts had yelled summonses down into the control room for him when the cloud looked like clearing, and four times he had been frustrated in his attempts to identify a planet or star. He had rough longitude –in the middle of the bloody Atlantic – but what he hadn't been able to fix for the past three days was latitude, how far north of the equator *U-395* was. And the old man was snapping at his heels as though the unending cloud was his fault. Even if the cloud did break, it would be a swine locating the horizon because the moon had set three hours earlier. The chances of the cloud breaking between him and the Pole Star were nil. He opened his eyes and could just discern the faint line of the horizon where jet black met mere black. Well, that was something.

'Break!' yelled a voice.

Brink's head snapped up and there was the milky white, shining disc of Jupiter, smack in the middle of a hole, looking like a motorbike headlight coming out of a tunnel. Such was the quartermaster's eyesight that he could even make out the gleaming string of the Galilean moons.

'Readings – Jupiter!' he yelled and snapped the sextant to his eye. 'Time!'

'Readings Jupiter timed at two-one-three-three!' the look-out yelled back.

'Get a gyro bearing on it!' Brink ordered.

A thread of cloud spread across the elusive disc. Brink's experienced fingers released the rack and pinion that controlled the index mirror and slammed the image of the giant planet down to the horizon.

Careful. Careful. This has got to be dead right – there might not be another opportunity for days.

He made minute adjustments so that Jupiter's rim was just touching the line of blackness, and then brought the image down a whisker so that the planet was neatly bisected. He was tightening the tangent locking screw just as the gleaming disc vanished for good, but it didn't matter – he had his fix.

'Elevation seven-six-decimal-five,' he called out, shining a penlight torch on the sextant's vernier quadrant.

'Elevation Jupiter – seven-six-decimal-five degrees timed at two-one-three-three,' said the lookout dutifully. 'Azimuth bearing two-five-six true.'

Brink took the readings and clattered down the ladder into the control room where he busied himself at the tiny chart table. The sighting had been taken at a bastard time of a planet at a bastard high elevation which meant a lot of calculating grind with the aid of his almanacs and a slide rule. After a few minutes he arrived at a position which he didn't believe, and had to start all over again.

Kessler wandered into the control room looking bleary-eyed and out of sorts. He hated Wednesdays because they were days of the week that were furthest from Tuesdays. 'Heard a scurrilous rumour that you might have a rough idea as to where we are, quartermaster.'

'I've worked out a provisional fix, Captain,' said Brink huffily, not looking up from the chart table. 'But I'd like to double check.'

Kessler moved to Brink's side and stared down at the pencilled cross on the chart. 'Forty by forty!' he said in astonishment. 'I don't believe it!'

'Nor do I, Captain,' Brink replied. 'That's why I'm double checking.'

'Much as I respect your abilities, quartermaster, I think you had better triple check, please.'

Brink wisely said nothing and carried on working. He straightened up after ten minutes and met Kessler's eye. 'Still the same, captain. Forty-one ten north, thirty-eight west, to be precise.'

Kessler was about to say 'Are you sure?' but checked himself. Instead he stared down at Brink's cross that was almost exactly halfway between Newfoundland and the Azores. He opened a pair of dividers to ten degrees and walked them across the chart to Lorient. It took three steps – thirty degrees. He twirled the pointers back to the cross and seemed lost in thought for a few moments, chewing ruminatively on his beard. 'My God, quartermaster,' he breathed at length. 'This means that the Gulf Stream has been giving us a steady three to four knots shove up the arse since the last fix.'

'So it would seem, Captain. *And* there's been a following trade – not that we've got much windage, but every little bit helps.'

Kessler's Wednesday mood evaporated. A broad grin escaped the confines of his beard. He clapped Brink delightedly on the back. 'Good news, everyone!' he boomed. 'We're less than two thousand miles from home!'

Dieter finished his watch at midnight and handed over to the sister in charge of the nuns.

'*Mucho frio,*' she commented, wrapping a large piece of awning around herself as she settled on the stern thwart.

Dieter said yes, it was indeed cold. He nodded in the direction of the U-boat from whence came snatches of song borne on the blustery wind. 'Something seems to have cheered them up.'

'Perhaps it's the colder weather?'

He agreed that that was the most likely explanation, and picked his way carefully over the sleeping forms in the near total darkness. The survivors had taken to sleeping under the awnings, so that it was hard to see where one body ended and another started.

He found his usual space beside Marco and crawled under his cover. The boy had been sleeping almost continuously for twenty-four hours. His forehead felt hot and dry. Dieter wondered if his mother knew but decided not to wake her. He bunched up his spare clothes into a serviceable pillow and was settling down to sleep when a slender arm crept around his waist and slid under his jersey. He turned to face the arm's owner but she burrowed deeper under the awning.

'Tammy?' Her answer was to press a warning finger to his lips. Dieter pulled the lightweight canvas over his head and wriggled down so that they were face to face, her hair tickling his cheek. He wished he could see her. 'You're supposed to be next to Mrs Montgomerie,' he whispered.

'She thinks I am.' She blew hot breath into his ear and bit his earlobe.

'You're a naughty girl.'

'Not yet.' She kissed him on the lips, lightly at first, and then with a steadily increasing intensity that he found frighteningly disorientating in the total darkness. Someone nearby coughed. The sudden sound triggered an instinct to pull away, but she stilled his panic by walking mischievous fingertips up and down his stomach and nibbling his lower lip. The kiss that followed seemed to last for ever. He brought his hand up and brushed his palm lightly over her nightdress. He guessed it was the one that she had worn in the sea when they had first made love. A nipple surged against the thin material to greet his questing fingertips. He spread his hand and found he could tease both nipples simultaneously with his thumb and little finger at full span. He rasped the engorged buttons of flesh back and forth; with each pass they rose up harder and harder. He remembered what she liked and sudden bore down quite roughly, pressing her breasts so hard that his fingers were enfolded deeply in the warm flesh. A little cry rose in her throat which he quickly stifled by renewing the intensity of their kiss.

'Turn your back on me,' he whispered in her ear. 'Slowly . . . naturally . . .'

She twisted around languidly like a sleeper shifting into a more comfortable position. Dieter carefully rearranged the awning over them while Tammy snuggled her head on his forearm and pressed his trapped hand over her breast. She wriggled her buttocks sensually into his groin, provoking a sudden completion of the response that had started with her kisses.

Marco stirred behind Dieter and wedged a foot or a knee into his back. My God, he thought, this is crazy – it can't be happening. But it was happening, albeit in a strange slow-motion that added a curious piquancy to the intensity of the heady sensations coursing through him as she lifted her leg and crooked it slightly backwards over his hip. He used his free hand to unhitch his trousers before encircling her waist. He then brushed his fingers slowly and gently along the inside of her parted thighs, starting just above the knee. His fingertips made careful little exploratory circles over her hip and around her navel. He marvelled at the silky smoothness of her flawless skin and had to stop his eager exploration, temporarily overwhelmed by the privilege of holding this lovely girl in his arms. She didn't stir when he cupped his hand over her pelvis or when he slipped his hand lower and carefully parted her soft folds. He felt like a schoolboy opening a forbidden book. His forefinger and the puckering, moistening ridge at her centre lay still together in the humid darkness for a few moments like sleeping lovers, secure in each other's contact. So saturated were his senses by this divine closeness that he didn't realise that she had been moving her hand between her thighs until her fingers closed around him, gently clasping and unclasping as though gauging his readiness. She moved forward a little, sacrificing some of their spoon-like contact, while her fingers eased him backwards until he felt a yielding membrane of heavenly warmth close softly around him. Such was their empathy at this intense moment that both denied their instincts by remaining still, allowing the lifeboat's motion to bring about total closeness. Tammy turned her head and bit gently on his forearm while his fingers teased her nipple by rolling it in and out.

Taking great care not to communicate his movements

beyond the confines of the awning, he began carefully massaging her fast-elongating ridge. Surprisingly, the instinct to start thrusting when he heard a tiny moan escape her lips was easily suppressed; he wanted to hear every sharp intake of her breath and for his fingertips to savour and cherish every startling change in the texture of her lovely skin beneath his insistent caresses.

Tammy's first climax came so slowly that for a moment Dieter thought that she had fallen asleep. Then her breathing quickened and was followed by a sublime surge of pelvic contractions of astonishing silent power. There was another moment of panic when he felt a cry rising in her throat but she choked it to a soft moan as her teeth sunk deeper into his arm. Her muscles gradually relaxed and he felt the hardened ridge shy away from his forefinger. The hand she laid on his wrist told him to stop.

They lay like that for timeless moments. Then Tammy's hand signalled for him to start again. She slipped her leg from his hip so that she was gripping him more tightly and seemed to be milking him by clenching and unclenching her buttocks. Her next climax came almost instantly and merged into a continuous stream of contractions of such power that the reserves of self-control he had to call on not to respond with frenzied thrusts left him drained and breathless. Her body suddenly relaxed and he sensed that she wanted him to stop even before her fingers clenched his hand into stillness. His own climax came as a surprise. The stream of sensations that raced up his spine and the inevitable release that followed was wholly unexpected because he had made no movement to encourage it. Tammy seemed to sense what had happened for she gave a little sigh, so faint that he hardly felt her breath on his arm.

The precious moments slipped by. Gradually her teeth relaxed their grip although little shudders continued to course through her. No doubt there would be a mark on his arm, possibly permanent. Dieter hoped so. Something else touched his arm. He brushed his hand over her cheek and realised that she was crying. He eased his arm from under her and kissed her on the temple. He tried to turn her to face him but she resisted.

'Tammy?' he whispered. 'What's the matter?' She didn't answer and his concern became a turmoil of guilt. 'Tammy . . . I'm sorry . . .'

She rolled over and flung an arm around him so that he had to hastily rearrange their covers.

'Hold me, Dieter. Don't say anything . . . Just hold me . . . Please.'

Later he would be unable to recall how long they lay together like that, not speaking or moving. It could have been a minute, or half an hour. Her voice was surprisingly calm when she eventually broke the long silence.

'What will happen to us, Dieter?'

He stroked her hair, the desire to see her face now a blind craving. 'We'll reach port. We're certain to, now.'

'No . . . After that.'

'You'll be well looked after. I'll see to that. I promise.'

'But what about Miss Angela? She's your enemy.'

'We're not animals, Tammy. She will be treated well. You all will.'

She began to cry again, more openly this time. He sat her up with his arm around her shoulders so that it would seem to any listener amid the sleeping forms around them that he was affording her the comfort that the survivors had shown for each other whenever one of them was distressed. He settled the awning around them like a shawl because the wind was strengthening.

'I love her so much . . . She's been my mother all . . . I can hardly remember my real . . .' Her shoulders shook uncontrollably and her sentences were lost in a flood of silent tears. Dieter said nothing. He continued holding her tightly, letting her tormented emotions run their course. The nun on watch heard or sensed Tammy's distress and called out in the darkness, asking if everything was all right. He assured her that it was.

'Dieter?' said Tammy in a small voice.

'Yes?'

'Will you promise to take me to see snow if there's none at Lor . . . at Lorient?'

The timid note in her voice and the child-like request brought his thoughts into sharp focus and crystallised his guilt over what he had just done. He had just treated her like a woman and yet she was a little girl. A frightened, lonely child whom he had selfishly taken advantage of to gratify his own needs.

She read his silence as a refusal. 'Oh, please, Dieter. Please take me to see snow.'

'I'll take you to the mountains,' he said, forcing himself to sound cheerful. 'There's snow all the year round there.'

'Like the mountains in my magazine? The big colour picture?'

His guilt came at him like a ravening monster.

God — a little child . . .

'Of course I'll take you to the mountains,' he whispered hoarsely.

61

No one aboard *U-395* watched the deteriorating weather over the next few days more closely than Haug although his mounting apprehension was more than matched by the survivors in the lifeboats. For them the misery of the appalling heat of the tropics was being inexorably replaced by cold. Not severe cold, that would come later, but the numbing cold that came from wind-whipped spray saturating their clothes and chilling them badly, especially at night. Marco contracted a fever and died quite suddenly — a terrifying warning to the other survivors as to the extent that long exposure had depleted their strength. The boy's distraught mother sobbed piteously for two days, refusing food and water, wailing in

Spanish that she wanted to join her beloved son. To watch a young woman lose the will to live was frightening, and her death came as an unspoken relief. Dieter realised that he didn't even know her name or how she had become separated from her husband.

The last day of January was marked by a series of violent squalls. Dense black clouds of driving horizontal rain that came hurtling from the south-west under a lowering sky with the speed and ferocity of starving wolves, the crests of the mountainous swells ripped to spindrift. For thirty minutes the survivors were held in terror and misery, then the squall was past and they could only await the next. During a lull Brink rowed around the tiny fleet to lengthen the towrope and to ensure that the survivors knew how to secure the lifeboats' storm covers should the weather deteriorate even more. The use of the heavy canvas covers had been delayed as long as possible because conditions under them soon became suffocatingly impossible.

By 14:30 the weather had moderated sufficiently for Maron to order the daily cooked meal to be ferried to the survivors. Now that conditions were more tolerable in *U-395*'s galley, he had ended the dusk ritual of cooking. It was his intention to be back on normal watches by the time they reached port.

U-395 lay stopped, rolling abominably while the tossing dinghy was loaded with canteens of squid stew, loaves of bread, and bottles of water. Haug's name had come up on the dinghy rota for that day. If he didn't act now, he would not have a another chance for five days, and then it might be too late. He half fell, half-jumped into the wildly gyrating inflatable.

'It would be better if just one of us went,' he told the rating manning the oars.

The young rating objected but Haug insisted that he could manage alone. The crewman shrugged and relinquished his place, his comrades helping him scramble back onto the casing. Haug rowed determinedly, Kessler's Luger stuffed inside his blouse, its heavy shape pressing insistently against his chest, colder than the spray that lashed his face.

As soon as the diesel was closed down, Pols settled his hydrophone headphones in place and used the respite from propeller noises for a careful 360-degree sweep. No one had asked him to do it but it had become part of his daily routine. First a rapid spin of the wheel to pick out the loud beat of a ship that could be just over the horizon, and then a more careful listen, turning the wheel a few degrees at a time. That he had never heard anything since the tow had started in no way affected his diligence. Today was different. Almost immediately he picked up the rhythmic pounding of several propellers.

'HE bearing three-five-five!'

Kessler was at Pols' side in an instant. He jammed the spare headphones to his ear. He didn't need Pols' expert diagnosis to separate the shrill whine of steam turbines from the heavy pounding of reciprocating engines from God knows how many ships.

'Holy shit!' Kessler exclaimed. 'We've got a convoy! Escorts – the whole damned lot! Give me its course as soon as you can!' He leapt into the control room, yelling orders.

A hundred and fifty metres from *U-395* the survivors in Lifeboat 1 were reaching out eager hands to help pull the dinghy alongside. Dieter sat warily in the stern. The days when it was Haug's turn to help ferry the meal always made him uneasy. That Haug was alone this time made him doubly uneasy.

The swell lifted the lifeboat and dinghy together and Dieter spotted Kessler's white cap appear on the bridge. The U-boat dipped from sight. On the next crest he saw that Erlicht had shinned up the periscope standard and was training his binoculars to the north.

'They've seen something, Mr Haug,' Dieter called out above the buffeting wind.

Haug glanced at *U-395*. 'They've got the Klaxon if they want to recall me,' he said curtly.

The canteens and loaves were passed across to Mrs Montgomerie. Tammy helped pour the thick squid stew into bowls while the nuns broke the loaves into halves. Haug's plan was brutally simple: he intended to shoot Dieter Rohland dead without preamble and then, keeping the gun trained on Tammy, demand that Mrs Montgomerie hand over the crystals. As with his seizure of the *Anaconda*, he would rely on the shock effect of the sudden killing to get his way. He grabbed the lifeboat's gunwale and pulled the pitching dinghy around so that he would have a clear line of fire. There was no point in delaying the business. He jerked the Luger from his blouse, slipped the safety catch, and aimed at Dieter's head. At a range of three metres, he could hardly miss.

A forest of mastheads danced briefly like duelling matchstick men above the rolling humps of the great army of swells that was marching on Europe.

Kessler kept his binoculars trained on the smudges of black smoke that stayed undispersed just long enough to provide a marker. The mastheads reappeared. 'Got 'em!' he breathed.

'Got a rough course, Captain,' Erlicht called down from his perch on the periscope standard. 'Between two-twenty and two-seventy degrees.'

Kessler had come to the same conclusion. 'A west-bound convoy,' he commented, his mind racing as he weighed up the pros and cons of going after the ships. There was the possibility that the convoy was being shadowed by other U-boats. Maybe the powerful radio transmitters in Western France had directed a whole pack into its path for a coordinated attack. He inwardly cursed his lack of a radio.

'They'd be empty,' the lookout petty officer observed.

'In ballast,' Kessler replied.

The petty officer chuckled. 'What have the British got left to export, Captain?'

'Blitzkrieg ballast. London rubble. West-bound ships sink fast, believe me.'

'Tanker!' Erlicht called down. 'Riding high. About ten thousand tonnes!'

That made up Kessler's mind. Any tanker, even an empty one, was a target no U-boat skipper could pass up. He thumbed the Klaxon button and gave a long blast to recall the dinghy.

'Seems to be a commotion around the lifeboats,' one of the lookouts observed.

'Damn Haug!' Kessler muttered, too preoccupied to spare the lifeboats a glance. 'We'll come back for them.'

He released the towline shackle and called down orders to the helmsman. Both diesels kicked into life. The conning tower air intake roared, the water under the stern was churned to vanilla candy floss, and U-395 set off at a brisk twelve knots to rejoin the war.

The sudden howl of U-395's siren and an unexpected drenching from a particularly large wave spoilt Haug's aim the instant he pulled the trigger. The round chewed harmlessly into the lifeboat's planking.

'No!' screamed Tammy. She dropped the flask of stew, leapt onto the lifeboat's gunwale, was about to launch herself at Haug just as he squeezed off another shot. The bullet penetrated her left breast. Its impact caused her to pirouette on one foot, her expression mirroring disbelief until the wind plucked at her magnificent tresses and wound them around her face as she toppled backwards. Before anyone could react, Dieter gave a bellow of rage and dived at Haug. One hand closed around the pudgy wrist that was holding the gun and other grabbed his throat. The dinghy overturned, and the two men, still locked together, were thrown into the icy sea. Dieter swallowed water and thrust his head above the surface, choking and gasping as Haug's free hand clawed savagely at his face. He would have lost an eye had he not fastened his teeth on Haug's fingers and clamped his jaw shut with all his strength until the bones crunched. There was a sudden cloud of crimson before his eyes. He heard a scream but Haug fought on with astonishing strength and almost succeeded in tearing his hand from between Dieter's teeth. Dieter felt himself losing control over the other hand that was clutching the Luger and realised that his strength was failing fast. He bit down even harder. Haug's scream was now a continuous howl of agony but the pain didn't distract him from slowly dragging his wrist between the two men and twist the gun around so that it was pointing at Dieter. With a superhuman effort, Dieter managed to lift himself so that his weight drove Haug under the surface. He was blinded by blood and saltwater and had no idea if Haug had let go of the Luger. A loud report against his chest answered the question. It was closely followed by two more. Dieter assumed that his body was too numb with cold for him to feel where he had been hit.

Suddenly Haug changed tactics by going limp, but Dieter wasn't fooled for an instant. He spread his fingers over his adversary's head to force him under the water and held it there while kicking wildly with his feet to keep his own head above the surface until he realised that Haug's sudden limpness wasn't a ruse. He grabbed the side of the dinghy and retched, hardly aware of the screams around him and the hands that were hauling him bodily out of the water. He fell sprawling on the duckboard, his diaphragm pumping impotently as he tried to inhale. He came close to panic when he realised that he couldn't breathe until a powerful blow in the small of his back unleashed a paroxysm of heaving coughs that expelled the seawater from his lungs.

'Tammy!' he croaked. He rolled over and opened his eyes. The faces staring down at him were wrong. He pulled himself up and, before anyone could stop him, flopped into the sea and found the strength to swim the few metres to Lifeboat 1. 'Tammy!' he gasped, hanging onto the side of the lifeboat.

'Tammy bad,' said one of the Spanish seamen who helped pull him aboard.

Unmindful of who he trod on or kicked in his haste, Dieter scrambled to Mrs Montgomerie's side. Tammy's head was cradled on her lap. One of the nuns had cut away the girl's clothes and was swabbing the blood that was welling from an ugly hole in her left breast. Her face was strangely relaxed, her eyes clear, and she even seemed to be smiling up at her nurses.

'*Leave us!*' Mrs Montgomerie snarled, her eyes blazing raw hatred. 'Haven't you and your kind done enough!'

'No – please, Miss Angela . . .' said Tammy softly. 'Let him stay . . . Please.'

Her voice sounded so normal that for an insane moment Dieter thought that the shot had done less harm than the terrible entry wound suggested. But her sentence ended in a little gurgle and a thin stream of blood oozed from the corner of her mouth which the nun wiped away. The woman looked at Dieter; her knowing eyes told him the worst.

'Dieter . . . the magazine . . .' Crimson bubbles frothed around the wound as Tammy spoke.

Dieter's eyes were blinded with tears as he scrabbled among the girl's pitifully few belongings. He found the magazine and held it in front of her. She tried to reach out to it but the effort proved too much. Mrs Montgomerie caught her hand as it fell.

'Show me the mountains, Dieter. With the family.' He watched through his tears as she focused her eyes on the picture. 'They look so . . . happy.' For the first time pain creased her lovely face as she reached out to trace the outline of the largest, snow-capped mountain with her fingertip. 'Snow,' she said in a faraway voice. 'You will take me to see it, won't you, Dieter?'

'Yes, Tammy. Of course.'

She smiled. The memory of that sweet, lovely smile would remain with him for the rest of his life. 'To that mountain . . . where the people are so happy.' Her hand fell to her side.

Dieter opened his mouth to speak, but her eyes suddenly

seemed to glaze – losing their precious lustre, and he knew that she would not hear his answer.

62

There was a price to be paid for the tanker that *U-395* sank.

For six unremitting hours the U-boat was pounded by depth charges dropped with uncomfortable accuracy by the convoy escorts. Instead of the usual pattern of an escort ship making Asdic contact and then losing contact as it charged forward to dump its deadly load, it seemed that one ship was designated to maintain contact. Several times Kessler managed to shake off the probing sonic beam using every trick drawn from his considerable repertoire of evasion manoeuvres, but each time he escaped from the unnerving pinging the Asdic found them again within minutes and the relentless torture by high explosive resumed.

'The British seem to have got themselves organised,' he observed to Maron after they had managed to evade a pattern of depth charges whose hydrostatic fuses had been set to explode too shallow. 'I do believe the cunning little buggers are queuing up to take pokes at us.'

Maron was too busy directing damage repair operations to answer. The control room was on emergency lighting and Kessler was the tranquil eye of a whirl of activity as ashen-faced ratings worked frantically to repair leaks and replace shattered gauges. Maron snatched down a microphone.

'Control room. Bow compartment, have you got that outer torpedo door closed yet?'

'Bloody hopeless,' a voice answered. 'It's jammed solid. The guides must be buckled to hell or the pressure hull's distorted.'

Maron relayed the news to Kessler who nodded and ordered an abrupt change of course. The news was more serious than Kessler's relaxed attitude suggested. His surface attack on the convoy just after midnight had been conventional: a fan of four torpedoes fired on the tanker's quarter so that one would be certain to hit the target, as indeed had happened. But what had been unexpected was the speed of the escorts' response. A destroyer intent on ramming *U-395* had loomed out of the darkness with such swiftness that it must have been closing for the attack before Kessler had fired the torpedoes. The warship had passed over the diving U-boat with centimetres to spare and its first terrifying pattern of depth charges had jammed the outer sliding door of torpedo Tube 2 when it was only half closed. It meant that the inner circular door in the torpedo room was exposed to the full brunt of depth charge detonations near the U-boat's bow. If it gave way the bow compartment would be flooded, and Kessler would be forced to blow all tanks and surface . . . that is if *U-395* was capable of surfacing with her forward compartment flooded.

The nerve-jangling crump of another pattern of depth charges intruded on his thoughts and decided his next course of action.

'Mr Maron!'

'Captain?'

'Time to try that ridiculous pill thing.'

Maron acknowledged and ordered the *Pillenwertha* to be ejected from the aft torpedo tube. The experimental device was like a huge Alka-Seltzer tablet: when it came into contact with water it formed a giant cloud of effervescing bubbles which was supposed to provide the enemy with a fat Asdic decoy target thus enabling the U-boat under attack to slip away. Like all the experimental devices that had been foisted on him, Kessler had little faith in it.

'Those British Asdic operators are good,' he had once commented. 'They know the difference between a cloud of bubbles and 750 tonnes of steel.'

His ordering of its use now was a measure of the seriousness of their predicament. But his mistrust was unfounded because the strange device actually worked. While the enemy warships were busy blasting away at the rising column of bubbles, U-395 sank to fifty metres, the deepest that Kessler dare take the boat with full outside water pressure bearing on an inner torpedo door and unknown damage to the pressure hull. Subsequent patterns of depth charges continued to explode too shallow, thus enabling U-395 to creep away from the scene at two knots.

Kessler grinned broadly around at the watch. 'Brilliant device,' he declared. 'Always thought it would work.'

U-395 surfaced at noon. Except for black squalls and freezing whiplash spindrift that ravaged the conning tower, the storm-racked sea all around was empty. To the west a strange glow was reflected off the underside of the leaden cloudbase.

'Our tanker,' Kessler commented to Maron, puzzled by his own lack of elation at the sight. And then he realised why. 'Crazy world . . .' he growled half to himself. 'We've spent the last few weeks doing our damnedest to save lives, and then we embark on an orgy of destruction that ends lives.' He lowered his binoculars and stared astern at the mountainous following seas that were foaming across the after casing and rolling around the conning tower. 'We'd better go back and look for our lifeboats. And please don't tell me that we expended too much of our fuel getting into position for the attack, Hans. Because I know.'

'I wasn't going to comment, Captain,' said Maron evenly.

Kessler glanced in surprise at his I.WO and decided that he was telling the truth.

63

'Look out!' Dieter yelled, but his warning was too late and ineffectual because it would not have stopped the heavy, broken sea from lifting the bows of Lifeboat 1 and bringing its steel-capped forefoot crashing down on what he supposed was Lifeboat 2. The force of the splintering impact knocked the torch from his hand. There were screams in the darkness as the second lifeboat capsized and its survivors were spilled into the heaving black water. He groped frantically around the sloshing duckboards. He recovered the torch but it was no longer working. He scrambled forward to the locker, found a flare, and yanked the igniter. The brilliant light climbed and was immediately swept downwind but it provided enough illumination for those in Lifeboat 1 to grab those survivors they could reach and haul them inboard.

'For God's sake fire another flare!' Mrs Montgomerie cried.

'Three left!' Dieter shouted. 'We'll need them if the U-boat is to find us!'

There were too many rescuers on one side of the lifeboat. A quick-thinking Spanish seaman averted a capsize by bellowing at the survivors to get away from the gunwale and followed through by stumbling the length of the boat, unceremoniously yanking rescued and rescuers amidships. A sea reared up in the darkness. It broke over the stern and sent bodies tumbling from one end of the lifeboat to the other. Dieter lashed out blindly as the sea carried him away. He would have been swept over the side but he managed to grab the bilge pump crank handle and hang on as the lifeboat slowly righted. The boat's motion felt wrong – unnaturally sluggish.

'Bail!' a woman screamed. It was one of the nuns. 'Everyone bail! We're sinking!'

The choking cries of those floundering in the sea were forgotten as searching fingers scrabbled blindly in the surging bilge water for mugs, bowls, dishes, anything that could hold water. Dieter started cranking the bilge pump and was relieved to feel it prime. It had proved its efficiency on a number of occasions.

'Francisco! Pepe!' he yelled. 'Get the storm cover fixed!'

One of the Spanish seamen shouted back that they were

already doing so. Amid the chaos the men had managed to unfold the storm cover without it blowing away, and were fastening it by its rope loops to the gunwale cleats and pulling it tight as they worked their way around the boat in the darkness. The cover provided a welcome respite from the savagery of the wind. Like departing spirits, the cries of those in the water had been swallowed by the storm before the cover was finally secured. The Spaniards left a flap open on the leeward side for the bailers but it was Dieter's continuous pumping that cleared most of the bilge water. His arms felt like leaden appendages that had been attached to his body as afterthoughts by the time the pump started sucking air. He stretched out his long legs across the duckboard and propped himself against the hull planking, too exhausted to think straight. Miraculously, someone managed to strike a match. For a few seconds the flickering yellow flame illuminated a mass of shapeless bodies and pinched, staring faces huddled beneath the cover. A boathook had been jammed upright under the canvas to form a ridge so that the seas breaking over the lifeboat were drained away. Dieter located Mrs Montgomerie just before the light was extinguished. She was sitting near him with her head resting on her knees, her whole demeanour one of an indominable spirit that had finally been crushed. Another matched flared. She lifted her head and their gazes locked. The light went out suddenly but not before Dieter had seen her look of terrible emptiness. He moved to her side in the darkness.

'Mrs Montgomerie?' She didn't answer until he spoke again. 'What do you want?' Her voice was devoid of emotion. 'I'm terribly sorry for what happened. Please believe me.' 'The bullet was meant for you.'

Dieter couldn't think of anything helpful to say and was wishing that he hadn't made this overture. He was glad of the darkness.

'Why should a Nazi scum like you be alive when my Tammy is dead?'

'Where is she, Mrs Mongomerie?'

'She was swept away. I made sure of that. I didn't want you or your kind to see her or touch her,' she paused. Dieter sensed that she was losing the struggle to hold back tears. 'My only regret is that she is sharing her grave with her murderer.'

Dieter could no longer bear the long silence that followed. He muttered something hopelessly ineffectual about being sorry and moved away. He sat in the darkness, alone with his misery, not hearing the shriek of the wind or the staccato hammering of spray on the cover. His confused thoughts were with Tammy. He relived her last moments over and over again, desperately willing the forces of the universe to turn back time so that he could do something to prevent Haug opening fire. If only he had handed over the crystals; if only he had never found them in the first place. If only . . . If only . . . If only . . .

The little strength he had left to resist the sickening rolling and pitching of the lifeboat finally deserted him, and he slept. It was a fitful slumber in which every particularly sharp motion of the lifeboat as the storm tightened his grip tilted him between alternate periods of dozing and deep unconsciousness in which he dreamed of Tammy. It was a strange dream without her face but with her warm, comforting presence in the darkness and the feel of her hot breath on his shoulder. He was dragged back to full wakefulness by someone tripping over him and cursing in Spanish. It was one of the seamen pulling back the cover. Dieter blinked in the strong light. As his eyes adjusted, he realised that the daylight filtering through the heavy, scudding clouds was not that strong. The storm had abated although a moderate sou'westerly was still spurring a heavy swell. The nuns were busy clearing up the mess made by the storm. They had even recovered some of the flasks of food and were sharing out the contents. Dieter was counting the survivors, working out which were new faces and which were old, when there was a loud report. The distress flare burned a trail of light into the sky.

'What do you think you're doing,' Dieter snarled angrily at the seaman who had fired the flare. 'We need those to signal the U-boat!'

The Spaniard looked nonplussed. 'But it is after midday. The boat has been gone many hours.'

'It's one o'clock,' said Mrs Montgomerie venomously.

'I'm sorry,' said Dieter dully. 'I didn't realise.'

'At least your conscience, if you have any, hasn't prevented you from sleeping.'

Dieter met the Englishwoman's eye. She looked quickly away and he sensed that she regretted the outburst. He turned to the seaman. 'It would be better if we waited another hour before firing the next flare.'

The Spaniard agreed and pointed. 'We have Lifeboat 2 but we don't know what has happened to Lifeboat 3 and the raft.'

Dieter glanced aft. Lifeboat 2 was floating upsidedown, tethered to their own boat by a long length of knotted rope. It looked undamaged.

'The wind has dropped a little more, we will try to right it,' said the seaman. 'We have recovered everything that we could find.'

Dieter nodded. 'You've done well.'

The seaman shrugged and watched Dieter stepping over the huddled shapes to reach the aft locker. The bag of crystals was safe, still lashed by a stout cord to the underside of one of the locker's cross-beams. The bilges beneath the duckboards were awash again. It was time for another session with the pump. Something caught his eye in the bilge water. He moved two survivors out of the way, lifted the slatted board, and recovered Tammy's now sodden magazine. He laid it carefully on the stern thwart to dry. It was open at the colour centre-page spread of the smiling family against the background of snow-capped peaks.

Seven miles to the north, a lookout on *U-395*'s bridge had spotted the brief flash of the distress flare. The petty officer of the watch alerted the control room and the U-boat altered course.

64

U-395 was lying stopped, stern down, while a team of Brandt's men struggled with club hammers and cold chisels to free the jammed outer torpedo door. The boat's rolling in the heavy swell was making their task impossible.

In the wardroom, Kessler listened, grim-faced and silent, as Dieter made his report while Maron took notes. On the fold-down table was the bag of crystals, Tammy's sodden magazine, and the empty Luger holster.

'So you don't know when Lifeboat 3 was lost?' Kessler pressed.

Dieter shook his head. 'I think it was before Number 2's capsize. I've asked everyone but no one knows for sure.'

A petty officer hovering outside the open door caught Kessler's eye and reported that Lifeboat 2 had been righted, and inspected, and that three sprung planks had been recaulked. 'And thanks to Erlicht who spotted it, we have also recovered the inflatable using the spare, Captain,' the NCO concluded.

Kessler expressed his thanks and dismissed him. He stared at Dieter for some moments, bleary-eyed from lack of sleep, while drumming his fingers on the table. 'Thirty-one survivors missing,' he said at length. 'Twenty-eight men and three women. One of the women shot. My God, what a mess. A damnable, stupid mess . . .'

'Will you look for them?' Dieter asked.

Kessler's unkempt black beard twitched. 'What's the bloody point in this visibility when you took their flares?' he snapped. He gave a despairing gesture and his flash of anger was gone as quickly as it had appeared. 'Oh hell . . . It's not your fault, Mr Rohland. Even if we had millpond conditions, I wouldn't be able to carry out a search. We're 1500 miles from France and we've just about enough fuel for 500 miles.'

Dieter stood. 'If you've no further questions, Captain, I'll return to my lifeboat.'

'You can stay on the boat,' Kessler offered. 'Haug's berth is free.'

The thought of sleeping in the same bunk as Tammy's killer was more than Dieter could stomach. 'Thank you. But I'd rather –'

'I have a few questions,' said Maron suddenly.

Kessler motioned to Dieter to sit. He subsided onto the settee and regarded Maron suspiciously.

'Mr Haug was your superior officer?'

'Yes.'

Maron tapped the bag of crystals with his pencil. 'Yet you wilfully disobeyed his lawful order to hand these over . . . Items that you had obtained in the service of our country and therefore are the property of our country?'

'I've handed them over now, Mr Maron.'

'But you disobeyed the orders of a superior officer?' the oberleutnant persisted.

Dieter found that he could out-stare Maron. 'Yes – I did.'

'In that case,' said Maron. 'If the captain approves, I am proposing that you consider yourself under arrest until we reach port, where you will be handed over to the appropriate authorities.'

'That will require some thought,' said Kessler diplomatically, inwardly cursing Maron's pedantic nature that seemed to be surfacing again.

Dieter rose. 'A small favour please, Captain.'

Kessler gave a wry smile. 'No doubt we can persuade Mr Maron to set up a committee to consider it.'

'The magazine belonged to Tammy. I'd be grateful if it could be dried out and returned to me.'

'Consider it done,' said Kessler generously, avoiding Maron's eye.

The three men returned to the bridge. it was now bitterly cold. Kessler had donned a sheepskin coat of such disreputable appearance that even its original owner would have disowned it. He and Maron watched Dieter being rowed back to the two lifeboats. Brandt was on the bow casing haranguing his repair crew who were still hard at work to free the jammed torpedo door. Despite *U-395*'s bow-high trim, seas surged and boiled around the men. All were secured to the jumping wire with lifelines. Two ratings were over the side helping steady a third who was swinging a club hammer.

Kessler picked up the loudhailer and requested a report when the chief was ready. Brandt acknowledged with a wave. Kessler turned up his moth-eaten collar and moodily surveyed Lifeboat 1. Mrs Montgomerie was still staring fixedly at the U-boat as she had been ever since it had returned. He raised his binoculars and studied the gaunt figure in close-up. All the other survivors were wearing the thick woollen jerseys and trousers that Maron had issued, but she had contemptuously spurned the extra clothing. Even under normal circumstances, a woman of her age and build would not be able to stand such cold for long; the weeks of exposure she had suffered would have surely reduced her resistance. She would inevitably succumb. Perhaps that was what she wanted.

Damn the woman!

Her bolt upright posture reminded him of the cartoon figures of Englishwomen he had once seen in one of Julius Streicher's tabloid rags, but there was nothing funny about the unbridled hatred he felt radiating from her.

'That Englishwoman,' he muttered to Maron. 'If looks were depth charges, we'd be sinking right now.'

The repair crew stopped hammering. Brandt climbed onto the bridge. Like Kessler, he looked in need of a week's sleep.

'Sorry, Captain. We can't shift it. There's a three-metre long rip in the outer hull below the waterline, and the pressure hull's distorted to hell. We've hammered the casing back as best we can to reduce drag, but the pressure hull's going to be a dry-dock job.'

As usual Kessler made light of the situation. 'Thanks, chief.

Oh well – might as well look on the bright side. A long refit means a long spell of leave.'

'And another daughter,' Maron added drolly.

Kessler sighed. *Three* jokes in two months. They were now coming thick and fast.

65

'Please, Mrs Montgomerie,' the sister pleaded. 'You must eat.'

The Englishwoman took her gaze off *U-395* and stared listlessly at the nun. 'Why?'

'You must eat to live.'

'Who said I wanted to live?'

The nun pressed the small enamel jug of cold stew into Mrs Montgomerie's hand and closed her emaciated fingers around it. The stubborn Englishwoman had refused food and water for two days since the tow had resumed and now her hands were like claws. Spray burst over the bows, soaking the two women. Like all the survivors, the sister was wearing an oilskin, but Mrs Montgomerie had continued to refuse additional clothing. To make matters worse, she had taken up a permanent position on the bow thwart – the most exposed place in the lifeboat.

The nun tried to lift the jug to Mrs Montgomerie's lips but she gave a snort of anger, snatched it from the nun's fingers and placed it at her feet. 'I said that I didn't want it and I meant it. Now will you *please* leave me alone!'

The nun shook her head, not knowing what to do or say. She made her way to Dieter's side. He had been watching with interest. It had been repeated every three hours for the past two days, albeit with slight variations save one.

'It's no good asking me,' he said. 'I'm the last person she'll listen to.'

'But she *must* eat. She will die.'

'I think she knows that, sister.'

'She will be eternally damned.'

'At least she didn't throw the jug down.'

'Everytime I go to her, I find that she has kicked it away. *Please*, Mr Rohland – you must speak with her.'

'I'll try,' Dieter promised.

A weak sun broke through the thinning cumulus the following morning. The welcome patches of blue and the wind's change from bone-chilling forty-knot gusts to a steady ten-knot blow did much to revive the survivors' flagging spirits. Clothes were peeled off and pegged out to dry. Soon the two lifeboats trailing behind *U-395* were festooned with a strange assortment of garments that had been donated by the U-boat's crew.

Mrs Montgomerie was still maintaining her vigil although her posture was much less rigid. She had slumped forward slightly and was supporting herself against the gunwale.

She ignored Dieter when he sat beside her. He was shocked by her appearance. Her lips were cracked and blistered, rimes of salt had encrusted her eyebrows and hair, and her cheeks and eyelids were swollen and grey from hours of exposure.

'Good morning, Mrs Montgomerie.'

She continued to ignore him.

'The nuns will be serving up some food soon. You really ought to eat.'

Silence.

Dieter reached down and picked up the jug she had kicked over. Some stew, certainly not a jugful, had been spilt across the slats of the duckboard and had run down the sides. But there was no sign of any stew in the bilge. There was no possibility of it having been washed away by bilge water sloshing about because the bilges were dry – he had seen to that.

He gave up after two more attempts to start a conversation and returned to his usual position. He regarded the hunched, forlorn figure slumped on the bow thwart and wondered what she was planning.

318

66

The sounds of the whispered argument between Brandt and Maron in the wardroom began to annoy Kessler as he brought the log up to date in his cabin. He threw down his pen, cupped his hands over his ears, and read what he had written. Normally he enjoyed writing the log – it helped bring his thoughts into focus – and he knew that the armchair sailors back at Kerneval liked his style. He had once offered his services just writing logs without the tedious business of actually having to take a U-boat to sea, but the suggestion had not been appreciated.

But now, for the first time, Kessler was beginning to have serious doubts as to whether anyone other than himself would ever read the log. The chief's daily fuel consumption figures made one line on the graph, and the distance covered each day made another. The lines crossed at a point that was six hundred miles west of Lorient – the outer reaches of the Bay of Biscay; the worst place in the entire Atlantic for a U-boat to be stranded because it was within range of the squadrons of Hudsons that the Americans were supplying to RAF Coastal Command. The British put everything that could fly into the air over the Bay of Biscay, even lumbering old Walrus amphibians, because damaged, exhausted U-boats returning from long patrols were easy pickings.

Kessler's contempt for his superiors hardened as the bleak evidence on the charts and graphs before him spelt out the danger facing his boat and his men. The idiots were too blind and too stupid to organise something as simple and as obvious as the RAF's Coastal Command to protect returning boats. They gave their precious egos a higher priority than the lives of the men serving under them.

He closed his eyes and allowed his temper to cool while trying to ignore the heated, whispered exchanges between

Maron and Brandt. It was so unusual for the two men to deign to talk to each other that he found himself straining to hear what they were saying. After five minutes he gave up and shambled into the wardroom in time to hear Brandt say that the 'old man' would never agree to such a mad idea.

'Agree to what?' Kessler asked, dropping onto the settee like a sack of potatoes and helping himself to a generous swig from Maron's bottle of apple juice.

'Mr Maron says he wants to turn us into a sailing boat,' said Brandt contemptuously.

'I said nothing of the kind, chief,' Maron responded mildly, toying with a sketch. 'I merely asked if we had the necessary timber should such a move become necessary.' He moved his bottle of apple juice out of Kessler's reach.

Kessler hiccuped and pulled Maron's sketch towards him. It showed a U-boat sporting a clumsy jury mast bearing a square-rigged lateen sail. The entire contraption was lashed to the U-boat's conning tower.

'A crazy idea,' Brandt muttered, confident that Kessler would agree.

'Well, perhaps not practical,' said Kessler, reaching across the table and draining the last of Maron's juice.

Brandt's self-satisfied smirk faded as Kessler continued: 'Square-rigs are fine for taking advantage of a wind on your quarter, but the problem is that your yard and the whole weight of the sail is at the top of the mast – at its weakest point.' He picked up Maron's pencil and made a few alterations. 'A simple genoa would be better. They're not triangular-shaped for appearance. Most of the wind loading and the weight of the boom or yard is at the foot of the mast where it's strongest. The really clever thing is that one mast can carry two genoas, rigged fore and aft. That balances the loading on the mast and saves on the weight and top hamper of a second mast and yard. The genoa sail was one of the great inventions of maritime history. Invented in Genoa, but I expect you've already worked that out.' He hiccuped again and grinned, pleased that he had navigated a diplomatic course between two conflicting reefs of opinion.

'Not as great as Rudolf Diesel's invention,' Brandt remarked sourly. 'Nothing like one of his inventions for sailing into the eye of the wind.'

'Or better still – two,' Kessler added, grinning.

'A pity he didn't invent the lifejacket,' murmured Maron.

It was all Kessler could do to prevent himself from laughing out loud. 'You know something, chief?' he said quickly before Brandt had time to explode. 'Mr Maron's idea isn't so impractical after all. A quarter of our displacement is ballast, including the batteries – that gives us enormous stability. Certainly enough to carry a considerable spread of canvas.'

'Except that we don't have much canvas,' said Brandt sardonically. 'Only a couple of square metres for repairing covers.'

Maron was unperturbed. 'How much canvas would we need to make a small genoa sail, Captain? But one that's large enough to be effective?'

Kessler chuckled. 'In the Doldrums or the Horse Latitudes it would have to be bloody enormous. But here, with a brisk trade blowing up our arse all day, then any area of canvas is going to transfer some wind thrust to the boat.' He made some more alterations to Maron's sketch by pencilling-in a genoa sail attached to a jury mast about twice the height of the conning tower. He was careful to keep the scale reasonably correct. 'But, as the chief has pointed out – we don't have any canvas.'

'The lifeboats' storm covers?' said Maron.

Kessler stared at his I.WO. He was about to speak when the control room petty officer appeared.

'Sorry to disturb you, Captain, but one of the survivors has been taken very ill.'

'Which one?'

'The Englishwoman. Mrs Montgomerie. She's unconscious.'

67

The stretcher with Mrs Montgomerie bound firmly in place was manoeuvred carefully down through the forward hatch and into the bow torpedo compartment. *U-395*'s remaining torpedoes were in their respective tubes and most of the supplies had been used, so there was sufficient room in the compartment to fold down additional bunks. Also, the sick from among the survivors had been transferred back to the two lifeboats.

Brink had a temporary screen rigged so that he could examine Angela Montgomerie without the benefit of coarse suggestions from the owners of a host of prying eyes.

'Exposure and malnutrition,' he reported back to Kessler on the bridge. He had to shout to make himself heard above the racket of sawing and hammering as Brandt and his men fashioned a jury mast and a boom from the engine-shoring baulks of timber that U-boats carried in their battery compartments.

'Malnutrition?' Kessler queried.

'According to other survivors in her boat, she hasn't been eating her food, Captain.'

Kessler was incensed. 'That's her own damned fault,' he growled. 'Chuck her out. I'll not have malingerers in my boat.'

'She won't be one any more, Captain. I pushed a tube into her stomach and poured some soup into her.'

'About the only way to get anyone to eat Ivy's soup,' Kessler observed. 'Didn't she object?'

Brilliant blue sparks hissed and crackled from two hooded welders using oxy-acetylene guns. They were working on the *wintergarten* deck, cutting up some steel to make a heel plate and mounting sleeve for the mast.

'She didn't have much choice,' Brink replied. 'I did it while she was still strapped to the stretcher.'

Kessler watched the working party for a few moments. He was not happy with the idea of an enemy national in his torpedo compartment. Not that the Type VIIC U-boat had many secrets – they were very conventional craft – but the notion of the enemy at the very heart of the one weapon that could destroy them disturbed him. 'How bad is she?'

'Well, she's certainly tough, Captain. Forty-eight hours in the warm with plenty of food in her, and she should be okay.'

'All right. Forty-eight hours, then we boot her out. Can't have women in the way if we engage a convoy.'

Brink wondered how Kessler expected *U-395* to launch any form of attack while sporting a sail and a mast. He would not have commented openly to his captain, but Kessler read his thoughts.

'Quartermaster ... So long as I have a U-boat and torpedoes, then I'll do my damnedest to sink any enemy ship that crosses my sights. Understood?'

The squeal of a hoist and the grating of blocks and tackle woke Angela Montgomerie. She opened her eyes. The appalling stench in the torpedo compartment no longer made her want to retch. Maybe she had got used to it. Without moving her head or drawing attention to herself, she took in details of the hateful killing machine into which she had inveigled herself: pipes, wires, gauges, valves. No doubt all of them were important, but which ones were vital?

It was the thought that she would soon be exacting a terrible vengence for the murder of Tammy that had enabled her to maintain rigid self-control when the brutes had lashed her to the stretcher, and when they had pushed a tube down her throat and forced food into her. They would pay for killing her beloved Tammy, and pay dearly. Also it would be one less murdering U-boat prowling the seas. She turned slowly onto her side in the narrow lower bunk and watched what was going on.

A party of sweating ratings in overalls had extracted a torpedo from one of the tubes. The weapon gleamed black and sinister in the harsh yellow light of the caged lamps. Hanging from slings attached to overhead rails, it swayed gently in harmony with the U-boat's motion as the ratings worked on it like termites attending their queen. Under the direction of a senior mechanic, they checked its batteries, oil reservoirs, and electrical connections to the torpedo director. They were too busy to notice that they were being watched by a pair of eyes that was committing everything they did to memory.

The torpedo was slid back into its tube. As soon as the handwheel was spun closed to lock the circular door, work started on extracting the second torpedo.

'Do any of you speak English?'

Paul Fischer, the senior rating, jumped and wheeled round. The Englishwoman was propped on one elbow, regarding him.

'I speak English a little,' he said proudly. 'You are feeling better I think?'

'Much better, thank you. Your name?'

Fischer told her and wondered what it was about the woman that made him obey her so promptly. 'I am sorry we are making such a noise, but it is necessary. We will be another one hour.'

'What exactly *are* you doing?' Mrs Montgomerie inquired.

Fischer explained that they were carrying out routine servicing of their torpedoes.

'So you're not about to fire them?'

The U-boat man grinned and shook his head. 'Just servicing. It has to be done every few days. If you will excuse me . . .' He turned back to his men and resumed work, uncomfortably aware that the Englishwoman was watching him and his men intently.

The third torpedo was slid back into its tube and the door secured by spinning the handwheel home. Clockwise, Mrs

324

Montgomerie noticed. The men started throwing their tools into steel boxes.

'You forgot one!' Mrs Montgomerie called out above the racket.

Fischer turned. The Englishwoman was pointing at Tube 2. A red rag was tied to its locking handwheel. He smiled self-effacingly. 'That tube – it is kaput. The outer door is stuck open.'

Under normal circumstances Mrs Montgomerie considered anything mechanical boring in the extreme, with the possible exception of canning machines. But on this occasion she was interested. Very interested.

'So there's a torpedo jammed in there? Oh dear.' She contrived to look frightened. 'Isn't that terribly dangerous?' She was playing to perfection the part of a disinterested woman deliberately holding a male's attention by keeping the conversation on a subject she knew would interest him.

'There is no danger,' said Fischer. 'Only water in there. It is not possible to load the tube because the outer door is stuck open so it is not possible to pump it dry.' He pointed. 'You see? There is a little water coming in around the seals.'

Mrs Montgomerie feigned shock. 'You mean the sea is just the other side of that door? Dear me.'

He assured her that it was a very strong door.'It is safe if we do not dive too deep.'

68

'Take the strain!' Brandt called out.

The eight ratings braced themselves against the rope like a tug-of-war team about to do battle. Maron and Kessler watched the proceedings from the bridge.

'And heave!'

The tug-of-war team hauled and the twelve-metre long mast that was lying on the after casing swung upright, teetered on the edge of its mounting sleeve that had been welded to the deck and dropped into place with a resounding crash, to the accompaniment of loud cheering. *U-395* now had a mast abaft the conning tower that was equal to the height of the attack periscope when fully extended.

'If it had been any heavier, the bloody thing would've gone right through the deck,' Kessler grumbled to Maron.

Brandt looked upon his creation with satisfaction. The mast had been made by scarf-joining together three lengths of square-section timber. It had been sanded smooth, the corners rounded, and treated with two coats of insulating shellac. The most difficult task had been routing the back-taper sail track groove which ran the entire length of the mast.

Once Brandt was satisfied that it was secure, the four main supporting shrouds were attached to deck eyes with bottle screws. The boom, a shorter length of timber, was then hooked into place on its swivel near the base of the mast and secured with cotter pins. Kessler climbed down from the bridge and walked aft to run a critical eye over the strange rig. While this had been going on *U-395* had maintained two knots. A stiff following wind was skimming spray off the swells.

'Excellent, chief,' said Kessler slapping the mast. 'Solid as a rock.' He glanced aft at the lifeboats, at the puzzled faces staring up at the new addition. 'Time for them to find out why we wanted their covers.'

Making the sail had been Brink's responsibility and had taken him and his ten-man sewing team fifteen hours' hard work with bodkins and twine. Their creation was unfolded and cleated to the mast track. A nod from Brink and two ratings hauled on the halyard. The sail was flapping before it was halfway up the mast and by the time it was fully hoisted it had taken on the aerofoil shape of a well-made genoa.

'Keep the boom centred,' Kessler ordered the ratings. 'Don't want her running away from us just yet.' He looked up. The sound of flapping canvas. Heaven.

Brink checked the tension of the shrouds, made a few adjustments to the bottle screws, and signalled to Kessler that all was well.

'Stop your engine, Mr Maron,' Kessler called up to the bridge.

U-395 lost way, the towline sagged, and the two lifeboats gathered near the stern.

'A sail,' Dieter commented to one of the nuns. 'You have to admire their resourcefulness.'

'Do you think it will work?'

'I think we're about to find out.'

Kessler gave the order to pay out the sheets. The blocks squealed. The wind caught the boom, swung it away from the U-boat's centreline and snapped the sheets taut. The sail filled and the mast gave an ominous creak as it took the load, but Brink was watching the shrouds closely and seemed happy.

To most of the crew *U-395*'s change of motion was imperceptible, but Kessler and Brink felt it and exchanged triumphant grins.

The towline lifted clear of the sea and tugged its charges awake like a puppet master picking up a marionette by its strings. The U-boat buried her bows in a sea. They lifted sluggishly with water streaming from the casing drains and promptly drove hard into the next sea. The sail groaned and the mast creaked, sounds that Kessler hadn't heard in years. He wheeled around and stared aft. Spray burst across the bows of Lifeboat 1 but he was watching the sea. There was no doubt about it:

Both the diesels were stopped and yet *U-395* was making a crisp, white-fringed wake.

69

At 02:00 activity in the bow torpedo compartment was at a minimum. Even this far from the engine room, it was strangely quiet without the incessant vibration of a diesel. Men were sleeping, some were reading or playing cards. They were used to survivors convalescing in their domain and paid little attention to the Englishwoman.

Mrs Mongomerie waited another fifteen minutes and decided that it was now or never. She climbed slowly out of the bunk and stood in the narrow gangway, clinging weakly to a bunk rail with one hand while holding the waist of the trousers they had given her with the other. Fischer lowered his book and looked inquiringly at her.

'I do not feel well,' said Mrs Montgomerie. 'I need to go to the lavatory.'

Fischer stood. 'I will put the screen up.'

'This time I need the toilet – not a bucket.'

The rating looked embarrassed. 'I am sorry, but you will have to use the bucket for that also. It is not permitted for survivors to use the toilet. The valves and levers are very complicated.'

She sat on her bunk and looked despairingly at the young rating. 'I'm too weak to move, anyway. Very well . . . But would you please turn the lights out for a few minutes.'

Fischer looked doubtful.

'*Please*, Mr Fischer. I will not take long, I promise.'

He hesitated.

'For God's sake turn the bloody lights out,' said a voice. 'No one wants to see her.'

The pleading look in the wretched woman's eyes decided Fischer. He flipped the master gas precaution switch that extinguished even the bow compartment's emergency lights. The darkness was total.

Mrs Montgomerie had planned every move and memorised the position of everything. She moved barefoot along the gangway, turning her body sideways so that she didn't brush against the bunks.

Four yards . . . Three yards. . . Two yards . . . She had reached the torpedo doors. Her hands searched frantically in

328

the darkness and found the rag tied to a handwheel, confirming that she had right door.

Quickly! Pull out the spring-loaded locking pin and turn anti-clockwise.

Her fear that she might lack the strength to move the handwheel proved unfounded: it turned easily and silently on its well-oiled screw thread. Twenty turns, she reckoned, but don't bother to count. Just spin the wheel as fast as possible and keep spinning until something happened. The sudden spray of icy water from around the door's seals caused her to give an involuntary gasp. A voice immediately behind her gave a yell and the lights snapped on at the exact moment that the door burst open and unleashed a wall of water. It hit Mrs Montgomerie in the chest and threw her backwards. She was trampled underfoot by yelling torpedomen who threw themselves on the door and wrestled it shut. Her head struck the corner of a bunk as she went down and she lost consciousness.

'Concussion,' Brink reported cryptically.

Kessler glowered. 'Will she live?'

'Oh, yes.'

'Pity. But at least she'll stand trial. Firing squad offence. Waste of bullets if you ask me; I'd cheerfully strangle the bitch. Keep her lashed to the stretcher in the meantime. Yes, Mr Maron?'

'Bow torpedo compartment pumped dry, Captain.'

Kessler grunted. The next problem was Fischer. He had already decided on his punishment and had made out a warrant. A petty officer marched the hapless rating to the threshold of Kessler's cabin. They stood side by side, shoulders touching. A U-boat did not lend itself to the usual formalties. Fischer stared white-faced over his captain's shoulder.

'You,' said Kessler slowly, 'are a prize cunt. Would you agree with that definition?'

'Yes, Captain,' said Fischer miserably.

'Your criminal stupidity endangered this boat and the lives of its crew. Such behaviour warrants the very harshest punishment that I have the power to mete out.'

Fischer said nothing but his face went even whiter when Kessler picked up a sealed envelope. It bore the captain's seal and that could mean only one thing. Such was his terror that he came close to fainting.

'This is the warrant for your sentence,' Kessler continued, grim-faced. 'It has been signed by me and has been properly witnessed by two officers in accordance with naval regulations. Sentence is to be carried out immediately. And may God help you.' He handed the envelope to the petty officer. 'Dismissed.'

The one job that Eric Handel loathed was cleaning. With both diesels now closed down, permanently it seemed, the chief had decreed that the opportunity should be used to ensure that the engine room shone. He also hated the silence. It wasn't right, not having an engine running. He was putting a shine on a copper fuel pipe when he felt a tap on the shoulder. He turned. Paul Fischer was standing there looking utterly miserable. The torpedo rating raised a piece of paper and read aloud:

'I, Paul Helmut Fischer, do hereby solemnly and truthfully declare that I am the biggest dummkopf that ever put to sea in a U-boat.' He turned around and bent over. 'You now have to kick me.' He added pleadingly: 'But not too hard, *please*, Eric – I have to go round to the entire crew.'

70

'You know, Hans,' Kessler confided. 'I almost long for the sighting of an aircraft to tell us that we're nearly home.'

The two men were on the bridge watching Brink take a noon sun sight now that the weather had moderated. The sail creaked and groaned. Many of its stitches had broken as a result of its four days' arduous service, strips of frayed canvas were flapping inefficently, and some sail cleats had parted company from the mast. But it was still driving *U-395* into the green, heaving swells at a steady three knots.

'I think I'd rather rely on the quartermaster's fix, Captain. The thought of an aircraft chancing on us with all that gear to dump makes me very worried.'

'It was a joke,' Kessler said mildly. 'I thought you now appreciated jokes.'

'I'm trying to break the habit,' Maron replied. 'I'll check on the aft watch.' With that he went down the ladder and edged past the sail. Since it had been hoisted, Maron had organised lookouts at the stern to compensate for the blindspot it created.

Brink disappeared down the forward hatch and emerged on the bridge a few minutes later. As usual, his expression was inscrutable.

'Well, quartermaster?'

'That sail's done a first class job, Captain. I didn't think it would, but I was wrong. Ten west.'

Kessler goggled. 'What!'

'Ten west. Forty-six north. We're 480 miles due west of Lorient.'

'My God – that means we can dump the sail tomorrow!'

'*Aircraft!*' The yell was right in Kessler's ear. A lookout was pointing north. The Klaxon howled and men poured out of the aft hatch. They had been drilled to perfection. Within sixty frantic seconds the pins had been pulled from the mast's heel where it was stepped into the mounting sleeve, the shrouds released, and *U-395* was diving as the mast keeled over: her electric racing at full power; her forward speed helping flood her ballast tanks. But an RAF Hudson could cover three miles in a minute, and it was on the U-boat, roaring in at 300 feet, its nose machine-gun yammering as Kessler struggled to release the towline. The shots went wide. The Hudson's belly gunner went to work but the aircraft was banking too steeply for

331

accurate fire. It came in low and fast for a depth charge run just as Kessler conned the boat to ensure it was clear. The last man jumped down the aft hatch. He would later swear that he heard the depth charge clang off the casing.

Kessler slammed and secured the hatch just as the explosion laid the boat nearly on her beam ends. He hung onto the commander's saddle in the attack kiosk and shut out the sounds of smashing equipment and men's shouts and curses. When he fell into the control room, the boat had taken on such a steep bow-down attitude that he was convinced the door on Tube 2 had failed. Suddenly the boat was levelling.

'Thirty metres,' a planesman intoned.

'No deeper, for Christ's sake!' Kessler yelled.

'That's the depth I ordered, Captain,' said Brandt. 'All we want now is for some of that crap to foul our props.'

Hearing the chief engineer's matter-of-fact voice was the best tonic Kessler could have had. He picked himself up and quickly took in the scene. The chart chest had broken free and several gauges were squirting water. He called for reports. The entire boat was a mess but there was no serious damage, and no one had been injured in the machine-gun fire. He was returning the microphone to its hook when the second depth charge exploded. The crump shattered the depth gauge and rocked *U-395* but that was all.

'Those Hudsons are like old men,' Kessler observed. 'Two pops and they're done for.'

Another explosion shook the U-boat.

'Virile old men,' he added.

The Hudson's gunners had ceased firing before their water-stitching .303 rounds reached the lifeboats. The aircraft banked hard and released a depth charge. To his astonishment, Dieter saw the canister hit *U-395*'s aft casing at an angle. It bounced into the sea and exploded, throwing up a huge plume that drenched both lifeboats. The remains of mast and rigging fell into the sea not fifty metres from Lifeboat 1.

U-395's conning tower was going down fast at a steep angle amid a welter of foam and jets of water squirting from the casing vents.

By the time the twin-engine aircraft had completed its turn and was coming in for another run, the U-boat had vanished.

'That bomb do the submarine a big favour,' commented a Spaniard when the spray cleared. 'It blow away all that rigging.'

Another approach and another depth charge dropped. The Hudson decided that it had done its best and circled the lifeboats like a wary hawk sizing up a mouse caught in the open. Dieter could see the face of the nose gunner staring down at them. A few survivors waved but the gunner made no attempt to return the gesture. The Hudson waggled its wings and flew away to the north.

'Perhaps they'll wireless for a ship to pick us up?' the sister suggested.

'With a U-boat in the vicinity?' said Dieter. 'I doubt it.'

The sun set at 18:30 and the wind that had been blowing steadily from the south-west freshened to a moderate gale.

'They have left us without storm covers,' said a bitter voice in the darkness.

Dieter remained silent, wishing that he knew Kessler better so that he could predict his actions. Somehow he didn't believe that the U-boat skipper would abandon them. Not so much because Kessler would be concerned for their lives, but because getting them to France now that they were so close would be a matter of honour.

That Dieter was wrong in his appraisal of Kessler's motives was academic. A few minutes after midnight *U-395* surfaced within two hundred metres of the two drifting lifeboats and resumed the tow.

71

'Two hundred miles!' Kessler exclaimed, thumping the wardroom table in delight. 'My God — we're going to do it!'

'Two hundred miles but only enough fuel for one hundred,' Brandt warned. 'Just under a tonne, Captain. That's all we've got.'

'What about your reserves?'

'That's what we're on.'

Nothing was going shake Kessler's good humour. 'Ah. But what about your reserve reserves?'

'Please, Captain. I ask you to believe me. I do not have any reserves or reserve reserves. What we have is one tonne of fuel. I give you my word that —'

A scream rang through the boat followed by a commotion aft. Kessler was on his feet and through the control room before Brandt could complete his sentence. Three men had Mrs Montgomerie pinned to the deck in the galley gangway. Despite the weight on her, she was struggling manfully and nearly succeeded in dislodging the lightest rating. Poison Ivy was leaning against the cooker clutching his left forearm. Blood was oozing past his fingers.

'What the hell happened?' Kessler demanded.

'The bitch slashed me!' Ivy protested. 'Carved a chunk out of my arm!'

The men pinioned Mrs Montgomerie's wrists together behind her back and snapped a pair of handcuffs in place. They were none too gentle hauling her to her feet. The buttons had been ripped off her tunic in the mêlée, exposing her breasts, but she didn't seem to care. She stared at Kessler in haughty disdain.

'So what happened?' Kessler asked again.

The youngest rating looked nervously at his comrades for support and found none. 'I was escorting her to the sickbay for her check-up, Captain. She's been no trouble so I agreed to take her handcuffs off.'

'She snatched up my best knife as she was passing and stabbed me!' said Poison Ivy belligerently. He made it sound as though he would not have minded being stabbed with any other knife.

'You'd better get the quartermaster to take a look at that arm,' Kessler advised him.

'But I won't be able to cook, Captain.'

'We'll manage somehow.' Kessler regarded Mrs Montgomerie in silence for some moments before speaking to the rating. 'Find her another jacket and bring her to me in the wardroom in five minutes. That's about as long as I need to make up my mind what to do with her.'

Kessler returned to the wardroom and sat deep in thought, going over what he would be saying. His English would have to be good. It could be if planned. The jokes about Poison Ivy's escapade were already under way in the control room and were certain to spread:

'Maybe she was fed up with his cooking?'

'It's not so bad that he deserves to be stabbed.'

'Isn't it?'

There was a movement outside. A petty officer thrust Mrs Montgomerie into the wardroom. Her wrists were still handcuffed. She ignored Kessler's gesture to sit. The petty officer helped her with a firm thrust on her shoulders.

'I have nothing to say,' she declared.

'Good,' said Kessler. 'Because you are to listen. We are near port. You will be tried for sabotage and attempted murder. The verdict and sentence is certain. For the safety of my crew, I wish to carry out the sentence now, but I have decided to give you a chance. I'm putting you in an inflatable boat with food and water for two days. You will be towed behind Lifeboat 2. You can do two things. Either you go with us into port in that manner, or you slip the tow. I will see that you have distress flares. The British haunt these waters with high-speed air-sea rescue craft and amphibious planes so your chance of getting found is good. Whatever you decide is up to you. Either way I will be rid of you.'

The sister sat beside Dieter. She was holding a handbag that he had not noticed before.

'This belongs to Miss Angela,' said the nun. 'Perhaps we can find a way to get it to her?'

The inflatable dinghy with the forlorn, lone figure sitting in it, appeared briefly on the crest of a swell and was lost to sight. Lifeboat 2 seemed to rise up to take its place.

'It is wrong to do this to her,' the nun continued. 'She is a good woman. She nursed those Germans and this how you repay her.'

Dieter was too depressed to argue. Now that they were nearing Lorient, he was preoccupied with the trouble he would be in when they reached home.

The nun fingered the handbag. 'Perhaps we could get someone in Lifeboat 2 to pull the rope in and give this to her?'

'Mr Maron was quite firm,' said Dieter seriously. 'No communicating with Mrs Montgomerie under any circumstances.'

'How could they deny a woman her handbag?'

He took the bag and promised to have a word with the petty officer when the food was ferried to them the following day.

Dieter never did have the chance to return the handbag. The first light of dawn showed that the inflatable dinghy with Mrs Montgomerie aboard had disappeared in the night. A survivor in Lifeboat 2 pulled in her towline and discovered that it had not frayed through as he had supposed, but had been untied.

The photograph of Tammy that Dieter found in the handbag served to deepen his depression. It was a studio picture of her sitting on a couch wearing a simple summer dress, white stockings and buckle shoes. She was just as he remembered when he had first seen her sitting on a trunk on the dockside at Montevideo, idly swinging her lovely legs and eyeing him speculatively. Not only had the photographer placed his lamps carefully to emphasise the glorious highlights in her hair, but he had captured her expression of sweet but mischievous innocence.

72

The port engine managed to outlast the starboard engine by fifteen minutes before it died. The sudden silence on the bridge was as eerie as the total blackness that engulfed *U-395*.

'That's it, captain,' Brandt's voice answered when Kessler called down to him.

'All gone?'

'Every drop.'

'Very good, chief. Motors grouped down and half-ahead both.'

The electric motors started and *U-395* regained way, shouldering her way through the sluggish oil-black swells at three knots.

'Weird,' Kessler muttered, staring into the night. 'I can smell land, I swear I can. Fish. Garlic. That cheap perfume the waitresses at the *Beau Sejour* wear. Freshly-mown hay.'

'Freshly-mown hay in February?' Maron queried.

Kessler screwed up his eyes as though it would improve his night vision. 'The poet in me smells what it wants to smell.'

The bantering small-talk covered their nervousness about mines – the one thing that Kessler loathed above all else even although he had laid a few in his time. He recognised their value but that didn't stop him from viewing them as the weapons of cowards.

'Quartermaster! Where's Brink? I said I wanted him on the bridge.'

'Right here, Captain,' said a voice at Kessler's elbow.

'How far to the islands?'

'Ten point four miles, Captain.'

'That's how far they should be if we were in the right place, but how far are they really?'

'Ten point four miles, Captain.'

Kessler knew that it was unfair to needle Brink. If anyone could make a perfect landfall after sailing across an ocean, Brink could. Damned nerves, he told himself. Damned mines. No radio. Christ – the navigation channel could be abandoned for all he knew. Maybe it was so infested with mines that a new one was in use. Maybe the flotilla had moved further south and there was no escort vessel anyway. Maybe there was a mine lying in wait dead ahead. Maybe he had been too long at sea. 'Send our recognition signal again,' he ordered.

Brink lifted the signalling lamp and rattled its louvres.

Another hour slipped by.

'Seven miles now,' said Brink, looking at his luminous watch. He sent the recognition signal again without being asked. A faint light responded from almost dead ahead.

Kessler was so keyed up that he was unable to restrain his elation. He gave a whoop of joy. 'That's it! They're there! My God – we've done it!' He was about to clap Brink on the back and tell him what a brilliant navigator he was but the quartermaster was busy exchanging lengthy signals with the distant light.

'Typical,' Kessler muttered. 'We hardly get a word out of him for weeks, months at a time. But put a lamp in his hand and he tells the world his life story.'

At 02:00 there were no brass bands to greet *U-395*'s overdue return as she nosed towards the quay. No smiling secretaries; no champagne; and no flotilla commander to make speeches, shake hands, and dish out a few medals. Instead the welcoming committee consisted of a hollow-eyed staff officer who resented being dragged from a bed which he had just persuaded a pretty French brunette to share; two ambulances together with two doctors and several nurses; a handful of indifferent dock workers, and a police car. A few lights were grudgingly switched on – enough to indicate where U-395 was to tie up and to illuminate her little string of pennants, each flag representing an enemy ship sunk.

A rating standing on the bow threw a line ashore to the dockers. U-395's motors went astern and brought the U-boat to a stop with her bow nudging a wooden pile. Stern lines were thrown to waiting hands, fenders were dropped into place to protect her saddle tanks, and U-395 sidled up to the dockside like a lost sheepdog returning home to an indifferent master.

Boathooks wielded by the dockers drew the two lifeboats towards a flight of slippery steps. The doctor and nurses helped the survivors up the algae-coated slabs. Few of them could walk unaided. One of nuns prostrated herself when she reached the top and kissed the glistening flagstones.

Maron had some figures ready. 'We've sailed 14,300 miles – more than halfway around the world, and we've beaten Horst's patrol duration record by twenty-two days.'

Kessler grunted disinterestedly. He bent over the voice pipe and told Brandt that he had finished with the motors. 'Bit of an anticlimax,' he remarked. 'The whole damned thing.'

Dieter's cell in the former dockyard police station at Lorient measured a little under two metres, which meant that his bunk was too short for him to stretch out properly. Not that he could have slept had they given him a four-poster bed and a feather mattress. For one thing the room kept rolling and pitching, and for another he couldn't banish Tammy from his thoughts. And yet another was the continuous grind of cement mixers as Todt Organisation workers laboured through the night on their mammoth task of adding several more metres of reinforced concrete to the roofs of the massive U-boat pens.

At 09:00 he was served with his first hot meal since his last dinner on the *Anaconda*. Fried eggs, toast, and so much

339

marmalade that he wondered if the British had invaded and everyone was keeping it a secret.

At 10:00 a doctor examined him and pronounced him fit. At midday another breakfast arrived, and at 18:00 the door was thrown open and a dapper little man entered, all smiles, a smart grey suit, and a large briefcase. He came forward and pumped Dieter's hand.

'Dieter Rohland. This a great pleasure. A great pleasure indeed. My word, your exploits have caused a ripple. More than a ripple – a stir. A plane was provided to fly me here and take you back to Berlin. That's how important you are. Yes, indeed.'

'I suppose you're my defence lawyer?' Dieter inquired when he had recovered from his initial surprise.

The little man looked taken back for a moment and then laughed. 'Goodness me, no.' He bowed, opened his briefcase, and handed some identification documents to Dieter. 'Oberleutnant zur See Karl Mahne at your service. Abwehr. Head of Branch I(C).'

'But that's my branch!'

'*Was* your branch, Dieter,' said Mahne, returning the papers to his briefcase and perching on the edge of the bed. 'You've been gone many weeks and your work has to go on. I was privileged to step into your shoes. But you'll be pleased to know that you've been promoted.'

'I'm under arrest,' Dieter pointed out, not believing that this conversation was taking place. 'Treason, wilful disobedience of orders, and God knows what else. Won't that jeopardise my promotion prospects?'

Mahne shook his head. 'The epic voyage of *U-395* is going to be headline news tomorrow. Goebbels will be milking it for all it's worth. "Brave U-boat rescues passengers and crew of a neutral ship sunk by the cowardly British." Just the sort of thing we need to keep relations with Franco on an even keel. No one associated with the story is in trouble, believe me, Dieter. The British picked up a woman in a dinghy who claims that the U-boat abandoned her, but I expect Goebbels' staff will deal with that in their usual way.'

'Mrs Montgomerie . . .' said Dieter. 'Is she all right?'

Mahne shrugged. 'It would seem so. The British are making a noise about her story. Our noise will be louder, of course.'

'Do you know about the crystals?'

Mahne tapped his briefcase. 'All safe. Perhaps not so important, but safe.'

Now Dieter knew that the conversation was unreal. 'What the hell do you mean, *not so important*? I used them as a bargaining chip, for God's sake!'

'You mean the new super Asdic the British are supposed to be developing?'

'They've probably got it working by now,' was Dieter's sour response.

Mahne became serious. 'I doubt it.'

'We've got the ASDIC committee papers. I collected them myself from Paris. My God – that was nearly two years ago! The British are certain to have their advanced Asdic working by now.'

Mahne looked doubtful and shook his head. 'We've gone through all the papers, Dieter, checking the lot. When you recovered these papers, you had limited resources. Remember the battle you had to get translators? You wrote a number of very forthright memos.'

Dieter nodded, wondering what was coming.

'A serious translation error was made on one of the more important documents.'

An icicle of foreboding formed in Dieter's stomach. 'Which one?'

'The mistake was not yours, Dieter,' said Mahne smoothly. 'You had poor quality translators.'

'*Which one!*'

'There was a summary that described the new set as having the capability to sweep an area one hundred miles square. Ten thousand square miles. Remember it?'

'Remember it!' Dieter echoed. 'Of course I remember it! It was the one document that led to the operation to recover those quartz samples from the British mine in Brazil!' He broke off and stared at Mahne. 'Are you saying that the document was wrong?'

'The translation was wrong,' said Mahne gently. 'The figure given in the original ASDIC document wasn't one hundred miles square. It said one hundred *square* miles . . . An area ten miles by ten miles.'

There was a long silence as the full import of Mahne's words sank in. The colour drained from Dieter's face as images from the last few weeks swam before him: the terror of groping around in a piranha-infested river for Joe Cleary's kitbag and finding his hideously mutilated body; the destruction of the *Anaconda*; the screams of the passengers and crew; making love to Tammy in the sea. And most vivid of all, Tammy's terrible death.

'My God,' he whispered. He tried to stand but suddenly the cell was spinning around. He slumped onto the bed and buried his face in his hands.

73

After two hours climbing the narrow mountain path, Dieter's calves and ankles were aching. The locals in the town had assured him that it was an easy ninety-minute walk. The last thirty minutes had been particularly hard-going: a miserable trudge on melting snow up a steadily steepening track in unsuitable boots. His feet were so numb with cold that he could hardly feel them. He stopped walking to get his breath and the cold alpine air started eating relentlessly through his parka. High above in the clear sky a lark was celebrating the arrival of spring.

He slipped the rucksack off his back and unfolded the map that the former magazine photographer had marked for him.

Only another five hundred metres to the summit, but the path had deteriorated to the point that it was virtually non-existent. Had he known what he knew now, he would have asked the photographer how he had managed to get the happy, smiling family and all their skiing gear up this impossible path in mid-winter.

Tracing the photographer who took the pre-war pictures in Tammy's magazine had been the result of unofficial use of Abwehr resources. Dieter had finally tracked him down to a Luftwaffe aerial photographic unit in Holland. Over watered-down beer in an Amsterdam bar the photographer had recalled that the original shoot had been for a ski-wear company that had switched to the production of parachutes at the outbreak of the war.

'A tremendous location,' the photographer had said, studying his double-page spread in Tammy's magazine. 'The joke about this picture is that it's not skiing country. But it's a fantastic view – absolutely stunning. I only wish that I'd used 120 film instead of 35mm, but I had decent wide-angle lenses for my Leica. Maybe when this lot is over I'll go back and do it properly.' He tried to turn the pages but the magazine was stiff and many pages were stuck together from its soaking in the lifeboat. 'What happened to this? Looks like it's been in the war.'

Dieter told him that it had.

He returned the map to his rucksack and resumed his pilgrimage to the summit, threading his way between massive outcrops of granite that obscured his view. Some wag had carved a sign advising climbers that they had only ten metres to go. Dieter staggered around the last outcrop and was brought up short by the splendour before him. He even stopped breathing so that the clouds of his breath wouldn't obscure the magnificent view. The soaring, snow-capped mountains shone like jewels in the clear air. The rucksack slipped from his shoulders and he leaned against a rock, the cold forgotten as he drank in every detail. He stayed like that for several minutes, trying to picture Tammy's reaction had she lived to see this. As he stood there he could hear her sweet laughter echoing across the distant valleys. Five minutes passed. During such contemplative moments he liked to recall every moment that he had spent in her company. He stared at the shining mountains and saw her finger tracing their outline. But now he had work to do.

He unfastened the rucksack, took out a small garden fork and a trowel, and looked around for a suitable spot. He found it between two rocks whose sides formed a frame of the scene that closely matched the cropping of the magazine photograph. It was an awkward to reach spot that was unlikely to be disturbed by tourists. The loess at the foot of the rocks was hard-packed. It took him twenty minutes to dig a deep enough hole. He reached into the rucksack and took out the miniature jewellery chest that he had purchased in Berlin, heavy from its lead lining. Inside he had placed the handkerchief Christmas card that Tammy had embroidered for him, the photograph of her that had belonged to Mrs Montgomerie, and a typewritten account of the girl's life and death that had taken him three evenings to write. The box had been carefully sealed with layers of electricians' tape. A slight enlarging of the hole with the trowel was necessary for it to fit. He pressed it into place and refilled the hole, carefully tamping down the loess and soil so that the ground looked undisturbed. He stood back to contemplate his handiwork.

Perhaps, one day in the distant future, when everyone on this war-torn planet was dead, archaeologists with advanced equipment would locate the little jewellery chest and dig it up. They would read about Tammy, look at her photograph, and think about her.

The thought was a great comfort.

He packed his gear and set off down the treacherous track without looking back.

A List of James Follett Titles Available from Mandarin

While every effort is made to keep prices low, it is sometimes necessary to increase prices at short notice. Mandarin Paperbacks reserves the right to show new retail prices on covers which may differ from those previously advertised in the text or elsewhere.

The prices shown below were correct at the time of going to press.